ALSO BY ANDREW VACHSS

FLOOD

STREGA

STREGA

a novel by

ANDREW VACHSS

19 87

ALFRED A. KNOPF

NEW YORK

THIS IS A BORZOI BOOK
PUBLISHED BY ALFRED A. KNOPF, INC.

LIBRARY OF CONGRESS CATALOGING-IN-PUBLICATION DATA

Vachss, Andrew.
Strega.
I. Title.
PS3572.A33S7   1987   813'.54   86-46019
ISBN 0-394-55937-1

Manufactured in the United States of America
FIRST EDITION

For Doc, who heard it all while he was down here.
For Mary Lou, who can hear it all now.
For Sam, who finally gave up his part-time job.
And for Bobby, who died trying.

Different paths to the same door.

ACKNOWLEDGMENT

To Ira J. Hechler, the master-builder content to allow others to engrave their names on the cornerstones of his achievements, I acknowledge my gratitude and proclaim my respect.

STREGA

1

IT STARTED with a kid.

The redhead walked slowly up the bridle path, one foot deliberately in front of the other, looking straight ahead. She was dressed in a heavy sweatsuit and carrying some kind of gym bag in her hand. Her flaming hair was tied behind her with a wide yellow ribbon, just as it was supposed to be.

Forest Park runs all through Queens County, just a dozen miles outside the city. It's a long narrow piece of greenery, stretching from Forest Hills, where Geraldine Ferraro sells Pepsi, all the way to Richmond Hill, where some people sell coke. At six in the morning, the park was nearly deserted, but it would fill up soon enough. Yuppies working up an appetite for breakfast yogurt, jogging through the forest, dreaming of things you can buy from catalogues.

I was deep into the thick brush along the path, safely hidden behind a window screen. It had taken a couple of hours to weave the small branches through the mesh, but it was worth it—I was invisible. It was like being back in Biafra during the war, except that only branches were over my head—no planes.

The redhead stopped on the path, just across from me, about twenty feet away. Moving as if all her joints were stiff in the early-spring cold, she pulled the sweatshirt over her head, untied the pants, and let them fall to the ground. Now she was dressed in just a tight tank top and a skimpy pair of silky white shorts. "No panties, no bra," the freak had told her on the phone. "I want to see everything you got bounce around, you got it?" She was supposed to do three laps around the bridle path, and then it would be over.

I had never spoken to the woman. I got the story from an old man I did time with years ago. Julio called me at Mama Wong's restaurant and left a message to meet at a gas station he owns over in Brooklyn. "Tell him to bring the dog," he told Mama.

Julio loves my dog. Her name is Pansy and she's a Neapolitan mastiff—about 140 pounds of vicious muscle and dumb as a brick. If her entire brain was high-quality cocaine, it wouldn't retail for enough cash to buy a decent meal. But she knows how to do her work, which is more than you can say for a lot of fools who went to Harvard.

Back when I did my last long stretch, the prison yard was divided into little courts—every clique had one, the Italians, the blacks, the Latins. But it didn't just break down to race—bank robbers hung out together, con men had their own spot, the iron-freaks didn't mix with the basketball junkies . . . like that. If you stepped on a stranger's court, you did it the same way you'd come into his cell without an invite—with a shank in your hand. People who don't have much get ugly about giving up the little they have left.

Julio's court was the biggest one on the yard. He had tomato plants growing there, and even some decent chairs and a table someone made for him in the wood shop. He used to make book at the same stand every day—cons are all gamblers, otherwise they'd work for a living. Every morning he'd be out there on his court, sitting on a box near his tomato plants, surrounded by muscle. He was an old man even then, and he carried a lot of respect. One day I was talking to him about dogs, and he started in about Neapolitans.

"When I was a young boy, in my country, they had a fucking statue of that dog right in the middle of the village," he told me. "Neapolitan mastiffs, Burke—the same dogs what came over the Alps with Hannibal. I get out of this place, the first thing I do is get one of those dogs."

He was a better salesman than he was a buyer—Julio never got a Neapolitan, but I did. I bought Pansy when she was a puppy and now she's a full-grown monster. Every time Julio sees her, tears come into his eyes. I guess the idea of a cold-blooded killer who can never inform on the contractor makes him sentimental.

I drove my Plymouth into the gas station, got the eye from the attendant, and pulled into the garage. The old man came out of the darkness and Pansy growled—it sounded like a diesel truck downshifting. As soon as she recognized Julio's voice her ears went back just a fraction of an inch, but she was still ready to bite.

"Pansy! Mother of God, Burke—she's the size of a fucking house! What a beauty!"

Pansy purred under the praise, knowing there were better things coming. Sure enough, the old man reached in a coat pocket and came out with a slab of milk-white cheese and held it out to her.

"So, baby—you like what Uncle Julio has for you, huh?"

Before Julio could get close enough, I snapped "Speak!" at Pansy. She let the old man pat her massive head as the cheese quickly disappeared. Julio thought "Speak!" meant she should make noises—actually, it was the word I taught her that meant it was okay to take food. To Julio, it looked like a dog doing a trick. The key to survival in this world is to have people think you're doing tricks for them. Nobody was going to poison my dog.

Pansy growled again, this time in anticipation. "Pansy, jump!" I barked at her, and she lay down in the back seat without another sound.

I got out of the car and lit a cigarette—Julio wouldn't call me out to Brooklyn just to give Pansy some cheese.

"Burke, an old friend of mine comes to me last week. He says this freak is doing something to his daughter, making her crazy—scared all the time. And he don't know what to do. He tries to talk to her and she won't tell him what's wrong. And the daughter—she's married to a citizen, you know? Nice guy, treats her good and everything. He earns good, but he's not one of us. We can't bring him in on this."

I just watched the old man. He was so shook he was trembling. Julio had killed two shooters in a gunfight just before he went to prison and he was standup all the way. This had to be bad. I let him talk, saying nothing.

"So I talk to her—Gina. She won't tell me neither, but I just sit and we talk about things like when she was a little girl and I used to let her drink some of my espresso when she came into the club with her father—stuff like that. And then I notice that she won't let this kid of hers out of her sight. The little girl, she wants to go out in the yard and play and Gina says no. And it's a beautiful day out, you understand? They got a fence around the house, she can watch the kid from the kitchen—but she's not letting her out of her sight. So then I ask her, Is it something about the kid?

"And then she starts to cry, right in front of me and the kid too. She shows me this brown envelope that came in the mail for her. It's got all newspaper stories of kids that got killed by drunk drivers, kids that got snatched, missing kids . . . all that kind of shit.

"So what? I ask her. What's this got to do with *your* kid? And she tells me that this stuff comes in the mail for weeks, okay? And then this *animale* calls her on the phone. He tells her that *he* did a couple of these kids himself, you understand what I'm saying?—he snatches the kids himself and all. And her kid is going to be next if she don't do what he wants.

"So she figures he wants money, right? She knows that could be taken care of. But he don't want money, Burke. He wants her to take off her clothes for him while she's on the phone, the freak! He tells her to take the clothes off and say what she's doing into the phone."

The old man's eyes were someplace else. His voice was a harsh prison whisper, but reedy and weak. There was nothing for me to say—I don't do social work.

"She tells me she goes along with it, but she don't really take nothing off, okay?—and the freak screams at her that he knows she's not really doing it and hangs up on her. And that's when she hit the fucking panic button—she believes this guy's really watching her. All the time watching her, and getting ready to move on her kid."

"Why come to me?" I asked him.

"You know these people, Burke. Even when we were in the joint, you were always watching the fucking skinners and the baby-rapers and all. Remember? Remember when I asked you why you talk to them—remember what you said?"

I remembered. I told the old man that I was going to get out of that joint someday and I'd be going back to the streets—if you walk around in the jungle, you have to know the animals.

"Yeah," I told the old man, "I remember."

"So what am I gonna fucking do, ask one of them psychiatrists? *You* know about freaks—you tell me what to do."

"I don't tell people what to do."

"Then tell me what's going on—tell me what's in his head."

"He isn't watching her, Julio," I told him. "He just figured she wasn't going along, that's all. He's a freak, like you said—you don't ever know why they do something."

"But you know *what* they're going to do."

"Yeah," I told him, "I know what they're going to do." And it was the truth.

We smoked together in silence for a bit. I knew Julio, and I knew there was more coming. Finally, he snubbed out his skinny, twisted black cigar on the Plymouth's faded flank and stuck it in his pocket. His old, cold eyes grabbed mine:

"He called her again. . . ."

"And . . . ?" I asked him.

"He told her to come to the park, you know, that Forest Park, near her house in Kew Gardens? And he says she has to go jogging in the park Friday morning, okay? And not to wear no underwear, so's he can watch her bounce around. He says if she does that, they'll be even and he'll let her kid off the hook."

"No," I said.

"No fucking *what*?" shouted the old man. "No, she don't go to the park—no, he don't let the kid off the hook . . . what?"

"The kid's not on the hook, Julio; this freak is. He's a degenerate, okay? And they never stop what they do. Some of them step it up, you understand? They get into more freakish shit. But they don't stop. If she goes into that park, he'll call again. And the next time he'll want more."

"He's gonna rape her?"

"No, this kind doesn't do that. He's a watcher—but he wants to hurt women just the same. He wants to make them dance to his tune. And the ones that dance, he speeds up the music."

The old man slumped against the fender. All of a sudden he looked ancient. But an old alligator can still bite.

"She's good people, Burke. I never had a daughter, but if I did I wish it would be her. She's got a heart like steel. But this kid of hers, Mia, she turns her to water. She ain't scared for herself . . ."

"I know," I told him.

"And she can't tell her husband. He'd wanna file a fucking *lawsuit* on the guy or something."

"Yeah," I agreed, sharing the old man's profound respect for citizens.

"So what do we do?" the old man asked me.

"Where did this 'we' come from, Julio?"

"You do bodywork, right? I heard around for years—you do this kind of work, like private-eye shit and all."

"So? This is different."

"What's so different? Just nose around and find out this guy's name for me—where he lives and all."

"Not a chance," I told him.

The old man looked into my eyes, slipping into a new game quicker than a striking snake.

"Burke, this is family."

"Yeah," I said, "*your* family."

"In the joint, we was like family," he told me, his voice quiet.

"You been reading too many books, old man. I was never in your fucking family."

"Hey, come on, Burke. Just 'cause you ain't Italian don't mean nothing to me," he said, with all the sincerity of a real-estate broker.

"I went to prison because I wasn't going to spend my life kissing ass," I said, "and kissing some old man's pinky ring don't race my motor either. A boss is a boss—I don't have much but at least I don't have a fucking boss, you hear me?"

The old man kept his face flat against this sacrilege, but his lizard eyes blinked. He said nothing, waiting for me to finish.

"I showed you respect then—and I show you respect now," I said, letting him save face. "But don't disrespect *me* with this bullshit about 'family,' okay?"

The old man thought he got it. "You want money?" he asked.

"For what—for doing what?"

"I want to make this freak stop hurting Gina."

"Will she do what you tell her?" I asked him.

The old man made a clenched fist, pounded his chest where his heart would be if he had one. It was all the answer I needed.

"I'll take a shot," I told him. "Tell her to go to the park on Friday, just like the freak told her to. I'll be around, okay?"

"Burke—you'll do it right?"

"There is no 'right' about this, Julio. I'll get it done or no charge, how's that?"

"How much?"

"Ten large," I told him.

The lizard eyes didn't blink. "You got it."

I climbed back into the Plymouth. It was only two days to Friday and I'd need some help for this one. The old man's small hand reached for my arm—I stared down at the hand the way you do in prison when someone touches you who shouldn't—it was boneless—nothing but parchment skin and blue veins.

The old man looked at me. "Burke," he pleaded, "take him off the count."

"I don't do that kind of work, Julio."

The old man's eyes shifted again. "You said thirty large, right?"

"I said *ten*, old man. I don't do that kind of work. Period."

Julio tried to look injured. "You think I'm wearing a wire?"

"No, old man, I don't think you're wired. But you know better than to ask me to drop someone. I'll do what I said I'll do. That's it. Say yes or say no."

"Yes," said the old man, and I backed out of the garage, heading back to the city.

2

I T TOOK us most of the night to get everything in place. I couldn't bring Pansy on a job like this—if I kept her in the blind with me and some fool let his dog lift a leg against a nearby tree, the emergency ward would have some new customers. She's perfect on a job when you're working people, but other dogs annoy the hell out of her—especially male dogs.

Max the Silent was somewhere in the nearby brush. He's a Mongolian free-lance warrior who works for only those he wants to, and walks where he will. Calling him a karate expert is like calling a politician crooked—it doesn't tell you anything special. A strange little guy we call the Prophet was trying to explain Max to some of the young guys on the yard once. He did it much better than I could—when the Prophet talks, it's like being in church, only he tells the truth:

"Max the Silent? Max the life-taking, widow-making, silent wind of death? Brothers, better to drink radioactive waste, easier to reason with a rattlesnake, safer to wear a gasoline overcoat into the fires of hell than to mess with that man. You go to fuck with Max, people, you best bring your own body bag."

But he's not called Max the Silent because he moves so quietly. Max doesn't speak and he doesn't hear. He may be able to read lips—nobody knows—but he communicates perfectly. I showed him some of the clippings the freak had mailed to the redhead; then I made the universal sign of the maggot—two palms pressed together, one opened to show a rock being overturned, and a disgusted face at what I was looking at underneath the rock. Then I made the sign of using the telephone, and started to unbutton my shirt with a horrified look on my face. He got it all, and he dealt himself in. We'd split the money.

It was quiet and peaceful in my concealed blind. It made me think of Biafra again—comfortable isn't the same as safe.

I watched the redhead jog off along the path, her face set and hard but her body doing what the freak wanted it to do. She'd make the three circuits, standing up all the way—just like Julio promised.

He had to be out there somewhere. I didn't know his name, but I knew him—he'd have to see the redhead dance for himself. But I'd been there for hours; if he was anywhere nearby, I'd know it by now. The bridle path was about a half-mile around. The freak could be anywhere out there—but so could Max the Silent.

Minutes passed, but I never moved. I'm good at waiting. Then I heard the car: someone was driving along the road parallel to the bridle path, moving too slowly to be an early commuter. I froze as I heard the tires crunch gravel—he was off the road now, heading over to right across from where I was hidden. Perfect.

The tan Pontiac rolled to a gentle stop deep into the branches on the other side of the path, about fifty feet from where I was hidden. The engine died and the forest went silent, wondering at this new intruder. The side window of the Pontiac was heavily tinted—I couldn't even see movement inside. Then the door opened and the freak cautiously stepped out. He was tall, well over six feet, and rail-thin. He was wearing one of those jungle camouflage outfits they sell in boutiques, complete with polished black combat boots. He had a military field cap on his head, and his eyes were covered with mirror-lensed sunglasses. A long survival knife was slung low on his left thigh.

The freak started chopping at tree branches with the knife, covering the nose of the car so it would be invisible. His movements were quick, frantic. Maybe in his mind he was a soldier building a sniper's roost— to me he looked like a freak in a raincoat bouncing up and down in his seat, waiting for a porno movie to start.

The little telescope brought his face right into the blind with me. I couldn't see his eyes, but his lips were working overtime. Then we both heard the measured slap of sneakers on the path and we knew the redhead was making another circuit. He dove back into the Pontiac. I watched until I saw the driver's window sneak down and there he was, his face swiveled on a scrawny neck, eyes glued to the bridle path.

The redhead came along at a dead-even pace, running in the middle of the path, looking straight ahead. The freak's head turned with mine as we watched her approach and watched her disappear around a bend. I could see his face, but not his hands—I knew what he was doing with them.

The freak never moved. His window stayed down. Now I had to wait—was one circuit enough for him to get where he wanted to go? Would he take off now? I couldn't read the license number on his car. If he took off I'd have to make my move without Max.

But he stayed where he was—going back for seconds. I slowly twisted my neck back and forth, working out the kinks from staying too long in one spot, getting ready to move out. I felt a sharp sting against my face—I slapped the spot, looking all around me for the offending hornet. Nothing. Then a snake's hiss, amplified a dozen times, penetrated my foggy brain and I knew Max was close by. It took me another half-minute to spot him, crouched motionless not ten feet from my blind. I pointed over to where the freak was parked and Max nodded—he knew.

I held up one finger to Max, telling him to wait a minute before he moved. Then I used the same finger to draw a half-circle in the air, made a motion as if I was getting to my feet, and grabbed my left forearm with my right hand. Circle around behind the freak, I was telling Max, wait for me to show myself, and then make sure the target doesn't move. I had grabbed my forearm instead of my throat for good reason—I wanted the freak to stay where he was until I could talk to him, not get planted there forever.

Max vanished. The park was still quiet—we had some time, but not much. How long does it take a woman protecting her cub to run a half-mile?

We both heard her before we saw her again, just like the last time. I knew where the redhead had left her gym bag, up ahead of where she rounded the corner. This would be the last time we saw her, but maybe the freak didn't know that. He had missed the first circuit—maybe he thought there was another lap still to come.

The redhead jogged past us exactly like before—a reluctant machine unable to overcome its programmer. I could feel the freak's eyes burning.

I waited a couple of seconds after she rounded the bend, watching carefully, but the freak didn't start his engine. I knew Max was in place. No point in trying to be quiet about this—it would take me ten minutes to slither out of the blind without giving myself away.

I grabbed both knees, rocked back until I was flat on my back, and kicked out with both feet. The blind went flying, the birds started screaming, and I heard the freak trying to start his car. His engine fired into life just as I was charging across the road to where he was hidden, but he never had a chance. His rear tires spun in a frantic dance, but his car never moved. It wouldn't go anywhere, not with the concrete wedges Max had stuffed in front of each front wheel.

The freak saw me moving toward him; his head was whipping wildly on its thin stalk of a neck looking for a way out, and then Max materialized at the side of the car. Another split-second and he reached into the car and pulled out the freak, the way you'd pull a dead fish out of a tank. The freak started to say something and Max twisted his neck—the something turned out to be a scream. Max flashed his spare hand into the freak's belly, palm out, and the scream turned to silence.

The Pontiac was a coupe, so I went around to the passenger side and climbed into the front seat. Then I pushed the driver's seat forward and Max climbed in too, holding the freak at arm's length until I shoved the seat-back forward to give him room. He deposited the freak next to me on the front seat, keeping his hand on the scrawny neck.

We all sat there for a minute. Nobody spoke. Three strangers at a drive-in movie with nothing on the screen. When the silence got too much for the freak, he opened his mouth—it only took a slight pressure from Max's hand for him to realize that talking would be painful. I reached over and snatched the mirror lenses from his sweaty face—I wanted to see his eyes. They darted around in their sockets like half-drunk flies on a Teflon pan.

"Give me your wallet," I told him, in a calm, quiet voice.

The freak hastily fumbled open his camouflage suit and handed me a billfold. Just what I expected—a miniature police badge was pinned to one side, almost two hundred in bills, an honorary membership card from the PBA, credit cards, and other assorted crap. The driver's license and registration were my targets, and I found them soon enough.

"Mark Monroe," I said, reading from the license. "That's a nice name

. . . Mark. You think that's a nice name?" I asked Max, who said nothing.

The freak said nothing too. I took my .38 from one pocket and the silencer tube from another. He watched as I carefully screwed them together, assembling a quiet killing machine.

I made a gesture to Max and his hand vanished from the freak's neck. "You made a big mistake, Mark," I told him.

The freak looked at me. He tried to talk but his Adam's apple kept bobbing into his voice box. "Just calm down," I told him, "take it easy, Mark." It took a while before he could speak.

"Wh . . . what do you want?"

"What do I want, Mark? I want you to leave people alone. I want you to stop threatening their kids. I want you to stop getting your kicks by torturing people like you did this morning."

"Could I explain this to you . . . could I tell you about . . . ?" he wanted to know.

"Mark, if you want to tell me you're a sick man and that you can't help yourself, I got no time to listen, okay?"

"No," he said, "I don't mean that. Just let me . . ."

"Or maybe you want to tell me how the bitch asked for it—or how she really enjoyed the whole thing—is that it, Mark?"

"Well, I just . . ."

"Because if that's it," I told him, leveling the pistol at his eyes, "I'm going to blow your slimy face all over this car, you understand?"

The freak didn't make a sound—I'd just used up his only two options and he couldn't think of another. I pulled the keys from the ignition and got out of the car, leaving him inside with Max. The trunk had two cartons of newspaper clippings about kids, plus an assortment of magazines that made *Penthouse* look like *House & Garden*—*Bondage Beauties, Women in Chains, Leather & Discipline*, all hand-job specials for long-distance rapists. I took the stuff out and piled it on the ground; then I got back in the car. The glove compartment had two canisters of the halfass "mace" they sell over the counter, a billy club, and a roll of Saran Wrap. A Saint Christopher's medal dangled from the rearview mirror. Still no surprises.

"Where do you work, Mark?" I asked him in a friendly tone.

"Con Edison. I'm an engineer. I've been with them for . . ."

"That's enough, Mark!" I said, jabbing him in the ribs with the silencer. "Just answer my questions, okay?"

"Sure," the freak said, "I just . . ."

I jabbed him again, harder than before. "Mark, you and me have got a problem, understand? My problem is how to stop you from doing this stuff again, okay? And your problem is how to get out of here alive. You got any good suggestions?"

The freak's words were tumbling all over themselves, trying to get to the surface. I guess he was better on the phone. "Look, I'll never . . . I mean, you don't have to worry. . . ."

"Yeah, Mark, I have to worry. People *paid* me to worry, you understand what I'm saying?"

"Sure, sure. I didn't mean that. I'll never call her again, I swear."

"Yeah, that's right—you won't," I told him. "Now get out of the car, okay? Nice and slow."

He never tried to run. Max and I walked him back deep into the woods until I found what I was looking for—a flat stump where the Parks Department had chopped down a monster maple tree for some stupid reason.

"Mark, I want you to kneel down and put your hands on the tree—where I can see them."

"I . . ." the freak said, but it was a waste of effort. Max's clenched hand drove him to the earth. I let him kneel there as though I had all the time in the world.

"Mark, I notice you're all dressed in survival gear—it's real nice. When you drive yourself to the hospital, you tell them you were out in the woods fucking around and you fell and hurt yourself, okay?"

"Hurt myself?" he whined.

"Yeah, Mark, hurt yourself. Because that's just what you did today—you hurt yourself. You always hurt yourself when you try and fuck with people, right?"

"Please . . . please, don't. I can't stand pain. My doctor . . ."

I nodded to Max. I saw his foot flash in the morning light and I heard the crack—now the freak only had one thighbone that went from end to end. His face turned dead-white and vomit erupted from his mouth, but he never moved his hands. Even slime can learn.

"Every time you try and walk straight, Mark, I want you to think about how much fun you had in the park this morning, okay?" I asked him.

The freak's face was contorted in pain, his lips bleeding where he had bitten into them. "Yes!" he gasped out.

"And every time you try and dial a phone, Mark, I want you to think about today—will you do that?"

"Yes, yes!" he blubbered again. Max reached over and took one of his hands gently from the tree stump. A quick twist behind the freak's back, another loud snap, and the arm was useless. They call it a spiral fracture—the doctors would never get it set right. The freak had opened his mouth wide, set for a desperate shriek, when he saw the pistol six inches from his face. The scream died—he didn't want to.

"Mark," I told him, "listen to me real good. I know your name, your address, your Social Security number . . . I know everything. If this ever happens again—if you ever so much as use a scissors on a newspaper or make a phone call again—I'm going to pull your eyes out of your head with a pair of pliers and feed them to you. You got that?"

The freak looked at me; his body was working but his brain was on the critical list. All he could say was "Please . . ." It wasn't enough.

"Mark, when you get to that emergency room, you better tell them you hurt *yourself*, right? You bring anyone else into this, and you're a piece of meat. We're going to be leaving in just a minute. You can still drive, and the pain will pass. But if you ever forget the pain, there's lots more coming, okay?"

"Yes," the freak said.

"Oh, just one more thing," I told him, "I got to make sure you don't forget, Mark. And, like I told you, pain goes away. So I'm going to leave you something permanent as a souvenir of your little war-games today."

The freak's eyes turned crazy when I pulled the butcher knife from my coat, watching his one hand resting on the tree stump.

"Don't move," I told him, but he whipped back his hand and tried to run. You can't run on a broken leg. This time we let him scream.

Max hauled him back to the chopping block, holding the freak's forearm down like an anvil on a feather.

"Now, see what you did to yourself, Mark?" I asked him. "You turned a nice clean broken leg into a compound fracture. You jump around too much now and you're liable to lose an arm instead of just a hand, okay?"

The freak's slimy smell mingled with his urine as he lost all control. He was making sounds but they weren't words. Max grabbed the freak's fingertips, stretching the hand out for me. I raised the butcher knife high above my head and brought it flashing down. The freak gasped and passed out.

I pulled the knife short, looked back at Max. He immediately grabbed the freak's hand and stretched it again, but I waved him away. If the freak hadn't learned from what had happened to him already, he was past anything we could do.

Time to go. Max picked up the two cartons of filth in one hand and we worked our way back to the blind. I pulled out the screen and carried it to the hidden Plymouth. Another two minutes and we pulled out of the forest onto the pavement. I left Max in the car and used some branches to sweep away the tire tracks.

Another five minutes and we vanished onto the Inter-Boro, heading for Brooklyn.

3

IT SHOULD have been over then, except for picking up the money. You don't get cash in front from a man like Julio—it's disrespectful. Besides, I know where he lives, and all he has for me is a pay-phone number in Mama's restaurant.

I gave him three weeks and then I called the gas station from a pay phone near my office. You have to call early in the mornings from the phone—it belongs to the trust-fund hippies who live in the loft underneath me. They generally stay up all night working on their halfass stabs at self-expression, and they usually fall out well past midnight, dreaming of a marijuana paradise where all men are brothers. Good thing they never ride the subways. I don't pay rent for the top floor and I never expect to, unless the landlord sells the building. His son did something real stupid to some people a few years ago, and I passed the information only as far as the landlord. Like I told him one time, the top floor has lots of room to store information like that, but if I had to move to a smaller place . . . you never know.

I don't abuse the privilege—never stay on the phone for more than a minute, no long-distance calls. I put a slug into the pay phone—another slug answered.

"Yeah?"

"It's Burke. Tell your boss I'll meet him tonight on the third shift."

"I ain't got no boss, pal. You got the wrong number," he said, slamming down the phone. The Strike Force is making all Italians nervous these days.

The "third shift" means eleven at night to seven in the morning, just like it is in prison. When you're doing time, you learn that each shift has its own personality. The first shift, the joint is on its best behavior; that's when the visitors are allowed in and that's the only time the Parole Board comes around. The jerkoff therapists and counselors and religious nuts all make their appearances on the first shift too. The second shift is where you settle all your disputes, if you're serious about them. Prison fights only last a few seconds—someone dies and someone walks away. If the guy you stab lives, he's entitled to a rematch. And the third shift is where you check out of the hotel if you can't stand the room—that's where the young ones hang up in their cells. Prison's just like the free world: bullshit, violence, and death—only in prison it's on a tighter schedule.

Maybe you never really get out of prison. I don't have bars on my back windows—the fire escape rusted right off the building years ago except for the stairs to the roof—and Pansy was ready to discuss the ethics of breaking and entering with anyone who might show up—but it was another day coming on and my only goal was to get through it.

Inside the walls, they don't leave you with much. That's why the body-builders treasure their measurements more than any fashion model.

You can die for stepping on another man's little piece of the yard—or on his name. You either stand up to what they throw at you or you go down—it's that simple. In prison, you go down, you stay down.

The redhead was a standup broad. She didn't like doing that number in the park, but she went the route for her kid. She did the right thing— it made what I did right too. I'd never see her again. I didn't want to— the whole thing made me think of Flood.

Until Flood came along, I had survival down to a science. Like the redhead, she had a job to do, and I got brought in. She took her share of the weight and carried it right to the edge.

Flood was a state-raised kid, like me. "I'm for you, Burke," she told me just before she went back to another world. I was okay before I met her—I knew what I had to do and I did it. You don't miss what you never had. But ever since Flood, the pain floats around inside me like a butterfly. When it lands, I have to do something to forget. A piece of that song Bones used to sing in his cell late at night came to me:

> I wish I had a dollar,
> I wish I had a dime.
> I wish I had a woman,
> But all I got is time.

"Maximum Security Blues," he used to call it. Bones wasn't used to big-city jailing. He'd done most of his time down in Mississippi, on the Parchman Farm, a thirty-thousand-acre prison without walls. They didn't need walls—a man can't run faster than a bullet. Bones said he got his name years ago when he was working the dice circuit, but we called him that because that's all there was of him—he was about a hundred years old, as sharp and skinny as an ice pick. Bones did things the old way— he'd be so respectful to the guards with his thick Southern voice that they'd never listen to what he was really saying.

One of the young city blacks didn't listen so good either. Bones was sitting on a box on one of the neutral courts in the Big Yard, playing his battered six-string and singing his songs. The young stud came up with his boys, all dressed in their bullshit back-to-Africa colors, "political prisoners" one and all. I didn't know mugging old ladies for their welfare checks was a revolutionary act, but what the hell do I know? The only Marx who ever made sense to me was Groucho. The leader insisted everyone call him by his tribal name, and the new-breed guards went along with it. He rolls up and tells Bones that he's a fucking stereotype—a low-life Uncle Tom ass-kissing nigger, and all that. And Bones just strums his guitar, looking past the punk to someplace else.

The only sounds on the yard were the grunts of the iron-jockeys and the slap of dominoes on wood—and Bones's sad guitar. Then we heard a loud slap; the guitar went silent but the rest of the joint started to hum. The cold gray death-shark was swimming in the prison yard, but the guards on the catwalks didn't know it yet. Men were getting to their feet all over the yard, drifting over to where the punk was standing over Bones, holding the old man's guitar in his hands.

"This thing is nothing but an instrument to play slave music with, old man," the punk leered at him, holding the neck in one hand and the body in the other. "Maybe I'll just snap it over my knee—how you like that?"

"Don't do that, son," Bones pleaded with him.

The punk looked back at his friends for approval, all alone in his power-world now, never seeing the human wall closing around him. I looked past Bones to where Virgil, my cellmate, was closing in. Virgil wasn't raised to take up for blacks, but he'd back my play like he was supposed to when it went down. I hated Bagoomi—or whatever the fucking fool called himself—anyway. His revolutionary mission didn't stop him from raping fresh young kids when they first came on the cellblock.

But I was too late. The ancient guitar snapped across his knee as easily as a toothpick and he held one piece in each hand, his gold-toothed mouth grinning down at Bones. The old man's hand flashed and the fool's smile died along with the rest of him. By the time the guards smashed through the dense clot of prisoners, all they discovered was one more weasel who'd found the only true path to the Promised Land, a sharpened file sticking deep between his ribs. The guards paid no attention to Bones holding the pieces of his guitar and crying to himself. Their investigation determined that someone had settled a gambling debt with the punk, prison-style, and that the old man's guitar had been a casualty of the collection method.

I didn't know Flood when I was doing time—I didn't know there were women like her on this earth. I should have known that when love came to me, it would only be for a visit.

When the blues come down on you this hard, you don't want to be locked up. In prison, I had no choice. But in prison, I never had the blues like this. It was time to hit the streets.

4

I CALLED Pansy down from her roof, locked the place up, and climbed down the stairs to the garage. Sometimes when I get the blues I sit and talk with Pansy, but she was being a real bitch lately. She was in heat again—I didn't want to have her fixed—and every time she went into heat she'd rip up pieces of the office until she got over it. It didn't change the look much, and my clients aren't the particular type anyway.

The docks were quiet—a few sorry hookers hiding empty faces behind cheap makeup, a leather-laced stud hustler not smart enough to know the action didn't start until it got dark, a few citizens late for work. I was looking for Michelle, but I guess she'd taken the day off.

I thought about going up to the Bronx and scaring up the Mole, but I wasn't in the mood for a conversation about Israel today. The Mole loved the *idea* of Israel, but he'd never go.

Then I thought I'd find Max and go on with our gin game. We'd been playing almost a dozen years now, and he still had every single score-sheet. I was about forty bucks ahead. But the warehouse was empty.

The light at Bowery and Delancey held me up—long enough for one of the bums to approach the Plymouth with a dirty rag in one hand and a bottle of something in the other.

"Help me out, man?" the bum asked. "I'm trying to get together enough to get back home."

"Where's home?" I asked him.

"Used to be Oklahoma—I don't know."

"This is home now, brother," I told him, handing him a buck and watching his face light up. Maybe I'll never buy the world a Coke—although I know some Colombians trying to do just that—but at least I can buy a man a drink. Even so, the blues were still winning.

Across Fourth Street near Avenue C, another light, another stop. Paul Butterfield was singing "I've got a mind to give up living" through my car's speaker and the music wafted out into the thick city air. I had lit a smoke, and was thinking my thoughts, when I heard her voice—"You like that sad old music, *hombre?*"—and my eyes were pulled to a Puerto Rican flower: glossy raven hair hanging loose and free, big dark eyes, lips as red as blood before it dries. She was perched on a stoop near the curb, a shiny white blouse tied just under her heavy breasts, creamy skin tapering to a tiny waist and flaring out dramatically in pink toreador pants. One spike heel tapped out a rhythm on the hot sidewalk.

"The blues are the truth, little girl," I told her—and she swivel-hipped her way up to the Plymouth to hear what else the stranger had to say.

She was fifteen years old—or thirty—I couldn't tell. But she'd never again be as beautiful. Every eye on the street followed her. I looked over to the stoop where she'd been sitting and I saw four men sitting. Watching.

The Puerto Rican flower was no whore—she was a fire-starter. She bit into her lower lip, making it swell against the pressure, leaning one perfect hip against the Plymouth.

I only had a minute to make up my mind, but it was no contest—she was for sale all right, but the price was a war with at least one of the watching young bloods. I wasn't buying—young blood gets hot, and hot blood gets spilled.

"What's your name, honey?" she wanted to know. And I knew she never would. I took one of her hands in mine, the red-lacquered nails gleaming in the sun. "Make today last, beautiful girl," I told her. I kissed her hand, and drove off.

It wasn't going to be my day—I knew the feeling. I drove aimlessly, the music playing, getting it under control. It wasn't nice, but I'd do the time—I'd done it before.

I went back across the bridge, past the House of Detention, telling myself that being depressed on the street was better than being depressed in jail, but it only worked for a couple of blocks.

I parked on Nevins Avenue to get some smokes, sat on the hood of the Plymouth, and lit one up. In no hurry to go nowhere. Right across from me were three old black guys—impossible to tell how old—wearing winter coats in the warm weather, sitting on some milk crates, passing around a bottle of wine, talking to each other about something. Minding their own business, sitting in the sun. Not all clubhouses have doors and windows.

Then I saw the pack of punks bopping up the street on the same side as the old men. Four white kids; they all had those weird haircuts, short and spiky in front, long in back, streaks of bright color and sticking up. They were dressed in short-sleeved leather jackets. One sported a long black cane with an eagle's head on top and probably a sword inside. Another one had a collar around his neck that looked like it belonged on a bulldog. They all were wearing black half-gloves, the kind that leave your fingertips out and knuckles bare. The punk with the cane came first, the others fanning out behind him. Then the biggest one moved up on the outside wing of the flying wedge, bouncing up the street throwing left jabs at anyone who came by—the others laughing as people fell over themselves to get out of the way.

As they passed by the old men, the big one fired a vicious jab square into the chest of one of them, knocking the old-timer right off his crate. I stepped off the hood of the Plymouth, reaching into my pocket for the roll of quarters I always keep there to pay tolls—but before I could move, the old man shook his head violently and struggled to his feet. He rubbed his face with both fists, drew a deep snarfling breath through his nose, and shuffled forward, suddenly hooking with both hands. The big kid threw up his own hands in some feeble imitation of boxers he'd seen on television, but he never had a chance. The old man drove the kid back against the side of a van like it was the ropes in the ring he must have fought in years ago, firing punch after punch to the kid's unprotected face and stomach—hard, professional punches, coming unpredictably from both hands. The big kid dropped to the street; the old man turned and went to a neutral corner, running on automatic pilot.

The street was quiet, but you could feel the joy swelling out of the bodegas and the bars. The big kid lay where he dropped—I scanned the street, but his running buddies were nowhere in sight. About what you'd expect. And the old man was back on his milk crate, being with his friends.

When the old man heard the bell, he knew what he had to do. Maybe he was past talking about it, but he could still do it. When I looked around again, the big kid was gone. And so were my blues.

5

THE THIRD shift was just getting started when I wheeled the big Plymouth up Flatbush Avenue to the gas station. I pulled up to the high-test pump, told the jockey to fill it up, and watched the shifty-eyed slob pour an extra twenty-eight cents' worth of gas down the side of my car just so the total would come out even and he wouldn't have to count to make change. When he came around to the window, I just said "Julio?" and he nodded toward the back. Before he could ask for his cash, I flicked the lever into Drive and took off.

As soon as I pulled behind the station and saw the white Coupe de Ville I knew Julio had sent one of his stooges to make the payoff—the old man's idea of a class act. The white Caddy had the driver's window down—the guy inside picked up the Plymouth and was opening his door even before I came to a stop. Just what I expected: a full-race Cheech— about twenty-five years old, blow-dried hair over a blocky face sporting an Atlantic City tan and dark glasses, white silk shirt open to his chest so I could see the gold chains, dark tight pants, shiny black half-boots. His sleeves were rolled up enough to show me muscular forearms, a heavy gold bracelet on one wrist, a thin gold watch on the other. Central Casting.

The Cheech stepped out of his Caddy, flicking the door shut behind him, strolling over to me.

"You Burke?" he wanted to know.

"Sure," I told him. I wasn't there for the conversational opportunity.

"I got something for you—from Mr. C."

I held out my left hand, palm up, keeping my right where he couldn't see it.

"I got ten big ones here," he said, tapping his front pocket.

I didn't say anything—the jerk was unhappy about something, but it wasn't my problem.

He peered into the Plymouth, watching my face. And then he came out with it. "You don't look so tough to me, man. Whatever you did for the old man—I coulda done it."

"Give me the fucking money," I told him pleasantly. "I didn't drive out here to listen to your soap opera."

"Hey, fuck you, you don't want to listen! Money talks, right?"

"I don't know, kid. But the money you're holding for me better *walk*, you understand?"—opening and closing my hand a couple of times so he'd get the message.

The Cheech took off his dark glasses, hooked them over his dangling chains, acting like he was really thinking about not paying me—or acting like he was really thinking, I couldn't tell which. Then he decided. He handed over the envelope without another word, something still on his mind. I tossed it into the back seat, giving him something else to think about. I took my foot off the brake and the Plymouth started to roll forward.

"Hey!" he said. "Wait a minute."

"What?"

"Uh . . . look, man. You ever use anyone else on jobs . . . you know. I could always use some extra coin, right?"

"No," I told him, my face flat as a prison wall.

"Hey, just *listen* for a minute, okay? I got experience, you know what I'm saying?"

"Kid," I told him, "I got warrants out on me older than you," and started to roll forward again.

The Cheech's hand went in his pocket again, but this time he came out with a snub-nosed revolver—he stuck it through the open window, holding it steady, about six inches from my face.

"Don't fucking *move*! You got that? You fucking sit there and you listen when I talk, you understand? I ain't no fucking nigger you can just walk away from—I'm *talking* to you."

I looked at him, saying nothing. There was nothing to say—Julio sent me a messenger boy with some dangerous delusions. It's hard to get good help nowadays.

"You show me some respect, huh?" barked the Cheech. "You ain't no fucking better than me."

"Yeah, I am," I told him, nice and calm and gentle. "I think about what I'm going to do before I do it. Now *you* think about it. Think about me coming here alone. Think about how you're going to get out of this alley if you pull the trigger. Think about what you're going to tell the old man. Think about it . . . then think about what you have to say—and say it."

The Cheech tried to think and hold the gun on me at the same time. It was too much work and his brain overloaded. The snub-nose trembled in his hand for a second and he looked at it as if it had tricked him. When his eyes came back up to me, he was looking at the sawed-off shotgun I was holding in my right hand.

"I'm listening," I told him. But he had nothing to say. "You know how to load that thing?" I asked him. "Or did someone do it for you?"

"I know . . ." he mumbled.

"Then fucking *un*load it, kid. And do it slow—or I'm going to blow your pretty gold chains right through your chest."

He pointed the pistol up, popped the cylinder, held it upside down, and slowly dropped out the bullets. They made a soft plopping sound as they hit the ground. There was so much wet garbage in that alley you could have dropped a safe from a ten-story building without too much noise.

"Listen to me," I said, calm as an undertaker. "You made a mistake.

You even *think* about making another one, go make out a will, understand?"

He just nodded. It was an improvement.

I tapped the gas and the Plymouth rolled out of the alley, heading home. By the time I crossed Flatbush Avenue, my hands had stopped shaking.

6

THE PLYMOUTH slowly made its way down Atlantic Avenue. It wasn't the fastest way back from Brooklyn, but it was the quietest. I eyeballed all the antique shoppes and trendo restaurants which had sprung to life in the last few months—the wino-rehab centers and storefront churches never had a prayer. The new strip runs from Flatbush all the way down past the Brooklyn House of Detention—pioneer-yuppie lofts with stained-glass windows sat over little stores where you could buy fifty different kinds of cheese. Some of the stores still sold wine, though not the kind you drank out of a paper bag. But news of the urban renaissance hadn't filtered down to the neighborhood skells yet—it still wasn't a good idea to linger at a red light after dark.

I turned up Adams Street, heading for the Brooklyn Bridge. The first streaks of filthy daylight were already in the sky. The Family Court was on my right, the Supreme Court on my left. It works good that way—when the social workers are done with the kids, the prisons can take them.

The newsboy was standing on the median strip just before the entrance to the bridge. He had a stack of papers under one arm, hustling for an honest buck. Motorists who knew the system beeped their horns, held their arms out the window, and the kid would rush over, slap a paper into your hand, pocket the change, and keep moving. Every once in a while a patrol car would decide the kid should work some other corner, but mostly the cops leave the kids alone.

I pulled into the Left Turn Only lane, ignoring the sign like everyone else. When I hit the horn, the kid came over. I pushed the switch to lower my window and took a close look: black kid, about fifteen, husky build, Navy watch cap over a bushy Afro. I waved away the *Daily News* he offered.

"Roscoe working today?" I asked.

"Yeah, man. He working. 'Cross the way, you know?"

I already had the Plymouth rolling, timing it so I'd get caught at the light. I watched the black kid fly back across the street to tell Roscoe he had a customer. The twenty-four-hour news station was saying something about another baby beaten to death; this one in the Bronx. So many cases like that now, all they do is give you the daily body count.

The light changed. The Plymouth rolled forward until I spotted Roscoe standing on the divider, a bunch of papers in one hand, a big canvas bag held by a thick strap around his neck. Roscoe's about thirty, too old to be selling papers.

He recognized the car—looked close to be sure he recognized the driver too.

"Paper, mister?"

"Yeah, give me *The Wall Street Journal*," I said, holding a twenty out toward him at the same time.

"Oh, yeah. I got one around here someplace," he mumbled, rummaging in his canvas bag.

While he was looking down at his bag, I did a quick scan of the streets, knowing he was doing the same. Nothing. I reached my left hand out for the paper Roscoe was holding over the open top of his bag, snapped the twenty toward him, and dropped the sawed-off into his bag at the same time. Gravity is one law nobody fucks with.

Roscoe comes honestly by his name, if not his income. I tossed yesterday's *News* on the front seat and drove off, heading for Chinatown. I don't like to carry heat across the border.

7

THE CHINATOWN streets were just getting organized: young men pushing hand trucks loaded with fresh vegetables, older women lumbering toward another day in the sweatshops. I spotted Hobart Chan cruising the Bowery in his sable Bentley, a shark looking for blood in the water. Even gangsters go to work early in Chinatown.

I rolled past Mama's checking the front window. The white dragon tapestry was in place—everything cool inside. I tooled through the narrow alley and left the Plymouth in its usual spot, right underneath some Chinese writing on the wall that warned the local hoods not to park there. It didn't bother me—it was Max's writing.

I went through the kitchen and into the back like I usually do. When I opened the door, one of Mama's alleged cooks smoothly slipped his hand inside his white coat—he pulled it back empty when he recognized me. I walked to the front, pulled the two-star edition of the *News* from underneath the register, and walked to my table in the back, next to the kitchen. No one approached my table pretending to be a waiter, so Mama was around someplace. I read through last night's race results from Yonkers and waited.

I caught a shadow across the newspaper and looked up. It was Mama—looking as though she just stepped out of a 1950s beauty parlor, hair black and glossy in a tight bun at the back of her head, plain high-collared blue silk dress that almost covered her shoes, a jade necklace setting off her dark-painted lips. She's somewhere between fifty and ninety years old.

"So, Burke. You come to eat?"

"To eat and to see Max, Mama. He around?"

"Burke, you know Max not come around so much anymore. Not since he take up with that bar girl. You know that bar girl—the one from Vietnam?"

"Yeah, I met her."

"That girl no good for Max, Burke. He not keeping his mind on business—not reliable like before, right?"

"He's okay, Mama. There's no problem."

"You wrong, Burke. *Plenty* problems. Problems for me, problems for Max, maybe problems for you, okay?"

"I'll talk to him," I told her, more to stop this broken record than anything else.

"Yes, *you* talk to him. I talk to him, he not listen, okay?"

"Okay. You got any hot-and-sour soup?"

But even the mention of her favorite potion didn't calm her down. Mama was a businesswoman in her heart. She wanted me to get on Max's case about the girl, but she hadn't been there when they first met. I had.

WE WERE working the box system that night on the subway: me lying across three empty seats on the uptown express, dressed in my Salvation Army suit and a smashed old fedora, Max right across from me wearing an old raincoat, staring straight ahead like he was on his way to some early-morning cook's job, the Mole at the other end of the car, Coke-bottle lenses fixed on pages and pages of his "calculations" on some greasy paper. I had the papers we had contracted to deliver sewn into the lining of my suit jacket. I don't carry heat on this kind of job. The Mole was packing enough high explosive to turn the F Train into a branch of the space shuttle. Max had only his hands and feet—he was more dangerous than the Mole.

I didn't need a disguise—it's no great feat for me to look like a used-up wino. And the Mole always looks like the lunatic he is—not the kind of human you'd want to make eye contact with on the subway. Max can adjust his posture and muscles in his face so he looks like an old man, and that's what he was doing.

The deal is this: If anybody hassles me, I take any amount of abuse that won't cripple me or make me lose the papers. If anyone moves on the Mole, Max steps in, leaving me carrying and clear. And if anyone moves on Max, me and the Mole just sit there and watch. It never takes long.

But that night we weren't alone in the subway car. First this Oriental woman gets on at 14th Street. She was wearing a black cape with a red silk lining over a white silk dress. It buttoned to the throat, but the straight skirt was slit to past mid-thigh. Heavy stage-type makeup, overdone eye shadow, spike heels. Maybe some Off Broadway lames were reviving *Suzie Wong*. She looked at me without expression, didn't even glance at Max or the Mole. She sat there primly, knees together, hands in her lap. Her eyes were unreadable.

And we rode together like that until we got deep into Brooklyn, where the wolfpack boarded the train. Two white kids and a Puerto Rican, dressed alike in the standard hunting outfit: leather sneakers, dungaree jackets with the sleeves cut off, gloves that left their fingertips exposed, studded wristbands, heavy belts with chains dangling. One carried a giant radio, the others were empty-handed. They checked the car quickly, eyeballing the girl.

But they were looking for money, not fun. A fast score from some working stiff. And Max was the target.

Ignoring me, they surrounded him. One sat down on each side; one of the white kids remained standing, facing Max. The spokesman.

"Hey, Pop—how about twenty bucks for a cup of coffee?"

Nobody laughed—it wasn't a joke.

Max didn't respond. For one thing, he doesn't speak. For another, he doesn't pay a lot of attention to bugs.

I glanced over at the Mole under the brim of my hat. The yellow-orange subway lighting bounced off his thick glasses as he buried his head deep into some papers. He never looked up. The skells weren't paying any attention to me, just concentrating on Max. One of the white kids snatched Max's old raincoat, jerking the lapels toward him to pull Max to his feet. But nothing happened—I could see the muscles ripple in the kid's arm as he strained, but it was like he trying to pull up an anchor. The other maggots crowded in, and the Puerto Rican kid snarled, "Give it up, old man!" The other white kid started to giggle. He pulled out a set of cheap brass knuckles, the kind they sell to kids in Times Square. He slowly fitted them over one hand, made a fist, smacked it into an open palm. The slapping sound brought the Mole's head up for a second. Max never moved.

The kid with the brass knuckles went on giggling to himself while the other white kid struggled to pull Max to his feet and the Puerto Rican kept up a steady stream of threats. None of them was in a hurry.

Then the girl got to her feet. I could hear the tapping of her spike heels as she closed the gap between herself and the maggots. They never looked her way until she hissed at them: "Hey! Leave the old man alone!"

Then they spun to her, delighted with new prey, abandoning Max. The Puerto Rican kid was the first to speak.

"Fuck off, bitch! This ain't your business!"

But the woman kept closing on them, hands on hips. Now the whole wolfpack had its back to Max, moving toward her. The white kid was still giggling, still slamming his brass knuckles into an open palm. The woman walked right into the center of the triangle they formed. As the white kid reached a hand toward the front of her dress, I lurched to my feet in a drunken stupor and stumbled into him. He whirled to face me, brass knuckles flashing. I threw up a weak arm to try and fend him off as the Oriental woman unsheathed her claws and the Mole reached into his satchel. But then Max the Silent shed his dirty raincoat like an old scaly skin and moved in. It was too fast for me to follow—a hollow crack and I knew the Puerto Rican kid would never reach for anything again without major medical assistance—the flash of a foot and the biggest white kid screamed like ground glass was being pulled through his lungs—a steel-hard fist against the skull of the punk with the brass knuckles and I saw the front of his face open like an overripe melon too long in the sun.

The subway car was dead quiet inside, rumbling on unperturbed toward the next express stop. The Mole took his hands out of his satchel and went back to whatever he was reading. The three maggots were on the ground, only one of them conscious enough to moan—it was the Puerto Rican kid, blood and foam bubbling out of his mouth.

The woman stood shock-still, her face drained of color, her hands frozen at her sides. Max the Silent looked into her face, and bowed deeply to her. She caught her breath, and bowed back. They stood looking at each other, seeing nothing else.

Max gestured for me to stand, pointed at his mouth and then at me. The Oriental woman's eyes flashed, but she seemed beyond surprise now.

She stood swaying slightly with the train's rhythm, balancing easily on the spike heels, dark-lacquered talons on silky hips. She watched the wino remove his hat and smooth out his tangled hair. If she was expecting another transformation, she was deeply disappointed. The distance between the real Max the Silent and a helpless old man was cosmic—the distance between the real me and a bum was considerably less. But I bowed to the woman too.

"My brother does not speak or hear. He can read lips, and those who know him can understand him perfectly. He wishes to speak with you, through me. With your permission . . . ?"

The woman's eyebrows arched, and she nodded, saying nothing . . . waiting patiently. I liked her already.

Max gestured toward her, two fingers held against his thumb. He turned that same hand back toward his heart, tapped his chest lightly, bowed, reached his left hand back to the old, discarded raincoat, held it in one hand, touched his eyes, one at a time, with the other. He touched his heart again.

"My brother says you are a woman of great courage, to protect what you thought was an old man against such dangerous people."

The woman cleared her throat, smiled gently with the side of her mouth. She spoke as gravely as I had, with just the trace of a French accent in her speech.

"Your brother is quite deceptive."

Max absently swung his foot into the rib cage of one of the maggots lying on the floor, never taking his eyes off the woman. I heard a sound like a twig snapping. He touched his eyes again, shook his head "no." He expanded his chest; his eyes flattened and power flowed from his body. He turned to me.

"My brother says a maggot cannot see a true man," I told her.

Still with the same half-smile, she asked, "Can a maggot see a true woman?"

Max took a pair of dark glasses from my coat pocket—he knows where I keep them—and put them on his face. He made a gesture like tapping with a cane, took off the glasses, threw both hands toward the woman, and smiled.

"My brother says even a blind man could see a woman such as you," I translated, and she was smiling too, even before I finished.

That's how Max met Immaculata.

8

To Mama, Immaculata was a "bar girl," her catchall phrase for anything from prostitute to hostess. A Vietnamese was bad enough, but one of mixed parentage was suspect beyond redemption. As far as she was concerned, a true warrior didn't need a woman, except on an occasional basis.

Mama never seemed to move from her restaurant, but nothing escaped her sight. She knew Max still lived in the back of the warehouse near Division Street, where his temple lay hidden upstairs. But he didn't live alone anymore. For Mama, anything that wasn't business was bad.

Immaculata had been working as a hostess in a Manhattan bar before she met Max. She had been trained as some kind of psychotherapist in France, but she couldn't practice in this country until she completed enough courses and got a license.

I saw her work one day when I went over to the warehouse looking for Max. I pulled the Plymouth into the garage on the first floor. It was empty—it always was. I got out of the car, closed the garage doors, and waited. If Max was around, he'd be there soon enough. If he didn't show in a couple of minutes, I'd just chalk a message to him on the back wall.

I heard the sound of fingers snapping, looked to my left, and there was Max. He was holding a finger to his lips—no noise. I climbed out of the Plymouth, leaving the door open, and walked over to where Max was standing. He motioned for me to follow him upstairs.

We padded along the narrow catwalk past the entrance to his temple. When we came to the blank wall behind the temple door, Max reached up and pulled back a curtain. We were looking through some one-way glass into what looked like a kid's playroom: kid-size furniture, brightly painted walls, toys all over the place. Immaculata was seated at a small table. Across from her was a little girl—maybe four years old. They were both in profile to us. It looked like they were playing with some dolls together.

I shrugged my shoulders, spread my hands, palms up. "What is this?" I was asking Max. He patted the air in front of him with both hands and pointed to his eyes: "Be patient and watch."

There were four dolls on the table. Two were bigger than an average kid's doll; the other two were a lot smaller. From their clothes and their hair I could see that two were male and two female.

Immaculata put the dolls to one side of the table and asked the kid something, looking calm and patient. The little girl took one of the small dolls and started to undress it, slowly and reluctantly. Then she stopped. She took the big male doll and made it sort of pat the little girl on the head. The little doll pulled away from the pat, but not too far. Finally, the big male doll helped the little girl doll get undressed. The big male doll unbuttoned his pants. It had plain white boxer shorts underneath. The child took off the shorts, revealing a set of testicles and a penis. The little girl doll was pushed over toward the big doll. The child kept lifting the male doll's penis, but it always flopped back. Finally, she put the little girl doll's mouth against the male doll's penis. A couple of dead-weight seconds went by. Then the child pulled the little girl doll away from the big doll. She put the little girl doll face down on the floor—then she had the big male doll pull up his shorts and pants and walk away.

The little girl was crying. Immaculata didn't move—but she was talking to the child. You couldn't hear a thing outside the window. She put out her hand to the child. The little girl took her hand, and Immaculata gently pulled her around to where she was sitting. She put the little girl on her lap, one arm around her back. She kept talking until the child nodded agreement to something.

Then Immaculata reached out for the big male doll and put it right in front of the child. The little girl grabbed the doll and started to shake it, screaming something. Her face was contorted in rage. She ripped at the big doll. Suddenly, the big doll's arm came off in her hand. The child looked at the arm she was holding, then back to Immaculata, who nodded something to her. The child ripped off the other arm. Then she started talking to the big, armless doll, shaking her finger in some kind of admonishment. Then she started to cry again.

Max motioned for me to follow him again. He pointed back toward his temple, telling me to wait for him.

I walked through the temple, being careful not to step past the black lines painted in a rectangle on the bleached wood floor. Then around to the back stairs, and from there into the small room that opened onto an alley behind the warehouse. I went over to the battered wood desk and pulled out the last score-sheet from our endless gin-rummy game.

I heard a knock at the back door. Then another. And then three raps, short and sharp. Max. I opened the door to let him in. If the three raps had come first, I wouldn't have opened the door without a gun in my hand.

Max and Immaculata came in together. She greeted me the way she always does—a slight bow of her head over her hands clasped in front. Always formal. She sat down across the table from me. Max went around behind me so he could watch her lips when she spoke.

"What was that I was watching?" I asked her.

"That was what we call a 'validation,' Burke."

"Validation?"

"That little girl has gonorrhea—a sexually transmitted disease. It was my job to find out how she contracted it."

"And she showed you?"

"Yes. The large doll is her father. Many children, especially very young ones, have no ability to use a narration. Most of them don't even have the words for what has been done to them."

"I never saw dolls like that," I said.

"They're 'anatomically correct' dolls. Under the clothes, the bodies have genitals proportionate to their size. They have to be specific, especially when the children don't speak."

"You mean when they're too young?"

"Not necessarily. The child you saw is almost six years old. But she had been told that the 'game' Daddy plays with her is their special secret and she isn't to tell anyone."

"Did he threaten her?"

"No. In fact, most incest offenders don't use threats until their victim is a lot older than this one. The child almost instinctively knows something is wrong with the activity, but the combination of guilt and fear is usually enough to ensure silence."

"What was that thing at the end—with the arms on the doll?"

"Just what it looked like to you. Rage. Sexually abused children are often consumed with anger at the person who hurt them. And sometimes at the person who failed to protect them as well. Part of the treatment process is letting them know it's okay to say 'No!'—it's okay to be angry. The arms and legs of the dolls are attached with Velcro; the children can tear them apart—and maybe put them together later, if they come that far."

"Doesn't the kid live with her father?"

"She lives with her mother. The incest happens during the time she visits him."

"No more visits for him?"

"That's really up to the courts. When the child showed signs of having been sexually abused, the mother took her to a doctor. She didn't know what was wrong, but she knew *something* was. The doctor didn't find anything physical—he never thought to check for V.D., it never occurred to him. The actual diagnosis wasn't made until weeks later—when the mother took the child to the emergency ward because of a vaginal discharge. The child was referred to a program where they do therapy and also teach the children physical and emotional self-defense. I work there too—I need the supervision to qualify for my license here. What I was doing in the playroom was preparing the child for supervised visitation with her father. She has to know she can confront her father and tell him to stop, and she has to feel protected if she is to do that."

"Why should this maggot get *any* visits with her?"

"That's a good question," she said. "The answer is that the child must work through her own rage at what happened to her. She has to recapture a sense of control over her life. The supervised visits are not meant to benefit the father—they are therapeutic for the daughter. And, at the same time, the father can start his own treatment."

"How about if he denies the whole thing?"

"They usually do, at first. But eventually, most of them do acknowledge what they have done—covering it, of course, with a thick layer of self-justification."

"What justification?"

"Oh, that the child was the instigator . . . that this was nothing more than showing his affection in a special way . . . minimizing. . . ."

"What bullshit. Is he going to be tested for gonorrhea?"

"Yes, he will be tested. But it takes less than twenty-four hours for all traces of the disease to disappear if he gets treatment. However, the courts will consider the presence of a sexually transmitted disease together with my validation. And find against him."

"You're telling me there really is treatment for these people?"

"That's one of the major arguments in the profession today—I don't know the answer."

"I don't know about incest like this. But the maggots who like sex with kids *never* stop."

"Pedophiles may well be incurable. I don't know. I work only with the victims."

Max crossed over to stand behind Immaculata. He shook his fist tightly to show me how proud he was of his woman. She looked up at him and I knew this wasn't a day for gin rummy.

9

Everything probably would have blown over between Immaculata and Mama except that Max brought his woman to the restaurant one night. In honor of the occasion, we all took one of the big tables near the back. There's no air conditioning in Mama's place, but the atmosphere was like a meat locker anyway. Mama wasn't insane enough to openly insult Immaculata, so they fought their battle with the subtle fire only women of character ever truly master.

One of the thugs brought a huge tureen of hot-and-sour soup. Mama bowed to Immaculata, indicating she should serve everyone—that's what bar girls do, right? But Immaculata never flinched—she took Max's bowl off his plate and spooned in a generous helping, being extra-careful to serve it properly, a full measure of all the ingredients, not just the thin stuff on top. Mama smiled at her—the way the coroner smiles at a corpse just before the autopsy.

"You serve man first, not woman. Chinese way, yes?"

"Not the Chinese way, Mrs. Wong—my way. To me, Max comes first, you see?"

"I see. You call me 'Mama,' okay? Like everybody else?"

Immaculata said nothing, bowing her head ever so slightly in agreement. But Mama wasn't finished.

"Immaculata your name? I say that right—Immaculata? Is that Vietnamese name?"

"It's the name the nuns gave me—a Catholic name—when the French were in my country."

"Your country Vietnam, yes?"

"Yes," said Immaculata, her eyes hard.

"Your father and mother both from Vietnam?" Mama asked innocently.

"I don't know my father," Immaculata responded flatly, "but I know what you want to know."

The table was dead quiet then. Max watched Mama, making up his mind—Mama had survived two wars but she was never as close to death as she was at that moment.

Max pointed one steel finger at my face, then opened his hands, asking a question.

I knew what he wanted. "No," I told him, "I don't know who my father was either. So what?"

Max wiped his hands together: "All finished," he meant. The discussion was over.

But he wasn't going to pull it off that easy. "You want to know my father's nationality, yes?" asked Immaculata.

"No," Mama said, "why I want to know that?"

"Because you think it would tell you something about me."

"I already know about you," Mama snapped.

"And what is that?" asked Immaculata, the air around us crackling with violence.

But Mama backed away. "I know you love Max—that good enough. I love Max—Max like my son, right? Even Burke—like my son too. Have two sons—very different. So what, yes?"

"Yes, we understand each other," Immaculata told her, as Mama bowed her agreement.

"You call me 'Mama'?" the dragon lady asked.

"Yes. And you call me Mac, okay?"

"Okay," said Mama, declaring a truce, at least when Max was around.

10

BUT MAX wasn't around now, so I'd have to leave the money with Mama. No big deal—anytime I make a score, I stash some of it with Max or Mama. It's not that I have such good savings habits—it's just that it's a long time between decent scores for me. I didn't mind working without a license, but I wasn't going to try it without a net.

The last time I went back to prison changed everything. When you're raised by the state, you don't think about the same things citizens do. You find out sooner or later that time is money—if you don't have money, you're going to keep on doing time. Most of the guys I came up with were doing life sentences on the installment plan. A few years in—a few months out.

I thought I had it figured out before I took my last fall. Up to then, I kept making the mistake of involving citizens in my business. There's a different set of rules for them and for us. You stab a man in prison, you might end up in the Hole for a few months—you stick up a liquor store on the street and you're looking at telephone numbers behind the walls, especially if you've been there before. I'd taught myself some things by then, and I knew better than to work with partners who wouldn't stand up. And I knew where the money was—if I wanted to steal without making citizens mad at me, I had to steal from the bad guys. Back then, the heroin business was strictly European—the blacks were only on the retail end and the Hispanics hadn't made their move. The Italians were moving pounds and pounds of junk all through the city, and they weren't too careful about it—they had no competition. Max wanted to hijack the gangsters when the money changed hands, but that wouldn't work—the Italians transported the dope without a care in the world, but they got paranoid as hell when it came to cold cash. Too many bodyguards—I wanted a nice smooth sting, not the O.K. Corral.

Finally, I came up with the perfect idea—we'd hijack the dope, and then sell it back for a reasonable price. It worked fine at first. Max and I watched the social club on King Street for a few weeks until we saw how they did it. Three, four times a month, a blue pastry truck with Jersey plates would pull up to the front door, and the driver would offload the covered trays of pastries and the metal tubs of tortoni and spumoni. Within a couple of hours, a dark blue Caddy would pull up outside and the same two hard guys would get out. They looked enough alike to be twins: short, muscular, with thick manes of dark hair worn a little too long in the back.

Max and I watched them walk up to the dark-glass front of the social club. If a couple of the old men were sitting outside—always wearing a plain white shirt over dark suit pants, polished shoes, talking quietly— the young guys would stop and pay their respects. They were muscle all right, but family muscle, working their way up the ladder.

The young guys would go in, but they wouldn't come out for hours. It didn't add up—boys like that might be allowed in the club to get an assignment, or on a special occasion, but the old guys wouldn't let them just hang around.

Max and I learned to be patient in different places, but we both learned it well. It took another few weeks to work our way around to the back of the club and find a spot where the constantly watching eyes in that neighborhood couldn't see what we were doing. Sure enough—

ten minutes after they went in the front door, the muscle boys went out the back. One carried a suitcase, the other held a pistol parallel to his leg, barrel pointed down. The guy with the suitcase tossed it into the open trunk of a black Chevy sedan, slammed it closed, and got behind the wheel while the gunman watched the alley. A minute later, the Chevy took off with both of them in the front seat.

I didn't have the Plymouth then, so Max and I followed them in a cab—me behind the wheel and Max as the passenger. I didn't mind taking some reasonable risks to make some unreasonable money, but I wasn't about to let Max drive.

The muscle boys took their time—they cruised up Houston Street to the East Side Drive. When they crossed the Triboro into the Bronx, I looked a question at Max, but he just shrugged his shoulders—they had to be going to Harlem sooner or later. Sure enough, they circled Yankee Stadium, hooked onto the Major Deegan Expressway, and took the exit to the Willis Avenue Bridge. At the end of the exit road all they had to do was make a quick right and they were back over the bridge and into 125th Street, the heart of Harlem. Another few minutes and they parked in the back of a funeral parlor. We didn't follow them any farther.

The next two runs followed the same route—we just had one more piece to check out and we were ready to operate. We met in Mama's basement—me, Max, Prophet, and the Mole.

"Prof, can you get a look at how they transfer the stuff? It's in the back of the Golden Gate Funeral Parlor on Twenty-first," I said.

"The next time the move goes down, the Prof shall be around," he assured us.

"Mole, we need three things, okay?" I told him, holding up three fingers to let Max follow along. "We need to disable their car real quick, get the trunk open, and get in the wind."

The Mole nodded, his pasty skin gleaming in the dark basement. "Tiger trap?" he wanted to know. He meant one of his bombs under the lid of a manhole cover—one flick of a switch and the street would open up, dropping the car into the pit. That would sure as hell disable the car, open the trunk, and give us all the time in the world to walk away. It wasn't exactly what I had in mind—the Mole's heart was in the right place, but it would take years of therapy to reduce him to a lunatic.

"Mole, we don't want to *kill* them, okay? I had in mind maybe the Prof gets their attention for a second, Max and me hit them from either side and brace them—you pop open the trunk, grab the suitcase, and slash the rear tires. How's that?"

"How does the trunk lock?" the Mole wanted to know. It was all the same to him.

I looked over to the Prof and he nodded—we'd know soon.

"You can get us an old Con Ed truck, Mole?" I asked him.

The Mole made a face like "Who couldn't?" It was true enough for him—he lived in a junkyard.

||

THE NEXT time the muscle boys stopped at the red light before they turned onto the bridge for Harlem, things were a little different. The battered Con Ed truck was nosed against the metal support for the traffic light, blocking most of the intersection. The black Chevy slid to a smooth stop—running red lights wasn't the best idea when you were carrying a trunkful of dream dust.

I climbed out of the driver's seat, wearing a set of Con Ed coveralls and a thick leather tool belt around my waist with another strap over one shoulder. My eyes were covered with blue-tinted sunglasses—I had pasted on a heavy mustache a few minutes ago. The Con Ed cap covered a thick blonde wig and the built-up heels on my work boots made me two inches taller. The Prof was slumped against a building wall, an empty bottle of T-Bird by his side, dead to the world.

I walked toward the Chevy, spreading my hands in the universal civil-service hostile apology: "What can I do?" The driver wasn't going for any delay—he spun the wheel with one hand to pull around the truck: I could get out of the way or get run over. His hard face said it was all the same to him. He was in control.

Then it all went to hell. I tore open the snaps on the coveralls and unleashed the scattergun I had on a rawhide cord around my neck just as the Mole threw the truck into reverse and stomped the gas. The truck flew backward right into the Chevy's radiator, and one chop from Max took out the guy in the passenger seat before he could move. The Prof flew off the wall, an ice pick in his hand. I don't know if the driver heard the hiss from his rear tires—all he could see were the twin barrels of the sawed-off staring him in the face from a distance of three feet.

I flicked the scattergun up a couple of inches and the driver got the picture—his hands never moved off the wheel. He didn't see the Mole slither out of the truck and around to the back of the Chevy—another couple of seconds and the trunk was open and Max had the suitcases.

I patted the air in front of me to tell the driver to get down in the front seat. As soon as his head started to drop, I cut loose with the scattergun right into his door. I blasted the second barrel where his head had been a second ago, taking out most of the windshield, and sprinted for the side of the warehouse where the cab was waiting. Max was at the wheel, with the Mole beside him, the engine already running. I tossed the empty scattergun to the Prof in the back seat, dove in beside him, and we were rolling. Everyone knew what they had to do—we were pretty sure there was no backup car, but it was too early to relax. The Mole had his grubby hands deep in his satchel and the Prof was already reloading the shotgun for me.

12

WE LEFT the suitcases with the Mole in his junkyard and split up. We didn't make our move for a few weeks—the mobsters were too busy murdering each other to answer anonymous telephone calls. I don't know if they dusted the driver and his partner or not—probably kept them alive long enough to make sure they were telling the truth, and then started looking. But they weren't looking outside the family. Me and Max and the Prof were sitting in Mama's restaurant when we read the headline in the *Daily News*—"Torched Building Was Gangster Tomb!" It seems someone had wiped out a whole meeting of the heroin syndicate and then set fire to the building—the Fire Department hadn't discovered the bodies for a couple of days, and it took another few days for the cops to make positive identifications. That kind of massive hit didn't sound like it was connected to our little hijacking, but we didn't know who we could ask.

The Prof looked up from the paper. "Sounds like Wesley's work to me," he whispered.

"Don't ever say that name again," I snapped at him. Wesley was a guy we had done time with before—if I thought he was operating in New York, I'd move to the Coast.

Anytime you pull a snatch-and-switch, the last part is the hardest. You can grab the goods easy enough—the mark isn't expecting the move— you just disappear and let them look in their own backyard. But when it gets down to exchanging the goods for cash, you got major troubles. It's easy enough to do if you don't mind losing some of your troops along the way, but our army was too small for that kind of sacrifice.

We agreed to wait another two weeks. It was fine with the Prof. Max looked unhappy. I spread my hands, asking him "What?" He just shook his head. He'd tell me when he was ready.

13

WE WERE in the sub-basement of Mama's restaurant, planning the exchange. It was simple enough—I'd make contact over the phone, explain my problem, and wait for the solution to come from them. Sooner or later they'd agree to use one of the free-lance couriers who work the fringes of our world. These guys worked off a straight piece, no percentage—maybe ten thousand to deliver a package and bring something back. You could move anything around the city that way—gold, diamonds, blueprints, funny money, whatever. None of the couriers were family people, although one was Italian. They were men of honor—men you could trust. Even back then, there were only a few of them. There's even fewer now. Anyway, the scam was for them to suggest some halfass plan that would get me killed, and for me to act scared and start to back out. They'd eventually get around to suggesting one of the couriers, and Max was on that list. We'd agree on Max, and that would be it. Simple and clean—the heroin for the cash. I laid it out for the others, figuring on scoring about fifty grand apiece when this was over.

"No," said the Mole, his pasty face indistinct in the candlelight.

The Prof chipped in, "Burke, you know what the people say—when it comes to junk, the Silent One don't play."

And Max himself just shook his head from side to side.

I knew what the Prof meant. Max would carry anything, anywhere. His delivery collateral was his life. But everybody knew he wouldn't move narcotics. If he suddenly agreed to do this, it'd make the bad guys suspicious. Even if they let him walk away, he'd have to make dope runs from then on. No matter what kind of sting we pulled off, if Max was the courier he was finished.

There wasn't much to say after that. I watched the candle flame throw shadows on the walls, burning up my plans to be free of this nickel-and-dime hustling once and for all. I wasn't going into the dope business, and I wasn't giving this up without another try.

"Prof, your cousin still work for the post office?"

"Melvin's a lifer, brother—he's hooked on that regular paycheck."

"Would he hold out a package for us if we paid him?"

"Have to pay him a good piece, Burke—he *loves* that joint. What's the idea?"

"The idea is, we *mail* the stuff back to them. Mole, how much was in the suitcases?"

"Forty kilos—twenty bags in each case. Plastic bags. Heat-sealed."

"Prof, that's worth what on the street?"

"Depends—how pure is it now, how many times you step on it. . . ."

"Mole . . . ?"

"It's ninety, ninety-five percent pure."

"Prof . . . ?"

"They could hit it at least ten times. Figure twenty grand a key, at the least."

"So they'd pay five?"

"They'd pay the five just to stay alive."

"That's two hundred thousand, okay? How about we mail them four keys, okay? No questions asked. Just to show good faith? And we give them a post-office box number, and tell them to mail us the money for the *next* installment. We keep running like that until we're near the end. All they can beat us for is the first and last piece, right?"

"No good," said the Prof. "They'd trace the box, or have some men waiting. You know."

"Not if Melvin intercepts the shipment. He still works in the back, right? All he has to do is pull their package of money off the line when it shows up."

"Melvin don't work twenty-four hours a day, man. He's bound to miss some of them."

"So what? We don't need *all* of them. Every exchange is twenty grand coming from them. If Melvin can pull ten out of twenty, it's *still* fifty apiece, right?"

"It's shaky, man. I don't like it."

I turned to Max. He hadn't moved from his place against the wall, standing with his corded forearms folded, no expression on his face. He shook his head again. No point asking the Mole. We were back to Square One. The Prof was looking at me like I was a bigger load of dope than the one we'd hijacked.

I lit a cigarette, drawing into myself, trying to think through the mess. Keeping the dope wasn't a problem—the Mole's junkyard was as safe as Mother Teresa's reputation, and heroin doesn't get stale from sitting around—but we took all this risk and now we had nothing to show for it. Waiting didn't bother Max, and the Prof had done too much time behind the walls to care. I watched the candle flame, looking deep into it, breathing slowly, waiting for an answer.

Then the Mole said, "I know a tunnel." He didn't say anything else.

"So what, Mole?" I asked him.

"A subway tunnel," he explained, like he was talking to a child, "a subway tunnel from an abandoned station back out to the street."

"Mole, *everybody* knows about those tunnels—in the winter, half the winos in the city sleep down there."

"Not a way in—a way out," said the Mole, and it slowly dawned on me that we could still pull it off.

"Show me," I asked him. And the Mole pulled out a mess of faded blueprints from his satchel, laid one flat on the basement floor, and shone his pocket flash for us all to see.

"See here, just past Canal Street? You come in any of these entrances. But there's a *little* tunnel—it runs from Canal all the way up to Spring Street . . . see?"—pointing a grubby finger at some faint lines on the paper and looking up as though even an idiot like me would understand by now.

When he saw I still wasn't with him, the Mole's tiny eyes blinked hard behind his thick lenses. He hadn't done this much talking in the last six months and it was wearing him out. "We meet them in the tunnel near Canal. We get there first. They block all the exits. We give them the product and we take the money. We go out heading west . . . see, here? . . . they go out heading east. But we don't go out the exit. We take this little tunnel all the way through here"—tracing the lines—"and we come out on Spring Street."

"And if they follow us?"

The Mole gave me a look of total disgust. He was done talking. He took his satchel, pushed it away from him with his boot, so it was standing between us. "Tick, tick," said the Mole. They wouldn't follow us.

Now I got it. "How long would it take us to get to the Spring Street stop?"

The Mole shrugged. "Ten minutes, fifteen. It's a narrow tunnel. One at a time. No lights."

Yeah, it could work. By the time the wiseguys figured we weren't coming out any of the Canal Street exits, they'd have to go back inside to look for us, and we should be long gone by then. They'd figure we'd be hiding out, waiting for darkness to fall, or that we'd try to slip away in the rush-hour crowd. And even if they did tip to the plan, we'd have too much of a head start.

"It's great, Mole!" I told him.

The Prof extended his hand, palm up, to offer his congratulations. The Mole figured the Prof wanted to see his blueprints, and tossed the whole bundle into the Prof's lap. Some guys are just culturally deficient.

I looked at Max. He was watching the whole thing, but his face never changed. "What's wrong *now*?" I asked him with my hands.

Max walked over to us, squatted down until his face was just a few inches from mine. He rolled up his sleeve, pulled off an imaginary tie, and looped it around his bicep . . . he put one end in his teeth and pulled it tight. Then he drove two fingers into the crook of his arm, where the vein would be bulging, used his thumb to push the plunger home, and rolled his eyes up. A junkie getting high. Max watched my face carefully. He folded his arms in the universal gesture of rocking a baby, then opened his arms to let the baby fall to the floor. And he shook his head again. Max the Silent wasn't selling any dope.

I pointed to my watch, spread my hands again. "Why *now*?" I wanted to know.

Max tapped his heart twice with a balled fist, nodding his head "yes." Then he rubbed his fingers together to make the sign for "money," moving his hands back and forth with blinding speed. He was a warrior, not a merchant.

Fuck! I threw up my hands in total disgust. Max watched my face, his own immobile as stone. I used my hands to shape the one-kilo packages of dope in the air, laid them end to end until Max got the idea. We had a whole pile of heroin between us. Then I rubbed my first two fingers and thumb together the way he had before. Money, right? Then I separated my hands, and crossed them in front of my chest, opening them as I did so. Exchanging one for the other. "How?" I wanted to know.

Max smiled his smile: just a thin line of white between his flat lips. He bowed to the Mole and the Prof, then to me. He made the same signs for the dope as I had, and followed it with a gesture that meant throwing something away. Okay, we disposed of the dope—maybe threw it in the river. And then?

Max pointed to the blueprints, nodding his head "yes." We'd make the meet in the tunnel like the Mole wanted, only we wouldn't have any dope with us. I spread my hands wide for him again—how would we get out of there with the money? Max bowed, stepped back out of the circle of light cast by the candle, and vanished. It was dead silent in Mama's basement. I watched the candle burn down, along with my hopes of making a respectable score for the first time in my life.

"Hey, Burke," called the Prof, "when Max comes back, I want you to say something to him for me, okay?"

"Yeah?" I asked him, too depressed to give a damn.

"Yeah. You know how to make the sign for 'chump'?"

The Prof was good at this. Plenty of times he'd cheer us all up on the yard when nothing was happening. It didn't even bring a smile this time.

It got darker and darker in the basement, so quiet I could hear water dripping off in the distance. All of a sudden, the Prof shot straight into the air as if he'd been hoisted by an invisible crane. "Put me down, fool!" he barked, his short legs dangling helplessly. Max stepped into the tiny circle of light, holding the Prof by his jacket in one hand. He opened the hand and the Prof unceremoniously dropped to the floor. I pulled a fresh candle from my pocket and lit up. The shadows flickered on the walls and the darkness moved back another few feet. Now I understood.

"You get it, Mole?" I asked.

"Yes."

"Prof?"

"Yeah. We meet them in the tunnel, Mole kills the lights, and Max does his thing, right?"

"Right."

Max bowed to each of us, waiting for recognition of his superior problem-solving ability. The Prof was right—he *was* a chump.

"It's no good," I told them. "It'll take too long. If Max jumps them all in the tunnel, we'll be running for our lives, okay? And even if we get away with it, they'll never stop looking for us. It doesn't play, okay? It's not what we planned."

"You mean it's not what *you* planned, man," countered the Prof. "We took the shot to score a lot. Max don't want to give them the dope, and you don't want to rough off the money. That leaves us with what?"

That's when I got my brilliant idea that saved me twenty years in the joint. "Mole, you said the stuff was near pure, right?" He didn't answer—the Mole doesn't say anything twice. "Okay, how do you know?"

"Test," said the Mole.

"Test?"

"Heroin is morphine-based. You add something to it, it turns a certain color, you know it's good."

"Mole," I asked him, trying to keep the hope out of my voice, "can you make it turn the right color even if it *isn't* real dope?"

The Mole went into one of his trances—lost in thought. We all kept quiet, like people do around a volcano that might go off. Finally he said, "There would have to be *some* of the morphine-base—or else they would have to pick the right bag to test."

"How far down could you cut in and still make it pass the test?"

"I don't know . . ." said the Mole, his voice trailing off. He pulled out a pencil as stubby and greasy as he was, and starting scribbling formulas on the side of the blueprints, lost to the world.

Finally, he looked up. "How will they pick a bag to test?"

"Who knows?" I told him, looking over at the Prof, who nodded in agreement.

"Two bags of pure," said the Mole, "six bags cut deep. The rest no morphine-base at all. Okay?"

"*Okay!*" I told him. The Prof's grin split the darkness. And then there was Max. But before he could say anything, I took a deck of cards out of my pocket, held it up for him to see, and motioned for him to come close with the others. I dealt out forty cards, one for each bag of dope. Then I separated the cards into four stacks, shoving one in front of each of the others, and keeping one in front of me. I reached over and took the stack away from Max, held it up before his eyes, made a motion like I was spitting on the cards, and tossed them into the darkness of the cellar. I did the same thing with the Mole's share. And then with the Prof's. From my stack, I slowly counted off two cards, then six more—the amount the Mole said he needed to work the scam. And I threw my other two cards away too. I looked at Max, caught his eyes, then took six cards from my little remaining stack and tore them into small pieces. I threw away the big pieces, leaving only scraps behind—and two untouched cards.

There was a long count. Then Max slowly nodded, and we had a deal.

14

I WAS only on the phone for a few minutes with the wiseguys. Two hundred thousand in cash in exchange for forty kilos of their product. And I told them where and when. The gangster who answered the phone listened patiently—I could feel his desire for my death coming over the wire, but he kept his voice quiet. Sure, sure . . . whatever we wanted, no problems . . . very reasonable.

The meet was for five-fifteen on a Thursday evening. Maximum rush-hour mess, so they'd think we planned to lose them in the crowds after we made the switch. We got there just after eleven the night before, set up camp, and started to do what we all did best—wait.

We waited at the apex of the tunnels. The wiseguys would have to come from the east, and they'd have people planted in the tunnel from the west. Plenty of room to do whatever they planned. All we needed was a few minutes to get lost, and I had something with me that would take care of that. I didn't care if they sent Godzilla down the tubes after us—we had it wired.

It was five-fifteen on the dot when Max snapped his fingers and pointed to the east. I couldn't see anything at first, but then I glimpsed a faint beam of light moving slowly in our direction—from the west, where they weren't supposed to come from. And then I heard footsteps, lots of footsteps, coming from the right direction. The Mole put his satchel on the ground, one hand inside. The Prof thumbed back the hammers on my sawed-off, and I fingered the baseball-shaped piece of metal in my jacket pocket. It was going down.

And then the wheels came off. "This is the police!" came a voice on a bullhorn. "You men are surrounded. Drop your weapons and walk toward the sound of my voice with your hands in the air!"

The miserable fucking maggots! Why take a chance of dealing with renegades when they could get their dope back and hand their cop pals some major felony arrests at the same time?

I had to stall them, get time to think.

"How do I know you're the cops?" I shouted back down into the tunnel.

"This is Captain Johnson, N.Y.P.D., pal. Precinct Number One. You are under arrest, you got it? You got two minutes—I don't see hands in the air, I'm going to see blood on the ground."

It was the cops all right, and not the Transit Police either—only the bluecoats talk like that—and only when they've got an audience.

I turned to face my brothers. There was nothing to discuss—the Mole wouldn't last an hour locked up. If the Prof took another fall, they'd hold him for life. And without someone to watch out for him, Max would kill a guard sooner or later. "Prof," I snapped at him, "hit the little tunnel, okay? Take the bags with the real dope with you, leave me the rest. You go first—make sure it's clear on Spring Street before you step out. The Mole follows you. Max brings up the rear in case anyone gets past me. You know where the car is. Got it?"

"Burke," the little man said, "I'm down for the next round. Fuck these blue-coated thieves!"

"Get in the tunnel, Prof. The Mole can't make it without you. Don't let Max do anything crazy."

"Come with us," the Mole told me, hefting his satchel.

"Not a chance, Mole. It won't give us enough time. It's the Man, brother, not the mob. We can't outrun a fucking radio. Go!"

"What're *you* going to do?" asked the Prof.

"Time," I told him.

The Prof looked back for a second, squeezed my arm hard, and hit the tunnel, the Mole right behind. That left Max. I pointed into the tunnel, patted my back to show he had to protect the others, and Max touched his chest, made a motion like he was tearing out his heart, and put his fist in my open palm. He didn't have to tell me—I knew.

I turned in the direction of the bullhorn. "I'm not going back to jail!" I screamed at them. "I'll hold court right here, you understand!" I'd been waiting to use that line since I got out of reform school the first time.

"Give it up, buddy!" came back the cop's voice. "You got no place to go."

"Any of you guys ever been in 'Nam?" I yelled down the tunnel shaft, buying time with every word.

Silence. I could hear mutters, but no words. They'd move in soon.

Finally a hard voice came back down the tunnel to me. "I have, friend. Eighty-seventh Infantry, Charlie Company. Want me to come back there alone?"

"Yeah!" I shouted back. "I want you to tell your cop friends what *this* is!" I pulled the metal baseball out of my pocket—a fragmentation grenade with the pin still in—and lobbed it down the tunnel in their direction. I listened to it bounce around the walls and then everything went quiet. It must have fallen onto the tracks.

"What was that, friend?" my Vietnam buddy wanted to know.

"Shine your light and see for yourself," I told him. "But don't worry—the pin's still in!"

The place went as quiet as a tomb—because that's what they all thought it had turned into. I saw flashlights bounce off the dripping walls of the tunnel, but none of them came closer to me from either side. Then I heard "Holy shit!" and I knew they'd found it.

"You know what that is?" I called out to them.

"Yeah," came back the infantryman's weary voice, "I seen enough of the fucking things."

"You want to see more, just come on back," I invited him. "I got a whole crate of them just sitting here."

More silence.

"What do you want?" he called down to me.

"I want you guys to clear out of this tunnel, okay? And I want a car full of gas at the curb on Canal Street. And a ride to J.F.K. And I want a plane to Cuba. You got it? Otherwise, the Number Six Train's going to have a major fucking detour for the next ten years."

Another cop yelled back to me. "I want to talk to you, okay? I want to talk about what you want. Let me walk toward you. Slow . . . okay? My hands in the air. I can't talk to you about this and scream down this tunnel. Okay?"

"Let me think about it," I told him, "but no fucking tricks!"

"No tricks. Just take it easy, okay?"

I didn't answer him, wondering where the Prof was by now.

I stretched it out as long as I could. Then I called down to the cop, my voice shaking more than I wanted. "Just one cop, okay? I want the soldier. Tell him to come *alone*, you understand—and *slow*!"

I heard the soldier's footsteps before I saw him. He rounded the bend in the tunnel from the east, shirt unbuttoned, hands over his head. He was short, built solid and close to the ground. I couldn't make out his features in the dim light.

"Stop!" I barked at him.

"Okay, friend. Just be easy, okay? No problems, nothing to worry about. All we're going to do is talk."

"I want to show you something first," I told him. I held another grenade in my right hand, high up, where he could see it. Then I palmed one of the spare pull-pins I had with me in my left. I reached over to the grenade and pulled hard; my left hand came away with the extra pin. I flicked it backhand at the cop, listening to it skim down the tunnel, like a kid skipping stones on a lake. "Pick it up," I told him.

I watched him bend down, grope around until he had it.

"Fuck!" he said—not loud, but clear enough.

"Now you got the picture," I told him. "I'm sitting on a couple dozen of these little bastards and I pulled the pin on the one I'm holding, okay? You get one of your fucking sharpshooters to drop me with a night-scope and the whole tunnel goes into orbit. Now, what about my plane?"

"Those things take time, friend. We can't just make a phone call and set things up."

"All it took was a phone call to set *this* thing up, right?"

"Look, friend, I just do my job. Like I did overseas. Like you did too, right? I understand what you're feeling. . . ."

"No, you don't," I told him. "Where'd you see combat?" I asked him.

"Brother, for all I know, I was in fucking Cambodia. They sent us into the jungle and some of us came back. You know how it is."

"Yeah, I know how it is. But I did my stretch in prison, not 'Nam. Too many times. And I'm not going again. I'm going to Cuba or we're all going to hell."

"Hold up!" he barked at me. "Give us a chance to work this out. I didn't say we *couldn't* do it . . . just that it takes a bit of time, all right? I have to walk back down and talk to the Captain, let him use the radio, call outside, you know . . . ?"

"Take all the time you want," I said to him, the most truthful words I ever spoke to a cop in my life. I watched him back down the tunnel.

A few more minutes passed. I was looking around, checking to make sure there was nothing left in the tunnel to add to my sentence, when I heard his voice again.

"Can I come back down?" he shouted.

"Come ahead!" I yelled back.

When he got back to where he'd been standing before, he was talking in a calm, quiet voice, like you'd use on a crazy person. Good. "It's all in the works, my friend. We've got the process started, but it's going to take some time, you understand?"

"No problem," I told him.

"Man, this might take *hours*," he said. "You don't want to sit and hold that thing without the pin for that long."

"I got no choice," I replied.

"Sure you do," he said reasonably. "Just put the pin back in. You can sit right by the grenades. You hear anyone coming or anything at all, you just pull it again. Okay?"

I said nothing.

"Come on, friend. Use your head. You're going to get what you want—we're doing it for you—we're cooperating. No point in blowing yourself up when you're *winning*, right?"

"How . . . how do I do that?" I said, my voice trembling badly. "You have the pin."

"I'll give it back to you, friend. Okay? I'll walk nice and slow toward you, okay? Nice and easy. We got a piece of wire—I'll wrap it around the pin and tie it to my holster belt, okay? I'll throw the whole thing down to you. Nice and easy."

"You won't try anything?" I asked, distrust all over my voice.

"What's the point, friend? We try something and you blow us all up, right? I'll be standing right here—I'll be the first to go, okay? I didn't walk through that fucking jungle to get killed on the subway."

"Give me a minute," I told him.

He gave me nearly five, playing out the string, doing what he was supposed to do. The cop and I were the same right then: I was holding the point for my brothers so they'd make their break—and he was a hundred yards ahead of the rest of his boys. It was only him and me that'd get blown to hell if this didn't work. The soldier had a lot of guts—too bad he worked with such a lame crew.

"You're really getting the plane?" I asked him.

"It's in the works," he said, "you have my word. One soldier to another."

Maybe he did understand it. I was running in luck—an infantryman would know all about falling on grenades. If he'd been a Tunnel Rat in 'Nam he'd be thinking flamethrowers by now. But he was just doing his job. I let him persuade me.

It took another ten minutes for us to work it out, but he finally came back down the tunnel with the belt and lofted it gently in my direction. I could see it gleaming in the tunnel's soft light. I reached out for it gingerly, feeling the sniper's telescope on my face. Fuck them—I'd have the last laugh in hell.

But they didn't shoot.

"I got it!" I yelled to him.

"Just like I promised," he shouted back.

"I'm putting it back in," I said, my hands shaking for just the right touch of authenticity. I swear I could feel all their breath let out at once when I went back into the blackness.

"I'm going to sit right here," I yelled. "Just like I said. If any of you come even *close* . . ."

"All you need now is patience, my friend," said the cop. "I'll sit right down here and wait with you." And he was right about both parts.

15

It went on for hours. I knew the game—the soldier kept coming back down the tunnel to talk to me, reassure me everything was okay, ask me if I wanted some cigarettes, some coffee, anything—waiting for me to get sleepy. They had all the time in the world.

It was well past midnight. Either my people had made it or they hadn't. I was seeing spots in front of my eyes, jumping every time the cops made a noise at their end. I don't drink coffee, but I knew what would be in the coffee they kept offering me, so I finally said yes.

The soldier brought two Styrofoam coffee cups down on a tray, halfway to me, turned around, and went back. I told them it wasn't close enough, so he brought it even closer.

Then he played out the string. "Pick one, friend. The other one's for me." It didn't matter which one I picked—they'd have pumped the cop so full of stimulants that I'd pass out before he would anyway. I popped open the lid of the one I picked and drank it all down like a greedy pig. The drugs hit me like a piledriver before I could even take the cup away from my mouth. I remember thinking just before I passed out how I wouldn't even feel the beating I was going to get.

16

So I WENT back to prison, but only for possession of explosives. Possession of thirty-two kilos of sugar and quinine isn't against the law. And even Blumberg the lawyer was able to make something out of the fact that I was drugged and unconscious at the time of my arrest, so they didn't hit me with too stiff a jolt.

I wasn't in population more than a week before one of Julio's gorillas asked me where I'd stashed the heroin. I told him I didn't know what he was talking about—as far as I knew, the cops had the stuff. And, anyway, I told him, it hadn't been me who roughed off the stuff in the first place. Some guy had contacted me—offered fifty grand for me to handle the exchange.

Another man came to see me in the prison about the dope, but this guy came through the front gate. When the hack told me my attorney was there to see me, I knew something was wrong—Blumberg wouldn't make the trip to Auburn even if I *had* paid him for representing me at the trial. This guy was all pinstripes and old school tie, with a pretty leather briefcase and a gold wedding band to match his Rolex. The new breed of mob lawyer, although I didn't know it then. He didn't even pretend he was representing me—he came there to be judge and jury, and I was on trial for my life.

Okay—I was ready for him. We went over the thing a dozen times. He had me tell my story out of sequence, did his best to trip me up—it always played the same. But slowly he got a few more details out of me.

"Tell me again about this guy who approached you."

"I already *told* you," I said. "About thirty years old, long hair, almost like a hippie, dirty army jacket. He was carrying a piece in a shoulder holster—didn't care if I saw it or not. Said his name was Smith."

"And he told you . . . ?"

"He told me he had this stuff, right? And it belonged to your people, okay? And I should make arrangements to sell it back to him for two hundred grand. And all I had to give him was one fifty—the rest was for me."

"You thought he stole it?"

"I didn't know *how* he got it, right? What did I care? I figured the old man would be happy to get his stuff back—I'd make some heavy coin—it'd be a wash, right?"

"You ever see this 'Smith' character again?"

"He didn't show up at my trial, that's for fucking sure."

"Mr. Burke, think back now. Is there *anything* about this guy that would help us find him?"

"You got pictures I could look through? Maybe he's one of your own. . . ."

"He's not," snapped the lawyer.

"Yeah, I guess you're right," I acknowledged. "He was like one of those buffs, you know? A real whacko."

"A 'buff'?"

"Yeah, like those guys who carry around PBA cards and pretend they're fucking off-duty cops and shit. You know what I mean."

His eyes flickered, just for a second, but I'd been watching for it. "Why do you think this individual was in that category?"

"Well," I said slowly, "two things, really. Besides the shoulder holster, he had another gun strapped to his ankle. And when he reached in his wallet to come up with the front money I wanted . . . for the supplies . . . I saw a gold shield. I guess it was one of those complimentary badges the cops give you if you make some contribution."

The lawyer screwed around for another hour or so, but his heart wasn't in it. I read in the *Daily News* three weeks later how an undercover narcotics officer was killed in East Harlem. Shot four times in the face, but they left his money alone. Only his gold shield was missing.

17

BUT THAT was years ago. Today I left seven grand with Mama. Max would know that five was for him and he should hold the rest for me. There was no time for Mama's endless nonsense about Max, but I did have time to eat before I went back to the office to change. I had a court appearance for the afternoon, and I wanted to look my best.

Even though it was just a preliminary hearing, I normally wouldn't go into a criminal court. There wasn't any point pretending I had a private investigator's license, and even a flyweight defense attorney would have a ball asking me where I'd spent twelve years of my life. I testify a lot in civil court, though—matrimonials and crap like that. And I'm a lot more honest than the lawyers: I charge a flat rate for perjury, not so much an hour. But this was a special case.

It really started in Family Court, where this woman came in to get an Order of Protection against her husband. Seems they were showing a film about child sexual abuse in school and one of her daughters started crying and the whole sleazy story came out. Anyway, she gets this Order, and he's supposed to leave the house, but he comes right back in and starts screaming at the kid how the whole thing is her fault and how she's going to go to an orphanage and stuff like that. And the poor little kid just plain snaps out—she was only ten years old—and they take her to this psychiatric hospital and she's still up there. The slimeball naturally takes off, and the woman hired me to find him. It only took a couple of days. I threw a quarter into a pay phone and the Warrant Squad picked him up.

Most of the time the D.A.'s office wouldn't even think about prosecuting a guy like this. They got more excuses than Richard Nixon: the guy's the family breadwinner, the trial would be too tough on the kid, all that crap. The bottom line is that they don't want to mess with their sacred conviction rates—most of these family-style sex cases only get prosecuted when the perpetrator confesses, and even then the D.A.'s office doesn't get too worked up about it. After all, the family unit is the bedrock of America.

But they finally formed this new unit—City-Wide Special Victims Bureau. It's supposed to cover all crimes against children, in all courts. I heard the D.A. in this case was really going to go for it, and I wanted to see for myself.

I walked in all dressed up: dark-blue pinstripe, white shirt, dark-red tie, polished black shoes—even an attaché case. I wasn't carrying a piece—in the Supreme Court, they use metal detectors at the entrance because some politically wired judge complained about the dangerous radicals who might invade his courtroom and shoot it out with the guards. This happens in the Supreme Court about every other century, but you can't be too careful. On the other hand, right across the street in the Family Court, the average litigant carries some kind of weapon and violence is an everyday thing, but there's no metal detectors. That's New York—even the *names* of the courts are total bullshit—the lowest trial court is the "Supreme" Court, and the place where we turn abused kids into monsters is the "Family" Court. In this city, the name means more than the game.

The Assistant District Attorney was one I hadn't seen before—a tall brunette with a white streak in her thick mane of swept-back hair, wearing a gray silk dress and a string of pearls. She had a sweet face, but her eyes were cold. She wasn't from the Manhattan office—I guess they sent her over because she was handling another case against the same guy over in Queens or something. The court officers all seemed to know her, though, so I guess she was a trial veteran—those are the only ones they remember.

I sat in the front row—the one reserved for attorneys only. Nobody asked any questions—they never do.

The defense attorney was a real piece of work. His haircut cost more than my suit, and diamonds flashed from everywhere. It looked like it was only going to be a hearing on bail, and the lawyer had a long list of reasons why his man should be let back out on the street—the defendant was employed, sole support of his family, active in Little League . . . and that stuff. He looked like a weasel. His eyes darted around the courtroom—caught mine, and dropped. His wife wasn't even there.

The only person I recognized was the court reporter—the guy who takes down everything they say on one of those machines that don't make any noise. He was a tall guy with big hands, slumped over his machine. He'd gone to Vietnam about the same time I last went to prison, and it burned him out. I'd watched him a lot of times and he never changed expression, no matter what went down. I asked him about that once and he told me the courtroom was the same as 'Nam—only here they did it with words instead of with bullets.

The argument went on and on, and then the defense attorney made a mistake. He put his client on the stand, figuring the guy's long list of social contacts would get over on the judge. And it might have too, until the D.A. took her shot.

She stood up at her table and began questioning the creep in a soft voice, just background questions about his job, and where he'd be staying while waiting for trial—crap like that. She shuffled through some papers at the table as if she couldn't think of the next question to ask; then she took a step closer to him.

"Sir, on April twenty-fifth, did you enter your wife's home?"

"It's *my* home," the creep smirked, "I paid for it . . . I'm *still* paying the mortgage on it."

"Objection, Your Honor," said the defense attorney. "What does this have to do with a bail application?"

"It has to do with credibility," shot back the D.A. Then she gave a little bow of her head to the defense attorney, and told the court, "I promise to connect it up to the issue before this court, Your Honor, and I will not oppose a defense motion to strike the testimony if I fail to do so."

The judge tried to look like he was thinking it over, glanced over at his assistant (they call them "law secretaries" in New York—they're all political appointees and they make more money than the judges in the "lower" courts), caught the sign, and said, "Proceed, counsel," just like they do on television.

"Will you answer my question, sir?" the D.A. asked.

Then he went into his rap. "Yes, I entered *my* home, with *my* key. Of course I did."

"And did you have a conversation with your child Marcy at that time, sir?"

"It wasn't a conversation. I just said she had caused a lot of trouble with all these lies. You see, if it hadn't been for that stupid movie they showed at her school . . ."

"No further questions," snapped out the D.A., leaving everyone in the courtroom puzzled.

"You may step down," said the judge to the creep. Then he turned to the D.A.

"Young lady, I don't understand your line of questioning. If you can't connect this up . . ."

"My name is Ms. Wolfe, Judge, or you may refer to me as the Assistant District Attorney," she said in a gentle voice.

The judge smiled, humoring her, and the defense attorney rubbed his hands together. They weren't good listeners—the lady was being quiet, not soft. You could see she was a pro. There was steel inside, but she wasn't going to waste her time showing it when there was no jury around.

"Very well, *Ms.* Wolfe," said the judge, hitting the accent so the low-lifes hanging around the bench wouldn't miss his sharp wit, "the court is *still* waiting for you to connect it up."

"Yes, Your Honor," she said, her voice hardening, "I have here a certified copy of an Order of Protection, signed by Judge Berkowitz of the Family Court. Among its terms and conditions are that this defendant remain away from the home and person of the victim."

"Bring that up to me," the judge said to one of the court officers.

He scanned the two sheets of paper, looking even more puzzled than ever. He couldn't see where the D.A. was going, and neither could the defense. The creep's lawyer barked out, "Relevance, Your Honor?" The judge looked down at the D.A., no longer smiling, waiting for her to respond.

"Your Honor, the defendant has just admitted, under oath, that he violated an Order of the Family Court. He has further acknowledged that said violation was willful, that he intended to act as he did, and that he was without just cause. Thus, pursuant to the Family Court Act, section 1072, subsection B, he may be ordered to jail for a term not to exceed six months."

The defense attorney finally woke up—and it wasn't the coffee he smelled. "Your Honor, this has nothing whatever to do with the question of bail in a criminal proceeding. Counsel is referring to a *Family* Court matter—that court has nothing to do with bail over here."

The lady D.A. went on speaking as if she hadn't heard the interruption. "The court has already heard evidence that this defendant fled when initially charged in the Family Court. In fact, he was located living under an assumed name in a hotel here in the city. The purpose of bail is to ensure the defendant's presence at trial. In this case, given the defendant's past actions, and the indisputable fact that he is facing a jail sentence in another court, the People respectfully request that any bail application be denied and the defendant summarily remanded until trial."

The creep looked like he'd been body-punched—a remand meant he'd sit in jail for a few months no matter how the criminal trial turned out. But his lawyer wasn't finished.

"Your Honor, the District Attorney is asking for a *remand!* That would be a travesty of justice for an individual with no criminal record, significant roots in the community, and, I might add, every anticipation of prevailing on the merits when we come to trial. It's not as though he were being charged with murder. . . ."

The D.A.'s head snapped back—an old trial-lawyer's trick—pulling every eye in the courtroom toward her.

"He *is* charged with rape, sodomy, incest, and sexual abuse, Your Honor. He *did* flee the jurisdiction of the court. And he *did* confess before this very court that he violated an existing Order of Protection."

"Judge, that was the *Family* Court!" yelled the defense attorney, firing his best shot.

It wasn't good enough. The D.A. let a dark undertone into her soft voice—it carried to the back of the room. "Surely Your Honor is not ruling that an order of one court is entitled to more respect than the order of another? A defendant who will spit on the lawful order of one court has displayed his true character and his utter disregard for the law. Indeed, if this court grants bail to this defendant, it will be providing him with a *motive* to flee. He is only *charged* in this court—he stands all-but-convicted in another. The People respectfully request a remand, not only for the protection of the victim herein, and for the protection of the community at large, but to give the Family Court the opportunity to impose such sentence as it deems appropriate for the violation. If bail is granted, and the defendant flees," and there she paused, holding it for a long count, "the child will certainly be in danger. This court should not provide such an opportunity."

"This is ridiculous, Your Honor," shot back the defense attorney. "Ms. Wolfe cannot know what is in my client's mind!"

"I don't *need* to, do I?" asked Wolfe. The message was clear.

The judge was caught. He scanned the courtroom quickly, looking for some help. I thought I'd give him some—I whipped out a reporter's notebook and started scribbling away. He looked closely, trying to figure out who I was, or what paper I worked for—and then he decided he couldn't take the chance.

"Defendant is remanded for transportation to the Family Court. If sentence is not imposed by that court, he shall be returned before me for additional bail arguments."

The creep looked wiped out. He looked to his lawyer for reassurance, listened while the lawyer told him he'd go right over to the Family Court, and then got shakily to his feet. The court officers moved to take him into custody, passing right by the court reporter's stand. The court reporter looked up from his machine. His combat-deadened eyes caught those of the freak. Making no effort to keep his voice down, the court reporter gave the officers some advice.

"Don't take away his belt," he said, getting off his stool and walking toward the back before the defense attorney had a chance to protest.

They took the creep away. The defense attorney went over to the D.A.'s table, preparing himself to play Let's Make a Deal.

"Ms. Wolfe?"

"Yes?"

"Ah . . . I assume you'll be going to Family Court on this personally?"

"Yes—and right now."

"Well, so am I. Could I give you a ride?"

"No, thank you," she told him in the same calm voice, stuffing papers into her briefcase.

"You've got no win on this one, you know," he told her.

Wolfe stood up, hands on hips, and stared him down. She'd been through this before. "You mean I can't *lose* this one, don't you, counselor? This is a fifteen-round fight, and your guy has to win every round. You win this trial—he'll do it again, and I'll get another shot. Sooner or later I'll drop him for the count. And when he goes down, he's going down hard."

The defense attorney's mouth opened, but nothing came out. She walked past him to the gate which separates the front of the court from the spectators, nodded to the officer who swung it open for her, and walked toward the exit. Her body swayed gently in the silk dress, and her high heels tapped the floor. I could smell her perfume in the air. A rare jewel, she was—never more beautiful than when she was doing her work. Like Flood.

18

I GOT downstairs before Wolfe did. I knew where she'd be parked, and I waited. The tapping of her heels echoed down the corridor just before she stepped into the sunlight on Baxter Street, behind the courthouse. I didn't want to spook her, so I made sure she had me in her sights before I said anything.

"Ms. Wolfe?"

"Yes," she responded, in exactly the same neutral tone she'd used with the defense attorney.

Now that I had her attention, I didn't know what to say. "I . . . just wanted to tell you that I admire the way you handled yourself in the courtroom."

"Thank you," she said, dismissing me and turning to go.

I wanted to talk to her again, make some contact with her—let her know we were on the same side—but nothing came out. I don't have many friends in law enforcement.

"Can I walk you to your car?" I asked her.

She gave me a brief flash of her smile. "That won't be necessary—it's only a short distance."

"Well," I shrugged, "this neighborhood . . ."

"It's not a problem," she said, and I caught the dull sheen of the thick silver band on her left hand. I knew what it was—a twine-cutter's ring, the kind with a hooked razor on the other side. The guys in the twine factories run the string through their hands and just flick the ring against the cord when they want to cut it. You put one of those things against a guy's face and you come away with his nose.

"You think that ring's going to keep the skells away?" I asked her.

She looked at me closely for the first time, seemed to be making up her mind about something.

"I appreciate your concern, Mr. . . . ?"

"Burke," I told her.

"Oh, yes. I've heard about you. . . ."

"Was it a good reference?"

"Good enough—Toby Ringer said you pull your own weight. And that you helped him on some cases."

"Maybe I could help you."

"I don't think so, Mr. Burke. Toby also said you work the other side of the street too often."

"Not when it comes to freaks," I told her.

"I know," Wolfe said, giving me just the hint of what I knew could be a beautiful smile—for someone else.

"It was me who found that dirtbag you just dropped inside, right? You think the Warrant Squad would've turned him up?"

"No," she admitted, "but this case is finished."

We were slowly walking toward her car—a dull, faded blue Audi sedan. The parking lot was bathed in sunlight, but the watchers were there. A pro wouldn't try to strong-arm anyone in the D.A.'s parking lot, but a junkie would.

"That's my car," Wolfe said, reaching in her pocketbook for the keys. I stepped ahead of her like I was going to hold the door—and a massive dark form shot up from the back seat. Its huge head was a black slab laced with gleaming shark's teeth. A Rottweiler—a good lapdog if you were King Kong. They look as if some mad scientist took a Doberman, injected it with anabolic steroids, and bashed its face in with a sledge-hammer. I froze where I was—this was one lady who didn't need an escort.

Wolfe opened the door and the Rottweiler lunged forward. "Bruiser! Down!" she snapped, and the beast reluctantly moved back to let her in. She turned to me over her shoulder. "Mr. Burke, if you ever get a case that I'd be interested in, give me a call, okay?"

It was a dismissal. I bowed to her and the Rottweiler, touched the brim of my hat, and moved back where I belonged. The huge beast pinned me with his killer's eyes out the back window as the Audi moved off.

19

I MADE my way back through the dirty marble corridors of the Criminal Court, thinking my thoughts. Wolfe reminded me of Flood—so did the Rottweiler.

It was late March, but the sun was already blasting the front steps of the court. Maybe a real summer this year, not like the whore's promise we'd been getting for the past weeks—the sun would shine but the cold would be right there too. Only city people really hate the cold. In the city, it gets inside your bones and it freezes your guts. In the country, people sit around their fireplaces and look at the white stuff outside—saying how pretty it is, how clean it looks. The snow is never clean in the city. Here, people die when the Hawk comes down—if the cold doesn't get them, the fires they start to keep warm will.

I reached in my pocket for a smoke, looking out over the parking lot across the street where I'd stashed my Plymouth. A black guy with a shaved head, resplendent in a neon-orange muscle shirt with matching sweatband, caught my eye. "Got a cigarette, pal?" he asked.

At least he didn't call me "brother." When I got out of prison in the late 1960s, that bullshit was all over the street. Being an ex-con was never too valuable a credential, but back then at least it was a guaranteed introduction to girls. And the Village was full of them—promiscuously sucking up every shred of revolutionary rhetoric like marijuana-powered vacuum cleaners.

I made a good living then. All you needed was some genuine Third World people for props and you could raise funds faster than Reverend Ike—telling hippie jerkoffs that you were financing some revolutionary act, like a bank robbery. It was open season in the Village. Better than the Lower East Side. The hippies who lived over there believed they were making a contribution with their plotting and planning and their halfass bombs and letters to the editor. They were too busy organizing the oppressed to see the value of cash transactions, but they never knew where to buy explosives, so I did business with them too. Good thing they never tried to take out the Bank of America with the baking soda I sold them.

That's how I got started finding missing kids. It may have been Peace & Love in the streets, but the back alleys were full of wolves. The worst of the animals didn't just eat to survive—they did it for fun. So I'd run some of the kids down and drag them home. For the money. Once in a while one of the wolves would try and hold on to his prey. So I made some money and I made some enemies. I used up the money a long time ago.

When the revolution died—when BMWs replaced jeeps and the hippies turned perfectly good lofts a human could rent for a little money into co-ops with six-figure down payments—I stopped being relevant. I was ready for it. Some of the Third World wasn't, and they took my place in the jailhouses. Those that didn't go quietly got the key to Forest Lawn instead.

When things got nasty in New York, I rolled the dice on Biafra. I figured I'd do the same thing over there I was doing in New York, only on a grand scale—save a bunch of kids and make myself a fortune in the process. I didn't do either one, but I beat the odds anyway—I walked away from it. It's what I do best.

That was then. The black muscleman asking me if I had a cigarette was now.

"You taking a survey?" I asked him.

Our eyes locked. He shrugged, shifted his position, and went back to scanning the street. He probably didn't even smoke—just keeping in practice. His act needed work.

20

THE PLYMOUTH was in the parking lot across the street. Even on a warm day, that lot's always cold. The three courthouses surrounding it make a perfect wind tunnel. The car's fresh coat of primer made it look like it had been painted with rust— the Mole always changes the color after the car is used on a job and we hadn't decided on what to use next. It looks like a piece of junk, but it's anything but, with its independent rear suspension, fifty-gallon tank, fuel injection, heavy-duty cooling and shocks, bullet-proof glass, rhino-style bumpers—all that stuff. It wasn't fast, but you couldn't break it no matter what you did. It was going to be the Ultimate Taxicab, but it didn't work out that way.

The woman was standing in front of the Plymouth, tapping her foot impatiently like her date was late. All I could make out was that she was female. She was wearing a tan summer trenchcoat over dark slacks, her head covered with a black scarf and her face hidden behind sunglasses with big lenses. Nobody I knew, but I put my hand in my pocket anyway—some people subcontract their revenge.

Her eyes were on me all the way up to the Plymouth, so I walked past it like it meant nothing to me. But when I heard "Mr. Burke?" I knew there wasn't much point.

I don't like problems out in public—especially when half the public is cops.

"What?" I snapped out at her.

"I want to talk to you," she said. Her voice was shaky but determined. Trouble.

"You got me confused with someone else, lady."

"No, I don't. I have to talk with you," she said.

"Give me a name or get lost," I told her. If she knew my face from the courthouse but didn't have a referral from someone I knew, I was gone.

"Julio Crunini," she offered, her face close to mine now.

"I don't know anybody named Julio, lady. Whatever you're selling, I'm not buying, okay?" And I reached past her to open the Plymouth's door and get the hell away from her and whatever she wanted. Julio's been out of prison too long, I was thinking—his mouth was getting loose.

She put her hand on my arm. Her hand was shaking—I could see the wedding ring on her finger, and the diamond sparkling in the sun next to it. "You know me," she said.

I looked into her face, and drew a blank. She must have seen what I was thinking—one hand went to her face and the sunglasses disappeared. Her face meant nothing to me. Her mouth went hard, and she pulled away the scarf—her flaming red hair fired in the sun.

"You know me now?" she asked bitterly.

It was the jogger from Forest Park.

21

Nothing changed in my face—I was raised in places where it isn't a good idea to let people know what you're thinking—but she wasn't looking for recognition.

"I don't know you, lady," I told her, "and I don't want to."

"You don't like my looks?" she challenged me. A real Mafia princess all right—she was used to this.

"I don't like your smell, lady. You stink of trouble, and I got enough of my own."

I pushed past her like I had someplace else to go. Her hand reached out and grabbed my forearm—I gave her the same look I'd given Julio in the garage, but she didn't have enough sense to know what it meant. Her hand was aristocratic—dark-red polish over manicured nails.

"If you don't talk to me here, I'll just come to Murray Street, Mr. Burke—to your hotel."

It was a good, hard shot—she thought. Julio must have opened up like the Red Sea. Only a few people knew I lived at the Deacon Hotel. Of course, those people were all wrong. The front desk would take a message for me from force of habit—the only force any junkie recognizes—but I hadn't lived there for years, ever since I got off parole. It didn't matter now—this broad was making word sounds from her mouth, but all I heard was "tick, tick, tick . . ."

Her face had the smug look of a woman with lots more cards to put on the table. Uncle Julio's halfass *omertà* was the modern version—rock-solid until it got a better offer.

"Get in the car," I told her, holding the Plymouth's door for her to slip past me.

"My car's right over there," she told me, gesturing toward the inevitable BMW sedan. "It'll be more comfortable—it's air conditioned."

"I don't care if it's got a waterbed, lady. You get in here, or you get in the wind."

She hesitated for just a second—the script wasn't going like she'd planned. Then the same tight-set look she had on her face when she'd started jogging around Forest Park appeared—she'd made up her mind.

Her reconstructed nose turned up at the Plymouth's interior but she slid across the vinyl bench seat without another word. I pulled out of the parking lot and headed toward the West Side Highway. I needed to find out what she knew, but I wasn't doing any talking until I was sure she was the only one listening.

I grabbed the highway at Chambers Street and turned uptown. The environmentalists had lost the first round—the old elevated structure was gone and along with it the shadows that provided the cover for the working whores. Michelle wouldn't be on the piers this time of day, and I needed her help. The new construction site on Eleventh Avenue a few blocks south of Times Square was my best bet.

The redhead opened her purse and started to rummage around. "Is it all right if I smoke?" she asked, still in that nasty-edged voice.

"As long as it's cigarettes," I told her.

"You have some religious convictions against marijuana, Mr. Burke?"

"Marijuana is against the law, lady," I told her, my voice toneless so the audience could get the sarcasm without the evidence to go with it. "If you have any illegal substances or objects on your person, I insist you remove them from this vehicle."

"Who're you trying to kid? After what you did in the . . ."

"Shut your fucking mouth!" I snapped at her. "You really want to talk, you'll get your chance, okay? You want to make some tapes for the *federales*, you make them someplace else. Got it?"

She got it. Her face got hard again, like I'd insulted her, but she didn't say another word. Two hard dots of red stood out on her cheeks—not her makeup.

The big Plymouth worked the city streets the way it was created to do . . . passing through traffic as anonymously as a rat in a garbage dump, eating the potholes, smoothing the bumps, quiet and careful. The tinted windows were up on both sides, the air conditioner whisper-quiet, watching the streets.

I spotted the first bunch of working girls on 37th. Business was always slow this time of day, but the girls who worked the trucks and cabs for a living had to try harder than their sisters across town. On Lexington Avenue, the girls wore little shorts-and-tops outfits—over on the West Side, they worked the streets in bathing suits and heels. Even that was more subtle than you'd find elsewhere in the city—over in Hunts Point, they work in raincoats with nothing underneath.

Nothing but hard-core pros over here—black women who hadn't been girls since they were twelve, white ladies too old or too out of shape for the indoor work. The pimps kept the baby-faces for the middle-class trade farther east—the runaways worked Delancey and the Bowery or strictly indoors. I love the words some of the jerkoff journalists use in this town . . . like "call girls." The only thing these ladies ever used a phone for was to call a bail bondsman.

I slid the Plymouth to the curb. A tall black woman with a silky wig swivel-hipped over to the window, wearing one of those spandex suits, the green metallic threads shimmering in the sun. Her bright smile never got near her eyes.

"Looking for something, honey?"

"For some*one*. Michelle. She around?"

"You her man, baby?" the whore wanted to know, casting a sly glance at the Plymouth—it wasn't exactly your standard pimpmobile.

"Only if someone gets stupid with her," I told her, just so she'd know.

"Honey, I'm out here in this heat about some *money*, you understand?"

"You find her and bring her back over here, I'll pay one trick's worth—deal?"

"I don't work blind, man," she said, all business now.

"Tell her Burke needs to talk with her."

She seemed to be thinking it over—looked past me to where the princess was sitting, nodding her head like she understood what was going on. Traffic was slow—her sisters strolled the sidelines, bored but watchful. It had been a long time since they'd seen anything new—or anything good. Finally, she made up her mind. "I get a half-yard for a trick, baby. That's the price for bringing Michelle around, okay?"

There was no trick in the world this woman could get fifty bucks for, but insulting her wasn't going to get the job done.

"I'll pay you *your* piece, okay? Let your manager go look for his commission someplace else. Fifty-fifty, right?"

She flashed me a quick smile and swivel-hipped her way back to the other girls. No car-trick whore splits fifty-fifty with a pimp, but letting her think I believed that myth was worth the discount—for both of us. It's a sweet life out on the stroll in this city—every street-whore has a guaranteed time-share in the jailhouse. And the emergency ward is her only pension plan.

I pulled the Plymouth through a wide U-turn into the mouth of the construction site, reached in my pocket for a smoke, and got ready to do some waiting.

22

THE REDHEAD wasn't good at waiting like I was—I could tell her life hadn't been like that. Too fucking bad.

I let my eyes roam around the flatlands, watching the whores work, checking for any backup the redhead might have brought along. It's easy to tail a car in the city, but anyone following us would have to be some distance away or I'd have spotted them by now.

She shifted her hips on the bench seat, recrossed her legs. The silk-on-silk sound was smooth and dry to my ears. Like a gun being cocked. "I've never been here before," she said. "What do you call this neighborhood?"

"After you talk to my friend, I'll talk to you, okay?"

"All I asked . . ."

"Don't ask me anything. Don't talk to me. When I know it's just me you're talking to, I'll answer, you understand? I'm not going to tell you again."

I was watching her face when I spoke to her. If she was wired and the backups were out of eyesight, she'd want our location to go out over the air—and I wasn't having any. Her face told me nothing—nothing except that she wasn't used to being talked to like that and she didn't like it. Well, I didn't like any of this, but if Julio was turning into a public-address system, I had to find out why. Everybody has rules they live by. Mine were: I wasn't going to die. I wasn't going to go back to prison. And I wasn't going to work a citizen's job for a living. In that order.

I spotted my bird-dog whore before I saw Michelle. She walked quickly over to the Plymouth, holding the wiggle to a minimum. She wanted to collect from me before a new customer took her for a ride.

"She'll be here in a minute, honey. You got my quarter like you said?"

"Right here," I told her, holding a twenty and a five in my left hand where she could see it.

The whore said nothing. I believed her that Michelle was coming— I'd had too good a look at her face for her to pull a Murphy game on me. That is, if she had any sense. But if she had any sense, she wouldn't be out here tricking.

Then I saw Michelle. The tall, willowy brunette was wearing pencil-leg red pants that stopped halfway up her calves—spike heels with ankle straps—a white parachute-silk blouse, the huge sleeves billowing as she moved. A long string of black beads around her neck and a man's black felt fedora on the back of her head. Like all her outfits, it would have looked ridiculous on anyone but her. That was the point, she told me once.

I released my hold on the bills and the whore flashed me a quick smile and moved back to her post. The redhead wasn't missing any of this, but she kept her mouth shut. I got out of the Plymouth and moved over to Michelle, my back blocking the redhead's view. I didn't have to watch her—Michelle would do that—she always knew what to do.

She put her left hand on my shoulder, reached up to kiss me on the cheek while her right hand snaked inside my jacket to the back of my belt. If there was a gun in there, she'd know the person inside the car was bad news. If I stepped to the side, the passenger would be looking at my pistol in Michelle's hand.

Michelle patted my back, whispered in my ear, "What's on, baby?"

"I'm not sure," I told her. "The redhead in the car braced me outside the courthouse. She's related to that old alligator—Julio. She wants something—I don't know what yet. The old bastard gave her some information about how to find me. She made it clear she was going to stay on my case until I talked to her."

"So talk to her, honey. You didn't drag me away from my lucrative profession to be your translator."

"I want to see if she's wired, Michelle."

Michelle's impossibly long lashes made shadows against her model's cheekbones; her fresh dark lipstick framed her mouth into a tiny circle.

"Oh," is all she said. Michelle's life must have been hell when she was supposed to have been a man.

"I'll pull over around the corner behind the trucks, okay? You get in the back with her—make sure she's clean. I'll check her purse."

"That's all?"

"For now."

"Baby, you know I started the treatments . . . but they didn't do the chop yet. Just the shots. And the psychiatrist—once a week. It's not cheap."

"You definitely going through with it?"

"If I was gay, I could *come* out, you know? But like I am, I have to *break* out. You know."

I knew. None of us had ever asked about Michelle, but she gradually told us. And the Mole had explained what a transsexual was . . . a woman trapped in a man's body. Even before she started getting the hormone injections and the breast implants, she looked like a woman—walked like a woman, talked like a woman. The big thing was, she had the heart of a woman. When you go to prison, the only people you could count on to visit you were your mother or your sister. I didn't have those people—it was Michelle who rode the bus for twelve hours one way and then walked through the ugly stares and evil whispering to visit me upstate when I was down the last time. She still worked the same car tricks—all she needed was her mouth. I knew what was in her purse—a little bottle of cognac she used for a mouthwash after each time. And the tiny canister of CN gas the Mole made for her.

"I don't have a price for this job, Michelle. It may not be a job at all, okay? But if she's got anything in her purse, we'll see about a donation."

"Close enough," she said, "but if she's got no cash, you take me to the Omega to hear Tom Baxter before he leaves town. Deal?"

"Deal," I told her, and she climbed into the back seat behind the redhead.

I found the dark spot in the shadow of the trucks and pulled in.

"Get in the back seat," I told the redhead.

"Why?" she snapped.

"Here's why," I told her. "I don't know you—I don't know what you want. My secretary back there is going to search you. If you're wearing a wire, out you go. It's that simple. She's here because I can't search you myself."

"I still don't see why . . ."

"Look, lady, you asked *me* to talk to you, okay? This is the way we do it. You don't like it, you take whatever business you have and you shake it on down the road."

The redhead softly scratched her long nails across one knee, thinking. I didn't have time for her to think.

"Besides," I told her, "haven't you had enough experience with men telling you to take your clothes off?"

Her eyes flashed at me, hard with anger, but she didn't say a word. I looked straight ahead, heard the door open, slam, open and slam again. She was in the back seat with Michelle.

"Toss your purse over the seat," I told her.

"What?"

"You heard me. My secretary's going to check your body; I'm going to check your purse . . . for the same thing."

The lizard-skin purse came sailing over the back seat and bounced off the windshield. I picked it up, unsnapped the gold clasp. Sounds from the back seat: zippers, the rustle of fabric. The purse had a pack of Marlboros, a gold Dunhill lighter, a little silver pillbox with six five-milligram Valiums inside, a tightly folded black silk handkerchief, a soft leather purse with a bunch of credit cards and a checkbook—joint account with her husband—and three hundred or so in cash. In a flap on the side I found thirty hundred-dollar bills—they looked fresh and new, but the serial numbers weren't in sequence. No tape recorder. Not even a pencil.

"She's clean," said Michelle from the back seat. I heard the door open and slam again, and the redhead was next to me.

"So . . . ?" I asked Michelle.

"All quality stuff. Bendel's, Bergdorf's, like that. The pearls are real. *Very* nice shoes. But that underwear is just *tacky*, honey. Nobody wears a garter belt outside a motel room . . . didn't your mother tell you that? And that perfume . . . honey, you need some heavy lessons in *subtle*."

The redhead snapped her head around to the back seat.

"From you?" she asked, trying for sarcasm.

"Who better?" Michelle wanted to know, genuinely surprised at such a stupid question.

"How much do I owe you?" the redhead asked Michelle in the same voice she would have used on the man who tuned her BMW.

"For what?"

"Well, you are a *prostitute*, aren't you? I know how valuable your time is."

"I see. Okay, Ms. Bitch—the handjob was on the house, but you can give me a hundred for the fashion advice."

The redhead reached in her purse. She never touched the new bills. She put together a hundred from the other supply and tossed it into the back seat. Michelle was dismissed.

She floated around to the redhead's open window, winked at me to say goodbye. Then she spoke in a soft voice to the redhead. "Honey, I may be a whore, but I'm not a cunt. Think about it." And she was gone.

23

"**W**HAT NEXT ?" the redhead wanted to know, in a voice meant to tell me she was just about out of patience.

"Now we drive someplace else, and you tell me your story," I said, throwing the Plymouth into gear. We drove over to the West Side Highway in silence. I turned south, looking for a safe parking place near one of the abandoned piers on the Hudson River. I wheeled the car off the highway, pulled up to the pier, and backed in. From that spot, I could see every piece of traffic except the boats. If the redhead had friends with her, I'd know soon enough.

I hit a switch on the dash and both front windows opened. Another switch locked her door, just in case.

I lit a cigarette, leaned way back in my seat so I could watch her and watch the street too. "Okay, lady, what is it you want?"

The redhead shifted her hips so she was facing me on the seat, her back to the window. "I want you to find a picture for me."

"A picture . . . like a painting?"

"A photograph—a photograph of a kid."

"Lady, will you just tell me the whole story? I don't have time to drag it out of you piece by piece, okay?"

"This isn't an easy thing to talk about."

"Then *don't* talk about it," I told her. "I didn't ask you to show up. I'll drive you back to your car and you find somebody else, okay?"

"No! It's *not* okay. Can't you give me a fucking minute to get myself together? It took me a long time to find you."

"Yeah. But you *did* find me, right? When you see Julio, tell him I'll remember this."

"Don't blame Julio. All he gave me was that phone number . . . the one the Chinese lady answers."

"I got your messages."

"So why didn't you call me?"

"Because I don't know you. I don't speak to strangers on the phone."

"That's why I had to find your car. Vinnie told me what you looked like—and your car. One of Julio's crew saw you at the courthouse this morning and he called me."

"Vinnie?" I said, thinking that I'd have to get the car painted and some new license plates.

"The guy who delivered the money to you from Julio."

"I don't know what you're talking about, lady."

"I told Julio why I needed to talk to you. He said it was none of his business—not family. He probably knew you'd never return my calls. So I told Vinnie to ask you for me."

"Nobody asked me anything."

"I know. He told me you wouldn't talk to him."

"I don't know what he told you. I don't care. I don't like people threatening me."

"Vinnie threatened you?"

"I don't know any Vinnie. *You* threatened me. In the parking lot, right? Either I talk to you or you keep hounding me."

"I didn't mean to threaten you."

"You're threatening me with this whole conversation. Julio's got his people on the street looking for me? Very fucking nice."

"Julio doesn't know anything about this. Vinnie did me a personal favor—and so did the guy who spotted you this morning."

"People like to do you these favors?"

She moved her lips in something between a smile and a sneer. "*Men* like to do me favors. You find that very surprising?"

"If this Vinnie is your idea of a man, no."

"You don't like any of us, do you?"

"Who's this 'us' you're talking about? An old man with a loose mouth? A punk kid? A woman who threatens me?"

"Us Italians."

"I don't like people who don't mean me any good, okay?"

"Okay," she said in a quiet voice, "but now that I went to all this trouble—now that we're here—will you listen to me and see if you're interested?"

"And if I'm not?"

"Then that's your decision. I won't bother you anymore."

"On your word of honor, right?"

Her eyes narrowed in on me. I thought I saw a tiny red dot in each one—it must have been the reflection from her hair. "You don't know me," she said.

"I don't *want* to know you," I told her.

She reached in her purse, fumbled around with her hand. Her eyes never left my face. "I'll pay you five hundred dollars to listen to what I have to say—why I want you to work for me. You don't take the case, you still keep the money. Okay?"

I took a minute to think about it. If I listened to her story and told her I wasn't interested, there was at least the chance that she'd go some-place else. And there was a filly pacer running at Yonkers that night that I just knew was going to break her maiden with a big win. She was due to snap a long string of losses. So was I.

"Okay," I told her.

The redhead ran her fingers through her hair in an absent-minded gesture. The diamond flashed on her hand. "My best friend has a . . ."

"Hold it," I told her. "Where's the money?"

"You listen to me first."

"No way."

"I thought only lawyers got money up front. You're only a private detective."

"Lady, you don't have the slightest idea what I am," I said, "but I'll give you a hint. I'm a man who's going to listen to your story—*after* you put five hundred dollars on the table."

Her hand darted into her purse. Out came five new century notes. She fanned them out—held them up. "Is this what you want?" she snapped.

"It's half of what I want."

"You mean you want a thousand?"

"I mean I want you to tell me your story and then get out of my life—like we agreed," I told her.

She released her grip on the money. It dropped to the seat between us. The street was still quiet—plenty of people around, but no problems. I picked up the money and pocketed it.

"So?" I asked her.

"My best friend, Ann-Marie. She has a little boy, only two years older than my daughter. He was in like a nursery-school thing during the day. Someone there did something to him. A sex thing. And they took pictures of him. We didn't even know about the pictures until the therapist explained it to us. But the boy, Scotty, he keeps saying they have his picture. Like they have his soul."

"This picture . . . he's doing something in it?"

"I think he must have been doing something . . . but he won't tell us. The therapist is working on it. I think if he got that picture, and we tore it up right in front of him . . . then maybe he'd be okay again."

"Just one picture?"

"That's what he said—he saw the flash."

"Lady, that picture's either in some freak's private collection or it's out on the street. For sale, you understand? It's just about impossible to come up with the stuff you want. And even if I found one print, the people who do the marketing make thousands of copies. It's a better business than cocaine: as long as you have the negative, you can make as many copies as you want."

"All we want is *one* picture . . . he's too young to know about making copies. I want to be there when we tear it up in front of him."

"It's a real long shot, you understand?"

"Yes. But it has to be done."

I looked directly at her—the little gangster princess wasn't going to take no for an answer. She wasn't used to it. "Why come to me?" I asked.

She had the answer ready. "Because you're friends with the Nazis."

24

I LOOKED straight ahead through the windshield, trying to get a grip on what she just said. If she knew about the Nazis, then she knew about some of the scores I'd pulled over the past few years—home-grown Nazis are a con man's delight. Knowing an old hotel address was nothing, it wasn't the trump card she thought it was. But the Nazi thing—she could hurt me. A cold wind blew through my chest. She held better cards than I thought.

Nothing moved in my face. I lit a cigarette, throwing the question at her out of the side of my mouth. "What're you talking about, lady?"

"Julio said you were friends with them. In prison. He saw it himself."

The weight came off my chest. *Those* Nazis were a different breed.

"Julio's got a lot of medical problems, doesn't he?" I asked.

"What medical problems? He's in perfect health, specially for an old man."

"No, he's not," I told her, my voice quiet and calm now. "His eyesight hasn't been good for a long time. He's losing his memory. And his mouth is out of control."

She understood what I was saying. I wouldn't have to do anything to the old man myself—if some of his bloody brothers got the word that Julio was writing his memoirs, he was gone.

"He only told me," said the redhead, her voice tight with tension, trying to convince me. "He wouldn't tell anyone else."

"Sure."

"I *mean* it. I *made* him tell me. I was desperate, okay?"

It wasn't okay. I took a close look at her. I might have to describe her someday and I didn't think she'd pose for a picture. The red hair framed a small, heart-shaped face. Her eyes were big and set far apart, the color of factory smoke. Her makeup looked like it was done by an expert: dark-red lipstick outlined in black, eye shadow that went from blue to black as it flowed from her eyebrows to the lashes, blended blusher on her cheeks, breaking right at the cheekbones for emphasis. Her teeth were tiny pearls—they looked too small for a grown woman, and too perfect to be real. Her nose was small and sharply bridged, slightly turned up at the tip. Piece by piece, she wasn't beautiful, but the combination worked. It was hard to think of that red slash of a mouth kissing anyone. Her hands were small, but the fingers were long, capped with long, manicured nails in the same shade as her lipstick. The redhead's eyes followed mine as they traveled over her—she was used to this.

"And you're *still* desperate, right?"

"Right," she said, as if that settled everything.

It didn't settle anything for me. I turned the ignition key, listened to the motor catch, and moved the lever into Drive. The Plymouth rolled off the pier, headed back to the courts.

"Where are we going?" the redhead wanted to know.

"*We're* not going anywhere. *You're* going back to your car."

"What about this job?"

"I said I'd listen to you. I listened to you. We're square—that's all there is."

She sat in silence for a couple of minutes. I could feel her eyes on my face. She cleared her throat a couple of times, but nothing came out. As we pulled onto Centre Street near the courthouse parking lot, she reached across the seat and put her hand on my forearm. I turned to look at her. Her big eyes were even bigger, as if tears were only a second away. It was a good trick.

"All this for a lousy picture?" I asked her.

"Yes."

"It doesn't add up for me."

She pulled at my arm so I'd look at her. "I gave my word!" she said, each syllable spaced and heavy.

Now it made sense. The redhead's ego was on the line. So what? Better her ego than my body. I wheeled next to her BMW and waited for her to get out. But she wasn't ready to give up. She shifted her hips, pulled her long legs up underneath her so she was kneeling on the seat facing me.

"What can I do to make you change your mind?"

"I haven't made up my mind, okay? Write your phone number down and I'll call you when I know."

"How do I know you'll call?"

"You don't."

Her face darkened under the makeup. "You call me. I know what you did in the park. One phone call . . ."

She let it hang there as she shifted position again and got out. Before I could pull away she was standing in front of the Plymouth, looking through the windshield. Then she came around to my side of the car, leaned in, and whispered to me: "I am very serious about this."

I locked eyes with her, spoke quietly. "I'm serious too, lady. Threats make me nervous. I'm likely to do something stupid when I'm nervous."

She didn't bat an eye. "I'm used to getting what I want. I'm spoiled—more than you'll ever know. I pay for what I want. You just tell me the price."

"Not everything has a price."

"That's a cliché," she whispered, her face close to mine. She put her head inside the car, kissed me lightly on the cheek, and quickly moved away. I watched her snake-hip her way back to the BMW. She looked back once before she pulled away.

"So are you, bitch," I thought to myself. As it turned out, I was half right.

25

THAT WAS the end of it, I thought.
The little princess wouldn't get what she wanted for once in her life and
she'd get over it. And I had five hundred bucks. It wouldn't balance the
scales, but it would do for today.

I parked behind Mama's apartment, opened the back door, and stepped
inside. The door's never locked, but when you open it some kind of bell
goes off in the kitchen. When I stepped through the doorway, the short,
squat Chinese Mama calls a cook was smiling at me, a butcher knife in
one hand. He was ready to chop something—when he saw it was me,
he settled for a slab of beef on the counter. I didn't bother to say hello
to him—he never answered.

The restaurant was about half filled. Mama was in her usual perch
by the cash register near the front door. I caught her eye and made a
motion like dialing a telephone. She bowed her head—all clear. I stepped
back inside the kitchen, went down a corridor to my right, and found
the pay phone.

My call went to another pay phone, the one in Julio's social club.

"Yeah?" barked the receptionist.

"Put Julio on, okay?"

"Who?"

"Julio, pal. You know the name. Tell him he's got a call."

"From who?"

"This is private business, okay? Just tell Julio. He don't want to talk
to me, that's his business."

I heard a thunk at the other end, telling me the receiver was swinging
against the wall in the club. Julio came on the line.

"Who's this?"

"It's me. You know my voice?"

"Yes," he said, clipped, but not cold.

"I need to talk with you."

"So?"

"Face to face."

"About . . . ?"

"About three o'clock tomorrow afternoon. At the Eastern District."

Julio didn't answer, just hung up. Anybody listening to the conversation would think Eastern District meant the federal courthouse in Brooklyn. What it meant to Julio was the pier at the end of Jay Street, only a few blocks from the courthouse, but in another world. And tomorrow meant in one hour. If I wanted two hours, I would have told him the day after tomorrow. It was a good place to meet, open on all sides—Julio wouldn't be coming by himself.

I dialed another number, let it ring until it was picked up by my broker.

"What?" Maurice snapped into the receiver.

"Burke. Yonkers, tonight, in the seventh. Two yards to win on Flower Jewel."

"Flower Jewel, two on the nose in the seventh at Yonkers, that right?"

"Right."

"Bring the cash by closing time tomorrow."

"What if I win?"

"Come on," he sneered, "you've already had your quota for this year."

"I haven't hit one fucking race yet this year," I told him.

"I know," said Maurice, and hung up.

I went back inside the restaurant, took the booth at the rear, the one I always use. I wrote Julio's name on a napkin, folded it around the money for Maurice, and waited. Mama spotted me. She left her post and walked back to the booth. I stood up until she was seated.

"So, Burke. You have soup, okay?"

"Yes, Mama. But not too much—I've got work to do."

"Good thing, work. Max work with you?"

"Uh . . . not on this, I don't think. But take this money and give it to him, okay? Tell him to give it to Maurice tomorrow if he doesn't hear from me." I handed her the napkin wrapped around two hundreds and a twenty. Max would keep the twenty for himself if he made the delivery. And he'd go see Julio if I didn't come back.

Mama didn't make a move, but one of the so-called waiters came over, listened to her rapid-fire Cantonese, and vanished. He came back in a couple of minutes with a tureen of hot-and-sour soup. Mama served me first, like she always does.

"I may have a new case," I told her.

Mama lifted her eyebrows, the soup spoon poised near her mouth.

"I haven't decided yet," I said in answer to her unspoken question.

"Good case?" Mama wanted to know—meaning was I going to get paid.

"Sure. Good case, bad people."

"That woman who call you here last week?"

"Yes."

"You say you not call her back, right? When I tell you who . . ."

"She found me, Mama."

"Oh. At your office?"

"No. She doesn't know about that place. But she looked all over and got lucky."

"That girl very angry."

"Angry? Why? At who?"

"I not know this. But very angry. You feel in her voice."

"She didn't seem angry to me."

"Angry," said Mama. "And dangerous."

"To me?" I asked her.

"Oh, yes," she said. She didn't say anything else while I finished my soup. When I got up to leave, Mama asked, "You take Max with you?"

"Not today."

"When you do work for this girl?"

"I don't know if I'm going to work for her yet."

"Yes, you know," said Mama, a little sadness in her voice. She bowed her head in dismissal and I went out the back to meet Julio.

26

I GRABBED the Brooklyn Bridge on the Manhattan side and drove across, staying in the right lane. I took the first off-ramp and kept bearing right until I hit the light under the overpass. To the right was the federal courthouse. It's a good spot to meet someone like Julio—nice and private, but too close to the *federales* for anyone to start shooting. I turned left onto Jay Street and kept rolling my way through the side streets until I was just past John Street, in the shadow of the Manhattan Bridge. I turned the Plymouth parallel to the water on the passenger side, dropped my window, and lit a smoke. The deserted slips hadn't seen a boat in years. I was about fifteen minutes early.

I only had a couple of drags on the cigarette when the white Caddy pulled up. It pulled up to the Plymouth, stopping only when it was nose to nose. The passenger door opened and Julio got out. I opened my door and started to walk away from the cars, my back to the Caddy. I heard one man's footsteps crunching on the gravel behind me. When I got to the railing, I turned so I could see both cars, looking past Julio to see if he was going to be stupid.

The old man had both hands in his overcoat pockets, collar turned up, hat pulled down over his eyes. Maybe he was cold.

"What's so important?" he wanted to know.

"Your friend's daughter—you told her where to find me?"

"Yeah."

"She wants me to do something for her."

"So you do it. You get paid. What's the problem?"

"What if I don't want the job?"

Julio turned away from me, looking out over the water. "Times have changed, Burke. Things aren't like they used to be. It's different inside too, you know?"

"I know," I told the old man. And I did: When I was a kid, it was always "Do the right thing." You couldn't go wrong if you did the right thing. When the new cons roll up on a new kid inside the walls today, they still tell him to "Do the right thing." But they mean get on his knees or roll over. Even the words don't mean the same things.

The old man just nodded, watching me.

"You told her about the Nazis too?" I asked him.

The old man went on like he hadn't heard me. "Remember how it used to be? If you was a rat in there, guys would shank you right on the yard . . . just to be doing it. You knew where you stood. Now guys come in *bragging* how they sold their partners for a better deal."

"What's that got to do with me, Julio?"

The old man was wasting away. His cashmere overcoat looked three sizes too large. Even his hat was too big for his head. But his alligator's eyes were still the same—a man on chemotherapy can still tell someone else to pull the trigger.

He looked me full in the face. "I always thought it was you that did the hijacking," he said.

I moved closer to him, my right hand on the handle of the ice pick I kept in my overcoat pocket. The tip was covered with a piece of cork, but it would come right off if I pulled it out. Julio had spent more time in prison than on the streets—he knew what it meant for me to stand so close. You spend enough time inside, you don't even think about getting shot—there's no guns behind the walls. It takes a different kind of man to stab someone—you have to be close to do it—you have to bring some to get some.

"You thought wrong," I told him, holding his eyes.

He looked right at me, as cold as the Parole Board. "It don't matter anymore. People do things . . . maybe it's the right thing to do when you do it . . . who knows? It don't matter to me."

"So why bring it up?" I asked him, my hand still on the ice pick, eyes flicking over to the white Caddy.

"I want you to understand that some debts get paid, okay? Whatever you did years ago, you always been a standup guy, right? Enough years go by, *anybody* should be off the hook."

I knew what he wanted me to say, but not why. "Yeah," I told him, "we all got a life sentence."

He gave me a chilly smile—he was lying about something and I was swearing to it.

"You told her about the Nazis?" I asked him again.

"Yeah," he answered again. His voice was dead.

"Why?"

"She's like my blood to me, you understand? I can't refuse her anything." He moved his shoulders in a "What can you do?" gesture.

"I can," I told him.

The old man didn't say anything for a while. He lit one of his foul cigars, expertly cupping his hand around the wooden match. He blew a stream of blue-edged smoke out toward the water. I just waited—he was getting ready to tell me something.

"When I was a young man, the worst thing you could be was an informer. The lowest thing. That's all over now—you can't count on anything," he said.

"You said that already. When I was a kid, it used to be 'Don't do the crime if you can't do the time.' Now it's 'Don't do the crime if you can't drop a dime.'"

The old man made a dry sound in his throat—it was supposed to be a laugh. "Only now it's a quarter," he said. The laugh never reached his belly, like the smile never reached his eyes.

"I still want to know what this has to do with me, Julio. It's your family, not mine."

"Yeah. My family." He took a breath, turned his flat eyes on my face. "Gina *is* my family," he said, as if that settled it.

"Whose idea was it to send that clown with my money?"

"Okay, it was wrong. I know. She wanted him to do it—I didn't see the harm. There was no disrespect. You got your money, right?"

I just nodded.

"Did Vinnie get stupid?" he wanted to know.

"Vinnie *is* stupid," I told him.

Julio didn't say anything. Being stupid wouldn't disqualify Vinnie from employment.

"The girl threatened me," I said. "Like I do her work or else . . ."

"She don't know no better, okay? When she wants something, she's like a crazy person. I'll talk to her."

"Do that. I'd appreciate it."

"It's done," he said. The old man put his hand in his pocket, came out with a roll of bills wrapped in a rubber band. He handed it to me. I pocketed the money, waiting.

"For your trouble," he said.

"My past trouble or my future trouble?"

"For the past. I apologize. I never thought she'd go all the way on this."

"You know what it is?"

The old man took a breath. The smoke came out his nose in two faint wisps. He took too long to think about the answer. "Yeah," he said. "That picture."

Now it was my turn to just nod. The jackpot question was still on the table.

"I just walk away? No problems?" I wanted to know.

"Burke, you want to walk, you walk. But if you did this thing . . . for the girl . . . if you did it, I would be grateful. You would have my gratitude, understand?"

I nodded again. A hundred feet away the two cars stood in silence. They looked like two giant dogs, nosing each other to see who was in control. It was a good question.

The old man walked over to the Caddy. He never looked back. His door closed; the Caddy backed away from the Plymouth and pulled out with a chirp of tires on the pavement. I was alone.

27

I sat in the front seat for a minute, lighting a cigarette and looking around. The pier was empty. I didn't expect anything else. There was no need for Julio to have me followed—

I don't advertise in the Yellow Pages, but people know where to find me if they want to bad enough.

The bridge was quiet too, that time of day. I drove slowly back to Manhattan, thinking my thoughts, trying to put it together. I was making the turn onto Allen Street when this old fool stepped right in front of the Plymouth. I hit the brakes just in time. Instead of apologizing, the old bastard gets red in the face and screams, "Why didn't you blow your horn?" A real New Yorker. "If I'd known you were fucking blind, I would've!" I shouted back. I live here too.

I pulled into the alley behind the old industrial building near the Hudson where I have my office. It's all been converted to "living lofts" and the landlord is making a bundle. Except on me. I unlocked the garage and drove the Plymouth inside. The back stairs go all the way up to the top floor, where I have the office. Steel doors block the stairway at the top and bottom. There's a sign that says the doors have to be kept unlocked in case of fire, but it's always too dark to read it. The top floor has a door near the front stairs and another near the back. The one near the back is sealed from the inside—I haven't tried to use it in years. The other door has a fat cylinder set into the middle—when you turn the key, a bolt drives into both sides of the doorframe and into the floor too. I never use it unless both Pansy and I are out. I don't carry the key with me either—I leave it in the garage.

I took the door-handle key out and twisted it hard to the left before I turned it to the right to make it open. I heard a low rumbling from Pansy as I stepped inside. "It's me, stupid," I told her as I stepped over the threshold. If I hadn't twisted the key to the left first, a whole bar of lights aimed at the door would blast off, and whoever entered would get a few thousand watts in their face and Pansy at their groin. She wasn't supposed to move unless the lights went on or if I came into the office with my hands up, but I didn't want to get careless with her—like I seemed to be with everyone else lately.

Pansy goes through personality splits whenever I walk into the office alone. She's glad to see me, but she's disappointed that there's nobody to bite. She followed me through to the back of the office. There's a door back there that would open out to the fire escape if this building still had one. The metal stairs go up to the roof. Pansy knew the way—she'd been dumping her loads up there for years, and I guess she still had room to spare. I keep telling myself that one day I'm going to go up there and clean up the whole damn mess. One day I'm going to get a pardon from the governor too.

The office is small and dark, but it never makes me depressed. It's safe there. A lot of guys I know, when they get out of jail after a long time, the first thing they do is find themselves some kind of studio apartment—anything with one room, so it feels like what they're used to. I did that too when I first hit the bricks, but that was because even one room was a strain on my budget. I was on parole at first, so my income was limited.

The office looks like it has two rooms, with a secretary's office on the left as you walk in. But there's nothing there—it's just a tapestry on the wall, cut so it looks like there's a way through. That's okay—there's no secretary either. Michelle made me up a bunch of tapes so I can have her voice buzz someone in from downstairs if I have to. I can even have her voice come over the phony intercom on my desk in case some client has to be reassured that I run a professional operation. To the right, it looks like a flat wall, but there's a door to another little room with a stall shower, a toilet, and a cot. Just like jail, except for the shower. It was supposed to be for when I had a big case running and I'd have to spend a lot of time in the office. I stopped kidding myself about stuff like that when Flood left. I stopped kidding myself about a lot of things—it's dangerous to lie to yourself, especially when you're as good at it as I am. I live in the office. I have a good relationship with the hippies who live downstairs. I don't know what they do for a living, and they don't know I use their phone.

The whole floor is covered in Astroturf. It's easy to keep clean, and the price was right. I can lock the front door with a switch on the desk in case I want to keep someone from leaving too quick. And the steel grate on the window makes it real tough for anyone to just drop in unless they bring along a cutting torch. Michelle always says it reminds her of a prison cell, but she's never been in prison. It's not a prison when you have the keys.

I left the back door open so Pansy could let herself back in when she finished on the roof. She lumbered over to me, growling expectantly. She was just looking for a handout, but it sounded like a death threat. Neapolitans were never meant to be pets. I checked the tiny refrigerator: I still had a thick slab of top round and a few slices of Swiss cheese. There's only a hot plate—I can't cook anything except soup. I cut a few strips from the steak, wrapped each one in a slice of cheese, and snapped my fingers for Pansy to come. She sat next to me like a stone lion—her cold gray eyes never blinked, but the drool flowed in rivers through her pendulous jowls. She wouldn't take the food until she heard the magic word from me—I didn't want some freak throwing a piece of poison-laced meat at her. I tossed one of the cheese-wrapped pieces of steak in the air in front of her. It made a gentle arc before it slapped against her massive snout, but her glance never flickered. Satisfied that she was in no danger of backsliding, I tossed her another piece, saying "Speak!" at the same time. The food disappeared like a junkie's dreams when he comes out of the nod. Her jaws didn't move but I could see the lump slip down her throat as she swallowed. "Can't you ever *chew* the damned food?" I asked her, but I knew better. The only way to make her chew was to give her something too big to swallow in one piece.

I sat there for a few minutes, patting her huge head and feeding her the rest of the steak and cheese. Pansy wasn't a food-freak like a lot of dogs. Most dogs will eat until they kill themselves if you let them. It's left over from being wild—wild things never know where their next meal is coming from, so they pack it in when they get the chance. When Pansy was a puppy, I got four fifty-pound sacks of the dry food she was raised on and lugged them up the stairs. I opened them all, dumped all the dog food in one corner of the office, and let her loose. She loved the stuff, but no matter how much she ate, there was always a big pile left. She ate until she passed out a couple of times, but once she got it that there would always be food for her, she lost interest. I always keep a washtub full of the dry food against the back wall of the office, near the door. And I have a piece of hose hooked up to the shower so her water dish refills itself every time the level drops. Now she eats only when she gets hungry, but she's still a maniac for treats, especially cheese.

The phone on my desk rang but I didn't move—it couldn't be for me. The Mole had hooked up an extension to the hippies' phones downstairs. I could make calls out when they weren't on the line, but that was all. I only had it ring to let me know if the line was in use, and to let clients think I was connected to the outside world. My clients never asked to use the phone—I don't validate parking either. The hippies didn't know I lived up here, and they couldn't care less anyway. All they cared about was their inner space, not who was sitting on top of their cave. It was my kind of relationship.

I glanced through the pile of mail left over from the last time I went to the drop and picked it up. It was the usual stuff, mostly responses to my series of ads promising information about opportunities for would-be mercenaries. When I get a legitimate response—one with the ten-dollar money order inside and a self-addressed stamped envelope—I send them whatever crap I happen to have lying around at the time. Usually it's a photocopied sheet of names and phone numbers in places like London or Lisbon. It's the real stuff, like "Go to the Bodega Diablo Bar between 2200 and 2300 hours, order a vodka tonic, and tell the bartender you want to speak to Luis." Sometimes I throw in a Rhodesian Army recruiting poster or a *National Geographic* map of what used to be Angola.

Don't get me wrong, I'm not in this just for the ten bucks—I keep a nice sucker list of anyone who replies to my ads. I've had a lot of careers, and as I get older I play it safer and safer. Stinging suckers and scamming freaks won't make me rich, but it won't make me dead either. And I'm much too old to go back to prison.

I used to sell other things, like handguns, but I stopped. I have to move between the cracks if I want to keep on being self-employed. Robbing citizens got me sent to prison, and the heroin hijacking almost put me down for the count. In the wild, when a wolf gets too old and slow to work with the pack, he has to go off on his own to die. If he's lucky, he gets captured and they put him in a cage to prolong his life. I already had that chance, and it wasn't for me. The way I figure it, I can always keep feeding myself if I work easier and easier game—prey without teeth. So what if the disturbos and petty crooks and outpatients don't ever add up to a retirement-level score? They might get mad, but they don't get even.

28

NONE OF this was getting me any closer to the answers I needed. I pulled out the roll of bills Julio had handed me at the pier. There was a century note on the outside, and it was no Chicago bankroll—every bill was the same, fifty of them, all used. Five thousand bucks. Too big to be a tip for the Forest Park job and not enough for the work the girl wanted me to do—but just the right amount for a warning. In case I missed the message, the last piece of paper inside the roll wasn't green—it had a phone number and the name "Gina" in a spidery, old-man's handwriting.

I went back into the other room and got a piece of mirror glass with a small red dot painted in the middle. I set it up so I was comfortable and sucked a deep breath in through my nose and down into my stomach, expanding my chest when I exhaled. I kept working on this, taking the air deeper and deeper each time, forcing it down to my lower stomach and then to my groin. I kept watching the dot, waiting to go inside, setting my mind to take this problem with me. The dot got bigger and bigger, filling the surface of the mirror. I concentrated on the sound of my own breathing, picturing the breath moving inside my body, waiting for it to happen. Images floated in: all gray tones—the prison yard, Julio's lizard eyes, a pool of dark water, a street in the rain. I came out of it slowly, feeling the cold spot between my shoulder blades. My hands were shaking.

I lit a cigarette, blew the smoke at the ceiling. The old man was trying to tell me something, and him wanting me to do the job for the girl was only part of it. I didn't need the dough, for a change. The girl wasn't going to lay off, and the old man wouldn't call her off. I should never have taken any work from Julio. My parole officer used to have a sign in his office: "Today Is the First Day of the Rest of Your Life." Sure. The trick is to make sure the first day isn't the last day.

I wanted to sleep for a while, but I knew what that meant. I wasn't tired, just depressed. And scared. It was safe in my office, so I wanted to stay. Some guys tried to sleep through their whole bit in prison. You could get all the medication you wanted from the unlicensed reject that passed for a doctor, and they let you have a TV in your cell too. But when they finally open the door, you could get killed while you were blinking at the light.

I always know what the right thing to do is—the hard thing. So I gave Pansy a pat, told her I'd bring her back a treat, and hit the street to buy some time.

29

I PULLED out of the garage thinking about what I'd need to cover my trail. The Plymouth is legally registered—to Juan Rodriguez, who lives in an abandoned building in the South Bronx. I wasn't worried about it being traced to me: in the South Bronx, every abandoned building has dozens of registered voters—they never miss an election.

You have to change with the times—using Juan Rodriguez as an alias today was like using John Smith thirty years ago.

The name "Burke" was legally registered too—I took some of the cash from a decent score a few years ago and invested fifteen grand in a piece of a junkyard in Corona, a Queens neighborhood that's Italian to the south and black to the north, with an expanding seam of Puerto Ricans down the middle. I'm on the books as a tow-truck driver. Every two weeks, the owner mails a check for my salary to the post-office box I keep at the main station, across from Madison Square Garden. I cash the checks at this bar near the junkyard and give everything but fifty bucks back to the junkyard owner. It's a good deal for both of us: he gets a business deduction for paying an employee and I get a w-2 form and a legit source of income in case anyone asks. The owner even throws in a set of dealer plates I can legally slap on any car when I do salvage work for him. I give the desk clerk at the hotel where I used to live ten bucks a week for insurance, and I'm covered all the way around. If I get arrested, the desk clerk verifies that I'm a permanent guest and the pay stubs do the rest—I'm a citizen.

I use money orders to pay the yearly registration on the Plymouth. Juan Rodriguez is a straighter shooter: he pays his bills, never gets a parking ticket, and he's never in an accident. He insures the Plymouth through this outfit in the Bronx which specializes in cheap coverage. He even votes regularly. Not only that, he lends me his car whenever I ask him, and he's in no hurry to get it back.

When I have to use the Plymouth on a job, I get the Mole to strip off the paint. The cops are used to seeing old cars in the process of getting painted, especially in the neighborhoods I work. I also have some vinyl sheets in different colors I can just press right over the paint. That kind of cover doesn't last long, but I only use it for a few hours and then pull it off. The Mole has thousands of license plates in his joint—he takes a couple of them and splits them in half, then welds two halves together to make a new set of plates that won't come up on any computer.

Julio wasn't the only reason I had to see the redhead—I had to find out what she knew about me and then go back and erase the tapes.

As I drove through Chinatown, afternoon was fading into evening. The streets were clogged with women making their way home from the sweatshops—their eyes were down and their shoulders slumped, the only hope in their hearts that their children would have a better life. And as they walked from the blackout-curtained rooms, where a straw boss watched their half-paralyzed fingers fly over the sewing machines, to their walk-up apartments with toilets in the hall, other children took over the streets. But these children had no dreams. The Blood Shadows—they took their name from the chalk outline the police coroner draws around a body on the sidewalk. Wearing their trademark black leather coats, silk shirts, and glistening black shoes, they were living proof that hell is cold. The newspapers called them a "street gang," but they were nothing like the bopping gangs from East Harlem or the South Bronx. No cut-off dungaree jackets with their colors on the back for these boys. And no social workers either. Every year Hong Kong disgorges more of them, nobody knows how they get here, but they keep on coming. And America tolerates it like any toxic-waste dump as long as there's money in it for somebody. The Blood Shadows disdain common street mugging—they don't do their gang fighting with knives and chains. Chinatown runs on gambling and dope—organized extortion of these industries forms the Holy Triad, and the Blood Shadows were the sole survivors of a territorial war with other cliques for vulture's rights. The other gangs either merged with the Blood Shadows or got very dead. That left the old guard—what was left of the Tongs.

The old men had first tried to recruit the Hong Kong boys to their own use, but that wasn't working anymore. The old men retreated deeper and deeper into the networks they had spent years developing—but all their political contacts were useless against young boys with flat eyes and hungry guns, kids who didn't play by the rules. The old folks didn't have a chance. They had to import muscle while the kids were growing their own.

I nosed the Plymouth through the alley in back of the warehouse. Clotheslines stretched across the alley, and children ran past, shrieking at each other in a mixture of English and Cantonese. The kids were like birds in a jungle—everything was safe as long as they were making noise. When they went silent, a predator was walking the trails.

I pulled around the front and into the garage. I left the engine running while I pulled the door closed behind me. The Mole had once offered to wire the door so a light would blink and tell Max someone was around, but Max bowed his thanks and said he didn't need it.

I wasn't going to call the redhead from anyplace that could be traced—with cocaine accounting for half the gross national product of the city, half the pay phones in town have been tapped by one agency or another. I'd have to wait for an hour or two anyway. When Max didn't materialize on the landing at the back of the garage, I made a pillow out of my jacket, put it against the passenger door, and stretched out. I put on a

Judy Henske tape and listened to her raw-silk voice sing "If That Isn't Love" while I smoked a cigarette in the soft darkness of the garage.

Max might be back in five minutes or five hours. In my life, time isn't important—so long as you're not doing it inside.

30

SOMETHING dropped onto the Plymouth's hood from upstairs, waking me up. I glanced through the windshield—it was a new deck of playing cards, still in the original box. Max was telling me he wanted a rematch of our last game of gin, and warning me not to cheat.

I pocketed the cards and went through the downstairs door all the way to the back. We had a little table back there and a couple of chairs. The table held a big glass ashtray and a chrome ghetto-blaster some would-be mugger had donated to Max. A true liberal, Max never called the police, realizing that the young man needed rehabilitative services instead. He left that task to the emergency ward.

Max floated in the side door, bowed to me, and made a motion like he was dealing the cards. I opened the new deck and riffled them between my hands, getting the feel. Max reached into one of the cabinets and pulled out one of those thick telephone message pads they use in government offices—we used the back for a score sheet. We play three-column gin: 150 points a game, twenty-five for a box, double for a schneid in any column, and double again for a triple. The stakes are a penny a point—first man to a million bucks wins the whole thing. I looked through our stack of tapes, asked Max which one he wanted me to put on. He pointed to Judy Henske. I slammed the cassette home and put the volume on real low. I know Max can't hear. I used to think he listened to music by feeling the bass line in his body or something, but Henske's voice doesn't get real low. One time I slipped a Marie Osmond tape on the player. Max listened for a minute, pointed to me, made a face to say

"You *like* that shit?" and hit the "stop" button. He reached in, pulled out the cassette, and crushed it in one hand. He threw the mess into a bucket we use for a garbage pail, folded his arms, and waited for me to display some better taste. I still don't think he can hear the music, but maybe he can feel how I react to it. Lucky there's no bluffing in gin.

We were about an hour into the game, with Max ahead for a change, when Immaculata came into the room from behind Max. Her long black hair was pulled back into a severe bun and her face was scrubbed clean of makeup. She was wearing a white jersey sweatshirt that must have belonged to Max—it was big enough for two of her. She bowed to me in greeting as she put one hand on Max's shoulder. Her long nails were lacquered a shade of purple so dark it was almost black. Max reached up to touch her hand, but he never took his eyes from the cards. The first time Immaculata had walked into our clubhouse like she belonged there, I felt a stab of something—but it passed. She did belong there.

"Hey, Mac," I greeted her, "we're almost done."

Max reached across the table and snatched the score sheet from in front of me. His score was under "X" and mine was under "O"—we'd started playing tic-tac-toe first, years ago, and Max wanted to keep the same identifications just because he won the last time—Orientals are superstitious people. He handed her the sheet. His meaning was obvious—it was me who was almost done.

That did it—being ahead was bad enough, but bragging about it was gross. I immediately knocked, going down with two aces and a deuce—four points. Max spread his cards: three queens, three fives, and three tens. The only other card was my missing ace—an under-knock—worth four boxes and fifty points . . . and the fucking third column too. The miserable thug couldn't keep the smile off his face as he handed me the pencil to total things up. Mac went to the hot plate in the corner to make some tea for her and Max—there was apple juice in the refrigerator for me. Max had cut deeply into his ongoing deficit with that last score.

I made the sign of a man rolling dice with his eyes closed to show that it was pure dumb luck, and Max made the sign of a man playing the violin to show how sorry he felt for me and my dismal lack of skill.

Max stashed the score sheet and lit a cigarette. He used to light up whenever he needed only one more card for gin. As soon as he realized I'd caught on to it, he just plain stopped smoking while we were playing— a typical fanatic. Immaculata brought the tea and the apple juice on a little tray and lit a cigarette of her own. I made the sign of talking into a telephone, telling Max I needed to plug into the phone system of the architects who had the building next door. I started to get up and Max held out his palm in a "stop" gesture. He turned to Immaculata, pointed to me, and waved his hands in front of his chest, fingers curling back toward his face. He was telling her to get on with it—whatever it was.

"Burke," she said, "I'm having a problem with my work. Max insists you could help me with it," she said, in a doubtful voice.

"I'll do what I can," I told her.

"I'm not sure there's anything you *can* do," she said. Her English was perfect, the mixture of French and Vietnamese in her voice sounding exotic but not foreign. "When I interview abused children . . . about what happened to them . . . like you saw with the dolls?"

I just nodded, listening.

"Well, if they're old enough to really talk, what I have to do is get it all on tape. You can't take notes . . . you just distract them if you do . . . they want to know what you're writing down. And we may have to use the tapes in court. You understand so far?"

"Sure," I said.

"Anyway, for these children, what we're working on is something we call 'empowerment.' It just means that sexually abused children have no sense of power over their own lives . . . these children are always in fear—they never feel really safe. The goal is for them to eventually be able to confront their abusers, and feel safe while they do it, okay?"

"Okay."

"So they have to feel in control. They have to believe that they're on top of the situation—even when they're working with the therapist."

"How come they don't feel in control when the freak isn't in the room with them anymore?" I asked her.

Immaculata looked at me, two long dark fingernails against her cheek, thinking. "Wait here, okay? I want to show you something."

She patted Max on the shoulder a couple of times, probably their signal that she was coming right back, and went out the way she came in. Max leaned back in his chair, looked over at me, and moved his fingers on the table top to make the sign of a trotting horse. He looked a question at me. I nodded in agreement. Sure, I was still betting on the horses—what was I supposed to do, open a fucking IRA? Max made the sign of opening a newspaper and glancing through it, and looked another question at me. He wanted to know which horse was the latest object of my interest. I shrugged—I didn't have a paper with me. The bastard moved his two fists like he was holding a steering wheel—didn't I have one in the car? Okay. I trudged out to the Plymouth, snatched the *Daily News* off the front seat, and went back to our clubhouse. I sat down and opened it to the right page as Max drifted around behind me. I ran my finger down the page until I came to the seventh race, showed him Flower Jewel, and waited. The line of Flower Jewel showed 8-4-3 reading across from her name—she had finished dead last a week ago, fourth the time before that, and third before that. Max pointed to the "8," put four fingers on the table, and moved them like a pacer would run, the two outside legs forward, then those on the inside—that's why they call them sidewinders. He paced halfway across the table, then broke into a gallop—the two front legs moving together. He looked a question at me. Yeah, I told him, the horse had broken stride in the last race. I held up my right fist to indicate my horse, started to move it across the table in a circle. Then I had my left fist cut in front, with the right veering off to the side. My horse had broken stride, but she had been interfered with by another—not her fault.

Max smiled knowingly. He rubbed the first two fingers and his thumb together in the sign for money, shrugged his shoulders, and spread his hands to ask how much I'd invested. I held up two fingers. Max reached over and pulled one toward him—he wanted to take half my action. The last time he'd done that was the first time he'd ever bet on a horse—back when Flood was here. And we'd won. I hadn't hit a horse since—maybe my luck was changing. But it was probably just that Max was standing up with me. He knew I'd been blue, and his own good fortune in finding Immaculata made him feel even worse for me.

When I wrapped up my sentence for the heroin scam, Max took me over to the warehouse and handed me an old airline carry-on bag. It was stuffed with money—almost forty thousand bucks. He took a paper packet of sugar out of his pocket, tore it open, and dumped the sugar on the table. He spread it flat, then divided it precisely in half with one fingernail. He swept half off the table into his hand, and pointed to the other half, and then to me. I got it—from the day I got arrested, he'd put away half of every score he'd made and saved it for me so I wouldn't have to start all over when I got out.

I didn't know what to say. Max cupped one hand on the table and used two fingers to burrow through it. The Mole. He put one hand on his chest, and spread the other wide in a gesture of impassioned oration. The Prof. The bag was half of everything they'd all made while I was inside. Then he touched his heart with his fist, and extended an open hand to me. Telling me that money didn't square the debt—he would always owe me.

I've done time with a lot of gangsters over the years. The cream of the crop, the real elite, were the "made men," the guys who get to cut their fingers and swear undying loyalty to some boss. They keep their mouths shut and do their time, just like the movies say. When they finally make it back to the streets, they get a kiss on both cheeks and a few bucks from their boss. And they call themselves "wiseguys."

31

IT WAS another few minutes until Immaculata came back. She had an armful of paper with her. "Look at this," she told me, and sat down next to Max.

They were kids' drawings: stick figures, crude crayons—they didn't mean anything to me.

"So?" I asked.

"Look at them again, Burke. Look closely."

I lit a cigarette and went through them again. "How come the pictures of the kids have no arms?" I asked her.

"That's it. Now you see. The children have no arms. And see how small they are next to the big figures? Look at this one. . . ."

It was a picture of a little child looking at a giant penis pointed at her face. The child had no arms—her mouth was a straight line.

"She's trapped," I said.

"Yes. She is without power, you understand? She is small, her abuser is huge. The penis is her whole world. She has no arms to fend it off. She has no legs to run. She's in a cage."

"How do you break her out?" I wanted to know.

Immaculata took a deep breath. "Some of them never do break out. We have to give them back a sense of control before that happens. If we start too late, they look for control with drugs, or they try suicide. Or they surrender."

"Surrender?"

"To the feelings. It's not just the loss of power. Children have sexual feelings too. If you awaken them too early, they get out of control, and the kids themselves look for sex . . . it's what they think is love."

"Fucking maggots."

Immaculata didn't say anything. Max reached across and took a couple of the wooden matches I used for my smokes. He broke one until it was about a third the size of the rest, and put it next to a full-size match. Then he took the big match and snapped it off until it was even smaller than the first one. He looked at Immaculata.

"It won't work. To the child, the abuser is always all-powerful. You can't make him small—you have to make the child big."

I took the tiny piece of match that was supposed to be the parent, lit another match, and touched it to the little piece. It went up in flames.

"That won't work either, Burke. You can make the perpetrator disappear from the earth, but not from inside the child's mind."

I didn't say anything. Immaculata's face was calm, her eyes watchful but showing nothing. I looked at Max—his face was a concrete mask. He wasn't buying this any more than I was.

"What's this got to do with the tape recorder, Mac?" I asked her.

"In my office, the child has to not just *be* safe, she has to *feel* safe. She has to learn she can control parts of her life. She has to learn she has the right to say 'No!' Okay?"

"Okay."

"Most of the kids have been involved in a conspiracy of silence. The offenders make them promise not to tell—keep it a secret. Or they make the kids believe something terrible will happen if they do. So I tell them if there's something they don't want to go on the tape recorder, all they have to do is reach over and turn it off. So *they* are in control."

"And they turn it off when they get to the stuff you need for court?"

"Sometimes they do," she said.

I lit another smoke and closed my eyes, buying some time to think. When it came to me, it was so simple I was sure they'd already thought of it.

"Use two tape recorders," I told Mac.

"Two tape recorders?"

"Sure. The one on top of the table—the one the kids can turn off if they want, right? And you keep another one out of sight, maybe under the table or something. And you let that one run all the time. So even when they turn off the first one, you still have everything on tape."

Immaculata put the two fingernails back against her cheek, thinking it over. "That would be dishonest," she told me.

"Better to let some scumbag walk away laughing?" I asked.

She waited a second or two. "No," she said. And a smile broke across her lovely face. "That's what we'll do."

Max made an "I told you so" gesture to his woman, now smiling himself. Immaculata reached over and squeezed my hand, and Max's smile broadened.

Immaculata was the first woman ever to come into our clubhouse. She'd be the last. Like all truly dangerous beasts, Max would mate for life.

I left them with each other and went in the back to make my call.

32

IT WAS just getting dark as I walked through the catacombs behind the warehouse. The cellar was one of many that ran under all the buildings on the block. The City Planning Office sold me a set of the plans years ago, and the Mole figured out how we could make all the basements connect to each other by drilling a few holes. It took almost a month for us to finish, but once you got to the warehouse basement, you could get out a dozen different ways. We originally did it just in case we had to leave quickly, but once we were under there, the Mole showed me how we could tap into the telephone lines in the other buildings. The warehouse is owned by some corporation Mama Wong set up, but it belongs to Max. His temple is upstairs, and the rest of the space is for whatever we need. For Mama, it's a warehouse. For me, it's the post office.

I found the metal footlocker, rooted through it past the stuff we kept there—coats, hats, glasses, anything to make you look different. I found the field telephone and the set of alligator clips. I walked through our cellar into the next basement. Above us was a firm of Chinese architects, and they never worked late. I clipped the field phone onto the junction points the Mole had shown me and I got a dial tone right away. I used the little box that looked like the face of a calculator and punched out the number Julio had written down, lit a cigarette, and waited.

I didn't have long to wait—she must have been sitting by the phone.

"Hello." It was the redhead.

"Hey, baby," I leered into the mouthpiece, "you free tomorrow night?"

She got it right away. "Sure. What time will you pick me up?"

"I'm going to be working late. I'll meet you, okay?"

"Where?"

"Same place—nine o'clock," I told her, and unplugged the phone.

I put everything back where it was supposed to be and walked back through the cellar. Our clubhouse was empty. I fired up the Plymouth, hit the garage-door switch, and backed out into the alley. I got out to go back inside and close up, but I saw the garage door slide down. Max was on the job.

I drove over to Mama's. I needed some food for Pansy and an alibi for tomorrow night.

33

I T WAS past midnight before I was ready to go back to the office. If Mama didn't hear from me by the same time tomorrow, she'd know the meeting had been a bust. Mama would tell Max, and call Blumberg to get a bondsman over to Arraignments in Queens. If I wasn't in jail, Max would go see Julio.

One more call to make and I could bring Pansy her Chinese food. I found a pay phone off Atlantic Avenue.

A young woman with a sweet West Indian accent answered. "A & R Wholesalers. We never close."

"Is Jacques around?" I asked her.

"Please hold one moment, sir."

It was cold in the phone booth, but the man's voice was as sunny as the Islands.

"Yes, my friend. May we be of service?"

"Jacques, this weather is really turning ugly out here, you know? I think I can move some of those portable electric heaters if I can get a good price."

"We may have some in stock, mahn—I'll have to check the inventory. And the price . . . it depends on how many you want, like always."

"If I can get some tonight, I'll take a dozen and try them out."

"That's not a big order, my friend. The more you take, the less they cost."

"I understand. But I'm not ready to risk a lot of capital—I have to see how they move this year, okay?"

"Whatever you want, mahn—we are here to serve. You are familiar with our line?"

"Sure. Now, look, I only want new merchandise, still in the original cartons."

"Of course, of course. You understand this too affects the price."

"I understand."

"Now, we have a good supply of the new automatic models—the ones which shut off by themselves if they tip over?"

"No, I only want the old-style. They throw plenty of heat."

"Yes, my friend," said Jacques, "but many customers prefer the advanced safety features."

"The new ones are too complicated for me. I want a product I can trust."

"We have just what you want, mahn," he assured me. "Do you at least want the ones that run on both twelve hundred and fifteen hundred watts?"

"Yeah, that's a good feature. Can I pick them up tonight?"

"We never close, my friend," he said. We both hung up.

I drove down Atlantic toward Queens. Soon it turned into a West Indian neighborhood. I turned left on Buffalo Avenue, past the abandoned bar on the corner, until I saw the storefront restaurant. There was a sign for Tower Isle Jamaican Meat Patties in the window, a pair of black Cadillacs parked in front. I turned into the driveway and pulled around the back. When I had the Plymouth's headlights aimed at the back door, I flashed the lights three times and turned them off.

The door opened and a man came out, both hands in the pockets of a big leather apron. I had the window down and my hands on the sill by the time he got close enough to see me.

"Jacques is expecting me," I told him.

The man said nothing. He backed away, still facing me, until he was inside the door. I lit a cigarette and got ready to do some waiting.

I was just lighting another when the door opened again. The leather apron came out first and walked over to me again. He said nothing. From behind him I could see another man—tall, with a little snap-brim hat. The other man was carrying a shopping bag in one hand.

I kept my eyes on the leather apron. The other man disappeared from view. I heard the Plymouth's door open and someone climbed inside.

"Is that you, Burke?" asked Jacques.

"It's me," I told him, turning to face him, my back to the leather apron like it was supposed to be.

Jacques hands me the shopping bag. Inside was a blue box. And inside that was a Smith & Wesson .357 magnum snub-nosed revolver. The blue steel even smelled new.

I popped the cylinder open, held my thumb in front of the barrel, and sighted down. The rifling was new too. Not a very accurate piece, but the best man-stopper at close range. It would take either .38 Special or .357 magnum slugs, and it had no safety. A lot better than the 9mm automatic Jacques had been pushing over the phone.

I nodded my head in agreement. Jacques held up his hand, palm out, fingers spread. I raised my eyebrows. He just shrugged.

It's good to deal with professionals—even if I was wired like a Christmas tree, nothing would go on the tape. Five hundred bucks of Julio's money changed hands. I slipped the pistol into my coat pocket, put the box it came in back into the shopping bag, and waited. The West Indian took out a box of shells, holding them in his palm. I shook my head— I had all the bullets I needed. Jacques touched a forefinger to his brow. I turned to face Leather Apron again. I heard the car open and close, but I didn't move until I saw the bodyguard start to back away toward the restaurant door. Then I got out of there.

I drove down Atlantic, one hand on the wheel, the other pulling up the rubber floor mat and groping around until I found the panel next to the hump for the transmission. I had loosened the ratchets before I drove to the restaurant. The magnum slipped inside and the rubber mat went back in place. There was nothing in plain view. I couldn't do anything about a cop stopping me, but if he found the piece it wouldn't stand up in court.

The magnum was a heavy-duty piece. Just looking at the business end would scare most people. But guns aren't for scaring people, they're for people who are scared. I was—I just didn't know of what.

34

I DROVE back carefully, speeding up
so I blended in with the late-night traffic. The streets were quiet, but if
you looked close, you could see things. Two guys standing against the
wall of a darkened gas station—the wool caps on their heads would turn
into ski masks when they pulled them down, hands in their pockets. A
lonely whore in a fake-fur coat with a white mini-skirt underneath,
looking to turn one last trick before she called it a night. A van with
blacked-out windows driving by slowly, watching the whore while the
two men in the shadows watched the van. In New York, the vultures
work close to the ground.

Back in the garage, I unscrewed the plate and took out the magnum.
I needed to test the piece and I didn't have time to run over to the Bronx
and ask the Mole. I broke the gun and loaded it with some .38 Specials
I keep in a jar full of nuts and bolts. The door to the basement is set
into the garage floor, like a manhole cover. I pried it loose and backed
down the stairs, reaching for the light switch with my hand. I heard the
rats running across the floor even before the light went on. Some of the
bolder bastards just looked at me—it was their place, not mine.

The walls are lined with sandbags donated from a construction site—
about four bags deep all around the wall and up to the ceiling. I don't
keep anything else down in the basement; there's no other way out except
for the tunnels the rats use. It's good for nothing but testing things that
make a big bang—you couldn't hear a cannon from the street.

There's a little workbench on the floor down there with a heavy-duty
vise attached and a reel of two-hundred-pound-test fishing line. I wrapped
the butt of the magnum in the vise, wedged it tight, and tied some of
the fishing line around the trigger. I aimed it at the far wall, cocked the
hammer, and ran the line back to the stairs. I climbed halfway up and
gave it a hard pull. There was a sharp *crack!* sound and a puff of dust
from one of the sandbags. I went over to look—just a nice round entrance

hole—the other side would be wide open, but I wasn't going to pull the whole thing apart just to take a look.

I pulled the magnum out of the vise, held it two-handed, and emptied it into the wall. It kicked a bit, but not as much as I expected from the short barrel. I broke the gun and dropped the empties into my hand. Jacques was still selling quality merchandise.

The rats were back doing business before I had the trapdoor closed.

35

I woke up the next morning and just stayed there on the couch for a bit, watching Pansy growl in her sleep at a patch of sunlight on her face. I'd been dreaming of Flood—I do it all the time since she left. When I was a kid in reform school I used to dream about getting out—staying out—being somebody important, like a major-league gangster. Now I just replay the tapes of my past inside my head—I can't erase them but I do enough editing to keep me sane.

I took my time getting ready to go out and get some breakfast. I wasn't in any screaming hurry to check out the race results.

The bakery was a couple of blocks away, still standing despite the invasion of yuppies. Newspaper columnists who never rode a subway still call my neighborhood the "mean streets," but the only danger out there is maybe getting hit by a flying croissant.

There was a new girl working in the bakery, about sixteen years old, with black hair and dark eyes. From the way the guy who runs the place was watching her, she had to be his daughter. I make sure I don't buy there too often—the owner thinks I make the trip all the way from Brooklyn just for his bread. If too many people know where you live, sooner or later you get visitors.

I picked out a semolina loaf for Pansy and a couple of hard rolls for me. Next door in the deli I got some pineapple juice and seltzer plus a slab of cream cheese. A lot of guys I did time with said when they got out they'd always start the day off with a real breakfast—bacon and eggs, steak, hash-browns, coffee, all that. I never did that—I'm particular about who I eat with.

I grabbed a *Daily News* off the stand. The newsdealer is blind. I handed him a five, telling him what it was. He put the bill face down on this machine he has, moving his hand so it forced the bill over some lights. "Five dollars," the machine said in a robot voice. The paper costs thirty-five cents now. The price of everything except human life has gone up a lot in New York.

Upstairs I tore open the semolina loaf and scooped out the guts. Most of the slab of cream cheese went inside. I looked over at Pansy. She was sitting like a stone, drooling. I tossed her the loaf, saying the magic word at the same time. As usual, she bit right through the middle so that the piece on each side of her jaws fell to the floor. It was gone before I had a chance to make my own breakfast. "You've got the table manners of an animal," I told her. Pansy never looked up—nobody respects my social criticism.

I mixed the seltzer and pineapple juice, opened the hard rolls, and put the last of the cheese inside. Finally, I turned to the race results. Sure enough, Flower Jewel was the first horse listed in the seventh race. But before I had even a split-second's worth of pleasure out of it, I saw the tiny "dq" next to her name. Disqualified. I went over the charts, trying to see how I was robbed this time. My horse tried to get to the top but was parked by another animal all the way to the half before she was shuffled back to fourth against the rail. Then she pulled out and was flying in the stretch when she broke stride. When she crossed the wire first she wasn't pacing like she was supposed to, she was galloping. Flower Jewel was out of an Armbro Nesbit mare by Flower Child, a trotting stallion. She had her grandfather's heart, but not her father's perfect stride. What the hell: *she* probably didn't know she didn't win the race. My love for the animal was unchanged—she did the right thing—much better to get there first by cheating than play by the rules and finish back in the pack. At least she'd get another shot next week.

It was still early enough for the hippies downstairs to be asleep. I picked up the phone and called over to the restaurant.

"Poontang Gardens," answered Mama Wong. Some soldier had suggested the name to her years ago and she's too superstitious to change it.

"It's me," I said. "Any calls?"

"Same girl. She say you be there."

"What?"

"She call, okay? I say you not here. She say, 'You tell him be there,' and she hang up."

"Thanks, Mama."

"Hey!" she snapped, just as I was about to hang up, "People tell you what to do now?"

"No," I said and hung up.

I called Pansy back from the roof and went into the other room. I got the little TV set and went back to the couch. I asked Pansy what she wanted to watch but she didn't say. All she likes are shows about dogs and professional wrestling. I found a rerun of "Leave It to Beaver" and kicked back on the couch. I was asleep before it was over.

36

WHEN I came to, there was some western on the screen. Two guys had just finished bashing each other's heads in and were getting ready to shake hands. Politicians do that too, but it comes natural to them—they're all dogs from the same litter.

I let Pansy out to the roof again and started to put together what I'd need for my date. If this was a regular case, I would have had her come to the office, where it's safer for me, but she was pushing too hard and I wasn't going to give her any more information about me than she already had. I set the magnum aside—I could put it back into the cavity next to the transmission hump just in case, but I didn't think I was walking into a shoot-out. Hell, I *wouldn't* walk into a shoot-out. The redhead wasn't really working together with Julio—if the old man wanted me put down he would have tried it already. He was just pushing on me the same way the redhead was, but not for the same reason.

I dressed like I was going to be arrested—when nothing feels right, you make plans for things going wrong. An old leather sportcoat; plain white cotton shirt, button cuffs; a black knit tie. All that camouflage wouldn't stop me from being rolled in, but it might stop the cops from being too forceful about it. If they only took me as far as the precinct, I still might be able to do something about it. But if they actually made an arrest, I'd be around for a while—my fingerprints would fall and they'd know I wasn't a citizen. Figuring the worst, I made sure I wasn't carrying anything that would make a problem for me. The ankle-high boots had zippers up the insides. They also had steel toes and one hollow heel. I folded five ten-dollar bills tightly to get them inside the heel. Soft money is the best contraband to have when you're locked up. A ten-dollar bill is just about right for a jailhouse transaction—more than enough to get me moved to another tier or for a supply of smokes and magazines. Twenty bucks would get me some private time on the phone and tap me into the rest of my money if it came to that. In jail they let you keep most of your streetside clothes. They don't take everything away until you get sentenced.

I took a shower and shaved carefully, listening to the radio say how warm it was for that time of the year. I've got a good watch, a gold Rolex some rich guy lost in his hotel room, but I didn't put it on. Times have changed—I was just a kid years ago, sitting in the holding cell, watching the cops bring a full-race pimp up to the booking desk. I was still handcuffed but they'd hooked me in front so I could smoke. I was splitting one of my last matches—you put your thumbnails carefully into the cardboard at the base of the match, then you pull up slowly until you have two matches with half a striking-head on each piece. The Puerto Rican kid next to me was holding the matchbook so we could get a light. When he leaned over for some fire he nudged me in the ribs so I'd look up. The pimp was raising hell, mouthing off about how the cops should be careful of his jewelry and how much it cost. The fat old sergeant at the booking desk acted like the pimp wasn't in the room. He picked up all the jewelry one piece at a time, read aloud what it was, and marked it down on the voucher sheet. They'd give it all back to the pimp when he paid his fine. It was all a dance. The sergeant made his list like a guy taking inventory: "One diamond bracelet, gold clasp. One signet ring, onyx and gold, initial 'J,' one pinky ring . . ." The pimp kept up a running fire about how much all that stuff cost. I think that was when I first got the idea that it was stupid to steal from citizens. The sergeant picked up the pimp's wristwatch. It was thin as a dime, with a dark-blue face and little diamonds all around the rim—a thing of beauty. He looked down at the pimp, who said, "Hey, my man, you best be careful with that watch. It cost more than you make in a year!" The cop looked thoughtfully at the watch for a minute, like he was trying to figure out how it could cost all that cash. Then he slammed it face down on the desk counter. The crystal cracked and little pieces went flying all over the place. The pimp screamed "Hey man!" like it was his head that got cracked. The sergeant looked at the pimp, said, "One man's watch—broken," and wrote it down on his sheet. His expression never changed. I wasn't worried about them doing that to my Rolex. Like I said, times have changed. Now they'd probably steal it.

It was almost six by the time I was ready to leave. The meeting was for nine, so the timing was just about right. I brought Pansy back downstairs and fixed things so she'd have food and water for at least a couple of weeks if I didn't come right back. I left the back door open a crack so she could get to the roof herself. The open door wouldn't help a burglar much—he'd have to be a human fly to get in the door, and a magician to get out.

I stopped at four different self-serve gas stations along Atlantic Avenue. The Plymouth has a fifty-gallon tank—if I filled it up at one place, they might remember me. Just before I made the turn onto the Inter-Boro I saw a gray stone building on my right. The windows were barred and there was barbed wire on the roof. The door looked like the entrance to Attica. The sign on the front said it was a Day Care Center.

It took less than an hour for me to finally get to the old spot in Forest Park. It was still light enough for the joggers and dog-walkers. I drove through the entire park a couple of times, looking for some other spots to park—and for people looking for me. I finally parked the Plymouth just off the road, opened the trunk, and put on the old raincoat and leather gloves I always keep in there. Then I changed the rear tire closest to the road, taking my time. It was a while before I was finished. I put everything back into the trunk except for the tire iron and the gloves, which I tossed into the back seat.

By the time I settled down to wait, the only thing that didn't belong in all that greenery was me.

37

WHAT WAS left of the weak sun filtered through the thick trees, making patterns of light and dark all around the Plymouth. By the time the shadows won the war I had stopped listening to my tapes. Headlights shot through the park, cars motored by. Once in a while I'd see a bicycle or even a late jogger wearing reflective foil on his warmup suit. I ground each cigarette out against the car door, putting the butts inside a plastic bag. No point in telling the cops how long I'd been waiting, if it came to that.

It was almost nine when I heard the whine of a car kept too long in a lower gear. The little BMW tore around the far curve and headed right at me. The redhead was running a pair of driving lights on the front bumper—the white light blasted into my windshield as she slammed on the brakes and skidded to a stop almost on top of me. As soon as I heard her engine shut off, I started the Plymouth. I heard her door slam and I watched her walk the way women do in high heels on a tricky surface. She was close enough for me to see her face when I pulled the lever into gear and started to creep forward. Her legs were spread wide, anchored to the ground, hands on hips. Her mouth was open to say something, but I pulled past the BMW and stopped, foot on the brake. She walked toward me again, and I pulled forward some more.

She got it. The redhead walked back to her car. I waited until she started it again; then I pulled out slowly so she could follow, heading for the better spot I'd found before. The Plymouth calmly drove through the park; the BMW stuck to my bumper, her damned driving lights flooding the rearview mirrors. I turned the inside mirror backward and made two tours through the park, just in case she brought some friends. I could hear the angry roar of the BMW in the night—she was so close I could have merged with her front end if I hit the brakes.

I found the spot I wanted and pulled all the way in, leaving the Plymouth with its nose pointing back out to the road. The redhead was right behind me, but she didn't have room to turn around—like I wanted it.

I killed the engine.

Her door slammed hard enough to rattle the glass. She stalked over to where I was sitting, her little fox face set and hard.

"You all through playing games?" she snapped.

I got out of the Plymouth, reaching for the flashlight I keep in the door panel. I walked past her to the BMW, opened the door, and shone the light inside. Empty.

"Open the trunk," I told her.

The redhead made a hissing sound, but she turned and reached inside her car for the keys. I shined the light on her to help. She was wearing what looked like half a normal skirt, reaching over to the middle of her thighs. It had vertical black and white stripes and was topped by a wide black belt. Her stockings had dark seams down the back of her legs. She bent inside the car to get the keys—it was taking too long.

"Having trouble?" I asked her.

She looked back over her shoulder. "Just wanted to make sure you got a good look," she said, a bright smile on her face.

"Just get the keys," I told her, an edge to my voice.

She gave her hips a sharp little wiggle, then turned around with the keys in her hand. She walked back to the trunk, opened it, and stood aside. I shined the light inside. Lots of junk, but no humans. I pulled up the carpet, looked inside the spare-tire well. Nothing there either.

I gave her back the keys. "Follow me to the street," I told her. "We'll find a place to park your car and you can come with me."

"No way!" she snarled. "Go with you *where*?"

"Someplace where we can talk, okay?"

"We can talk right here."

"*You* can talk here if you want. You want me in on the conversation, you come with me."

"And if I don't?"

"Then we don't talk."

She ran her fingers through her fiery hair, front to back, thinking.

"Julio . . ." she started to say.

"Julio's not here," I said.

The redhead gave me one of those "You better not be fucking around with me" looks, but that was her last shot. She climbed back into the BMW and started the engine. I pulled the Plymouth away and headed out of the park.

38

I FOUND an empty spot on Metropolitan Avenue, pulled past it, and waited. She wrestled the BMW into the space, put a big piece of cardboard in the side window, and walked over to me. I got out and went over to look at what she left. It was a hand-lettered sign—"No Radio." I thought all BMWs came with those signs straight from the factory.

She slammed the Plymouth's door closed with all her strength. I made a U-turn on Metropolitan back toward the Inter-Boro eastbound. We pulled onto the highway, following the signs to the Triboro.

"We're going into the city?" she asked.

"Just keep quiet," I told her. "We'll talk when we get there."

She didn't say anything else. I checked the mirror. It was a relief not to have her driving lights burning in my eyes. Just before the turnoff to the Long Island Expressway, I pulled off into Flushing Meadow Park. She opened her mouth to say something, but I held my finger to my lips.

Nobody was following us, but I didn't want her saying where we were going in case Michelle's search had given her some ideas.

"How come you use those driving lights even when there's traffic in front of you?" I asked her.

"They look nice," she said, as if that settled things.

I circled the park slowly until I came to the parking lot on the east side. A few cars were already pulled in, facing the sewage the politicians named Flushing Bay. The cars were spaced well apart, the windows dark. The cops used to make a circuit through here, flashing their lights. If they saw two heads in the window they kept on going. They stopped when the merchants on Main Street complained they needed more coverage of their stores.

Couples used to park back in the bushes too, but a gun-carrying rapist working the area stopped all that. Wolfe had tried the case against the dirtbag when they finally caught him. She dropped him for twenty-five to fifty, but people still stuck close to the water's edge.

I pulled in between an old Chevy with a jacked-up rear end, "José and Juanita" painted on the trunk in flowing script, and a white Seville with fake wire wheels. Lights from the incoming planes to LaGuardia reflected off the black water.

I cracked my window and lit a cigarette. By the time I turned to the redhead, she was already unbuttoning her blouse.

39

WHAT THE HELL are you doing?" I snapped at her, my voice louder than it should have been.

"What does it look like?" she asked. "I'm showing you I'm not wearing a wire." She smiled in the darkness, her teeth so white they looked false. "Unless you have your little whore-friend with you in the back seat . . ." she said, looking over her shoulder.

"There's nobody here," I told her.

She kept unbuttoning the blouse like she hadn't heard me. She wore a black half-bra underneath, the lace barely covering her nipples. The clasp was in front. She snapped it open and her breasts came free, small and hard like a young girl's, the dark nipples pointed at me in the cool air. I didn't say anything, watching her. When I felt the cigarette burn my fingers I pushed it out my window without looking back.

The redhead reached behind her and pulled the wide belt loose. "I have to unzip this. I've got a big ass for such a small girl and the skirt won't go up. I'm sure you noticed."

I wanted to tell her to stop but . . . maybe it was a bluff . . . maybe she was wired and this was a game. I kept quiet.

The zipper made a ripping sound. She wiggled in her seat until the skirt was down past her knees. Her panties were a tiny black wisp, the dark stockings held up by wide black hands across her thighs. If she was wired it had to be inside her body.

"Yes?" she asked.

I just nodded—I'd seen enough. But she took it the other way. She hooked her thumbs inside the waistband of her underpants and pulled them down too. There wasn't enough light to see if her flaming hair was natural.

"Look out the window—smoke another cigarette," she hissed at me. I heard her struggling with her clothes, muttering something to herself. A tap on my shoulder. "Okay, now," she whispered, and I turned around.

"You have another cigarette for me?"

I gave her one and struck a wooden match. She came close to catch the fire. She didn't move her face, but her eyes rolled up to look at me.

I reached over and took her purse from her. She didn't protest while I went through it. She had her own cigarettes, a matchbook from a midtown restaurant, a few hundred in cash, and some credit cards. And a metal tube that looked like lipstick. I pulled off the top. Inside was a nozzle of some kind and a button on the base. I looked a question at her.

"Perfume," she said.

I pointed it outside the window and pressed the button. I heard the thin hiss of spray and smelled lilacs. Okay.

"I'm listening," I told her.

The redhead shifted in her seat so her hips were wedged into a corner, her back against her door, legs crossed, facing me.

"I already told you what this was about. I want you to do something for me—what else do you need to know?"

"Is this a joke? You're nothing to me—I don't owe you anything."

"It's not a joke. I'm not a joker." She drew in hard on her cigarette, lighting her face for a second. "You don't owe me . . . but you owe Julio, right?"

"Wrong."

"Then why did you do that other thing?"

"What other thing?" I asked her.

"In the park . . ."

"You're riding a dead horse, lady. I don't know anything about a park. You got me confused with someone else."

"Then why did you come out here at all?"

"Because you're pushing me. You're playing some silly rich-girl's game. I want you to get off my case, and I wanted to tell you to your face so you'd get it."

"I *don't* get it," she snarled at me. "And I *won't* get it. You work for money—like everyone else—I've got money. And I need you to do this."

"Get someone else," I told her.

"No!" she snapped. "You don't tell me what to do. Nobody tells me what to do. You think I *want* to use you for this? I told you, Julio said you know the Nazis."

"What's this about Nazis? It sounds like Julio lost it during his last stretch."

"Julio never loses anything," said the redhead, "and you know it. It's got to be you, and that's it."

"Because of these 'Nazis'?"

"Yes. And because they're the only lead I have."

I lit another cigarette. The air in the car felt charged, like just after a hard rain. The redhead sounded like she wasn't playing with a full deck, but what she had left were all wild cards.

I got out of the Plymouth and walked down toward the water's edge, not looking back. Before I got more than a few feet I heard the car door slam angrily behind me. I heard the tap of her high heels on the pavement and then felt her hand on my arm.

"Where do you think you're going?" she said, trying to pull me around to look at her.

"To the water," I told her, as if that explained everything.

She kept pace with me, tottering on the heels when we hit the grassy area, but hanging on.

"I want to talk to you!" she snarled.

The moon was out—almost full. Maybe it was making her crazy, but I didn't think so. Maybe she just didn't know how to act. I stopped at the water and grabbed her tiny chin in my right hand, holding her face so she couldn't move. I put my face close to her. "I don't give a flying fuck *what* you want, understand? You're not my boss. Julio's not my boss. You and me are square, okay? You think I'm some senile old uncle like Julio, you make a big mistake."

She squirmed in my hand, twisting her face but keeping her hands down. Her eyes slashed at me, but she didn't open her mouth.

"And if you think I'm some halfwit cock-hound like Vinnie, you're even stupider than you've been acting, understand?" I said, giving her face a quick shake. Her eyes flashed—I knew it hadn't been Julio's idea to send the Cheech with my money.

"Let. Go. Of. Me," she whispered, every word a separate sentence.

I pushed her face away from me, hard. She went sprawling away from me, lost her balance, and hit the ground. I walked away from her until I found one of the vandalized benches and sat down. Looked at the water. Tried to think my way out of the box I was in.

It was another couple of minutes before she sat down next to me, fumbling in her bag for a cigarette. I didn't light this one for her.

"You get your kicks shoving women around?"

"I wasn't shoving you around, princess—I was shoving you *away*."

"Don't do that," she whispered, her face close to mine again. "Don't do that—I can make it all right, just give me a chance, okay?"

I didn't say anything, waiting.

"I want this so bad," said the redhead. "I don't have much to go on.

If I go to some private detective agency they'll just rip me off. I know that. I know the whole thing's a long shot."

I kept staring at the water, waiting.

"Let me just sit here with you. Like I'm your girlfriend or something—let me tell you the whole story. If you don't agree to help me when I'm done, we're quits. You take me back to my car and that's the end."

I lit another cigarette, still quiet. She put her hand on my arm—a fat diamond sparkled in the moonlight—cold fire.

"You swear?" I asked her.

"I swear," she said, her eyes big and glowing and full of lies.

I looked down at the diamond. "Tell me," I said.

40

SHE GOT off the bench and walked around behind me. She leaned over against my back, her elbows on my shoulders, her lips near my ear. Like she'd been doing it all her life. Her voice was breathy, but she wasn't trying to be sexy now—she just wanted to get it all out.

"This is about Scott. He's my friend's little boy, like I told you. He's the sweetest little boy in the world—blond hair, blue eyes. He's a perfect little boy, always has a smile for everyone. Nobody's spoiled him yet— he loves everyone. He loves my Mia the most.

"My friend took him to a kids' party at the mall—where all the stores have clowns and singers and storytellers and all that, you know? Scott was having a great time until one of the clowns came up to him. All of a sudden he starts to scream and he runs away. His mother has to run and catch him. He won't tell her anything—he just wants to go home.

"He seems okay after that—like he just had a bad day or something. But a couple of weeks later, one of his father's friends comes over to the house. He has a Polaroid camera with him and he's taking pictures. When Scott comes downstairs, he sees the camera, and he goes rigid . . . like catatonic . . . he just freezes up. They take him upstairs and soon he's like okay again, but by then my friend figures something's really wrong and she takes him to a therapist.

"But he won't talk to the therapist. I mean, he won't talk about what's wrong. It's like he's himself most of the time, but something's really eating at him. He doesn't want to do things like he did before—he doesn't want to play, doesn't want to watch TV . . . nothing. The poor little guy is so sad.

"Anyway, my friend brings him over. She figures . . . he just *adores* my little Mia . . . maybe he'll play with her. But he doesn't want to do that either. And now Mia gets all upset too. 'Fix it, Mommy,' she says to me. What was I supposed to do? Mia . . . I *had* to fix it."

The redhead turns her face, gives me an absent-minded kiss like she's telling me "Don't move." She walks back around to the front of the bench and climbs into my lap—snuggles in to me like she's cold. Like I'm a piece of furniture. Her face is against my chest but I can still hear her when she talks.

"I tell my friend to stay in my house and I take Mia and we go out and buy a Polaroid. I come back to the house and I get this big hammer from the garage. I bring everything out to the patio and then I take Scott by the hand and bring him outside with me. I open the box and show him the camera and he starts to pull away from me. Then I take the hammer and pound that fucking camera until it's just a bunch of little parts all over the patio. I must have gone crazy for a minute. . . . I'm screaming something at the camera . . . I don't even know what. And little Scott . . . he comes over to me. I give him the hammer and he smashes the camera too. And then he starts to cry—like he's never going to stop. I hold him and Mia too—all together.

"Finally he stops. I ask him, 'Is it all okay now, baby?,'" and he says, 'Zia Peppina, they still have the *picture!*,' and he cries until I tell him I'll get the picture for him. I *promise* him. I *swear* to him on my daughter. On Mia, I swear to him I'll get this picture for him.

"And then he stops. He smiles at me. The little guy's got heart for days—he knows that if I swear that, it's done—it's done. He has trust in me."

She was quiet against my chest. I reached in my pocket, took out a smoke for myself, and lit it. She pushed her face between my hand and my mouth, took a drag from my hand. Waited.

"You know what's in the picture?" I asked her.

"Yeah. I know," she said.

"Because he told you or . . . ?"

"I just know."

"You did something to find out, right?"

She nodded against my chest.

"What?" I asked her.

"He used to go to this day-care center. Out in Fresh Meadows. One day they took him someplace—he says out in the country—in the school-bus they use. There was a guy dressed in a clown suit and some other stuff. He can't tell me. He had to take his clothes off and do something—he won't tell me that either. And someone took pictures of him."

"Where was this place?" I asked her.

"I don't *know!*" she said, fighting not to start crying, biting her lower lip like a kid.

I patted her back in a careful rhythm, waiting until it matched her breathing. "What else did you find out?"

"A woman came there. An old woman, he said. She had two men with her. Big, scary men. One had a little bag—like a doctor's bag? With money in it. The old woman took the pictures and the clown got some of the money."

"And . . . ?" I prompted her.

"Scott couldn't tell me what the men looked like, but he saw the hands of the man who carried the little bag. There was a dark-blue mark on one of them. Scott drew it for me." She fumbled in her purse and pulled out a piece of paper. It was covered with all kinds of crosses and lines, drawn in crayon like a kid did it. Down in one corner was something in blue, with a red circle around it. I held the match closer. It was a swastika.

"This was on the man's hand?" I asked her.

"Yes."

"Back of his hand?"

"Yes."

"What did you do?" I asked her.

The redhead took a breath. "I showed the drawing to Julio. He took one look and said, 'Jailhouse tattoo.' I asked him if there were Nazis in prison. He said he really didn't know too much about it. I pressured him—I made him tell me. And that's when I got your name—he said you knew them."

41

IT WAS cold out there by the water, especially along my spine. We had a deal—I had listened to her story and now I could walk away. But I wanted to buy some insurance—make her understand that I wasn't the man for the job anyway.

"Julio's full of shit," I told her in a flat voice.

"I know," she said, quiet and soft.

"I mean about the Nazis. I don't know them—they were in prison with all of us—nobody knows them—they keep to themselves, you understand?"

The redhead twisted in my lap until she was facing me. She grabbed the lower half of my face like I had done to her. I could smell the perfume on her hand. She put her little face right up against me, grabbing my eyes with hers.

"You're lying to me," she whispered. "I know all about men—I know more about men than you'll ever know. I know when a man is lying to me."

I met her stare with no problem, even though the moon was dancing in her crazy eyes.

"I'm telling you the truth," I said.

She leaned against me, shoving her lips hard against mine. I could feel her teeth. Then her tongue. She stayed like that for a solid minute, her hands somewhere on my chest. "Please?" she whispered.

She pulled her face away. "No," I said. I started to get up but she was still sitting on my lap. She put her face against me again, opened her mouth, and bit into my lower lip with all her strength. The pain-jolt shot through me like electricity—I stiffened two fingers and a thumb and drove them into her ribs. She grunted and pulled away from me, blood on her mouth.

The redhead rolled off my lap and bent double at the waist. I thought she was going to throw up, but she got herself under control. Her head came up. She was chewing on something—a piece of my lip.

"Mmmmm," she said, "it's so *good*." I watched her swallow a part of me. Her smile had red in it, like smeared lipstick.

I got up from the bench and walked back to the Plymouth, leaving her where she was. She didn't move until she heard the engine kick over. Then she walked to the car, taking her time.

She got in the passenger side, opened her window, and looked out—away from me. She didn't say another word until we pulled up next to her BMW.

42

METROPOLITAN Avenue was quiet. The BMW was sitting there undisturbed. It was that kind of neighborhood.

The redhead turned to me. "Can I say one thing to you before you go?"

I just nodded, tensing my right arm in case she decided she was still hungry.

"One hundred thousand dollars. In cash. For you."

She had my attention, but I didn't say anything.

"One hundred thousand dollars," she said again, like she was promising me the most erotic thing in the world. Maybe she was.

"Where?" I asked her.

"I have it," she said. "And it's yours if you find me that picture."

"And if I don't? I mean, if I look and come up empty?"

"How long will you look?"

"*If* I look, I'll look four, five weeks. After that, there's no point. You could run some ads, shake some trees . . . but if it's around, still local, that's all the time there is."

"How do I know you'll really look?" she asked.

"You don't," I said, "and *that's* the fucking truth."

"Five thousand a week?"

"Plus expenses."

"For a hundred grand, you can pay your own expenses."

"If I find the picture," I said, "the hundred grand covers it all, okay? But if I don't, you pay five grand a week for a max of five weeks, plus expenses."

The redhead stroked her own face, soothing herself, thinking. Finally she said, "Ten grand up front and you start tonight."

"Twenty-five up front and I start tonight," I shot back.

"Fifteen," she offered.

"Take a walk, lady," I said. "I shouldn't have started this in the first place."

"You walk with me," the redhead said. "Back to my house. I'll give you the twenty-five."

"And a picture of the kid?"

"Yes. And all the other stuff I put together."

"And then you're out of it? I do my work and I let you know the result?"

"Yes."

"And then you forget you ever saw me?"

"Oh, I'll do that," she said, "but you'll never forget you saw *me*."

Even in the car I was still cold. "You have the money at your house? Your husband . . . ?"

"Don't worry about it. He won't be home tonight. Is it a deal?"

"No promises," I told her. "I'll take my best shot. I come up empty . . . that's all, right?"

"Yes," she said again. "Follow me."

She got out of the Plymouth and into her car. I let the engine idle while she started up. She pulled out and I followed her taillights into the night.

43

THE REDHEAD drove badly, taking the BMW too high in the lower gears, backing it off through the mufflers when she came to a corner, torturing the tires. The Plymouth was built for strength, not speed—I drove at my own pace, watching to see if she attracted attention with her driving.

The BMW ducked into the entrance for Forest Park. I lost sight of her around a curve, but I could hear tires howling ahead. I just motored along—there was no place for her to go.

She turned out of the park and into a section of mini-estates—not much land around the houses, but they were all big bastards, set far back from the street, mostly colonials. The redhead took a series of tight, twisting turns and stopped at a flagstone-front house with a wrought-iron fence. She got out and walked to the entrance, never looking back. Something from her purse unlocked the gate. She waved me around her car and I pulled into the drive. I heard the gate close again behind me and then the BMW's lights blinded me as she shot past me, following the curve of the driveway around to the back of the house—it opened as we approached—it must have had some kind of electronic eye. The light came on inside the garage. Only one stall was occupied—a Mercedes sedan.

I watched her slam the BMW into the middle space. I brought my car to a stop, and reversed so the Plymouth's rear bumper was against the opening of the garage. She motioned for me to pull all the way inside. I shook my head, turned off the engine. She shrugged the way you do at an idiot who doesn't understand the program and pointed for me to follow her inside.

The redhead pushed a button against the garage wall and the big door descended from the ceiling and closed behind us. She opened a side door and started to climb some stairs, flicking her wrist at me in a gesture to follow her.

The stairs made a gentle curve to the next floor. Soft light came from someplace but I couldn't see any bulbs. The redhead's hips switched almost from wall to wall on the narrow staircase. I thought about the magnum I'd left in the Plymouth.

She took me into a long, narrow room on the next floor. One whole wall was glass, facing the backyard. Floodlights bathed the grounds— there was a rock garden around a patio in the back; the rest faded into the shadows.

"Wait here," she said, and moved into another room.

She hadn't turned on a light in the big room but I could see well enough. It looked as if her interior decorator had a degree in hospital administration. The whole room was white—a low leather couch in front of a slab of white marble, a recliner in the same white leather. There was a floor lamp extending over the recliner—a sharp black stalk with a fluted wing at the top. A black glass ashtray was on the marble slab. Against the far wall was a single black shelf running the full length, the lacquer gleaming in the reflected light. I saw four floor-standing black stereo speakers but no components—probably in another part of the house. The floor was black quarry tile and there were two parallel strips of track lighting on the ceiling—holding a series of tiny black-coned spots. The room was a reptile's eye—flat and hard and cold.

I sat down in the recliner and lit a cigarette. My mouth burned with the first drag. I pulled the butt away—there was blood on the filter. I wiped my mouth on my handkerchief and sat there waiting. I heard the tap of her heels on the tile, turned my head without moving. I tasted the blood on my lip again. She was wearing a black silk camisole over a pair of matching tap pants. The whole outfit was held up with a pair of spaghetti-straps—they made a hard line against her slim shoulders. The redhead had a pair of black pumps on her feet—no stockings that I could see. She was all black and white, like the room.

"You want a drink?" she asked.

"No."

"Nothing? We have everything here."

"I don't drink," I told her.

"A joint? Some coke?" she asked me, an airline stewardess on a flight to hell.

"Nothing," I told her again.

She crossed in front of me, like a model on a runway for the first time, nervous but vain. She sat down on the couch, crossed her long legs, folded her hands over one knee. "We have a deal?" she asked.

"Where's the money?" I said in reply.

"Yeah," she said absently, almost to herself, "where's the money?"

She flowed off the couch and walked out of the room again, leaving me to my thoughts. I wondered where her kid was.

The redhead was back in a minute, a slim black attaché case in one hand. She looked like she was going to work. In a whorehouse. She dropped to her knees next to the recliner in a graceful move, crossing her ankles behind her on the floor, and put the attaché case on my lap. "Count it," she said.

It was all in fifties and hundreds—crisp bills but not new. The serial numbers weren't in sequence. The count was right on the nose. "Okay," I told her.

She got to her feet. "Wait here. I'll get you the pictures," she said, turning to go. "Play with your money."

As soon as she was out of the room I got up and took off my coat. I transferred the money from the attaché case to a few different pockets, closed the case, and tossed it on the couch. Lit another cigarette.

She was back quickly, her hands full of paper. She came over to the same place she'd been before, kneeled down again, and started putting the papers in my lap, one piece at a time, as if she was dealing cards.

"This is Scotty like he looks today. I took this last week. This is Scotty like he was a few months ago—when it happened. This is the drawing he did—see the swastika? This is me and Scotty together—so you can tell how big he is, okay?"

"Okay," I told her.

She handed me one more piece of paper, covered with typed numbers. "These are the phone numbers where you can reach me . . . and when you can call. Just ask for me—you don't have to say anything else."

"Any of these answering machines?"

"No. They're all people, don't worry."

I took a last drag of my smoke, leaning past her to snub it out in the ashtray, ready to leave. The redhead put her face next to mine again, whispering in a babyish voice, more breath than tone, "You think I'm a tease, don't you?"

I didn't say anything, frozen there, my hand mechanically grinding the cigarette butt into tobacco flakes.

"You think I'm just teasing you, don't you?" she whispered again. "Dressing like this . . ."

I pulled back to look at her but she hung on, coming with me. "You do what you want," I told her.

"I will if you close your eyes," she said in my ear. "Close your eyes!" she said, a baby demanding you play a game with her.

I was still so cold. Maybe it was the room. I closed my eyes, leaned back. Felt her stroke me, making a noise in her throat. "Sssh, ssh," she murmured. She was talking to herself. I felt her hands at my belt, heard the zipper move, felt myself strain against her hand. I opened my eyes a narrow slit; her red hair was in my lap. "You promised!" she said in the baby voice. I closed my eyes again. She tugged at the waistband on my shorts, but I didn't move—she was rough and clumsy pulling me through the fly, still making those baby noises in her throat. I felt her mouth around me, felt the warmth, her tiny teeth against me, gently pulling. I put my hands in her soft hair, and she pulled her mouth off me, her teeth scraping the shaft, hurting me. "You don't touch me!" she whispered, the voice of a little girl.

I put my hands behind my head so they wouldn't move. And she came back to me with her mouth, sucking hard now, moving her mouth up and down until I was slick with her juices. My eyes opened again— I couldn't help it. She didn't say anything this time. I opened them wider. The redhead's face was buried in my lap, her hands clasped tightly behind her back. My eyes closed again.

I felt it coming. I pushed my hips back in the chair, giving her a chance to pull her mouth away, but she was glued to me. "Just this!" she mumbled, her mouth full, a little girl talking, a stubborn little girl who made up her mind and wasn't giving in. My mind flashed to a girl

I met once when I was on the run from reform school. This was all she'd do too—she didn't want to get pregnant again. Somehow I knew this wasn't the same.

It was her choice. She shook her head from side to side, keeping me with her. I felt the explosion all the way to the base of my spine, but she never took her face away—never reached for a handkerchief—I could feel the muscles in her cheeks work as she took it all.

I slumped back in the chair and she let me slide out of her mouth but kept her head in my lap. Her little-girl's whisper was clear in the quiet room. "I'm a good girl," she said, calm and smug. "Pat me. Pat my head."

My eyes opened again as I brought my hand forward, stroking her red hair, watching her hands twist behind her in the handcuffs she'd made for herself.

Her head came up. She was licking her lips and her eyes were wet and gleaming. Her hands came forward, taking one of my cigarettes and lighting it while I pulled myself in and zipped up. She handed me the lit cigarette. "For you," she said.

I took a deep drag. It tasted of blood.

"I have you in me now," she said, in her own voice. "Get me that picture."

I had to get out of there. She knew it too. I put on my coat, patting the pockets, putting the pictures and the other stuff she gave me inside.

"Come," she said, taking my hand, leading me back to the garage.

The Mercedes had a regular license, but the one on the BMW said JINA. "Is that the way you spell your name?" I asked her. "I thought it was Gina—G-I-N-A."

"They named me Gina. I didn't like it. When I have something I don't like, I change it."

"Who's Zia Peppina?" I wanted to know.

"Me. Auntie Pepper, you *capisce*? When I was a little girl, I was a chubby, happy child—always running, getting into mischief. With my red hair, they used to call me Peppina. Little Pepper. But when I got older, when I got to be myself, they stopped calling me that baby name. I only let Scotty call me that because he's special to me."

"People call you Jina now?"

"No," the redhead said, "now they call me Strega."

The side door slammed behind me and I was alone.

I drove too fast getting out of her neighborhood, cold speed inside me, rushing around like cocaine. Even the twenty-five grand in my coat couldn't keep out the chill. *Strega*. I knew what the word meant—a witch-bitch you could lust after or run from. You could be in the middle of a desert and her shadow would make you cold. And I had taken her money.

44

I SLOWED the Plymouth into a quiet, mechanical cruise when I hit the Inter-Boro. A dark, twisting piece of highway, paved with potholes. Abandoned cars lined the roadside, stripped to the bone. I lit a smoke, watched the tiny red dot in the windshield, feeling the tremor in my hands on the wheel. Not knowing if I was sad or scared.

The blues make a rough blanket, like the ones they give you in the orphanage. But they keep out the cold. I shoved a cassette into the tape player without looking, waiting for the dark streets to take hold of me and pull me in, waiting to get back to myself. When I heard the guitar intro I recognized the next song, but I sat and listened to the first call-and-answer of "Married Woman Blues" like the fool I was.

> Did you ever love a married woman?
> The kind so good that she just has to be true.
> Did you ever love a married woman?
> The kind so good that she just has to be true.
> That means true to her husband, boy,
> And not a damn thing left for you.

That wasn't Strega. She wasn't good and she wasn't true—at least not to her husband. I popped the cassette, played with the radio until I got some oldies station. Ron Holden and the Thunderbirds singing "Love You So." I hated that song from the first time I'd heard it. When I was in reform school a girl I thought I knew wrote me a letter with the lyrics to that song. She told me it was a poem she wrote for me. I never showed it to anyone—I burned the letter so nobody would find it, but I memorized the words. One day I heard it on the radio while we were out in the yard and I knew the truth.

I never had to explain things like that to Flood. She knew—she was raised in the same places I was.

There was too much prison in this case—too much past.

I tried another cassette—Robert Johnson's "Hellhound on My Trail" came through the speakers. Chasing me down the road.

45

B Y THE next morning, the magnum was back in my office and all but five thousand of the money was stashed with Max. I told him most of what happened the night before—enough so he could find the redhead if things didn't work out. I couldn't take Max with me on this trip—he was the wrong color.

I took Atlantic Avenue east through Brooklyn, but this time I rolled right on past the Inter-Boro entrance, past the neighborhood called City Line and into South Ozone Park. In this part of Queens, everybody's got territory marked off—the gangsters have their social clubs, the Haitians have their restaurants, and the illegal aliens have their basements. When you get near J.F.K. Airport, you move into the free-fire zone—the airport is too rich a prize for anyone to hold it all.

I pulled into the open front of a double-width garage. A faded sign over the door said "Ajax Speed Shop." A fat guy sat on a cut-down oil drum just inside the door, a magazine on his lap. His hair was motorcycle-club-length; he had a red bandanna tied around his forehead. He was wearing a denim jacket with the arms cut off, jeans, and heavy work boots. His arms bulged, not all from fat. He'd been a body-builder once; now he was slightly gone to seed.

A candy-apple-red Camaro stood over to my right, its monster rear tires filling the rear tubs under the fenders. The garage specialized in outlaw street racers—guys who made a living drag racing away from the legal strips. The back of the joint was dark.

I didn't wait for the fat guy. "Bobby around?" I asked.

"What do you need, man?" he wanted to know, his voice still neutral.

"I want to try a nitrous bottle. Bobby told me he could fix me up."

"For this?" he wanted to know, looking at the Plymouth's faded four doors. Street racers use nitrous oxide—laughing gas—for short power-bursts. You need a pressurized tank, a switch to kick it in, and enough *cojones* to pull the trigger. They're not illegal, but you want to fix things up so your opponent won't know you're carrying extra horses. The Plymouth didn't look like his idea of a good candidate—or maybe it was the driver.

I pulled the lever under the dash and the hood was released—it popped forward, pivoting at the front end. The fat guy went around to the passenger side as I got out, and we lifted the entire front end forward together. The whole front-end assembly was Fiberglas—you could move it with two fingers.

The fat guy looked into the engine bay, nodding his head.

"Three eighty-three?" he wanted to know.

"Four forty," I told him, "with another sixty over."

He nodded sagely. It was making sense to him now. "One four barrel?" he asked—meaning, Why just one carburetor for so many cubic inches?

"It's built for torque—got to idle nice and quiet."

"Yeah," he said, still nodding. The Plymouth wasn't for show—just the opposite. He walked around the car, peering underneath, noting that the dual exhausts never reached the bumper. The rear undercarriage puzzled him for a minute. "It looks like an I.R.S. Jag?"

"Home-built," I told him. Independent rear suspension was better for handling, but it wouldn't stand up to tire-burning starts—drag racers never used it.

And that was his next question. "Whatta you run with this . . . thirty-tromp?"

You can race from a standing start or side-by-side at a steady speed and then take off on the signal. Thirty-tromp is when each driver carries a passenger—you reach thirty miles an hour, make sure the front ends are lined up, and the passenger in the left-hand car screams "Go!" out the window and both cars stomp the gas. First car to the spot you marked off is the winner.

"Twenty's okay," I told him. "It hooks up okay once you're rolling."

"You want the nitrous bottle in the trunk?"

"Where else?" I asked him. I opened the trunk to let him look inside.

"Motherfucker! Is that a fuel cell?"

"Fifty-gallon, dual electric pumps," I told him. The kid who built it would have been proud.

The fat guy's suspicions were gone—he was in heaven. "Man, you couldn't run this more than one time—it's a fake-out *supreme!* Where do you race?"

"Wherever," I said, "as long as they have the money."

"What do you duel for?"

"A grand—minimum," I said.

The fat guy scratched his head. He was used to guys spending thousands and thousands to build a car and then racing for fifty-dollar bills. Guys who put a good piece of their money into the outside of their cars—like the Camaro sitting there. He'd heard about guys who treated the whole thing like a business—no ego, all for the bucks—but he'd never seen one before. "I'll get Bobby for you," he said, "wait here."

I lit a smoke, leaning against the side of the Plymouth. I let my eyes wander around the garage but kept my feet where they were. I knew what was in the back.

46

I HEARD a door slam somewhere and Bobby came out of the darkness, hands in the pockets of his coveralls. A big, husky kid—with his long hair and mustache, he looked like an ex–college football player. He came on slowly, not hesitating, just careful. The fat guy was saying something about the Plymouth, but Bobby wasn't listening.

He got close enough to see. "Burke! That you?" he yelled.

"It's me," I said in a quiet voice, knowing what was coming.

The kid crushed me in a bear hug, almost lifting me off my feet. "Brother!" he yelled. "My brother from hell!" I hate that stuff, but I hugged him back, mumbling some words to make it okay.

Bobby turned to the fat guy. "This is my man. Burke, say hello to Cannonball."

"We met," I told him.

"Yeah . . . right. What's *happening*, man?"

"He wants some nitrous . . ." the fat guy said.

"My brother don't want no nitrous . . . do you, Burke?" Bobby said in a superior tone.

"No," I said, watching the fat guy. Bobby's eyes dropped to my right hand. It was balled into a fist, the thumb extended, rubbing a tiny circle on the Plymouth's fender. The jailhouse sign to get lost.

"Take a walk, Cannonball," Bobby told him.

"You oughta get the nitrous, man," Cannonball said by way of goodbye. He went off into the darkness in the back.

Bobby reached into my coat, patting around like he was doing a search. I didn't move. He pulled out my pack of cigarettes, lit one for himself. A prison-yard move—okay if you were tight, a spit in your face if you weren't.

"You want to move cars?" Bobby asked. The back of his garage was a chop shop. He took stolen cars and turned them into parts in a couple of hours. A good business, but it takes a lot of people to make it work.

"I'm looking for a couple of your brothers, Bobby," I told him.

The garage got quiet. "You got a beef?" he asked.

"No beef. I'm looking for somebody they might have done some work for. That's all."

"They're not in it?"

"They're not in it," I assured him.

"What *is* in it?" he wanted to know.

"Money," I told him.

"Same old Burke," the kid said, smiling.

I didn't say anything, waited. "You got names?" the kid asked.

"All I got is this, Bobby. One of them had the lightning bolt on his hand. Big guy. And they did some work for a woman. Older woman. Delivering money."

"With her?"

"Yeah. Bodyguard work."

"We do that . . ." he mused, thinking. Bobby rubbed his forehead—saw my eyes on his hand. The hand with the twisted lightning bolts—twisted into something that looked like a swastika.

"You never joined us," he said, no accusation in his voice. Just stating a fact.

"I joined *you*," I reminded him.

47

Bobby's first day on the Big Yard, he was just off Fish Row, where they lock all the new prisoners. A happy kid despite the sentence he was just starting. Not state-raised—he didn't know how to act. Virgil and I were standing in the shadow of the wall, waiting for some of our customers who had miscalculated the results of the World Series. Bobby walked in our direction, but he was cut off at the pass by a group of blacks. They started some conversation we couldn't hear, but we knew the words. Virgil shook his head sadly—the stupid kid even let a couple of the blacks walk around behind him. It was every new kid's problem—they test you quick and there's only one right answer. The next time he hit the yard he'd better be packing a shank—or spend the rest of his bit on his knees.

The whole yard was watching, but the kid couldn't know that. "Take my back," said Virgil, and started over to the group. Virgil was a fool—he didn't belong in prison.

Virgil strolled over to the group, taking slow, deliberate strides, not in a hurry, keeping his hands where you could see them. I was two steps behind—he was my partner.

"Hey, homeboy!" Virgil shouted out. The blacks turned to face us. Their eyes were hot, but they kept their hands empty. The kid looked at Virgil, a blank, scared look on his face.

Virgil shouldered in next to the kid, put his arm on the kid's back, guiding him out of the circle. One of the blacks stepped in his way. "This is your man?" he asked.

"He surely is," said Virgil, his West Virginia accent like the coal he used to mine—soft around the edges but hard enough to burn inside.

"This your *homeboy* too?" the black guy asked me, sarcasm dripping from his lips. One of his boys chuckled. The yard was quiet—we all listened for the sound of a rifle bolt slamming a shell home, but even the guards were just watching.

"That's my partner," I told him, nodding at Virgil.

"You sure he's not your jockey?" the black guy sneered, forcing it.

"Find out," I invited him, stepping back, hearing footsteps behind me, unable to look for myself.

But the black guy could—right over my shoulder.

"Not today," he said, and walked off, his boys right behind.

I shot a glance behind me—a gang of warrior-whites were rolling up. They didn't give a flying fuck about me personally, but even the off-chance of a race war got them excited. When they saw the black guys walk away they stopped. Stood there with arms folded. They knew, but the kid didn't. He came back over to the wall with me and Virgil and we started to school him right then about what he had to do.

48

Bobby took a seat on the hood of the Plymouth. "I remember," he said. "You calling in the marker?"

"There *is* no marker, Bobby. I'm asking an old friend for a favor, that's all."

"The guys you want to meet—you know who they are?"

"Yeah," I told him.

"Say the name," Bobby shot at me, a lot of memories in his eyes.

I put it on the table. "The Real Brotherhood," I said, my voice quiet in the empty garage.

"You didn't say it right, Burke. It's the *Real* Brotherhood."

"That's how *you* say it, Bobby."

"That *is* how I say it. That's how it is."

"I told you I got no beef with them. I just want to talk."

I let it hang there—it was his play. He reached into my pocket and helped himself to another smoke. I saw the pack of Marlboros in the breast pocket of his coveralls—we were still friends. Bobby took the fired wood match I handed him, lit up. He slid off the fender until he was sitting on the garage floor, his back against the Plymouth. The way you sat in prison. He blew smoke at the ceiling, waiting. I hunkered down next to him, lit one of my own smokes.

When Bobby started to talk his voice was hushed, like in church. He bent one leg, resting his elbow on the knee, his chin in his hands. He looked straight ahead.

"I got out of the joint way before you did. Remember I left all my stuff for you and Virgil when they cut me loose? I got a job in a machine shop, did my parole, just waiting, you know? A couple of guys I know were going to the Coast. See the sights—fuck some of those blondes out there—check out the motors, right? I get out there and everybody's doing weed—like it's legal or something. I fall in with these hippies. Nice folks—easygoing, sweet music. Better than this shit here. You see it, Burke?"

"I see it," I told him. And I did.

"I get busted with a van full of weed. Two hundred keys. Hawaiian. And a pistol. I was making a run down to L.A. and the cops stopped me. Some bullshit about a busted taillight."

He took a drag of the smoke, let it out with a sigh. "I never made a statement, never copped a plea. The hippies got me a good lawyer, but he lost the motion to suppress the weed and they found me guilty. Possession with intent. Ex-con with a handgun. And I wouldn't give anybody up. They dropped me for one to fucking life—do a pound before I see the Board."

Bobby locked his hands behind his head, resting from the pain. "When I hit the yard I knew what to do—not like when you and Virgil had to pull me up. I remembered what you told me. When the niggers rolled up on me, I acted like I didn't know what they were talking about— like I was scared. They told me to pull commissary the next day and turn it over." Bobby smiled, thinking about it. The smile would have scared a cop. "I turn over my commissary—I might as well turn over my body so they could fuck me in the ass. I get a shank for two cartons— just a file with some tape on the end for a grip. I work on the thing all night long, getting it sharp. In the morning, I pull my commissary. I put the shank in the paper bag with the tape sticking up. I walk out to the yard with the bag against my chest—like a fucking broad with the groceries. The same niggers move on me—tell me to hand it over. I pull the shank and plant it in the first guy's chest—a good underhand shot. It comes out of him when he goes down. I run to get room. Turn around . . . and I'm alone . . . the niggers took off. I hear a shot and the dirt flies up right near me. I drop the shank and the screws come for me."

"You should of dropped the shank when you ran," I said.

"I know that *now*—didn't know it then. Things are different out there." Bobby ground out his cigarette on the garage floor, took one of his own, and lit it. "They put me in the hole. Out there, the fucking hole is like a regular prison—it's *full* of guys—guys spend fucking *years* in the hole. Only they call it the 'Adjustment Center.' Nice name, huh? There's three tiers on each side. Little tiny dark cells. The noise was unbelievable—screaming all the time. Not from the guards doing work on any of the guys—screaming just to be screaming.

"I was sitting in my cell, thinking about how much more time I'd get behind this, even if the nigger didn't rat me out. I mean, they caught me with the shank and all. Then it started. The niggers. 'You a dead white motherfucker!' 'You gonna suck every black dick in the joint, boy!' All that shit. I yelled back at the first one, but they kept it up, like they was working in shifts or something. And then one of them yelled out that the guy I stabbed was his main man—he was gonna cut off my balls and make me eat them. They were fucking *animals*, Burke. They never stopped—day and night, calling my name, telling me they were gonna throw gasoline in my cell and fire me up, poison my food, gang-fuck me until I was dead."

Bobby was quiet for a minute. His voice was hard but his hands were shaking. He looked at his hands—curled them into fists. "After a couple of days, I didn't have the strength to yell back at them. It sounded like there were hundreds of them. Even the trustee—the scumbag who brought the coffee cart around—he spit in my coffee, *dared* me to tell the Man.

"They pulled me out to see the Disciplinary Committee. They knew the score—even asked me if the niggers had hit on me. I didn't say a word. The Lieutenant told me stabbing the nigger was no big deal, but I'd have to take a lockup—go into P.C. for the rest of my bit. You know what that means?"

"Yeah," I said. "P.C." is supposed to stand for "protective custody." For guys who can't be on the main yard—informers, obvious homosexuals, guys who didn't pay a gambling debt—targets. To the cons, "P.C." means Punk City. You go in, you never get to walk the yard. You carry the jacket the rest of your life.

"They kept me locked down two weeks—no cigarettes, nothing to read, no radio—nothing. Just those niggers working on me every day. They never got tired, Burke—like they fucking *loved* that evil shit. Screaming about cutting pregnant white women open and pulling out the baby. One day it got real quiet. I couldn't figure it out. The trustee came with the coffee. He had a note for me—folded piece of paper. I opened it up— there was a big thick glob of white stuff inside. Nigger cum. I got sick but I was afraid to throw up—afraid they'd hear me. Then one of them whispered to me—it was so quiet it sounded like it was in the next cell.

'Lick it up, white boy! Lick it all up, pussy! We got yard tomorrow, punk. The Man letting us all out, you understand me? You lick it all up, tell me how good it was!' He was saying all this to me and all I could think of was, there was no way to kill myself in that lousy little cell. All I wanted was to die. I pissed on myself—I thought they could all smell it."

Bobby was shaking hard now. I put my hand on his shoulder, but he was lost in the fear. "I got on my knees. I prayed with everything I had. I prayed for Jesus—stuff I hadn't thought of since I was a kid. If I didn't say anything, I was dead—worse than dead. I looked at that paper with that nigger's cum on it. I went into myself—I thought about how it had to be. And I found a way to die like a man—all I wanted.

"I got to my feet. I stood up. My voice was all fucked up from not saying anything for so long, but it came out good and steady. It was so quiet everybody heard me. 'Tell me your name, nigger,' I said to him. 'I don't want to kill the wrong nigger when we go on the yard, and all you monkeys look alike to me.' As soon as the words came out of my mouth I felt different—like God came into me—just like I'd been praying for.

"Then they went fucking *crazy*—screaming like a pack of apes. But it was like they were screaming on some upper register . . . and underneath it was this heavy bass line, like in music. A chant, something. It was from the white guys in the other cells—some of them right next to me. They hadn't made a sound through all this shit, just waiting to see how I'd stand up. I couldn't hear them too good at first—just this heavy, low rumbling. But then it came through all the other stuff. 'R.B.! R.B.! R.B.!' "

Bobby was chanting the way he'd heard it back in his cell, hitting the second letter for emphasis . . . "R.*B*.! R.*B*.!" . . . pumping strength back into himself.

"They kept it up. I couldn't see them, but I knew they were there. There for *me*. They didn't say anything else. I started to say it too. First to myself. Then out loud. *Real* loud. Like prayer words.

"When they racked the bars for us to hit the exercise yard—one at a time—I walked out. The sunlight hit me in the face—I almost couldn't see. I heard a voice. 'Stand with us, brother,' it said."

Bobby looked at me. His eyes were wet but his hands were steady and his mouth was cold. "I've been standing with them ever since, Burke," he said in the quiet garage. "If you got a beef with them, you got one with me."

49

I GOT TO my feet. Bobby stayed where he was. "I already told you—I got no beef with your brothers. I want to ask some questions, that's all. I'll pay my own way."

Bobby pushed himself off the floor. "You think you could find the Brotherhood without me?"

"Yeah," I told him, "I could. And if I was looking for them like you think, I wouldn't come here, right?"

He was thinking it over, leaning against the car, making up his mind. Bobby made a circuit around the Plymouth, peering into the engine compartment, bouncing the rear end like he was checking the shocks. "When's the last time this beast got a real tune-up, Burke?"

"A year ago—maybe a year and a half—I don't know," I said.

"Tell you what," he said, his voice soft and friendly, "you leave the car here, okay? I'll put in some points and plugs, time the engine for you. Change the fluids and filters, align the front end. Take about a week or so, okay? No charge."

"I need the car," I said, my voice as soft and even as his.

"So I'll lend you a car, all right? You come back in a few days—a week at the most—your car will be like new." I didn't say anything, watching him. "And while I'm working on your car, I'll make some phone calls. Check some things out, see what's happening with my brothers. . . ."

I got the picture. The Plymouth could be a lot of things—a gypsy cab, an anonymous fish in the slimy streets—whatever I needed. This was the first time it would be a hostage.

"You got a car with clean papers, clean plates?"

"Sure," he smiled, "one hundred percent legit. You want the Camaro?"

"No way, Bobby. I'm not planning to cruise the drive-ins. You got something a little quieter?"

"Come with me," he said, walking to the back of the garage. I followed him to a door set into the back wall, watched him push a buzzer three times. The door opened and we were in the chop shop—bumpers and grilles against one wall, engines on stands against another. Three men were working with cutting torches, another with a power wrench. The pieces would all come together on other cars, building a live car from dead ones, Frankenstein monsters that looked like clean one-owners. I followed Bobby through the shop. He opened another door and we stepped into a backyard surrounded with a steel-mesh fence. Razor-ribbon circled the top, winding itself around barbed wire rising another two feet off the top. "Reminds you of home, don't it?" he asked.

In the backyard there were three cars—a dark-blue Caddy sedan, a white Mustang coupe, and a black Lincoln Continental. Bobby made an offhand gesture in their direction. "Pick one," he said.

I passed over the Caddy without a second glance. The Mustang had a shift lever as thick as a man's wrist growing out of the floor, topped with a knob the size of a baseball. Another dragster. The Lincoln looked okay. I nodded.

Bobby opened the door, reached in the glove compartment, and pulled out some papers. He handed them over—the registration was in his name.

"You get stopped, you borrowed the car from me. I'll stand up on it. I got all the insurance, recent inspection. You're clean on this one."

Sure I was—if Bobby told the cops he lent me the car. If he said it was stolen . . .

"Is it a deal?" he wanted to know.

"One week. I make those phone calls. Then we'll see," he said.

"What do you get for a stolen-car rap these days?" I asked him.

"Figure maybe a year—two at the outside."

"Yeah," I said, looking at him. He had me in a box, but not one that would hold me for long. "I'll show you the security systems on the Plymouth," I said, holding out my hand for him to shake.

"You won't know your own car when you come back, Burke," Bobby said, his hand on my shoulder, leading me back to the front garage.

"I always know what's mine," I reminded him.

We had a deal.

50

THE LINCOLN was a big fat boat. Driving it was all by eyesight—you couldn't feel anything through the wheel—like they used Novocain instead of power-steering fluid. The odometer had less than six thousand miles showing. Even the leather smelled new.

I stopped next to a pushcart restaurant, loading up on hot dogs for lunch. There wasn't any point hiding the car—even if Bobby had called it in stolen, the plates wouldn't bounce unless they pulled me in for something else. I was in his hands—for now. He could make the Plymouth disappear easily enough—but if he fucked me around I could make him disappear too. I get real angry if someone makes a move on me when I'm playing it square. The way I have to live, I don't get angry too often.

When Pansy came back downstairs I gave her four of the six hot dogs, chewing on two of them myself, washing them down with some ice water from the fridge. Putting it together in my head—finding the little boy's picture would be like finding a landlord who gives too much heat in the winter. I had to have an angle, and Bobby was my best shot.

I keep my files in the little room next to the office. Six cabinets, four drawers high, gray steel, no locks. There's nothing in there that would get me in real trouble—no names or addresses of clients, no personal records. It's all stuff I pick up as I go along—stuff that could help me at some point. Gun-runners, mercenaries (and chumps who want to be), heavy-duty pimps, kiddie-porn dealers, con artists, crooked ministers. I don't keep files on crooked politicians—I don't have enough space, especially since I have to sleep in that same room.

But I do keep files on the flesh-peddlers—they can't run to the cops when they get stung, it's not in their program. Those merchants sell two products: people and pictures. I checked the magazine file—the kiddie-porn rags were all the same, mostly kids doing things to other kids, smiling for the camera, playing with fire that would burn their souls. Occasionally an adult would intrude on the fantasies of the freaks who bought this stuff—an anonymous cock in a little kid's mouth, a thick hand holding a kid's head down in a dark lap. The pictures were all the same—recycled endlessly behind different covers. The kids in those pictures would all be at least teenagers by now. Recruiting other kids.

The underground newsletters kept the pictures pretty clean. Lots of arty photography—nude kids posing, playing volleyball, wrestling with each other. Plenty of contact information—post-office boxes, mail drops, like that. But every Vice Squad cop in the country was probably on the mailing list and it would takes months to work my way through the maze and actually make a decent buy. They'd try me out first—tame stuff, semilegal—with a ton of rhetoric about "man-boy love" for me to wade through.

I looked through my list of overseas addresses. Almost all kiddie porn used to come from places like Brussels and Amsterdam. The European countries are still a safer harbor for pedophiles, but the real heavy production was all home-grown now. Kiddie porn is a cottage industry. You can walk into a video store and come out with enough electronic crap to make a major motion picture. I didn't need the expensive stuff—a Polaroid was all the kid told Strega about. That was all I needed, and a lot more than I had.

Crime follows dollars—that's the way of the world. No buyers—no sellers. The professionals in the hard-core business have the technology to supply the huge amounts of filth humans want to buy, but the professionals were too big a target for me. Too spread out, too detached. The organized-crime guys were into kiddie porn for the money—if I wanted to find one lousy Polaroid, I'd have to go to someone who was in it for love.

51

I was just past midday, probably early enough to risk using the hippies' phone, but I was going out anyway. Pansy was sprawled out on the Astroturf, an expectant look on her ugly face. "You can come with me later," I told her. I was going to see the Mole, and I couldn't risk turning my beast loose near the junkyard—if she didn't get into mortal combat with the dogs the Mole keeps around she might just decide to stay.

I called the Mole from a pay phone a few blocks from the office. No point in wasting a trip if he wasn't around, and only God knew the Mole's hours.

He answered on the first ring the way he always does—he picks up the phone but he doesn't say anything.

"Can I come up and talk with you?" I said into the mouthpiece.

"Okay," came the Mole's voice, rusty from lack of use. He broke the connection—there was nothing else to say.

The Lincoln drove itself north on the East Side Drive. I set the cruise control to fifty and motored up to the Triboro Bridge. A decent suit on my back, no gun in my pocket, and a set of clean papers for a car that wasn't stolen—I hadn't been this much of a citizen since I was ten.

I met the Mole when I was doing a job for an Israeli guy, but I didn't really get to know him until I did another job, much later. Another one of those anonymous Israeli guys came to my office one day. He wasn't the same guy I'd met the first time, when they wanted me to find some ex-Nazi, a slimeball who'd worked as a concentration-camp guard. I did that job, and now they wanted a gun-runner. The Israeli said he wanted to buy weapons and needed me to set up the meet. Somehow I thought there was a bit more to it. The man he wanted to meet sold heavy-duty stuff—shoulder-fired missiles, antitank cannons, stuff like that. And he sold them to Libya.

I told the Israeli I wouldn't meet with the guy myself—I didn't do business with him and I didn't want any part of someone else's beef. When I said I didn't trade with the gun-runner, the Israeli asked me if I was Jewish. He's the only guy I ever met who asked me that.

It was the Israeli who took me to the junkyard the first time. They left me alone in the car, the dog pack cruising around me in the night like sharks lapping against a rubber raft. I don't know what they talked about, but the Israeli got back into my car carrying a little suitcase.

The Mole has no politics—he doesn't consider blowing up Nazis political. After the second job, I was a friend to Israel. And after a lot of years, I was the Mole's friend too. After I took the weight down in the subway tunnel, I was his brother.

I threw a token into the Exact Change basket, hooking a left and then a right to Route 95. But I ducked into the warehouse district off Bruckner Boulevard, finding my way to the Mole's junkyard. Hunts Point—New York's badlands. Topless bars. Diesel-fuel stations. Whores too raunchy to work Manhattan stalked the streets and waved at the truckers, flashing open their coats to show their naked bodies, then closed them quickly before the customers got a good look. I heard pistol shots, spaced a couple of seconds apart. Over to my right, two men were standing a few feet away from an abandoned old Chrysler, pumping shots into the body. Glass flew out of the windows; the old wreck's body rocked with each shot. It wasn't a homicide going down—just a seller demonstrating his goods for a prospective buyer. Hunts Point is a dead zone for police patrols—no citizens allowed.

I turned the corner near the entrance to the Mole's joint, driving slowly, scanning the street with my eyes. I heard a horn beep. The Mole's head popped up in the front seat of a burnt-out Volvo sitting at the side of the road. He climbed out, wearing his dirt-colored jumpsuit, a tool belt around his waist and a satchel in his hand. He looked like another part of the wrecked car.

He walked over to the Lincoln and climbed into the front seat. "Mole!" I greeted him. He nodded, confirming my diagnosis. We drove around to the side entrance, a rusting old gate secured by a dime-store lock. It wouldn't keep a self-respecting thief out for ten seconds. The Mole jumped out, selected a key from the several dozen he had on a saucer-sized ring, and popped the lock. I pulled the Lincoln inside while he locked up behind me. I kept the windows up as we pulled deeper into the junk-yard—I couldn't hear them, but I knew they were around. I glanced in the rearview mirror—the ground around the gate was already covered by a thick blanket of dogs. More of them loomed up from the dark depths of the yard, padding forward slowly, all the time in the world. The gate wouldn't keep a thief from getting in, but no power on earth was going to get him out.

The dogs were all sizes and shapes. I remembered the old Great Dane—a black-and-white Harlequin monster, now missing an ear. A matched set that looked like boxers approached from the front with something that might have once been a collie on their flank. But the real pack bounded up on my side of the car—lupine heads closer to wolves than German shepherds, alert, intelligent black faces over broad chests, thick tails curled up on their backs. Their coats looked like brown fur dipped in transmission fluid, matted and heavy. Only their teeth looked clean, flashing white in the dim sunlight. The pack had been working and making puppies in the South Bronx jungle for so many years that they had evolved into a separate breed—the American junkyard dog. They never saw a can of dog food. Or a vet. The strongest survived, the others didn't.

There were safer places to walk around than the Mole's junkyard—like Lebanon in the busy season.

The Mole jumped out of the Lincoln, shifting his head for me to follow. I slid over and got out his side. The Mole blundered through the dog pack like a farmer walking through a herd of cows, me right on his tail.

The dogs nosed my legs experimentally, wondering how I'd taste. One of the pack growled a threat, but the Mole ignored it like he does everything else they do. The Mole's underground bunker was on the other side of the junkyard—we weren't going there.

A red Ford station wagon was sitting in a patch of sunlight ahead of us, its entire front end smashed all the way into the front seat—a head-on hit. The back seat had been removed, propped up against the rear bumper. A cut-down oil drum was on one side, a thick book with a plain blue cover on top. The Mole's reading room.

A dog was asleep on the Mole's couch—a massive version of the others in the pack, his neck a corded mass of muscle. He watched us approach, not moving a muscle. Only his tail flicking back and forth showed he was alive.

"Simba-witz!" I called to him. "How's by you?" The huge beast's head came up, watching me. His ears shot forward, but his tail kept the same rhythmic flicking—back and forth, like a leopard in a tree. A bone-chilling snarl came from his throat, but it wasn't meant for us. The pack stopped dead.

The Mole walked over to his couch, sat down, half on top of Simba-witz. The beast slipped out behind him, sniffed me once, and sat down on the ground. I sat down next to the Mole, reaching for a cigarette, glad it was over.

The Mole reached in his jumpsuit, came out with a slab of fatty meat, and tossed it to the dog. Simba-witz tossed it in the air, caught it, and burst into a run, holding his prize aloft. The pack swung in behind him, yipping like puppies. We sat quietly until they disappeared. They wouldn't go far.

"Mole," I told the pasty-faced genius, "I need your help on something."

I paused, giving him a chance to ask what I needed his help for—it was a waste of time.

"I got a job," I said. "This little boy—he was in a day-care center or something, and someone took a picture of him. With a Polaroid. I need to get the picture back."

"Who has it?" the Mole asked.

"I don't know."

The Mole shrugged. He was good at fixing things, or making them work. And especially at blowing them up. But he didn't know how to find things.

"It's a sex picture, Mole."

"What?" he asked. It didn't make sense to him.

"Mole, these people forced the kid to do a sex thing with a grown man, okay? And they took a picture of it. To sell."

The Mole's little eyes did something behind the Coke-bottle lenses he wore. Or maybe it was the sunlight.

"Who does this kind of thing? Nazis?"

To the Mole, every evil thing on the planet was the work of the Nazis. If Bobby did get me a meeting with the Real Brotherhood, I'd have to go without the Mole.

"Kind of," I said, "kind of the same thing. People who go on power trips, right? In the kid's mind, as long as they have the picture, they have his soul."

"If you find the people . . ."

"I know, Mole. That's not the problem now. I need to find the picture."

He shrugged again—what did I want from him?

"I have to find the picture. It's like a scientific problem, right?" I asked, reaching for a way into his megawatt brain, probing for the switch to turn on the light.

"Scientific problem?"

"You once told me that to solve a problem in science you take all the known facts, then you work out some possible outcomes, right? And you keep testing until you prove . . . whatever you said."

"Prove the hypothesis?" the Mole asked.

"Yeah," I said, "the hypothesis."

The Mole sat slumped on his couch, watching the smoke curl from my cigarette. Quiet as concrete.

"You need a scenario," he finally said.

"What are you talking about, Mole?"

"A way something *could* happen. You take the result—what you already know—and you reason backward. You eliminate whatever wouldn't work until you are left with what the past had to have been."

The Mole took a breath—it was a long speech for him.

"I don't get it, Mole," I said. "You mean, if you have a problem, you reason backward and see how the problem started?"

"Yes."

"Could you figure out where cancer came from like that?"

"Yes," he said, again.

"So where did it come from?" I asked him.

"It would be too complicated for me to explain it to you," the Mole said.

"You mean I'm not smart enough?" I asked him.

The Mole turned his face slightly toward me, trying to explain. "You're smart enough. You don't have the background—the scientific knowledge. If it was in your world, you could do it."

"This picture is in my world," I told him.

"I know," he said.

I lit another cigarette, looking around the junkyard.

"Mole, show me how to do it."

The Mole sighed. "You understand—it only works if you have enough data."

I nodded.

"You know the Socratic method?" he asked.

"Where you ask questions to get at the truth?"

"Yes," he said, barely able to keep the surprise from his voice. You spend enough time in prison, you read more than comic books.

"Can we try it?"

"Yes. But not on cancer. Let me think."

I stubbed out my cigarette in the dirt next to the couch, waiting.

"You know about AIDS?" the Mole asked suddenly.

"Yeah, I guess. A superkiller."

"Where does it come from?"

"Nobody knows," I told him.

"I know," said the Mole.

I sat bolt upright on the couch. If he knew where AIDS came from, we could all be rich. "Tell me," I said.

The Mole held up his fist, index finger extended. He grabbed the finger with his other hand. Point number one.

"Did AIDS come from God? Is it God's punishment for something?"

"No," I said.

"How do you know?" he asked.

"God's been on vacation for fifty years from New York," I said. "You try Dial-a-Prayer here, all you get is a busy signal."

The Mole didn't say anything, still waiting for a Socratic answer.

"Okay," I said. "It's not God's punishment because little kids have it too. If God is punishing babies, we should have new elections."

The Mole nodded. It was good enough for him. He didn't hate the

Nazis out of any religious conviction. The Mole worshiped the same god I did: revenge.

"How do people get this disease?" he asked.

"Sexual contact, blood transfusions, dirty needles," I said.

"If it comes from sex," he asked, "how did the first person get it?"

"It's something in the blood, right? Something where the blood doesn't make immunities like it's supposed to. . . ."

"Yes!" he said. "There has been some interference in the chromosomes to create the first cases. But how did that interference take place?"

"Nuclear testing?" I asked.

"No," he came back. "If that were so, far more people would have been affected. Especially people near the site of the tests."

"But what about if some people are . . . susceptible to radiation. You know . . . if it has a different effect on them than on other people."

"That is better—a better hypothesis. But it is too broad, too weak. Think of more experiments—experiments on people."

"Like they used to do on prisoners—like with malaria and yellow fever and stuff?"

"Yes!" he barked. "Experiments on people."

"Like the Nazis did in the camps?"

The Mole's eyes changed shape, like there was a different fuel in his reactor. "They experimented on us like we were laboratory rats. To make twins from the same egg . . . eliminate what they called genetic defects . . . test it on us before they used it on themselves."

"AIDS came from Nazi experiments?"

"No. They didn't have the scientific knowledge. Sadistic amateurs. They just wanted to torture people. They called it science. When doctors help the torturers . . ."

I had to get the Mole off that topic. When he thought too much about the Nazis, the blood lust blocked everything else.

"So some other experiments?" I asked. "Something going on now?"

"Maybe . . ." he said.

"They don't let prisoners volunteer for that stuff anymore. They let us test some crap that was supposed to grow hair on bald people when I was down the last time . . . but no real heavy stuff."

"Where would the drug companies test?" he asked.

"Well, they test in Latin America, right? That fucking formula they wanted mothers to use instead of breast-feeding . . ."

The Mole was coming around again. "Yes. Yes, now you are working. What else do we know about AIDS?"

"Haitians, hemophiliacs, heroin addicts, and homosexuals . . . the 4-H Club, right?"

"And why do the drug companies test in foreign countries?" the Mole asked.

"It's illegal here, right? But some countries—they let you do what you want as long as you got the bucks."

"In democratic countries?"

"Okay, Mole, I get it. The best country would be some outrageous dictatorship where the people do what they're told or they get themselves iced."

"Like . . ."

"Like . . . I don't know . . . Iran, Cuba, Russia."

"Haiti?" the Mole wanted to know.

"Hell, yes, Haiti. I did time with a guy from Haiti. He told me this Papa Doc was the devil, straight up. And that his kid was the devil's son."

"Close to the United States?" said the Mole.

"Yes."

"Need money?"

"Sure."

"Dictatorship?"

"Yeah!"

"Would the leader care if some of his people were exposed to the grave risk of biochemical experiments?"

"No fucking way," I said. The Haitians who try and cross the ocean on rafts aren't looking for better social opportunities.

"Who goes to prison in Haiti?" asked the Mole.

"Anybody Baby Doc wants to put there," I said, thinking. "And dope fiends. Sure!"

"Homosexuals?"

"You better believe it, Mole. Damn!"

The Mole smiled his smile. It wouldn't charm little children. "The drug companies seek a cure for cancer . . . or any other great disease. The cure will make them rich beyond our imagination. This is the fuel that drives their engine. The scientists want to experiment, and they don't have the patience to test rats. And rats are not people."

I lit another smoke, saying nothing. The Mole was on a roll.

"So they make arrangements in Haiti to test their new drugs. On prisoners. Many of them in prison because of heroin addiction or homosexuality, yes? And they alter the genetic components of the blood with their experiments. The homosexuals do what they do inside the prisons. When they become obviously ill, the government disposes of some of them. But the drug companies don't want them all killed. Like when the government let those black men with syphilis go untreated years ago—they never treated them because they wanted to study the long-term effects. Some of the infected Haitians come to America. And when they have sex with others, the drug companies lose control of the experiment."

"And we have AIDS?" I asked him.

"It's one scenario," the Mole said, still thinking it over.

"Son of a bitch," I said, almost to myself.

Simba-witz rolled back into the clearing—we'd been there a long time. He saw us both sitting quietly, flicked his tail over his back, and faded away again.

"Mole," I said, "I've got a scenario about this picture I need to find. The way it was taken . . . Polaroid camera and all . . . it was for sale. If it goes in a magazine, then it's in the stream of commerce and there's nothing I can do about it."

The Mole looked up, listening.

"But I don't think that's the deal," I told him. "I think it was taken for a collector—a private thing. If they put it in a magazine, someone could see it. Cause a lot of problems. I need some freak who gets off looking at this stuff. Not some money-makers. You understand? Someone who's got shoeboxes full of pictures like that."

The Mole nodded. It made sense—at least so far.

"So I need to talk to a collector—a serious, hard-core pedophile. Someone with the money to buy things like this. This is a no-consent picture, right? The freaks might trade copies back and forth, but I don't think it will get commercially produced."

"I don't know anyone like that," he said.

"Mole," I said, keeping my voice level, "you have friends . . . associates, anyway . . . people I did some work for a couple of times . . . when we first met." No point mentioning the name the man from Israel had given me—whichever branch of the Israeli Secret Service made contact with the Mole was likely to be a pure wet-work group anyway.

The Mole turned so he was facing me. "So?" he said.

I was talking fast now, trying to get this all out, get the Mole to agree. "So they have to keep files on freaks like that. Blackmail, whatever. They have to know what's going down on the international scene—know who the players are. I know they don't do law-enforcement or vice-squad shit, but *information* . . . that's something they always want. Anything to give you a leg up . . . a handle."

"So?" he said again, waiting.

"Mole, I want you to ask your friends to give you the name of such a person." I held up my hand before he could speak. "*If* they know . . . okay? Just a name and an address. I want to talk to this person. It's a real long shot he would have the picture, but he sure as hell could put me into the pipeline of people who might."

I was done talking.

The Mole got off the couch, hands in his pockets, and walked toward the Lincoln. I followed him. The pack followed me, materializing out of the shadows.

"Is the little boy Jewish?" the Mole asked.

"He wants his soul back," I said.

I opened the door of the Lincoln, climbed inside. I hit the power window switch, looking at the Mole.

"All I can do is ask," he said. "I'll call you at the restaurant."

The Mole turned and walked back into his junkyard.

52

DARKNESS was dropping its blanket over the city by the time I crossed back over the bridge into Manhattan. I got off at 96th Street and worked my way through Central Park, heading for the West Side. It was still too early for the yuppies to start their mating rituals, but the neon was already flashing by the time I got into the West Fifties—humans who buy their sex in New York expect twenty-four-hour service.

The Lincoln cruised Broadway, hugging the curb. A block-long video-game parlor washed the sidewalk with flashing strobe-lights. Electronic war-sounds poured through its doors, a harsh wave dividing the kids lurking on the sidewalk. Black teenagers were standing to one side in little groups, their pockets emptied of quarters by the machines inside, alert for another penny-ante score so they could go back inside. The white boys on the other side of the doors were younger—they cruised quietly, hawk eyes watching the cars for a customer. The groups never mixed. The black rough-off artists knew better than to move on the little stud-hustlers—a kid peddling his under-age ass and telling himself he's not really homosexual will be happy to stab you to prove it.

Hookers don't work the main drags in the Square after dark—they have the massage parlors for that. Lexington Avenue was their turf. The customers know where to go.

I cut off from Broadway over to Ninth Avenue, kept heading down-town. The fast-food joint I was looking for stood next to a theatre specializing in kung-fu films, a heavy streamer of red and blue lights making a banner over its canopy. I slid the Lincoln to the curb behind a dark Mercedes stretch limo, waiting my turn.

It didn't take long. Three little kids bounded up to the passenger window, arranging their faces into smiles. The Hispanic kid was working with a partner, a blond boy a little taller but even thinner. The dark-haired boy had eyes like dinner plates; his curly hair glistened in the neon. He probably told the johns his name was Angel. Wearing a red T-shirt over a pair of jeans with a designer label on the back pocket. He turned like he was talking to his partner to show me. I couldn't read the designer's name but I knew what the label said: "For Rent." The blond kept his hands in his pockets, eyes down, heavy shock of hair falling in his eyes. They looked about twelve years old.

I pushed the power window switch and slid over to talk to them. The third kid was a redhead, freckles on his round face, a trace of colorless lip gloss on his mouth. He was wearing a white sweatshirt with a "Terry" in script on the front, black pants. New white leather sneakers on his feet. His skin was already a pasty color from a steady diet of junk food and freak-sperm.

I nodded my head to the redhead and the two other boys didn't waste another minute fading back to the front of the fast-food joint. They weren't there for conversation.

"You want to go for a ride, Terry?" I asked him.

The kid didn't blink, his eyes shifting to the back seat and up again to my face, smelling for trouble, the mechanical smile still in place.

He knew the code. "I have to ask my uncle," he said. "Will you buy me something nice if I go with you?"

"Sure," I said, "where's your uncle?"

"I'll get him," the kid said, his soft white hands on the windowsill of the Lincoln. "Don't talk to any of the other boys while I'm gone, okay?"

"Okay," I told him, lighting a cigarette like I was prepared to wait.

It didn't take long. The redhead disappeared inside the joint, emerged in another minute with a man in tow. The man was in his early twenties, wearing a white sportcoat with the sleeves pushed up to display heavy forearms and a jeweled watch. He had an orange silk T-shirt on underneath, wide flowing white pants, the cuffs billowing over his shoes. The new look for kiddie-pimps—Miami Lice. The man's hair was so short on the sides it almost looked shaved, but the top was grown out and flowed down his back. As he rolled up on the Lincoln, he grabbed the redhead by the waistband on his jeans and hoisted him onto the front fender with one hand. The waistband of the pimp's pants was wide, like a cummerbund. He hooked his thumbs inside the band, pressing his hands together to force the blood into his arms and chest. He wasn't a power-lifter: his waist was too small for that. He could lift the little redhead with one hand, but he was built for show, not go.

The pimp leaned into the Lincoln, his chiseled face filling the open window, sending me a message. "Terry says you want to take him out for some pizza?"

I let a tremor of fear into my face, mumbling, "Uh . . . yes, I just wanted to . . ."

He cut me off. "I know what you want. I'm responsible for the boy, see? You leave a deposit with me—just to make sure you bring him back on time, okay? Then you go and buy him that pizza."

"A deposit?"

"A hundred dollars," the pimp said. He wasn't going to discuss it.

I put my hand in my pocket like I was reaching for my wallet. Hesitated, watching his eyes. "What I *really* want . . ." I started to say.

"None of my business," he said, holding out his hand, turning his head casually to watch the street around us.

I cast my eyes down, looking at his open hand. "Pictures," I said.

The young man was getting impatient. "You want pictures, you take pictures, okay?"

"I want to *buy* some pictures," I said. "I'm a collector," as if that explained everything.

It did. "We got pictures of Terry. Candid shots. He's a beautiful boy," the young man said. He could have been describing a Chevy.

"How old is he?"

"Terry is"—thinking how low he could pitch this—"he's ten." The young man must have thought I looked dubious. "He's just tall for his age."

"You have pictures of . . . younger boys?"

"Pictures? Look, man. Take the boy here out for some pizza, okay? Take your own pictures. Anything you want."

"I just want the pictures," I said. "I . . . can't take them myself."

The young man rolled his eyes up, silently bemoaning the difficulties of his business. "I might be able to get you some pictures. It's a lot of work. Could be pretty expensive."

"I don't care," I assured him.

"Tell you what. You take Terry for his pizza, right? Bring him back to the big ships—you know the West Side Highway, near Forty-fifth? Where they have those navy ships you can walk around on?"

I nodded, eager to please.

"I got a red Corvette. A new one. Drive down to the pier, say around midnight? Look for my car. You bring back Terry—I'll have some pictures for you."

"How many?" I asked.

"How many you want, friend? They're expensive, like I told you."

"How many could I buy for . . . say, a thousand dollars?"

The young man's eyes flared for a split-second. Only a Class A chump would bargain like I was. "You want action photos or just poses?"

"Action," I whispered, my eyes downcast.

"That's four for a thousand," he said.

"Four different boys?"

"Four different. Action shots. Color."

"I have to go home and get the money," I said.

"Take Terry with you," the young man said. "After you buy him some pizza."

I just nodded, moving my Adam's apple in my throat like I was gulping it all down.

The pimp put his hand on the back of the redhead's neck. The little kid's face contorted in pain, but he didn't say anything. "You be a good boy, now," said the pimp in a dead-flat voice. The kid nodded.

The young man opened the door of the Lincoln, shoved the boy inside. He held out his hand for the hundred dollars.

I handed it over. Making my voice brave, I said, "How do I know you'll be there?"

"You've got my merchandise," the pimp said, pocketing the hundred and walking away in the same motion.

53

PULLED out into traffic, grabbing a quick look at the boy sitting next to me. He was huddled against the passenger door, head down. The digital clock on the dash said seven-fifty-six—about four hours until I got to meet the man with the pictures.

I hit the power-door lock button—the boy jumped when he heard it click home. He looked at me, twisting his hands together in his lap. "Are you going to hurt me?" he asked in a calm voice. He wasn't looking to talk me out of it, just asking what was going to happen to him.

"I'm not going to hurt you, kid," I told him in my own voice.

His face shot up. "Are you a cop?"

"No, I'm not a cop. I'm a man doing a job. And I want you to help me."

"Help you?"

"Yeah, Terry. Help me. That's all."

The boy was scanning my face, looking for the truth—probably wouldn't recognize it if he saw it.

"What do I have to do?"

"I'm looking for someone. Out here. I'm going to drive around the streets, looking. I want you to look too, okay?"

"Really?"

"Really."

"Who are you looking for?"

"You know the little black guy with no legs—the one on the skateboard . . . pushes himself along with his hands?"

His face brightened up. "Yeah! Yeah, I know him. I talked to him once. He asked me if I wanted to run away."

"What did you tell him?" I asked.

"I was still talking to him when Rod came along."

"Is Rod the guy who I was talking to?"

"Yeah, that's him. He kicked the little black guy right off the skateboard. He has legs, you know," the kid said, his voice serious.

"I know," I told him. "You keep your eyes peeled now—we want to find him."

"How come?" he asked.

"He's going to help me do something tonight," I said.

"You're not going to hurt me?" he asked again.

"No, kid. I'm not going to hurt you," I promised him again, keeping my distance.

I made a couple of slow circuits through the cesspool, cruising between Sixth and Ninth on the cross streets, my eyes passing over the action, searching for the Prof. A police car pulled next to us; the cop's eyes were bored. Almost all the people on the street were male—dream-buyers looking for sellers, wolfpacks looking for prey. Hell eats its tourists.

I looped around at 39th, heading back uptown on Eighth. We were across 44th when the boy shouted, "I see him!," pointing excitedly at the front of a gay movie house. The Prof was on his cart, working the traffic, begging for coins with his cup, watching from ground zero like the cops never could. I ran the Lincoln into the curb, pulled the ignition key, and locked the door behind me, leaving the boy inside. The Prof heard my footsteps pounding toward him and looked up, his hand inside his long ragged coat. When he saw it was me, he grabbed some sidewalk and gave himself a heroic shove in my direction. In our world, when someone moves fast, there's trouble behind.

"Prof, come on," I told him, "we got work to do."

"If you're singing my song, please don't take long," he bopped out, ready for whatever, telling me to get on with it.

I grabbed his outstretched hand and pulled him along on his cart to the Lincoln. I opened the trunk. The Prof climbed off his cart and we tossed it inside. I opened the passenger door and the Prof jumped in. He pulled his own door shut as I went around to the driver's side. We were back into the uptown traffic in a minute.

"Terry," I said to the boy, "this is the Prof."

"The Prof?" the kid asked.

"Prof is short for Prophet, my man," said the little black man, pulling off his misshapen felt hat, his spiky Afro shooting up out of control. "I never fall because I see it all."

The kid's eyes were wide, but he wasn't afraid. Good.

"What's on?" the Prof wanted to know. He didn't use my name.

"Tell you soon, Prof. First we need Michelle. You know where she might be working?"

"Avenue C ain't the place to be."

(The Lower East Side was a dangerous place to work.)

"Working the docks is only for jocks."

(The gay hustlers had West Street sewn up.)

"So if you want sex, it's got to be on Lex."

I swung the Lincoln east, moving crosstown on 48th. I lit a cigarette, letting the big car drive itself. The whores wouldn't be working until we got into the Thirties.

"Can I have one?" asked the boy.

I handed him the pack. "How old you are, boy?" the Prof asked, not happy with my child-care techniques.

"I was smoking when I was his age," I told him.

"Yeah, and look how you turned out, bro'," came the response.

A smile flickered across the boy's face, as fleet as a memory. He handed the pack back to me.

The side streets crossing lower Lexington were so clogged with whores that the Lincoln had to creep its way through. I knew Michelle wouldn't be running up to a car—it wasn't the way she worked. The Prof knew it too. "A racehorse don't run with the mules," he said. "Racehorse" was the ultimate compliment for a working girl, reserved only for the very best.

It took us another half-hour to find her, lounging against a lamppost, a tiny pillbox hat on her head, a half-veil covering her face. She had a black-and-white-checked coat that came halfway down her hips over a black pencil-skirt. Ankle straps on her spike heels. Like a bad girl from World War II.

I pulled the Lincoln up to the lamppost, but Michelle never moved. She brought a cigarette lighter to her face, letting the tiny flame show off her perfect profile. If you wanted a ten-dollar slut, you were in the wrong neighborhood.

I hit the power window switch. "Michelle!" I called to her.

She sauntered over to the Lincoln. "Is that . . . ?"

"Don't say my name," I told her, before she could finish. "I've got company."

She kept coming, leaning into the car, kissing me on the cheek, looking past me to the front seat.

"Hello, Prof," she said, "who's your friend?"

"This is my man Terry," he said. The kid's eyes were round. Even for him, this wasn't a regular night.

"Get in the back, Michelle. We got work."

I climbed out, pulling the kid along with me by his wrist. I found the release lever and the driver's seat slid forward. I put the kid in the back, moving my hands so Michelle could follow him, like I was holding the door for a countess.

"Hi, baby," Michelle said to the kid.

"Hello," Terry said, not a trace of fear in his voice for the first time that night. I don't know how Michelle does it, and I'll never learn.

By the time the Lincoln was halfway to my part of town, they were whispering together in the back seat like the Prof and I weren't there.

54

I NEEDED to set things up for later on. Michelle was the only babysitter I could trust. Someone had to watch the boy, and I didn't want him to see my office or anything else. I tooled down to the pier we always use for private conversations, off the Hudson just before the Battery Tunnel turns Manhattan into Brooklyn. I pulled over, cut the engine. A working girl detached herself from a small group and started to saunter over to the Lincoln. She stopped in her tracks when the Prof and I got out. Whatever we were, we weren't the customers she wanted.

"Be right back," I said to Michelle, motioning for the Prof to follow me.

I lit a smoke, handed the pack to the Prof, and looked at the dark water, thinking of the dark water in Flushing Meadow Park. Thinking of Strega. I was getting off the track.

"What's going down?" the Prof wanted to know.

"I'm looking for a picture. Kiddie porn. My client is concerned that a picture was taken of a certain kid. She wants it back."

"Why don't you just look for a fish out there?" he said, pointing at the silent Hudson.

"I know it's odds-against, Prof. I said I'd try, okay?"

"Where do I come in?"

"I hit the Square, asking around. The kid in the back seat with Michelle? He's hustling. I spoke to his pimp, told him I wanted to buy some pictures. He's going to meet me by the big ships around midnight. I'm supposed to bring a grand in cash, buy four pictures."

"Of who?"

"Who the fuck knows. The freak probably *has* some pictures. If he figures me for a customer, I'll buy the pictures, ask him for some more. Tell him what I'm looking for."

"And if he figures you for a tourist?" the Prof asked.

"That's where you come in. The Lincoln has one of those power trunk releases, okay? Michelle holds the kid in the front seat, keeps her head down. I climb out, she slides over where I was sitting. Any trouble— she pops the trunk and you come out. I got a scattergun you can use."

"I ain't dusting nobody, Burke," he said, trying to convince himself.

"I didn't say you had to take him out, Prof. Just keep me from getting stomped on, okay? Show him the piece, maybe break a cap in the air . . . that's all."

The Prof sucked cigarette smoke into his chest. "You going to play this one square?"

"If he's got real pictures, I'll buy and I'll ask him some questions. But if he moves on me and you have to brace him, we'll see what's he got on him. Okay?"

"What if he has backup?"

"He's driving a 'vette. Easy to check. And Michelle will be keeping the peek from the car."

"It sounds like a job for Max," he said.

"It's a job for us, Prof. You in or out?"

"I may talk some jive, but I never took a dive," he snapped, insulted.

I patted him on the back. "We'll get Michelle to drop us off near my office. Get the stuff we need, hang out a bit. Okay?"

"Right on," said the little black man, "but if the hound is going to be around . . ."

"Pansy's cool, Prof. You just have to get to know her."

He looked dubious, but he wasn't arguing. We walked back to the Lincoln—Michelle and the kid were still rapping away in the back.

"Michelle, how about you drop me and the Prof off? Take the car and meet us back around eleven?"

"Terry and I need to get something to eat anyway," she said. "Give me some money."

I handed her two fifties. The way Michelle ate she probably wouldn't bring back any change.

I drove to within a couple of blocks of the office and pulled over to the curb. Michelle climbed out to stand next to me, leaving the Prof inside the car with the boy.

"Walk a bit with me," I told her. She took my arm and we strolled out of earshot.

"The kid's hustling . . ." I began.

"I know," she snapped. "We talked."

"I'm supposed to bring him back around midnight. Do a deal with his pimp. Cash for merchandise. The pimp might get stupid—the Prof's going to ride shotgun in the trunk. You handle the kid—keep him with you for a couple of hours till you pick us up. Okay?"

"Burke," she hissed, her eyes flaming, "you're not giving that boy back to a pimp!"

"Michelle, I'm not giving him back to anyone, okay? No matter what goes down tonight, you leave with the kid. Take him to the cops. Let him find his home."

"The only cop I'm dealing with is McGowan," she said. McGowan is a detective with the Runaway Squad. By me, most cops would have to step up in class to be garbage, but McGowan plays it fair. You could drop off a kid with him and he'd never put the deliveryman in his report.

"Any way you want, babe. It's up to you. Just make sure the little bastard doesn't take off while he's with you. He's the reason I'm sure the pimp is going to show."

"Any money in this?" she wanted to know.

"If the pimp plays it square, I'm going to pay him and that's all. If he gets stupid, we'll take what he has. Split it three ways. Deal?"

"You think I was standing under that streetlight because I lost something, honey?"

I threw up my hands in surrender, reaching for my shirt pocket.

"Honey, I have told you time and time again not to carry cash in your shirt pocket—only dice players do that. It's bad enough you dress like a bum."

"Hey!" I said. "This is a good suit."

"Burke, it *was* a good suit. It's yesterday's news, darling. Like your haircut," she said, a smile playing with her painted lips.

"We can't all be on the cutting edge of fashion, Michelle."

"Don't I know it," she retorted, taking the wad of bills and counting off a few fifties for herself. If I ever paid taxes, Michelle would be one hell of a deduction. She reached up to kiss me on the cheek. "Thanks, baby. That's one step closer to Denmark for me."

"Sure," I said. I'd heard it before.

Michelle climbed behind the wheel of the Lincoln as the Prof got out. She turned and said something to the boy. He scrambled over the back seat to sit next to her. She was saying something to him as they pulled away—probably telling him to keep his feet off the upholstery.

55

WHEN THE Lincoln wheeled around the corner, I was waiting. The kid was sitting next to Michelle on the front seat, eating an ice-cream cone. I climbed in and Michelle slid over, changing places with the kid so he was between us. I found the release lever, popped the trunk, and waited for traffic to pass.

As soon as it got quiet, I climbed out like I was getting something out of the trunk. "Okay," I hissed into the darkness. The Prof came out, dressed in one of those padded suits guys wear for working in meat lockers. He was carrying his own coat in one hand, the shotgun wrapped inside.

The light went on inside the trunk when I lifted it up. I took a roll of quarters out of my pocket and put it against the light. When I smacked it with the flat of my hand, the light went out. It wouldn't come on again.

The Prof checked out the interior—it was clean and new, covered with carpet. Even the spare tire was buried under the flooring. "I lived in worse places," he said, and climbed in without another word.

I worked my way back to the West Side Highway. Michelle sat with her arm around the boy, listening to me explain the deal.

"The kid sits straight up in the seat, okay? You lay down, below the windshield. When I get out, you slide over and put your hand on this release. You hear me raise my voice for *any* reason . . . no matter what I'm saying . . . you pop the lever."

"Terry is coming back with us," she said. Her voice was calm—just stating a fact. I glanced over at the kid—if this wasn't okay with him he was a hell of an actor.

"There won't be any problem," I told them both, the magnum heavy in my coat. "This guy doesn't try and hurt me, he won't get hurt."

"I hope he does try and hurt you," Michelle said, her voice soft.

I shot her a dirty look, but she wasn't paying attention. "Do you know what he did to Terry? You know what he makes . . ."

"I know," I told her.

When we crossed 14th Street I told Michelle to get down. "You just stay in the car no matter what happens," I told the kid.

"Terry knows what to do," Michelle snapped at me, sliding into position. The boy held her hand.

I nosed the Lincoln into a dark spot in the shadows cast by the big ships. No sign of the pimp. I hit the window switch, waiting.

It didn't take long. Headlights on high beam flashed behind me—the red Corvette. I climbed out of the car, walked around toward the trunk. Where I'd stash the pictures if I got any.

The Corvette hit the brakes, sending the machine into a controlled skid across the back of the Lincoln, blocking me in. The pimp revved his engine before he shut it down, climbing out in almost the same motion. The passenger seat looked empty. I walked over toward him to get a better look.

The pimp stood next to his car, hands balled into fists. I walked right up to him, stepping in his space, looking down like I was afraid. The inside of his car was empty. Good.

"The pictures?" I asked him.

He reached in a shirt pocket, coming out with a pair of sunglasses. He took his time adjusting them on his face, making me wait.

"The money?" he said.

I took out the thousand from my coat pocket, handed it to him. Put my hand back in the same pocket like I was guarding the rest of my money. Felt the magnum waiting there.

He handed me four Polaroids, watching me turn my back to him so I could catch some light. They were all of the boy. Terry. Three had him naked, sucking on another little boy who was doing the same thing to him. The last picture was a side view of a kid being penetrated in the rear—you couldn't see his face. My hands shook.

"You only take pictures of your own boys?" I asked him.

"That's the best way, man. From me to you—no problems and no complaints."

He took a leather notebook from his pocket. Flipped it open and pulled out a gold pen. Started writing.

"What are you doing?" I asked him.

"Writing down your license number, man. Just in case I want to get in touch with you again." His eyes were hidden behind the glasses.

I quickly looked around. Quiet as a graveyard. "Don't do that!" I yelled, and the trunk of the Lincoln popped open. The pimp grabbed a fistful of my coat, drawing back his other hand to shut me up. I hooked him deep in the belly with the hand holding the magnum, trying to drive it through him and scratch the finish of his red Corvette. He grunted and doubled over, catching a kick on the temple from my steel-toed shoe. The pimp's glasses flew off—he was reaching for something in his jacket when the Prof put the scattergun in his face.

The pimp just lay there while I checked his equipment. A little .32-caliber automatic, a pretty silver color. A diamond ring, a wafer-thin watch. A tiny leather address book. A key ring with a bunch of keys. A wad of bills in a wallet so thick it was almost a purse. A silver vial with a screw-on top. No identification. I pocketed it all.

He was gasping for breath by then, but watching me closely. Wondering what the game was.

I went around to the Corvette, shoved the lever into neutral, and put my shoulder to it. It moved forward a few feet—more than enough to get the Lincoln out. I pulled the keys from the ignition, walked back, and held them in front of the pimp's face.

"I'll leave these under the streetlight over there," I told him, pointing to my left. It was about a hundred yards away.

The pimp was still quiet—the shotgun was his whole world.

"You fucked with the wrong kid," I told him, and walked to the Lincoln. I started it up, backed it out, spun around so the passenger door was at the Prof's back. Michelle opened it from the inside and the Prof jumped in as I took off.

The Lincoln shot toward the streetlight. I hit the brakes hard. "He's still down," the Prof called out. I threw the vial out the window.

If the maggot remembered the license number of the Lincoln, he could ask the Real Brotherhood for his car keys.

56

I WANTED the Lincoln off the streets in case the pimp decided to make a phone call.

"Can you call McGowan from your place?" I asked Michelle.

"I'll handle it," she said from the back seat. The boy was quiet. I glanced in the mirror—he was trembling, Michelle's arm around him, his face in her chest.

I tossed the pimp's wallet into the back seat. "Have to throw the rest of his junk away," I said. The Prof nodded agreement.

The Lincoln rolled north on the highway, heading for 125th Street, where I'd make the sweep and head back to our part of town.

"Almost six thousand," Michelle said, a happy note in her voice. The wallet came sailing over the seat, landing on the dashboard.

"Take your cut," I told the Prof. The scattergun was stashed under the seat.

"Cash from trash," he said, sounding religious, "cash from trash."

He pulled a pair of cotton gloves from the freezer suit and started to work on the pimp's little gun, wiping it clean. He pulled out the clip, then jacked the slide, catching the unfired slug in his hand.

"One in the chamber," he said. The little automatic had been ready for work.

"One piece at a time," I said. The Prof nodded, hitting the switch to lower his window. First the bullets, then the clip. The silver gun was the last to go.

The Prof handed me my share of the pimp's money, softly clapping his hands together to say all the work was done. I let him off on Second Avenue in the Thirties, opening the trunk to let him take his cart and leave the freezer suit. The Prof strapped his cart to his back like it was a knapsack.

"Watch yourself, Prof," I told him.

"The street is my home, and that ain't no poem," he said. The pimp might see him again, but nothing would register. We pressed our palms together, chest high. The way you say goodbye in the visiting room in prison. Through the bullet-proof glass.

I rolled up outside Michelle's hotel, opened the door to let her out as if I was a chauffeur. The little boy was holding on to her hand like a lifeline. Maybe it was.

Michelle kissed me on the cheek. "Keep the change, honey," she said, and started up the steps.

I had the Lincoln back inside my garage in another fifteen minutes.

57

THE PIMP'S watch had some fancy engraving on the back. "L to R. All ways." Probably from the freak who turned him out the first time. No point trying to sell it. I opened it up, keeping only the timing mechanism—the Mole could always use something like that—pushing the rest to the side of my desk. The diamond ring was another story—a heavy white-gold base holding what looked like a two-carat stone. I screwed the loupe into my eye socket and took a closer look—no blemishes that I could see, nice fire. I pried the stone loose, pushing what was left of the ring over next to the wreckage of the watch.

The key ring was useless to me, but I took my time with the little leather address book. All first names or initials, with phone numbers next to them. In the right-hand column there was a single-digit number next to each name. Some kind of code for what the customer usually wanted? I copied everything from the book onto a yellow pad. I'd keep the book itself—it might turn into a poker chip sometime.

I went out to the metal stairs leading to the roof, calling for Pansy. The moon was a crescent, clear against the night sky. I lit a cigarette, watching the moon hang up there, a million miles from this junkyard we live in. I like to look at the moon—you never get to see it in prison.

Pansy lumbered downstairs. She saw me standing on the iron landing and put her paws on the railing. Standing like that, her face was almost level with mine. I scratched the back of her ears absently, trying to get a grip on my search for the picture. In the morning I'd see a guy who would get me the names and addresses to go with the phone numbers from the pimp's book, but it wasn't likely to give me anything. I had to wait on the Mole and Bobby, couldn't push them to move any faster. The only way to get more information was to talk to the kid myself.

I'd need Immaculata for that.

And Strega.

58

THE NEXT morning I went to work. First to Mama's, where I called Strega.

"It's me," I said, when she picked up the phone.

"You have what I want?" she asked.

"I'm still working. I have to talk with you—get some more information."

"What information?"

"Not on the phone," I told her. "You know the statue on Queens Boulevard, on the north side, just before the courthouse?"

"Yes," she said.

"Tonight. At six-thirty, okay?"

"Yes," she said again, tonelessly. And hung up.

I went back inside to the restaurant. Mama glided over to my table. "No serve breakfast," she said, smiling. I looked stricken. "But not too early for lunch," she told me. One of the alleged waiters materialized next to me, bowed to Mama. She said something in Cantonese to him. He just nodded.

"Hot-and-sour soup?" I asked.

"You speak Chinese now, Burke? Very good."

I didn't bother to answer her—Mama was only sarcastic when she was annoyed about something.

"You want me do something for you, Burke? Get Max over here?"

"Yeah, Mama. I want Max. But I could find him by myself, right? I came here to give you something."

Her eyes opened slightly, looking a question at me. I put the diamond I took from the pimp on the table between us. Mama picked it up, held it to the light between her fingers.

"Man's stone," she said.

"Your stone," I told her. "A small gift to show my great respect."

A smile lit up her face. "Very nice stone," she said.

I bowed my head, saying the matter was closed. "Tell me about new case," Mama said.

"I'm looking for a picture," I said, and told her what kind of picture and why I was looking.

Mama put her hands in the sugar bowl, tossing a pinch of the white powder on the table top, using her fingers to push it into a long narrow column.

"Everybody do *something*," she told me, drawing her finger through the bottom of the column, drawing a line. "Some people do more things, okay?" Drawing another line, leaving more than half the column between us. "Gambling, funny money, jewels," she said, each time flicking more sugar off the column. "Guns, stealing . . ." More flicks of her finger— less sugar on the table. "Protection money, killing . . ." More sugar vanished. "Drugs," she said, and the last of the sugar was gone.

I got it. Everybody has to make a living. Everybody draws a line somewhere. The people who do kiddie porn are over the line no matter where you draw it. "I know," I told her.

"Business is business," said Mama, quoting her favorite psalm. "Every-thing has rules. Do the same way all the time. Reliable, okay?"

"Yes," I said, waiting.

"Even with war . . . rules," Mama said. I wasn't so sure—I'd been in one, but I let her go on.

"These people . . ." Mama shrugged, her face set and hard.

The soup came. Mama dished some out into my bowl. Gave some to herself. She bowed over the plates like she was saying grace.

Mama looked up. "No rules," she said.

"No rules," I agreed.

59

IMMACULATA came in the front door of the restaurant, made her way past the customers to our table.

"Hello, Mama," she said.

Mama smiled at her—a real smile, not the cat's grin she usually showed Max's woman. "You sit down with us, okay? Have some soup?"

Immaculata bowed. "Thank you, Mama. I have been told your soup is the finest of all."

That put the cap on it for Mama. "You help Burke on his case, yes? Very good. Very important case. Sit with me," she said, patting the seat next to her.

Immaculata shot her hips sideways and was next to Mama in a flash. She must have been working with Max—he'd been trying to teach me karate for a long time—I hoped he was having better luck with her. Mama gave her a generous helping of the soup, watching her bow over the food before eating, nodding her head in approval.

"Max coming?" she asked.

"Yes," Immaculata answered.

"Max good man. Fine warrior," Mama opened.

"Yes," said Immaculata, waiting.

"Good man. Make good father, yes?"

Immaculata's eyes were calm, but her golden skin flushed. She looked directly at Mama.

"You know? Even Max doesn't know."

"I know," said Mama, patting Immaculata's arm, her whole face smiling.

Immaculata watched Mama's face, then broke into a smile of her own. Without a word being said, she knew she wasn't a bar girl to Mama anymore.

60

MAX CAME out of the kitchen, bowed to everyone at the table, then slammed into the booth next to me, almost driving me through the wall. He pulled out a tattered copy of the *Daily News*, spread it on the table, and pointed to the charts of Flower Jewel's race with a thick finger. He spread his hands to ask a question—what did this "dq" crap mean anyway?

I used the sugar bowl and the salt and pepper shakers to show him how it had happened. Max nodded, moving his right hand in the "hit me" gesture blackjack players use when they want another card. We were going to bet on Flower Jewel the next time she raced. It wasn't like I had any choice—I handed Max a hundred, ignoring Mama's broad grin and Immaculata's look of benign interest.

Max made the sign of a galloping horse, checked to see that all eyes were focused on him. Then he pounded his chest over his heart, balled his right hand into a fist, and laid his forearm on the table with the underside up. The veins looked like electrical cords. He touched a vein, touched his heart again. Made the sign of the horse.

I got it. Since the blood of Mongol warriors ran in his veins, he claimed to have a natural kinship with horses. I should listen to him.

Mama nodded in agreement. "Good blood," she said. Immaculata blushed again, but Max was too busy proving he knew more about horses than I did to pay attention.

Mama got to her feet as Immaculata stood to give her room to exit.

She took Immaculata's hand, turned it over to see the underside of her forearm. She tapped the delicate veins there, nodded her head sharply. Smiled. "Good blood here too," Mama said, and kissed Immaculata on the cheek.

Max looked at me, puzzled. I didn't say anything—Mac would tell him when it was time for him to know.

I lit a cigarette as the waiter took away the soup bowls, and started to explain why I needed Immaculata.

61

BY THE TIME I was finished, it was mid-afternoon. Only the clock on the wall gave me a clue—daylight never reached the back booths in Mama's joint.

"You really think you can do it?" I asked her.

"It's not an interrogation, Burke. The little boy has information about what happened to him, but it's not so easy for him to talk about. He feels all sorts of things about the assault . . . guilt, fear, excitement. . . ."

"Excitement?" I asked her.

"Sure. Children are sexual beings, they respond to sexual stimulation. That's why, if we *don't* treat a child who has been sexually abused, he's likely to go on looking for the same experience."

"Even if it hurt him?"

"Even so," she said.

"What would make him talk?" I asked her.

"You don't *make* him talk. He *wants* to talk about it; he wants to get it outside of him . . . put down the pain. But first he has to feel safe."

"Like that nobody can hurt him anymore?"

"That's it. Exactly."

"So it's easier if he was assaulted by a stranger, right? So his family can protect him?"

"Yes, it is easier if the assault wasn't by a family member. If someone you trust hurts you, it changes the way you look at the whole world."

"I know," I told her. "If I can get the kid, where would I bring him?"

"Bring him to SAFE, the Safety and Fitness Exchange—where I work. I told you about it, remember? It's the best place for this—lots of other children around, and we know how to act around boys like this one. He'll know nobody can hurt him when he's with us."

"You think he'll come with me?" I asked her.

"Probably—I don't know. It would help if someone he trusted said it was okay for him to go—promised him he'd be all right. Probably the best way would be for you to bring the child's parent, or anyone he trusted, with you. We work with relatives of abused children all the time."

"You wouldn't want to work with this one," I told her.

Max tapped his chest, folded his arms. The kid would sure as hell be safe with him, he was saying. I tapped my fist against his shoulder to thank him, bowed to Immaculata, and went back through the kitchen to Bobby's Lincoln.

62

I STASHED the Lincoln in my garage. Strega had already seen one car; that was enough. Pansy chomped on the heavy beef bones Mama had given me for her, snarling anytime she felt the slightest resistance. Her life would have been perfect right then if I could have gotten pro wrestling on the tube, but only the cable networks carry it during the day. The hippies downstairs must have cable—their lives wouldn't be complete without MTV. I'd have to get the Mole to make the necessary adjustments.

It was getting near time to leave. There's only two ways to ride the subways in New York: dress up like a carpenter or a plumber—anyone who routinely carries tools around with him—or carry a gun. I didn't handle tools like I knew what I was doing, and if I got dropped holding a piece I was looking at some serious time upstate. I put on a dark suit over a blue chambray shirt with a darker-blue knit tie. A hard-working architect. I pulled my new attaché case from under the couch. Its black fabric sides expand to hold a lot of stuff, but that's not why I wanted it. This attaché case is made of Kevlar—the same stuff cops use for bullet-

proof vests. It looks like nylon, but it'll blunt a knife and stop a bullet—
it even has a shoulder strap so you can keep your hands free.

I unzipped the case and threw in a pack of graph paper, some pencils,
an old blueprint of a sewage plant, and a little calculator. I added a
telescoping metal pointer, the kind architects use to point out features on
their blueprints; it works just as well for keeping people from getting
close enough to stab you. Then I hunted around until I found the clear
plastic T-square the Mole made for me. It looks like the real thing, but
if you wishbone the two ends in your hands and snap hard, you end up
with a razor-edged knife. Perfect for stabbing and not illegal to carry.
The CIA uses these knives to beat airport security machines, but their
best feature is the way they break off inside a body—you can put a hell
of an edge on plastic, but it stays very brittle.

I caught the E Train at Chambers Street, under the World Trade
Center. That was the end of the line—the return would take me right
out to my meeting with Strega without changing trains. And I got a seat.

The first thing I did was open my briefcase and take out my blueprints
and T-square. I made a desk of the briefcase in my lap and sat there
watching. During rush hour, the trains belong to the citizens. By the
time we got into midtown, the car was packed with people. An Oriental
man, his dark suit shiny from too many cleanings, face buried in a book
on computers, shut out the train noises and concentrated. A dress-for-
success black woman was reading some kind of leather-bound report—
all I could read on the cover was "Proposal" stamped in gold letters. A
pair of middle-aged women sat facing each other, arguing over whose
boss was the biggest asshole.

The E Train has modern cars—blue-and-orange plastic seats set per-
pendicular to each other instead of lined up against the side like the older
versions . . . subway maps set behind thick clear-plastic sheets . . . stainless-
steel outer skins. Even the air conditioning works sometimes. By the time
the train hit the long tunnel connecting Manhattan and Queens the car
looked like a forest of newspapers and briefcases—gothic romances and
crossword puzzles covered faces. A transit cop got on at Queens Plaza,
a young guy with a mustache, carrying fifty pounds of equipment on his
belt. His eyes swept the car for a second; then he started writing something

in his memo book. The car was thick with people, but no skells—nobody smoking dope, no portable radio blasting. Working people going home from work. I felt like a tourist.

Roosevelt Avenue was the next stop on the express. The transit cop got off—Roosevelt Avenue was the Queens version of Times Square—the only thing free out on the streets was trouble. Next came Continental Avenue, where most of the yuppies made their exit. The train goes all the way out to Jamaica; by the time it got to the end of the line there wouldn't be too many white faces left.

I got off at Union Turnpike, stuffing the T-square back into my briefcase, checking my watch. I still had almost fifteen minutes to wait for Strega.

63

THE SUN was dropping into the west as I made my way across Queens Boulevard to the statue. The courthouse was to my right, a squat, dirty piece of undistinguished architecture that hadn't been put up by the lowest bidder—not in Queens County. Looming behind it, the House of Detention cast a shadow of its own, six stories of cross-hatched steel bars, cannon fodder for the processing system citizens call Justice. The guys inside—the ones who can't make bail—call it "just us." Wolfe's office was somewhere in the courthouse complex.

I found a seat at the base of the statue—some Greek god covered with tribute from the passing pigeons. I lit another smoke, watching my hands holding the wooden match. Citizens passed me without a glance—not minding their own business because it was the right thing to do, just in a hurry to get home to whatever treasures their VCRs had preserved for them. The statue was right behind a bus stop, just before the boulevard turned right into Union Turnpike. The human traffic was so thick I couldn't see the street, but I wasn't worried about missing Strega.

I was into my third cigarette when I felt the change in the air—like a cold wind without the breeze. A car horn was blasting its way through the noise of the traffic—sharper and more demanding than the others. A fog-colored BMW was standing right in the middle of the bus stop, leaning on its horn and flashing its lights.

I walked over to the passenger door. The window glass was too dark to see through. The door wasn't locked. I pulled it open and climbed inside. She had the BMW roaring into the traffic stream while I was still closing my door, the little car lurching as she forced it into second gear. We shot across to the left lane, horns protesting in our wake.

"You were late," she snapped, staring straight ahead.

"I was where I said I'd be," I told her, fumbling for my seat belt.

"Next time wait at the curb," she said. Telling the cleaning woman she missed a spot.

She was wearing a bottle-green silk dress, with a black mink jacket over her shoulders, leaving her bare arms free. A thin black chain was around her waist, one end dangling past the seat—it looked like wrought iron. Her face was set and hard behind the makeup mask.

I leaned back in my seat. Strega's skirt was hiked to mid-thigh. Her stockings were dark with some kind of pattern woven into them. Spike heels the same color as the dress. She wasn't wearing her seat belt.

"Where are you going?" I wanted to know.

"My house. You got a problem with that?"

"Only if it isn't empty," I said.

"I'm alone," said Strega. Maybe she was talking about the house.

She wrestled the BMW through the streets to her house, fighting the wheel, riding the clutch unmercifully. The car stalled on Austin Street when she didn't give it enough gas pulling away from the light. "God-damned fucking clutch!" she muttered, snapping the ignition key to get it started again. She was a lousy driver.

"Why don't you get a car with an automatic transmission?"

"My legs look so good when I change gears," she replied. "Don't they?"

I didn't say anything.

"Look at my legs!" she snarled at me. "Aren't they flashy?"

"I wouldn't get a car to go with my looks," I said, mildly.

"Neither would I—if I looked like you," she said, softening it only slightly with a smile. "And you didn't answer my question."

"What question?"

"*Don't* my legs look good?"

"That isn't a question," I told her. And this time I got a better smile.

64

SHE PULLED the BMW around to the back of her house and hit the button on a box she had clipped to the sun visor to open the garage. I followed her up the stairs to the living room, watching her hips switch under the green dress—it looked like a slip in the soft light. She carried the black mink like a dishrag in one hand, tossing it in the general direction of the white couch as she went by.

Strega passed through the living room to another flight of stairs, and climbed toward a light at the top, not saying a word. The bedroom was huge, big enough for three rooms. The walls were a dusky-rose color, the wall-to-wall carpet a dark red. A Hollywood bed, the kind with a canopy over the top, was in the precise middle of the room, standing on a platform a few inches off the carpet. It was all in pink—pink gauze draped from the canopy almost to the floor. The spread was covered with giant stuffed animals—a panda, two teddy bears, a basset hound. A Raggedy Ann doll was propped against the pillows, its sociopath's eyes watching me. A bathroom door stood open to my right—pink shag carpet on the floor, a clear lucite tub dominating the room. A professional makeup mirror was against one wall, a string of tiny little bulbs all around its border. A walk-in closet had mirrored doors. It was half yuppie dream-scene, half little girl's room. I couldn't imagine another person sleeping there with her.

"His bedroom is on the other side of the house," she said, reading my mind. "This is just for me."

"Your husband works late hours?" I asked.

"My husband does what I tell him. I give him what he wants—he does what I want. You understand?"

"No," I told her.

"You wouldn't," she said. Case closed.

I patted my pockets, telling her I wanted to smoke. I couldn't see an ashtray anywhere.

"I don't smoke cigarettes in here," she said.

"So let's go somewhere else."

Strega looked at me like a carpenter checking if there was enough room for a bookcase.

"You don't like my room?"

"It's your room," I replied.

Strega slipped the straps of the green slip over her shoulders, pulling it down to her waist in one motion. I heard the silk tear. Her small breasts looked hard as rocks in the pink light. "You like my room better now?" she asked.

"The room is the same," I said.

She took a breath, making up her mind. "Sit over there," she said, pointing to a tube chair covered in a dark suede—it looked like something growing out of the carpet. I shrugged out of my coat, holding it in one hand, looking toward the bed. "Put it on the floor," she said over her shoulder as she walked out of the room.

She came back with a heavy piece of crystal, kneeling in front of me to put it on the carpet. Whatever it was supposed to be, it was an ashtray then. She was as self-conscious about being topless as two dogs mating—you wanted to look, that was your problem.

"You want something besides that cigarette?"

"I'm okay," I told her.

She was putting a smoke together for herself, loading a tiny white pipe—tiny brown pebbles mixed with the tobacco. "Crack," she said. Super-processed, free-based cocaine—too powerful to snort. She took a deep drag, her eyes on me. It should have lifted her right off the carpet, but she puffed away, bored.

"You wanted to talk to me?" she asked.

I watched her walk back and forth in front of me, the green slip now a tiny skirt just covering her hips, her heels blending into the carpet. The tube chair had a rounded back, forcing me to sit up very straight.

"I need the boy," I told her. "I need to have him talk to some people. Experts. He knows more than he told you—he might have the key in his head."

Strega nodded, thinking. "You're not going to use drugs on him?"

"You mean like sodium amytal—truth serum? No. It's too dangerous. It could get him to where it happened, but we might not be able to get him back."

"Hypnosis?" she asked.

"Not that either," I said. "There's people who know how to talk to kids who've been worked over by freaks. It doesn't hurt—might make him feel better."

"He's okay now," she said. "All he needs is that picture."

"He's not in therapy . . . not getting treatment from anyone?"

"He doesn't need any of that!"

"Yeah, he does. Or at least someone who knows what they're doing should make the decision."

"Not about this," she said, her voice flat.

"Look," I said, "you don't know anything about this, right? Treatment could make all the difference."

"I know about it," she said. Case closed again.

I took a deep drag of my smoke. "I need to have somebody talk to the boy, okay?"

"I'm going to be there when they do."

"No, you're not. That's not the way it's done. Nobody's going to be there."

She puffed on her little crack-laced pipe, flame-points in her eyes.

"He wouldn't trust you."

"He would if you said it was okay, right?"

"Yeah. He'd do whatever I said."

"You bring him to a place, okay? I'll meet you there. I'll have the therapist with me. You hand him over—tell him to be a good boy, okay? I'll bring him back in a couple of hours."

"That's it?"

"That's it," I said.

Strega rubbed her eyes as if she didn't like what she was seeing. "What if I don't do it?"

"You do what you want," I told her. "But you're paying me money to get something done—you don't bring the boy, it makes it harder. And it's tough enough already. It's up to you."

She took a last drag on her pipe, came over to me, and sat in my lap. She put one slim arm around my neck and leaned down to drop the pipe in the ashtray. "I'll think about it," she said, grinding her butt deep into my lap. Heat flashed below my waist but my shoulders stayed cold.

"When's your husband coming home?" I asked her.

"He can't come back here until after midnight."

"Can't?" I asked her, looking the question into her little face.

She buried her face in my chest, whispering so softly I could barely hear her. "We have a deal. I do him good. I'm what he needs. I know his mind. On his last birthday I brought a girlfriend of mine over for him—we did a threesome." She was wiggling frantically in my lap, whispering in that little-girl's voice. "All men are the same," she purred, reaching for my zipper, pulling it down, slipping her hand inside, stroking me, scraping a long thumbnail down the shaft. "A hard cock makes a soft brain."

The big house was quiet as a tomb. "Do I get the boy?" I asked her.

"Pull up my dress," she whispered, lifting her butt from my lap. It slid up to her waist as if it was oiled—the green silk made a thick band around her waist; only her dark stockings showed underneath.

She fit herself around me, never changing her position, her face still buried in my chest. She contracted the hard muscles in her hips, pushing back against me. "Say my name!" she whispered into my hair.

"Which name?" I asked her, my voice not as flat as I wanted.

"You know!" she cried, her voice years younger than her body.

"Strega," I said, holding one of her breasts gently in my hand, feeling myself empty into her. She ground herself hard against me, groaning like I was hurting her. In another couple of seconds she was quiet, still welded to me, leaning her head back, letting a long breath out with a sigh.

I rubbed my hand softly over her face. She took a finger in her mouth, bit down hard. I left my hand where it was. She shifted her hips. I popped out of her with a wet sound. She twisted in my lap, her face buried in my chest again. "I'm the best girl," she said. I patted her head, wondering why it was so cold in that pink room.

65

WE STAYED like that for some time. I couldn't see my watch. "Have another cigarette," she said, climbing off my lap and walking into her bathroom. She closed the door. I could hear the tub filling.

She came out wrapped in a white terry robe, her red hair tousled above the thick collar. She looked thirteen years old. "Now you," she said.

When I came out of the bathroom the bedroom was empty. I heard music from downstairs. Barbra Streisand. Too bad.

Strega was sitting on the white couch, now dressed in a black pleated skirt and a white blouse. I walked past her to the steps. She came off the couch and held my arm, grabbing her mink with her free hand. I went down the steps first, feeling her behind me, not liking the feeling. We got into the BMW without a word.

She pulled into the bus stop, hitting the brakes too hard. "The boy?" I asked her, one more time.

"I'll do it," she said. "Give me one day's notice." Her eyes were somewhere else.

"Good," I told her, getting out of the car, looking back at her.

Strega made a kissing motion with her lips to say goodbye. It looked like a sneer.

66

I T WAS STILL a half-hour shy of midnight when I grabbed the subway heading back to Manhattan. The day-shift citizens were gone but the same rules applied—look down or look hard. I alternated between the two until the train screeched to its last stop under the World Trade Center. I stayed underground, following the tunnel a few blocks to Park Place, found the Lincoln just where I'd left it, and drove back to the office.

I let Pansy out to the roof, searching the tiny refrigerator for something to eat. Nothing but a jar of mustard, another of mayonnaise, and a frozen roll. I poured myself a glass of cold water, thinking of the mayonnaise sandwiches we used to make in prison, stuffing them inside our shirts to eat in the middle of the night. Sometimes it was hard to keep my mind from going back to doing time, but I could control my stomach anyway. I'd eat in the morning.

The pictures of Strega's boy Scotty were on my desk—a happy little kid. Like she had been, she said. There's a big slab of corkboard on one wall of my office, just over the couch. There was plenty of room for the boy's pictures. I tacked them up to help me memorize his face—I didn't want to carry them around with me. I lit a cigarette, my eyes sliding from the burning red tip to the boy's pictures.

Working on it. Drawing a blank.

The back door thumped—Pansy was tired of waiting for me to come up on the roof. I let her in, turned on the radio to get the news while I put some more food together for the monster. Then I lay back down on the couch. The radio was playing "You're a Thousand Miles Away" by the Heartbeats. A song from another time—it was supposed to make you think of a guy in the military, his girl waiting for him back home. It was a real popular song with the guys doing time upstate. I thought of Flood in some temple in Japan as I drifted off.

67

I WOKE UP slowly to the smell of dog food. Pansy's face was inches from mine, her cold-water eyes unblinking, waiting patiently. Something was floating around at the top of my brain—where I couldn't reach it. Something about the boy's pictures. I lay there, ignoring Pansy, trying to get it to come back to me. No good. Lots of dreams never come to you again.

I took a shower and went out to get some breakfast, still trying to figure out what was bothering me. Whatever it was would have to get in line.

Pansy ate her share of the cupcakes I brought back. It wasn't until I put down the paper that I realized I hadn't even looked at the race results. Depression was coming down as surely as the Hawk—what people around here call the winter. They call it that because it kills. I had to get word to Immaculata that I was going to have the boy for her to interview. And after that, I had to wait.

I stopped at a light at the corner of the Bowery and Delancey. A big black guy with a dirty bandage over half his face offered to clean my windshield for a quarter. A used-up white woman with a cheap wig riding over her tired face offered to clean my tubes for ten bucks. I paid the black guy—V.D. isn't one of my hobbies.

The alley behind Mama's joint was empty, like it always is.

I slumped down at my table in the back, catching Mama's eye. One of the waiters came out of the kitchen with a tureen of soup. I waved him away—I wasn't hungry. He put the tureen down in front of me anyway. Bowed. If Mama told him to bring soup, he was bringing soup.

Mama came back in a few minutes, hands in the side pockets of her long dress. "You no serve soup?" she asked.

"I'm not hungry, Mama," I told her.

"Soup not for hunger. Not food—medicine, okay?" she said, sitting across from me. I watched her work the ladle, giving us each a generous helping. Women don't listen to me.

"I have to call Mac," I said.

"I do that. You want her to come here?"

I just nodded. "Good," said Mama. "I want to talk to baby."

"Mama, she won't have a baby for months yet."

"Too late—talk to baby now—prepare baby for everything, okay?"

"Whatever you say," I muttered. I wasn't in the mood for her voodoo that morning.

I ate my soup, keeping quiet as Mama loaded the bowl again, smiling her approval. I lit a cigarette, looking at Mama. "You going to call Mac today?" I asked.

"Call soon," she said. "You get call here. Last night."

I looked at her, waiting. "Man say he has name for you. Say to call the Bronx."

The Mole. "Thanks, Mama," I threw over my shoulder, heading for the phones in the back. I dialed the junkyard—he picked up on the first ring.

"You have a name for me?"

"Yes."

"Can I come up?"

"I'll meet you. At the pad."

"When?"

"Day after tomorrow," the Mole said, and cut the connection.

I walked back inside the restaurant. The Mole would be at the helicopter pad just off the East Side Drive past Waterside Towers in two hours. With a name. It was a stupid place to meet, but there was no point arguing. The Mole loved helicopters.

Mama was still at the table. "I get Immaculata now?" she asked.

"Sure. Thanks, Mama."

"You feel better, Burke?"

"Yeah," I told her. And I did.

68

I WAS HALFWAY through a platter of roast duck, spare ribs, and fried rice when Immaculata came in. I got up from my seat, bowed to her, and indicated she should sit down and have something to eat. I was piling some of the fried rice onto her plate when Mama appeared over her shoulder. She shoved in next to Immaculata, pushing the plate away from her, barking something in Chinese. Another of the waiters came on the run. I don't know what Mama said to him, but he immediately started taking all the food off the table except for the plate in front of me. He was back in another minute, carrying a couple of plates with metal covers on top. Mama served Immaculata ceremoniously, arranging the food on her plate like an interior decorator.

"What was wrong with my food?" I asked her.

"Okay for you, Burke. You not mother, right?"

Immaculata smiled, not arguing. "Thank you, Mama," she said.

"Only eat best food now. For baby. To be strong, okay? No sugar, okay? Plenty milk."

I polished off the rest of my food, pushed the plate away, lit a cigarette.

"Smoke bad for baby too," Mama said, glaring at me.

"Mama," I told her, "the kid isn't here yet."

"Be here soon enough," Mama replied, "yes, baby?" she said, patting Immaculata's flat stomach.

I ground out the cigarette. "You think it will bother the baby if I *talk* to Mac?" I asked Mama.

"Talk in soft voice," Mama said. "And pay baby respect when you talk, okay?"

"What?"

"You talk to mother—first you tell baby hello, right? You finish talk, you tell baby goodbye. Very easy—even for you, Burke."

I rolled my eyes to the ceiling, looking back at Immaculata for sympathy. She looked back, her eyes clear. It apparently made sense to her too.

I bowed slightly to Mac. "Good morning, honorable infant," I said. "I have to speak to your beautiful mother, who is going to help me with something very important. You are the most fortunate of babies to have a mother and father so committed to you. I am certain you will have your mother's beauty and intelligence and your father's strength and courage. May all your days on this earth be blessed with love. I am Burke, your father's brother."

Mama nodded approval. Immaculata bowed slightly, the faintest of smiles playing about her lips.

"Mac, you know the kid I told you about? I figure he saw a lot of things when they took that picture of him. If you speak with him, maybe he'll tell you things he hasn't told anybody yet."

"He might," she said. "But it sometimes takes a while. The safer the child feels, the more he can tell us. His own therapist would be in the best position to get this information."

"He's not in therapy."

"Why is this?"

"His mother . . . other relatives . . . they feel the best thing is for him to forget it . . . go on with his life."

"That doesn't work," she said. "Kids who have been sexually abused have a lot of issues to work through. Guilt, fear, anger. Especially the anger. It's abusive not to give the child this opportunity."

I was thinking of prison again. If a kid was raped inside the walls, he had a shortage of choices: Keep on getting fucked by anyone who asked. Escape. Take a P.C. for the rest of his bit. Kill himself. Or kill the guy who did it to him. Only the last choice made any sense—the only way to get back to being treated like a human being. Instant therapy.

"Could you treat this kid?" I asked her.

"The interview you want me to do—that is the beginning of treatment. It would be unethical for me to simply work with the child to get some facts and then abandon him. It doesn't have to be me that works with him, but *someone* has to."

"I'll make that part of the deal," I told her. I glanced at my watch—

time to get on the road and meet the Mole. "When can we do this?" I asked.

"Tomorrow afternoon I have some time free. Can you bring the child to SAFE around three o'clock?"

"Can we make it the day after, Mac? The kid's people need a day's notice."

"Okay. Thursday, then. But make it four instead."

"You got it." I stood up to leave, bowed to Mama and Mac. Mama's eyes were hard on me. "Goodbye, baby," I said to Mac's belly. "It has been a pleasure to be in your company once again."

Mama smiled. By the time I was halfway to the kitchen, she was deep into a discussion with Mac about cribs. I couldn't wait for Max to show up—Mama would probably want him to open a bank account for the kid's college education.

69

I TOOK the East Side Drive to the 23rd Street exit, appreciating my cigarette even more than usual thanks to Mama's new edict. A guy on the radio was blubbering something about a political scandal in Queens—in the Parking Violations Bureau this time. Political corruption in New York isn't news, but they keep reporting it the same way they keep telling you the weather. People like to know about things they can't do anything about.

There's a big outdoor parking lot near the pad where the helicopters land and take off. The attendant was a ferret-faced little hustler. "You need a ticket, man?" he asked.

"I don't know," I said to him. "Do I?"

"Give me five and park it over there," he said, pointing to an empty corner of the lot. "Keep your keys." The sign on the lot said seven dollars for the first half-hour. A New York transaction—a little bit for you, a little bit for me, and fuck the guy who's not there when the deal is made.

I walked over to the edge of the helicopter pad. A blue-and-white copter sat there waiting for passengers—mostly tourists who wanted a different view of Manhattan than you get from the Circle Line boats which berthed on the West Side. I was into my second smoke when the Mole materialized from behind one of the cars. He was wearing a filthy white set of coveralls, with a tool belt around his waist, the usual satchel in his grubby paw. He didn't look dangerous.

"Mole," I said by way of greeting. When he didn't reply, I asked him, "You have that name and address for me?"

The Mole nodded his head in the direction of the highway, turned, and started to walk away. I followed him, wondering why he didn't want to talk by the launch pad. He led me to a South Bronx special—a battered old Ford, half primer and half rust, sagging on broken springs, no hubcaps, a hole already punched in its trunk from the last burglary attempt. The Mole climbed inside without unlocking the door. I followed him. He started the engine, put the car in gear, and pulled off.

"You think it's safe enough to give me that name now?" I asked.

"I have to go with you," he said.

"How come?"

"You can't hurt this person," the Mole said. "My friends, the ones who set this up—they make the rules. You can't hurt him. I have to go with you—make sure."

"Is he going to talk to me, Mole?"

"It is all arranged. He will talk to you, but only about his . . . thing, in general. You understand? Not about what *he* does, about what *they* do. 'Deep background,' my friends call it."

Great. "Can I threaten him?" I asked.

"He will know you can't hurt him. It won't do any good."

I lit another smoke, saying nothing. But the Mole read my thoughts. "You will know his address. He wanted the meeting to be where he lives. But if anything happens to him, my people will blame you. He is important to us."

"Slime like that is important?"

The Mole's eyes flashed behind his thick glasses. "We have a saying—the tree which bears fruit does not care about the fertilizer. And we must grow food in the desert. Okay?"

"Okay," I said. My one option.

The Mole drove the way he walked through his junkyard—like he wasn't paying attention, just blundering along. But he handled the Ford well, negotiating the traffic, paying no attention to the angry horns when he cut someone off, just being himself. We found a parking spot on 9th Street on the West Side. The Mole shut down the engine, looked over at me. "You have anything with you?" he asked.

"I'm clean," I told him.

"The cigarette lighter I made for you?"

I didn't say anything—he meant the throwaway butane lighter he had filled with napalm.

"Leave it here," the Mole said. I opened the glove compartment, tossed it inside.

"You going to leave your satchel in the car too?" I asked him. The Mole looked at me as if I should be on medication.

70

THE MOLE stopped in front of a lime-stone-front townhouse just off Fifth Avenue. It was three stories high, level with the rest of the buildings on the block. Maybe thirty-five feet wide. A seven-figure piece of property in that neighborhood. Four steps took us to a teak door, set behind a wrought-iron grating that looked custom-made. The Mole's stubby finger found the mother-of-pearl button, pushed it once.

We didn't have long to wait. The teak door opened—a man was standing there, waiting. You don't need a peephole when you have a couple of hundred pounds of iron between you and whoever's at the door. I couldn't see into the dark interior. The guy at the door was tall and slender, both hands in the pockets of what looked like a silk bathrobe.

"Yes?" he asked.

"Moishe," the Mole said.

"Please step back," said the man. He had a British accent.

The Mole and I went back to the sidewalk so the iron grate could swing out. We walked past the man inside, waited while he bolted the iron grate shut and closed the door. We were in a rectangular room, much longer than it was wide. The floor was highly polished dark wood, setting off overstuffed Victorian furniture, upholstered in a blue-and-white floral pattern. Only one light burned off to the side, flickering like it was gas instead of electricity.

"May I take your coats?" the man said, opening a closet just past the entranceway.

I shook my head "no"—the Mole wasn't wearing anything over his coveralls.

"Please . . ." the man said, languidly waving his hand to say we should go up the stairs before him. I went first, the Mole right behind me. We were breaking all the rules for this human.

"To your right," his voice came from behind me. I turned into a big room that looked smaller because it was so stuffed with things. A huge desk dominated the room, set on thick carved stubs at each corner. They looked like lion's paws. An Oriental rug covered most of the floor—it had a royal-blue background with a red-and-white design running from the center and blending into the borders. A fireplace was against one wall, birch logs crackling in a marble cage. The windows were covered with heavy velvet drapes the same royal blue as the rug. Everything was out of the past—except for a glowing video terminal on a butcher-block table parallel to the desk.

"Please sit anywhere," the man said, waving one arm to display the options in the room as he seated himself behind the big desk. I took a heavy armchair upholstered in dark tufted leather. A bronze-and-glass ashtray was on a metal stand next to the chair. The Mole stood near the door, his eyes sweeping the room. Then he sat on the floor, blocking the door with his bulk, putting his satchel on the ground. He looked from the man to where I was sitting, making it clear that we had an agreement. Then he pulled out a sheaf of papers and started to study some of his calculations—taking himself somewhere else.

"Now, then," said the man, folding his hands in front of him on the desk. "May I offer you some refreshment? Coffee? Some excellent sherry?"

I shook my head "no." The Mole never looked up.

"A beer perhaps?"

"No," I told him. I'd made a deal not to threaten him, but I didn't have to pretend I was his pal.

The man reached for a cut-glass decanter on his desk. Something that looked like a silver leaf dangled from just below the neck of the bottle, attached by a silver chain. He poured himself a wineglass of dark liquid from the bottle, held the glass up to the light from the fireplace, took a small sip. If he was any calmer he would have fallen asleep.

It was hard to make out his face in the dim light. I could see he was very thin, balding on top, with a thick pelt of dark hair around the sides of his head. Heavy eyebrows jutted from his skull, hooding his eyes. The face was wide at the top, narrowing down to a small chin—a triangular shape. His lips were thin—his fingers long and tapered, a faint sheen of clear polish on the nails.

"Now," he said, taking a sip from his glass, "how may I help you, Mr. . . . ?"

"I'm looking for a picture," I told him, ignoring the request for my name. "A picture of a kid."

"And you think I have this picture?" he asked, his heavy eyebrows lifting.

I shrugged. I should be so lucky. "Not necessarily. But I hope you can tell me about that kind of thing in general. Give me an idea where to look."

"I see. Tell me about this picture."

"A picture of a kid. Little chubby blond-haired boy. About six years old."

The man sat behind his desk, patiently waiting. I hadn't told him enough.

"A sex picture," I said.

"Um . . ." he mumbled. "Not such an unusual picture. Little boys in love do things like that."

Something burned inside my chest. I felt the Mole's eyes on me, got it under control, took another drag on the cigarette. "Who would have a picture like that?"

"Oh, just about *anyone*. It all depends on *why* the picture was taken."

"Why?"

The man made a tent of his fingers, his English accent making him sound like a teacher. "If the picture was taken by his mentor, then it wouldn't be circulated commercially, you understand?"

"His mentor?"

"A mentor, sir, is one who teaches you, guides you through life. Helps you with problems . . . that kind of thing."

I just looked at him, picturing a little dot of cancer inside his chest, keeping my hands still. I raised my own eyebrows—a question.

"Men who love boys are very special," the man said, his voice reverent. "As are the boys who love them. It is a most unique and special relationship. And very little understood by society."

"Tell me," I said, my voice flat.

"When a boy has a sexual preference for men, he is at grave risk. The world will not understand him—many doors will be closed to him. It is the task of a dedicated mentor to bring the tiny bud to full flower. To help nourish the growth of the boy into manhood."

"By taking pictures of the kid having sex?"

"Do not be so quick to judge, my friend. A true mentor would not take such a picture for commercial purposes, as I said before. The pictures are taken to preserve a unique and beautiful moment. Children grow up," he said, his voice laced with regret for the inevitable, "they lose their youth. Would not a loving parent take pictures of his child, to look upon in later years?"

I didn't answer him—I didn't know what loving parents did. Mine took a lot of pictures of me—they're called mug shots.

"It's capturing a moment in time," the man said. "It's a way of keeping perfect times always with you, even when the person is gone."

"You mean people . . . people like you . . . just want to *keep* the pictures? Not sell them or anything."

"People like me . . ." the man mused. "Do you know anything about 'people like me'?"

"No," I said. The deal was I couldn't hurt him—nobody said I had to tell him the truth.

"I am a pedophile," the man said. The same way an immigrant would one day say he was a citizen, pride and wonder at being so privileged blending in his voice. "My sexual orientation is toward children—young boys."

I watched him, waiting for the rest.

"I am *not* a 'child molester,' I am not a pervert. What I do is technically against your laws . . . as those laws now stand. But my relationship with my boys is pure and sweet. . . . I love boys who love me. Is anything wrong with that?"

I had no answer for him, so I lit another cigarette.

"Perhaps you think it's simple," he said, his thin mouth twisted in contempt for my lack of understanding. "I love boys—you probably assume I'm a homosexual, don't you?"

"No, I don't," I assured him. It was the truth—homosexuals were grown men who had sex with other grown men; some of them were standup guys, some of them were scumbags. Like the rest of us. This freak wasn't like the rest of us.

He watched my face, looking for a clue. "You believe my preferences to be unique? Let me say this to you: some of the highest-placed men in this city share my beliefs. Indeed, were it not for my knowledge of such things—of powerful men with powerful drive-forces in their lives—I would not have the protection of you people," he said, nodding his head in the Mole's direction.

The Mole looked straight at him, expressionless.

"Any boy I love . . . any boy who returns that love . . . benefits in ways you cannot understand. He grows to youth and then to manhood under my wing, if you will. He is educated, both intellectually and spiritually. Prepared for the world at large. To such a boy, I am a life-changing force, do you understand?"

"Yes," I said. It wasn't a lie this time.

"And I would . . . I *have* taken pictures of my boys. It gives us both pleasure in later years to look at this icon to our love, as it once was. A boy is a boy for such a short time," he said, sadness in his voice.

"And you wouldn't sell these pictures?"

"Certainly not. I have no need of money, but that is not the point. It would cheapen the love . . . almost immeasurably so. It would be a violation of the relationship . . . something I would never do."

"So nobody would ever see the pictures you have?" I asked him.

"Nobody outside my circle," he replied. "On some rare occasion, I might exchange pictures of my boys with others who share my preferences. But never for money."

"You mean you'd trade pictures? Like baseball cards?"

The man's eyes hooded again. "You have a crude way of putting things, sir. I know you do not mean to be offensive. . . ."

I nodded my head in agreement. I didn't want him to stop talking. The Mole's head was buried in his papers, but I could feel him telling me to watch my step.

"My boys *enjoy* knowing they give me pleasure. And it gives me pleasure to show their love for me to other men who believe as I do." He took another sip of his drink. "To be sure, there may be an element of egotism in exchanging photographs with others . . . I *am* proud of my success. But—and I'm sure you understand—one must be very discreet at all times."

I understood that all right . . . gave him another nod of agreement.

"There *are* those who produce pictures of children for purely commercial purposes. Not those who share my loves . . . my life style, if you will. But no true lover of boys would buy such pictures. They are so impersonal, so tasteless. One knows nothing of the boy in such a picture . . . not his name, his age, his little hobbies. Commercial photographs are so . . . *anonymous*. Sex is only a component of love. One brick in a foundation. Do you understand this?"

"I understand," I told him. It was true that the devil could quote the Scriptures, as the Prof was always saying. "Would a person ever destroy his pictures . . . like if he was afraid there was a search warrant coming down or something?"

"A true pedophile would never do that, my friend. I can assure you that, if the police were battering down my door at this very instant, I would not throw my memories into that fireplace."

"But the pictures are evidence. . . ."

"Yes. Evidence of *love*."

"People get convicted with evidence of love," I told him.

A smile played around his lips. "Prison is something we face all the time. A true believer in our way of life accepts this. Simply because something is against the law does not mean it is morally wrong."

"It's worth going to prison for?" I asked him.

"It's worth *anything*," he said.

"The people who . . . exchange . . . pictures of boys. You'd know how to get in touch with them?"

"We have a network," the man said. "A limited one, of course. You see the computer?" he asked, nodding his head toward the screen.

I nodded.

"The device next to it, with the telephone? It's called a modem. It's really quite complicated," the man said, "but we have something called an electronic bulletin board. You dial up the network, punch in the codes, and we can talk to each other without revealing our names."

I gave him a blank look.

"As I said, it's really quite complicated," he said smugly. I could feel the Mole's sneer clear across the room.

"Can you show me?" I asked.

"Very well," he sighed. He got up from behind the desk, bringing his glass with him. The man seated himself before the computer. He took the phone off the hook and placed it face down into a plastic bed. He punched some numbers into a keypad and waited impatiently, tapping his long fingers on the console. When the screen cleared, he rapidly tapped something on the keyboard—his password. "Greetings from Santa" came up on the screen in response, black letters against a white background.

"Santa is one of us," the man said, by way of explanation.

He typed in "Have you any new presents for us?" The man hit another key and his message disappeared.

In another minute, the screen blinked and a message from Santa came up. "Seven bags full," said the screen.

"His new boy is seven years old," said the man. "Are you following this?"

"Yes," I told him. Santa Claus.

The man went back to the screen. "This is Tutor. Do you think it's too early in the year to think about exchanging gifts?"

"Not gifts of love," came back the answer.

The man looked over his shoulder at me. I nodded again. Clear enough.

"Later," the man typed into the screen. He pushed a button and the screen cleared once more. He returned to his seat behind the desk. "Anything else?" he asked.

"If the boy's picture . . . the one I want . . . was taken for sale . . . not by a pedophile . . . I couldn't find it?"

"Not in a million years," the man said. "The commercial pictures . . . they sell them to just *anybody*. Besides, those pictures are not true originals, you see? They make hundreds and hundreds of copies. The only way to find an original is if it was in a private collection."

"Say I didn't give a damn if the picture was an original, okay? If I showed you a picture of the boy, would you ask around . . . see if you could find the picture I'm looking for?"

"No," he said. "I would never betray the trust of my friends." He looked at the Mole for reassurance. The Mole looked back, giving nothing away.

"And you don't deal with any of the commercial outlets?"

"Certainly not," he sniffed.

This freak couldn't help me. "I understand," I said, getting up to leave.

The man looked at me levelly. "You may show yourselves out."

The Mole lumbered to his feet, standing in the doorway to make sure I went out first.

"One more thing," the man said to me. "I sincerely hope you learned something here. I hope you learned some tolerance for our reality. Some respect for our love. I trust we can find *some* basis for agreement."

I didn't move, willing my hands not to clench into fists.

"I am a believer," the man said, "and I am ready to die for my beliefs."

"There's our basis for agreement," I told him, and turned my back to follow the Mole down the stairs.

71

I stopped at a pay phone off the Drive to call Strega—tell her I would need the boy for the day after tomorrow. Her line was busy. I lit a smoke, took a couple of drags, and dialed her number again. She picked up on the first ring.

"Yes," she breathed into the receiver, her voice as hard and seamless as her body.

"It's me," I said. "Thursday afternoon, okay? Like we agreed? Bring him to the parking lot across from the courthouse in Manhattan, where we met the first time."

"What time?"

"Four o'clock. If the lot's too crowded, I'll be standing in front of the Family Court. The dark-gray building on Lafayette. You know what I'm talking about?"

"I'll find it."

"Make sure he understands that it's okay to be with me."

"He'll be all right," she said, in a mechanical tone.

"See you then," I said, getting ready to put the receiver back in its cradle.

"That's for then," Strega said. "What about tonight?"

"It's too soon. I need time to set this up."

"What about me?"

"What *about* you?"

"I'm here by myself tonight. All alone with myself. You want to come over and talk to me?"

"I can't come over. . . . I'm working."

"Maybe you just want to *come*," she whispered into the phone, playing with the last word. I could see the sneer on her painted lips, glowing in a dark room.

"Some other time," I told her.

"You can never be sure," said Strega. I heard the phone slam down at her end.

I headed back to the office, wondering where her sacred child was all the time.

72

I SPENT the next day taking care of business. American Express was threatening to sever the line of credit I maintain in several names unless they got some prompt payments. There's only one way to respond to such a legitimate request—I typed out some new applications, checking my list to make sure I didn't duplicate any of the old names. Then I placed some ads—my new mail-order company was offering the latest version of the Navy Seal Survival Knife for only twenty-five bucks. No CODs. My company doesn't take checks either—too many dishonest people out there. I checked my file of birth certificates for people who died within a year of their birth. I had some of them apply for Social Security numbers, others for driver's licenses. When I got back the paper, I'd move it into various productive activities—passports, disability payments, unemployment benefits. As long as you don't get too greedy, it goes on forever.

Finally, I checked my rent roll. I have a few apartments around the city—when a tenant in a rent-controlled building dies, the super calls me, money changes hands, and I'm the new tenant. Then I sublet the apartments to yuppies happy to pay several times the base rent, positive they're beating the system. Michelle works the phones for me. I split the rent each month with the super and everybody's happy. Sooner or later the landlord finds out what's going down and moves to evict the tenant. Then the yuppies are on their own. I don't collect any more rent from them. I don't return their security deposits either.

I took Pansy down to the piers on the Hudson, working her off-leash obedience to keep her tuned. Then I took her with me to Pop's poolroom, letting her watch in baleful disapproval as I dropped fifty bucks at the table in the back. The one right under the "No Gambling" sign.

Killing time. It's a lot easier when you're not in a cell.

73

At FOUR o'clock the next afternoon, I parked the Lincoln in the courthouse lot. Immaculata was next to me on the front seat, Max lying down in the back, hands clasped behind his head, staring at nothing.

"You want to go over it one more time?" I asked Mac.

"It's not necessary, Burke. I know what you want. But it's like I told you—disclosures often come slowly. I can't promise you the child will tell me everything on a first interview."

"How long does it take?"

"It depends on the child . . . and the extent of the trauma. Some children never tell the whole thing."

"Can't you put some pressure on him?"

Mac's eyes narrowed. "Of course I could do that. But I won't. That's not the way we work. This first interview—the one where we validate that the child has been sexually abused—it's not just to gain information—it's part of a process. The real goal is to treat the child."

"Yeah, okay," I said, lighting a cigarette.

"That is what we agreed," Mac said, tapping her long nails on the dash. She wasn't going to discuss it anymore.

"You told Max what he has to do?" I asked her.

Immaculata smiled. "He knew," she said.

The courthouse parking lot doesn't discriminate. Porsches stood next to Chevies—a limo took two spaces. So did a gypsy cab.

A Spanish guy walked by my open window. "Smoke?" he asked, looking past me. I didn't reply and he moved on, working the parking lot. If you had the cash, you could buy just about anything around the courthouse.

Immaculata and I got out of the Lincoln and walked over to the Family Court. A steady stream of humans walked out of the revolving doors—a fat Puerto Rican woman with tired eyes came out with a kid who looked about twelve years old, sporting a gang jacket and a black beret on his head. "You hear what the judge told you?" she said. "Fuck the judge," the boy replied, neatly dodging her feeble attempt to slap him, smiling a kid's smile. A guy dressed in a phone-company uniform was pulling at his lawyer's arm, mumbling something about "another goddamned adjournment." The lawyer shrugged. Another guy stormed out the front, a woman trailing him by a couple of feet, tentatively reaching out to touch his arm. He was slamming a clenched fist in his palm over and over, looking down.

I was watching for Strega's little BMW, so I didn't pay any attention to the beige Mercedes cruising back and forth through the parking lot until I heard the door slam. She was standing across the street, a black kerchief on her head, wearing a full-length black coat. She looked about sixteen years old. Her arms were extended to each side, a child holding each hand. A boy and a girl. She bent to say something to the little girl. The child waved merrily at me and they started to cross.

It wasn't that cold on the streets, but Strega's cheeks were flushed and glowing. "Hi!" she called out in a voice I hadn't heard before, holding out a gloved hand to me. I took it—she squeezed down hard.

"This is Scotty," she said, pulling a round-faced little blond boy close to her side. "And this is my Mia." She smiled. The little girl was wearing a black coat and scarf like her mother. Flaming red hair peeked out, a halo for a happy little face.

"What's your name?" she asked me.

"Burke," I told her.

"That's a funny name," she said, still smiling.

"So is Mia," I replied.

"It's a *special* name," the little girl said, a trace of a pout on her lips.

"It's a lovely name," said Immaculata, stepping forward.

"This is my friend, Immaculata," I told them all, spreading my hands to introduce her.

Immaculata gracefully dropped to her haunches, her eyes level with the children's faces.

"Hi, Scotty. Hi, Mia," she said to them, holding out her hands. Mia took her hand right away, babbling on like they were old friends. Scotty hung back. "It's okay," said Strega. He came slowly to Immaculata. "You smell good," he said.

Strega's eyes lashed at me. "This is your *friend*?"

"Immaculata is going to work with Scotty. Like we agreed," I said, nothing else in my voice.

Her big eyes never shifted. "I'm trusting you," she said.

I met her gaze. Our faces were a hundred miles above Immaculata and the children. "You got any time problems?"

"Just tell me where to meet you."

"How about right back here. About seven-thirty, eight o'clock?"

"Whatever you say."

I lit a cigarette while Strega patted Scotty on the head, telling him he was going with me and Immaculata and that she'd meet him later with Mia. They'd all go to McDonald's and then for ice cream.

"Okay, Zia Peppina," the boy said, holding Immaculata's hand. His eyes were still cloudy with worry but he was going to stand up.

"Say your name again," Mia asked Immaculata.

"It is Im-mac-u-lata," she said, "but my friends call me Mac."

"That's easier," said Mia.

"It is always easier to be friends," Mac told her gravely.

"I know," said the child.

It was time to go. "It was a pleasure to meet you," Strega said to Immaculata.

"And to meet you as well," Mac told her, bowing slightly. "You have a beautiful and charming daughter."

Strega's eyes lit up at this. She bowed back to Immaculata before she realized what she was doing. Mac had that effect on people.

"Let's go, Scotty!" Immaculata said, taking the boy's hand and starting across the street to the Lincoln.

"Are you Mommy's friend?" Mia asked me.

"What did your mother tell you?" I replied.

"She said you were."

"Does your mother ever lie to you?"

"Oh, no," said the child, her mouth rounded in an O of surprise.

"Then you know," I told her. I held out my hand to Strega again.

She smiled at me, trying to crush my fingers into Jell-O. "Bye-bye," she said, turning her back on me, Mia in tow.

I lit a cigarette, watching the two little girls in their black coats cross the street to their Mercedes. Then I started across myself.

74

WHEN I GOT to the Lincoln, Scotty was standing on the front seat looking at Max seated in the back. "Do it again!" he yelled, clapping his chubby little hands.

"Do *what* again?" I asked him, sliding behind the wheel.

"Max is a *protector*," Scotty said. "He's here to make me safe."

"That's right," I told him, watching Immaculata nod in approval.

"Max is the strongest man in the whole world!" Scotty practically shouted at me. "Do it again. *Please!*" he shouted at Max. I don't know what kind of father Max might be, but he sure as hell wouldn't get disturbed by the noise kids make.

Scotty was waving an old iron horseshoe in one hand. Max reached over the seat and took it from him. The Mongol held one end in each hand, breathed deeply through his nose with a clean, whistling sound, and pulled the horseshoe apart until it was just a straight piece of metal. He bowed his head, handed it back to the child.

"See?" Scotty asked.

"That's amazing," I told him.

"Max could lift this whole *car* if he wanted to, couldn't you, Max?" he said.

Max pressed his fingertips together, shooting his biceps full of the blood. The muscles leaped in his arms, more than a match for the thin casing of skin around them. Max pulled his hands to his chest, as if he was rocking a baby. He smiled. Then he flexed a bicep in a body-builder's pose, a vain look on his face. He shook his head "no."

"What is he saying?" Scott asked Immaculata.

"He is saying that great strength is only for protecting people, not for showing off."

"Oh." The kid thought for a minute. "Then why did he bend the horseshoe?" Whatever else they had done to Scotty, they hadn't made him stupid.

"Remember I told you that Max would be your protector?" Immaculata said, and watched the boy's solemn nod. "Well, I had to show you that Max was a *good* protector. We are friends, you and me. But you shouldn't trust new friends until they prove they are telling you the truth. Isn't that right?"

"Yes . . ." he said, a sad look on his face.

"I know," Immaculata said, patting his shoulders. "You are safe now. We're going to make it all better. Okay?"

The boy nodded dubiously. Max put his huge, scarred hand on the boy's shoulder. Just letting it lay there. And Scotty smiled as we drove through the city to the place on Broadway where we'd make it all better.

75

SAFE WAS in the Village, not far from the courthouse. I found a parking spot a few doors down and we all got out together, Immaculata leading the way, holding Scotty's hand. A tall black man was seated at a desk just inside the double glass doors. He got to his feet when he saw Max and me come in behind Immaculata. "They're with me," she said, smiling. The black guy sat down again.

We walked up a long flight of stairs to what must have been a factory loft years ago. A huge room, maybe forty by a hundred feet. Gym mats in the corner. A bunch of little kids working out, practicing some form of karate, screaming their lungs out with every move. Even younger kids were playing in a sandbox at one end of the room. Some were doing finger painting. One little boy was knitting something. It seemed like hundreds of kids, all hyperactive. Sounded like a happy subway tunnel.

A young woman detached herself from one of the groups of kids and walked over to us. She was maybe five feet tall with short dark hair flying around her face as she came over. Another pretty Italian lady— the other side of Strega's coin.

"Boss lady," Immaculata whispered to me. "Lily."

"Hi, Mac," the woman said. "And you must be Scotty," she said to the boy, coming down on her haunches the way Immaculata had in front of the Family Court. "My name is Lily," she said, holding out both hands. Scotty took her hands, but his eyes were riveted to the other kids. "You can play with the other kids later," Lily said, reading his mind. "First we're going to go to a special playroom. You have a *reservation*." She made it like a big deal, and Scotty responded, feeling important.

She took Scotty by one hand. Immaculata took the other. On the way down the hall to the back office the two women lifted Scotty off his feet, swinging their arms. The kid giggled like he'd found heaven.

We turned into a small room stuffed full of kids' stuff—toy animals, a three-panel screen with puppies playing on its surface, dolls, coloring books. All the furniture was child-size.

"This is where you and Immaculata get to talk," Lily told Scotty.

"About the bad things?" he asked.

"If you want to, Scotty. We don't make you do anything you don't want to here, okay?"

He just nodded, subdued now.

"You go inside with Immaculata, and we'll all wait for you out here, okay?"

"Max too!" the boy said, tugging the Mongol forward.

Max picked the boy up by his belt and tossed him in the air. Scotty screamed in delight, never doubting for a minute that Max would catch him. Max caught the boy in his arms and carried him inside. Immaculata bowed to Lily and me and followed, closing the door behind her.

There was a long window in one wall. I could see the three of them inside. Scotty was sitting on Max's lap, Immaculata talking to him.

"One-way glass?" I asked Lily.

"Yes," she said. "We have graduate students observing all the time."

"You videotape the interviews?"

"We don't have the facilities to conceal the cameras here. And many of our children are phobic for video. You understand?"

"Sure," I told her. Kids who had been stars in porno movies could freak out if they saw a camera.

The boy was drawing something, holding the picture up for Immaculata and Max to see every couple of seconds.

"My name is Burke," I told her.

"I know who you are," she said, mixed feelings running through her words.

"You have a problem with me?"

She gave it some thought, looking directly into my eyes. "No . . . not a problem. In fact, a couple of our older girls said you pulled them off the streets. And McGowan says you're okay too."

"So?"

"Mr. Burke, when we work with children at SAFE we don't edit their disclosures."

I stood there, watching Scotty make word pictures with his hands for Max. Max's arms were folded on his chest, his eyes slitted in concentration. I was waiting for this woman to tell me what her beef was.

"You know a girl named Babette?"

I nodded. I was in a mess a few months ago and she ended up going off with McGowan. I guess she landed at SAFE. It was fucking sure she couldn't go back to the stepfather who paid me to find her.

"In group one day Babette told us how she happened to get free of her pimp," Lily said. "She said you shot the man."

"I thought he was reaching for a gun," I said lamely.

"Babette said your gun didn't make any noise," Lily told me, eyes level.

I didn't say anything. If I hadn't had the silencer, it might have been some uniformed cop coming to that hotel room instead of McGowan. Shooting a pimp should only be a petty misdemeanor anyway—like hunting without a license.

"Don't worry," she said. "Nobody's going to testify against you."

"I'm not worried," I told her. The Prof had visited the pimp in the hospital—given him the word.

"We don't allow guns at SAFE," Lily said, watching me.

"You want to search me," I grinned at her, opening my coat.

"No. I want your word."

"You got it."

We both turned back to the window. Scotty had his hands on his hips and was shouting something at Immaculata. Suddenly he struck out; his little fist pounded on her shoulder. Max didn't move.

"It's okay," Lily said. "It's probably a re-enactment."

I looked a question at her. "When the child relives the experience . . . some of them find it easier than talking about it at first. Or maybe he's already past it . . . maybe he told the secret. . . . Some of our kids fly into a rage when the truth is out . . . they have so much anger."

"So why's he hitting on Immaculata?"

"We encourage them to do it. At first. Then they progress to the self-defense classes. It all has to come out—first the secrets, then the anger."

"The secret is what happened to them—what people did to them?"

"No. That's what they call the 'bad stuff' or the 'scary stuff.' The secret is that the offender told them never to tell anybody about what happened. They usually make it so that if the child tells, something horrible will happen."

"To the kid?"

"Usually not. To their parent, or a puppy . . . even to some character on TV the child loves."

"The kid believes it?" I asked. When I was Scotty's age, I didn't believe anything.

"Of course. The offender is all-powerful. He can do anything. And the secret is helped by the guilt too."

"Why should a kid feel guilty if somebody did that to him?"

"Because they *like* some of it . . . it arouses new feelings in them. And, for some of them, they believe the person who is doing these things actually loves them. A parent will tell a child that if the secret comes out the parent may go to jail . . . and it will be the child's fault. You see?"

"Yeah, they make the kid take the weight."

Scotty was crying, his face buried in his hands. Immaculata was bending over him, talking to him, patting his back.

"You know a D.A. named Wolfe? With the City-Wide Special Victims Bureau?"

"Sure," said Lily. "She's the best. I do a lot of work for her office."

"You think you might be willing to put in a good word for me?"

"Are you looking for a job as an investigator?"

"No. I just want to talk with her about this case, maybe get some help. And I don't know too many people on her side of the fence."

"I could tell her what I know about you—that's all."

"Hey!" I said. "I brought the kid out safely, didn't I?"

"Yes, you did. Your methods left a bit to be desired, didn't they?"

"I don't know," I told her. "Why don't you ask Babette?"

Lily smiled. "I'll talk to Wolfe," she said, and we shook hands.

Scotty wasn't crying anymore. His tear-streaked face was turned to Max, his little hands flying. Max took some picture from Scotty's hands— it looked like crayon scribbles to me. Then he pulled the round wooden top off one of the tables, held it so the edge was facing the floor, and wedged it into a corner of the room. Max tested it with his hands to be sure it was solid. He wet his thumb and pasted the picture against the round surface. He bowed to Scotty, spun his wrists so the palms were facing outward, and flicked his fingers to his side. Telling them to stand back.

Lily was standing next to me at the window. "I never saw this one before," she said.

Max glided forward onto his left foot, twisting as it hit the ground. His right foot came around in a blur, shattering the wooden table like it was glass. He walked to the corner, pulled Scotty's drawing out of the wreckage, and turned to face the boy. Max tore the picture in half, throwing a piece to each side like it was garbage. The little boy's smile was wider than his face.

The door opened. Max stepped out first. He rubbed two fingers and a thumb together, pointing at me. "How much for the table?" I asked Lily.

"It's on the house," she said, a smile on her face too.

Immaculata came out with Scotty holding her hand. "I got the bad stuff out," he told Lily proudly.

"That's wonderful!" she said. "Would you like to play with the other children outside while we talk?"

"Can Max come?" Scotty asked.

Nobody answered him. "Come *on*, Max," he said, tugging at the Mongol's hand.

Immaculata nodded almost imperceptibly. Max and Scotty walked down the hall together to play.

76

LILY TOOK us to her office, at the end of the corridor. It looked like a kid's playroom except for the computer screen on the desk. I looked at the keyboard—there was no lock-out device. "How do you keep someone from getting into your records?" I asked her.

She laughed, tapping some keys. "Want to play a fast game of Zork before we get down to business?" The screen had some kind of mazes-and-monsters game on it.

"That's all you have it for?"

"Sure," she said, looking at Immaculata as if I was an idiot.

I lit a cigarette, looking around for an ashtray. "Use this," Lily said, handing me an empty water glass.

Immaculata sat behind the desk; Lily perched on a corner. I stood against the wall and listened.

"Scotty was going to a day-care center every day after school. He'd get there around one in the afternoon and his mother would pick him up when she got out of work. Around six o'clock. One day a woman came to the center. Scotty said she was an 'old lady,' but that could mean anyone older than his mother. She had a van and a driver—a big, fat man with a beard. She told the kids she was going to take them to see the clowns and who wanted to go? Scotty went with some other kids. It took what he said was 'a long, long time' to get there. A big house with a high fence around it. There was a clown there—a big, fat clown, like the driver. His face was all made up like a clown, and he had presents for all the kids. The clown and the old lady took Scotty out of the group where he was playing with the other kids. They took him into the basement, where they had a puppy. They told him he could have the puppy if he would be a 'good little scout.'

"To be a good scout you have to take your pants off. They let him keep his shirt on. It was red and black stripes. He has it in his closet at home," Mac said, answering one of the questions I'd told her to ask.

"The clown took off his pants too. His penis was very large. It scared the boy. They asked him if he wanted ice cream. They rubbed some on the clown's penis and told Scotty to lick it off. He started to cry. The old lady told him if he didn't do what he was told, they would hurt the puppy. He still refused. The clown strangled the puppy in front of him. Scotty didn't want to watch but he had to. He has bad dreams about the puppy. He's always scared."

The cigarette burned into my fingers. I threw it on the floor, stepped on it. Immaculata's face was closed—a soldier doing her job.

"The man put his penis in Scotty's mouth—told him to suck very hard. The woman took a picture with a Polaroid and a flash. White stuff came out. Scotty cried. The old woman told him if he ever told anyone about this his mother would get very sick and die. They took him back upstairs and put him into the van with the other kids. The other kids all had a great time."

"How does he know it was a Polaroid?" I asked.

"He doesn't know the name, but he said a camera where the picture comes out the front."

"Did he see the picture?"

"I think so. At least the fact that there *was* a picture." She took a breath. "Scotty never told anybody—he was scared something would happen. But his mother took him to a therapist, and he told the therapist about bad dreams. That's all. He was afraid of the therapist—he had a beard like the big, fat clown.

"Later he told some of it to the redheaded woman who brought him to the parking lot today—he calls her 'Zia.' He told her that the old lady came to the day-care center with a big, strong man who had a leather bag. The man took money from the leather bag and gave it to the lady who runs the day-care center. And there was some strange mark on the big man's hand. That's it," she said.

"He's going to need help with the dreams," Lily said.

"I know," Immaculata replied.

"He's not still afraid of anything happening to his mother?" I asked her.

"No," she said, smiling faintly, "Max told Scotty he would guard his mother."

"What was that bit with the table, Mac?" Lily wanted to know.

"Scotty drew a picture of the big, fat clown. Max told him he was going to find the clown and break him in little pieces. He was showing Scotty what he meant."

I lit another cigarette. "Does he have any idea at all where the big house is? You think he could find it if we went over the route?"

"Not a chance," Mac said. "He wasn't paying attention on the drive out there—and he was too scared on the way back to the center."

"If this woman is running a big operation, maybe Wolfe would know about her," I said, looking at Lily.

"I'll talk to her," Lily replied.

I felt a tap on my shoulder. Max. He held one hand to his eye, tapped his finger against the hand. Taking a picture. He pointed at me, made binoculars of his fists around his eyes.

"Yeah, I'm looking for that picture," I told him.

Max tapped his chest, dealing himself in.

We all left the office together to pick up the boy.

77

SCOTTY WAS in the middle of a group of kids, all trying to push a giant beach ball in different directions. "We have to go?" he asked Immaculata. Not so happy about it.

"We'll come back, Scotty. And we'll play some more and talk some more, okay?"

"And Max too?" the kid demanded.

Immaculata took his hand. "Max has to work sometimes, Scotty. But he's never too far away. And his work is very important."

"Like watching Mommy?"

"Yes, like that. Okay?"

Scotty smiled. Max smiled too—the way an undertaker does. The boy waved goodbye to his new friends. Lily gave him a hug. And we were out the door.

Scotty was cheerful on the drive back. It was almost eight by the time I pulled up right in front of the Family Court. The Mercedes was sitting there, smoke coming from its exhaust. The driver's door popped open and Strega climbed out, Mia in tow. I got out too, halfway between the cars.

"I have to talk to you for a minute," I said.

"Mia, take Scotty and wait in the car, okay, sweetheart? Mommy will be there soon."

The little girl looked at me. "You're not handsome," she said solemnly. "My daddy is very handsome."

"Good," I said.

"In the car, Mia," Strega told her. She took Scotty's hand and went off. Immaculata stayed in the Lincoln, looking straight ahead.

"What happened?" the redhead asked.

"It went well," I told her, picking my words carefully. "We got a lot of information. But the more he gets comfortable with these people, the more we find out, understand? He needs to come back, like once a week for the next few weeks at least."

"Not for therapy?" she asked, a warning note in her voice.

"For information," I told her, lying as smoothly as the rug on that pedophile's floor. "If you want the picture . . . ?"

"You got it," she snapped. "I want to talk to her"—pointing to the car.

I waved Immaculata over—no point in Strega seeing Max.

They didn't greet each other this time. "Is Scotty going to be all right?" Strega asked.

"In time, yes. He had an ugly experience. It's a process. You *are* going to bring him back?"

"Once a week, right?"

"Yes." Immaculata watched Strega's face, making up her mind about something. "You should not attempt to debrief this child," she said, her voice clear as crystal and just as hard.

"Debrief?"

"Ask him what he said, what we talked about. He will not want to do this now. In his own time, it will come. If you put pressure on the child now, you will set back his progress, yes?"

"If you say so," said Strega.

"I *do* say so. It is very important. Scotty is a strong child, but this whole thing was a severe trauma. You, as his mother . . ."

"I'm not his mother," Strega snapped.

"This is his aunt," I said to Immaculata. "Zia."

Immaculata smiled. "You must be very close with this little boy for him to have told you what he did. He loves you and he trusts you. When the time comes, we will need you to help us with the last stages of the healing. Will you do that?"

"I'll do whatever Scotty needs done," Strega said, a faint smile touching her lips. Responding to praise just like a kid.

I took Immaculata's arm to go back to our car. Strega plucked at Mac's sleeve.

"Is Burke your boyfriend?" she asked.

Immaculata smiled—a beautiful thing to see. "Good God, no," she said, and bowed to Strega.

We watched as the redhead climbed in her Mercedes and drove sedately off.

78

I LET Immaculata and Max off at the warehouse and drove back uptown looking for Michelle. She wasn't working any of her usual stands. The Prof was off the streets too. Like a hard wind was coming down and they had enough sense to get out of the way.

I thought about catching some of the later races up in Yonkers, but the thought slid by. The digital clock on the Lincoln's dash said it was ten-fifteen—a couple of hours gone. I thought about Flood—like biting into your own lip to make sure your teeth are working. When I started to think about calling Strega, I realized I had to talk to someone.

Dr. Pablo Cintrone's clinic would be open until at least midnight. Pablo is a Harvard-educated psychiatrist, a Puerto Rican who battled his way through the stone walls of prejudice circling the miserable slum that liberals love to call *el barrio*. He is a man without illusions—the pieces of paper he got from Harvard would fly him out of the neighborhood, but he'd have to make the trip alone. The people in his community call him *"el doctor"* in reverent tones. And if they know he runs an organization called Una Gente Libre they don't discuss it with the law.

Una Gente Libre—A Free People—a very low-profile group as terrorists go. They didn't pull armored-car robberies, no bank jobs, no bullshit "communiqués" to the newspapers. UGL wasn't interested in symbolic bombings or ego politics either. What they did best was take people out—simple, direct homicides—no "trademark" assassinations, no revolutionary slogans left at the scene. Somehow, people always knew when it was a UGL hit, though the *federales* were never sure. They knew the group existed, but they could never get inside. Without informants, they couldn't catch Jesse James if he was still doing trains on horseback.

A few years ago a suspected UGL triggerman was busted for blowing away a dope dealer who took his business too near an elementary school. The *federales* offered him pure immunity—a walkaway if he'd testify about the organization. No sale.

The gunman's trial was no revolutionary showcase—very straight-forward. He pleaded "not guilty," claimed the dealer had a gun too and was beaten to the draw. Pablo was just one of a dozen character witnesses, all neatly dressed, solid citizens. No revolutionary slogans, no picketing, no clenched fists in the air.

The defense attorney was good—a hard piece of work. A heavy-set, bearded guy from midtown, he pounded away at what a slimeball the dead dealer had been, never compromising, fighting the prosecutor and the judge every step of the way. The gunman was tried for murder—the jury was out three days and finally came back with manslaughter. The judge gave the gunman five to fifteen.

Everybody walked over to congratulate the defense attorney. He'd done a hell of a job to pull this one out—if the gunman fell for murder, he was looking at twenty-five to life. The lawyer sat at the counsel table, tears in his eyes, bitter that he hadn't won the whole thing. Not too many lawyers like that left, and they're worth whatever they cost.

The gunman went upstate and did some *good* time—a man of respect. He never had a blank visiting day, his commissary account was always full to the brim. And his wife hit *bolita*—the Spanish numbers game—for a big piece of change. Just lucky, I guess, but it took good care of his family while he was down.

When he hit the bricks, they threw a block party for him that lasted four days. He's still on parole, a driver for the ambulance service that works out of Pablo's clinic. To the cops, he's another ex-con. To his people, he's a POW returned to his home country.

If it was business, I would have called first. From a safe phone. But I just wanted to talk. I pulled the Lincoln into the empty space that's always in front of the clinic. Before I could even turn off the ignition there was a tap on the window. The glass whispered down into the door with a push of the little button. The guy tapping on the window wasn't too tall, but his width matched his height. A head the size of a basketball grew out of massive shoulders without benefit of a neck. Half his face was covered with old razor scars surrounding a glass eye—and that was his good side. The guy was ugly enough to need an exorcist.

"No parking here, *hombre*," he snarled.

"I'm here to see Pablo . . . *el doctor?*"

"Who you?"

"Burke," I said.

The monster held out his hand, palm up. I pulled the keys from the ignition and handed them over. He growled something and left.

He was back in a couple of minutes, his lips twisted in what he probably thought was a smile—his teeth were broken stumps. He jerked a thumb in a hitchhiker's gesture. I climbed out of the Lincoln. A young guy in a bright-red shirt worn outside his pants came up. The monster handed him the keys and the young guy climbed inside. They'd leave the Lincoln someplace—I could pick it up when I left. UGL's version of valet parking.

The monster gently shoved me ahead of him, guiding me through the maze of cubicles inside the clinic. A Spanish woman in a white nurse's uniform sat at the reception desk, the hard lines in her face the price of survival, not marring her beauty. The monster nodded to her as he prodded me forward, paying no attention to the activity around him. Phones rang, people yelled at each other, doors slammed. The people in the waiting room looked subdued, but not dead the way they do in the city hospitals.

Pablo's office was all the way in the rear. He was typing something on an ancient IBM when we came in. His eyes sparkled behind the round glasses he wore as he jumped to his feet to greet me. Pablo's got to be damn near as old as I am, but he looks like a young man. With his clear brown skin and neatly cropped hair he could get by any Puerto Rican mother in the world. He has four children that I know about and he's financed more abortions than Planned Parenthood.

"Hermano!" he shouted, grabbing my right hand in both of his, then embracing me in a hug.

The monster smiled again. *"Gracias, chico,"* Pablo said, and the monster threw a salute and went back outside.

"I got to talk to you, Pablito," I told my brother.

"Not business?"

"Just in my head," I said.

Pablo pointed to a couch in a corner of his office, sitting back down behind his desk.

"Tell me," he said.

79

RED NEON from the bar next door to
the clinic banked its ugly light against the window behind Pablo's desk.
It was a mark of pride for the clinic that no bars were on the windows.

"It started with a picture," I began.

Pablo looked a question at me.

"Kiddie porn," I answered.

Not all psychiatrists practice with poker faces—violence danced a
storm in Pablo's eyes.

"Yeah," I said. "Like that. A little boy, six years old. They used him
only the one time, but he knows they took the picture and it works on
his mind."

"You took him to that place downtown . . . SAFE?"

"Sure. And he's going to get better—they know what they're doing.
But it'll never really be square in the kid's mind—like they have a piece
of his soul, you know?"

Pablo nodded patiently.

"Anyway, I'm looking for this picture, right? And I come across this
freak. A collector. I figure I'll ask him what makes him tick—get a line
on who might have the picture I'm looking for."

"He spoke freely with you?"

"Oh, yeah. He's protected—they had a guard in the room with me—
I don't even know his name."

"Too bad," said Pablo.

"His time is coming," I said. "From the people who are protecting
him now. But that's not the thing—he tells me he's going to keep doing
what he does. Forever. It's what he *wants* to do. He says he loves the
kids."

"And you don't understand?"

"Do you?"

"Yes . . . but what I understand is the rationalization, not the drive.

The medical profession knows a good deal about the workings of the human body, but the study of the mind is essentially political."

I raised my eyebrows—Pablo thinks "No Parking" signs are political.

"It is true, *hermano*. We no longer treat physical diseases with leeches, but we still treat mental disorders as though they exist in a vacuum. This is not logical, but it is comforting to the citizens. If we say that mental illness is biochemical, then people believe that the correct medication is the answer to all questions."

"Like methadone?"

"Sure. You understand. Of course, heroin addiction is a product of many, many things . . . but heroin was first really introduced into this country by the United States government. After World War I, too many of our soldiers returned addicted to morphine. Heroin was the wonder drug that would make them all well again."

"It sure raised hell with the fighting gangs," I said.

"You remember the heroin monster, sweeping through our communities, turning young people into zombies? This was because the street gangs had begun to reach a kind of political awareness."

"Some political awareness," I said. "I came up in the fifties—all we ever wanted to do was keep other clubs off our turf, drink a little wine, play with the girls. Nobody even mentioned politics."

"Not then," Pablo said, "but soon after. The fighting gangs were in every part of the city. Independent units, yes? If they had ever *combined* . . ."

"Not a chance," I told him. "I don't think I ever knew a word for a black guy except 'nigger' until I was out of reform school."

"Racism is like heroin, Burke—it divides people from their true needs—it pacifies them with promises of foolishness."

I held up a hand like a traffic cop. "Hold it, brother. You're going too fast for me. What's this got to do with a baby-raper?"

"It's the same thing. Politics controls the reality which is presented to the public. Look, Freud taught that sex between children and adults was simply a fantasy—something in the minds of the children—something they imagined as a way of dealing with their own sexual feelings toward their parents. Now we know these feelings actually exist—the

Oedipus complex, for example. But just because all children have such thoughts does not mean that reports of actual incest were a fantasy. It took us a long time to learn this truth. Politically, it was better that incest be thought of as a fantasy. This meant we gave treatment to the victim, but this 'treatment' was bogus—it made the children believe a lie and doubt the reality of their own senses."

"That would make them . . ."

"Crazy. Yes, that is what it *did* do. And those children who acted crazy were displayed as proof of the fact that they were crazy to *begin* with. *Comprende?*"

"But why? Who wants to protect people who fuck their own kids?"

Pablo sighed, disgusted as always with my political ignorance. "Look at it this way. Suppose a slave were to escape from the South and make it to New York. Suppose we put him into psychotherapy—suppose we convinced him that the whole experience of slavery was nothing more than a bad dream—do you not see the political value? We would not have to confront the slave-keepers—we could continue to practice trade and commerce with them, maintain our own self-interest economically. Yes?"

"But slaves . . ." I said, groping for the clincher to prove Pablo wrong, "they'd still have the scars. . . ."

"You think an incest victim would not have scars?" he said.

I lit a cigarette, thinking of Flood and the scars she made on herself to replace the brand of a rapist—how she poured gasoline on herself over the tattoo the gang put on her, lit a match, and held on to her one friend in the world until the fire made them free. "What good would it do to trick a kid like that?" I asked.

"Children don't vote," he said.

"And Freud said there was no such thing as incest?"

"Freud did not make a conscious decision to accept the women's stories as fantasies—he lived within a political climate and he responded to it."

"But we *know* it happens."

"Now we know. But to truly *know* it then, you had to experience it."

"So if you thought the experience was all in your mind . . ."

"Yes," said Pablo, grateful that I was finally seeing the light that shone so brightly for him.

I got to my feet, pacing uncomfortably in the small room. "Forget politics for a minute," I said. "We know people do these things to kids, okay? Do we know *why?*"

Pablo tilted his head until he was gazing at the ceiling. "I will tell you everything we actually know—it won't take long. We know people have sex with children—the children of strangers and also their own. We know this has something to do with power—the power grown people have over children. In fact, sex with children is not sex as *you* would understand it, Burke. It is not, for example, the kind of adaptive mechanism which could cause a man to turn to other men when there are no women—like in prison. This is another dimension entirely. The pedophile—the one who has sex with children—he may be able to have sex with women, or with grown men. But he does not *prefer* to do this. The more intelligent the pedophile, the more skillfully he may rationalize his behavior, but the truth is really simple—he knows what he does is wrong and he does it anyway."

"I thought those freaks couldn't help themselves?"

"No! They can stop—they choose not to."

"It can't be that simple," I told him. "Who the fuck would *choose* to pass up women and force little kids to . . . ?"

"All that is within them is within you and me, my friend. If every man who felt sexual violence toward a woman acted on that feeling, New York would not be a city—it would be a graveyard."

"You mean it's not?"

"You joke when you do not understand. Just because some of the lower beasts walk our streets does not make our community into a jungle—not so long as people struggle against the beasts."

Pablo took a dark bottle down from a shelf and poured himself a glass of that jungle juice he drinks all the time. I passed up his offer with a shake of my head.

"To rehabilitation!" he said, tossing down half the glass.

"You ever try that with one of these freaks?" I asked him.

"One time. One time we did just that," he mused, his eyes somewhere else. "My people brought a man in here years ago. He had been molesting children in the neighborhood, and it was thought best to turn him over to our clinic."

"Why not the cops?"

"My people wanted justice, Burke. And they knew the man would probably never be prosecuted. His victims were not important."

"What did they expect *you* to do?"

"The man agreed to go into treatment with us. He made a specific contract that he would cease his activity while we tried to do something about his behavior."

"Behavior?"

"Only his *acts* were a danger to our community—his motivations are so deep inside him that it would take years of treatment for them to surface. And even then we could probably do nothing about them. We asked only that he stop."

"Did he?"

"No. We cannot know why he made his choice—what forces were within him. We can only assume that he tried to walk the line. One day he slipped and fell."

"What did you do then?"

"Nothing. At that point, it became a matter for the police."

"I thought you said the cops couldn't do anything."

"They could in this case, *compadre*. When he slipped and fell for the last time, he was on a rooftop." Pablo held his glass in a silent toast to the only rehabilitation that really works.

We sat in silence for a minute—each waiting for the other. Pablo took another sip of the jungle juice. "*Hermano*, in truth we have been talking about crime, not about psychiatry. And you know more about the behavior of such people than I do. Many times we have called upon you to predict the actions of such evil people—our paths originally crossed for that very reason, yes?"

I nodded—it was the truth.

"And you have become my brother, *verdad*? Do you think I call a man my brother and do not understand him?"

"No—I know you understand."

"Then maybe you should tell me why you have come to talk with me," Pablo said.

I took a last drag on my cigarette, feeling the cold wind eddying in the corners of his office, stirring the dust, making its own howling only I could hear. And I started to tell him about Strega.

80

I TOLD HIM everything. It didn't take as long as I'd thought it would—maybe there wasn't so much to tell. Pablo took off his glasses, carefully rubbed them on the lapel of his white coat, waiting to be sure I was finished.

"What is so puzzling to you, my friend? A person with a task to do uses the weapons he has, no? This woman wants you to do something— she obviously believes the money is not strong enough to bind you to her will. The sex is nothing more than a chain she tosses over your neck— a leash you put on a dangerous dog."

"It doesn't work like that. If she was working me to make sure I did the job, the sex would be a *promise*, right? A reward. Something to look forward to when the job was done."

"A promise, then? Not a performance?"

"It always *seems* like a promise . . . but it's not."

"The woman promises nothing?"

"Nothing."

Pablo looked at the ceiling, thinking it through. "She has already paid you some of the money, yes? If you took the money and didn't do the job . . . what could she do?"

"Nothing. Maybe she thinks she could, but . . . nothing."

Pablo shrugged. "I cannot see what makes this so difficult for you. Perhaps the woman is just covering her bets—making sure your nose is open—that you keep coming back for more. Remember when we were young men . . . how much we would risk for a night of love with a woman?"

"I'm not young anymore," I said. I couldn't remember ever being that young.

"Listen to me, Burke. It is not reality which controls our lives, it is the perception of that reality."

"More politics?"

"You cannot dismiss truth by mocking it," Pablo said, his voice hardening. "So long as my people believe their life is acceptable, then it *is* acceptable. My people live on a slave island, but their chains are food stamps and welfare programs."

"This is getting away from me," I told him.

"Because you are ignoring your senses—because you will not listen to what you have already learned."

"I *am* listening. I told you everything, Pablo."

"You have told me nothing. You said only what you *saw*—and you have been precise in your reporting, like an investigator. But you have told me nothing of what you *feel, comprende?*"

"No," I lied.

"What does this woman make you feel—that is more important than the sum total of everything else. Close your eyes, Burke. Think her name into your mind. *Feel* it . . . let it come to you."

I closed my eyes, playing it square. Letting it come into me. Pablo floated away from me—I could feel him in the room, but we weren't alone.

"What?" he asked.

"A cold wind," I told him. "A chill . . ."

"All this sex, and no fire?"

"No fire. Dark sex. It happens like it's supposed to, everything works, but nobody smiles. Only part of her is with me . . . like she's standing somewhere else . . . a movie director. . . . She's someone else when she wants to be."

Pablo was quiet, waiting for me to say something else. But I was tapped out.

"Burke, when you make love with her—do you think of making a baby?"

"It can't be. I can't say why . . . but we couldn't make a baby with what we do. . . . She has the only child she wants. . . . It's like . . . if she wanted . . . she could make acid run inside her."

"Even her kiss is cold?"

"I never kissed her," I said.

Pablo watched as I lit another cigarette, his eyes playing over the pictures of his children sitting on his desk. "You know that Puerto Ricans are a special tribe, my friend? You know we are not 'Spanish' like some gringos think we are? And like some of us wish to be? Puerto Ricans are African, Indian, Spanish. . . . Our roots are in many continents, and the knowledge of our people is that mixture in our blood. We call it 'racial knowledge,' and it is deeper than you could ever imagine."

I looked at Pablo—at his dark skin and tightly curled hair. I thought back to when the cops would bust the fighting gangs when we were kids. The dark-skinned Puerto Ricans would never speak English—they didn't want to be taken for black. I thought of the black face of the soldier on São Tomé, talking to me in a bar just before we went over the water to Biafra. Showing me a picture of his wife, smiling. Saying *"Muy blanco, no?"* to get my approval. Liberals wanted to find their roots—survivors wanted to keep from getting strangled by them.

"When you first talked about this woman, I thought you were describing a Santeria priestess. You know them—they mix voodoo and Christianity the way a chemist mixes two drugs. But this woman, she is nothing like that. Her rituals are in her head—they are not handed down from another—they are her own creation."

"Yeah. But . . ."

"What does she call herself, my friend?"

"That's a funny thing—her name is Gina, the name her people gave her. But when she got older, they started to call her something else. Strega. You know what it means?"

"*Sí, compadre.* But it means nothing . . . or everything. It depends on who is talking. On the tone of their voice—their relationship to the woman. We have the same word in Spanish. *Bruja.* It means . . . witch, perhaps. A woman with great powers, but maybe with evil in her heart. It can even be a term of affection . . . a bitch with fire in her eye and the devil in her hips, you understand?"

"Witch. Bitch. It doesn't help me."

"One is inside the other—but, remember, the witch includes all else. A woman who is a witch can be anything she wants to be—she can take many forms. An old woman, a child. A saint, a devil. And this is always her choice. We can never see such a woman—only the manifestation of herself she allows us to see. If ten men see her, they see ten different women. And each will believe he has seen the truth. A man cannot see a witch."

"Pablo, come on. You believe that shit?"

"I believe what is true," he said, his voice grave. "I believe this wisdom handed down to us over the years has survived for a reason. To ignore the truth is to fail to understand why the truth has survived."

Survival. My speciality—my birthday present from the state. "What does she want?" I asked him.

"Only she knows that, Burke. *Bruja* is a fire—she must have fuel."

I ground out my cigarette. "The best thing for me to do is make tracks, right?"

Pablo nodded.

"But I have this job to do," I told him.

"You will not always be this confused, Burke. When *Bruja* manifests herself to you, it will be clear. You will know the truth. She will not attempt to hold you without the truth—you cannot be tricked by such a woman—they disdain the wiles of normal women. All their slaves are volunteers."

"Who would volunteer to be a slave?"

"A man who fears freedom," Pablo said, getting to his feet to embrace me. It was a goodbye.

81

THE LINCOLN was standing out in front of the clinic as if it had never moved. The driver's door was open, the engine running. I can take a hint. I was off the block in seconds.

It was deep into the hours past midnight—still not too late to go to Mama's joint, but I wasn't hungry. The Lincoln turned itself north toward the Triboro—I was going to loop around and head back to the office. But I found myself on the long span heading for Queens instead. The bridge was quiet. I passed the Brooklyn-Queens Expressway, my last chance to head back downtown. But the Lincoln kept rolling, past LaGuardia. By then I knew where I was going.

Strega's house was still and dark as I let the Lincoln drift to the curb—maybe her husband and her daughter were allowed to return to the castle after midnight. I hit the power window switch, leaving the engine running. Lit a cigarette and watched the red tip in the darkness like it was a book I wanted to read, listening to the night sounds. A Yellow Cab rattled past—a late-arriving passenger from the airport going home to the wife and kids.

I threw my cigarette into the street, watching her house. A tiny light came on in an upstairs window, barely visible behind a gauzy curtain. I looked hard, trying to fix the exact location. The light went out.

I pushed the gas pedal down, letting the big car take me back to where I was safe. It felt as if she was playing with me in that upstairs room—letting me go. This time.

82

THE NEXT morning was no better. Strange days. The big part of staying off the floor is knowing how to wait. When you hit the floor in my neighborhood, there's no referee giving you time to get your brain back together. I knew how to stay off the floor, but this case was all bent and twisted. I had money in my pocket, nobody was looking for me—I should have been golden. Julio's weak threats wouldn't make me lose sleep. I could just wait a few weeks, keep my head down—tell Strega I came up empty. And walk away.

But when you spend your life lying to everyone from streetside suckers all the way to the Parole Board, you learn that lying to yourself is a self-inflicted wound.

I drove over to one of the post-office boxes I keep around the city in various names. The one in Westchester County is the one I use for kiddie-sex freaks. It's in Mount Vernon, just over the border from the Bronx, maybe forty-five minutes from the office. All I found were some "underground" newsletters and a magazine. The newsletter never quite crosses the line—just some pictures of kids mixed with whining about this repressive society. One even had a column supposedly written by a kid himself—bragging about how his life was enriched by his "meaningful association" with an older man. That dirtbag the Mole had brought me to would have approved. Most of it reminded me of the stuff the Klan puts out—who got arrested recently (and why he was innocent), what politicians are trying to make a name for themselves with "anti-kid" legislation . . . that kind of crap. Some freaks burn crosses, some burn kids. The feature story was about some priest in Louisiana doing time for sodomizing a bunch of altar boys—the newsletter said the real issue was freedom of religion.

It was a waste of time. I knew it would be. Someone once said people in hell want ice water. If that's all they want, maybe they deserve to stay there.

I pulled the car over on the West Side Highway, near 96th Street. It was peaceful there—a few guys working on their cars, one crazy bastard casting a fishing line into the oil slick, a young woman throwing a stick for her dog to fetch. The dog was an Irish setter. His coat gleamed coppery red in the sunlight as he dashed in and out of the water, chasing the stupid stick. The woman called to the dog—time to go. The dog stopped and shook himself, water flying from his coat in a fine spray. I threw away my cigarette. That was what I needed to do—shake off this witch-woman and get back to myself.

I spent the next two days asking soft questions in hard places. Marking time until the week was up and I could return Bobby's Lincoln. I called him from a pay phone on Twelfth Avenue, near Times Square.

"It's Burke. My car ready?"

"Yep. Running like a watch. When's the last time that thing had a decent tune-up?"

"I don't know—didn't think it needed one."

Bobby made a growling sound in his throat—abusing good machinery made him crazy.

"You have any luck with that other thing?" I asked him, heading off a lecture on auto mechanics.

"Sure. No problem. Pick up your car this afternoon. About four, okay? We'll talk then."

"I'll be there."

"By yourself," he reminded me.

"I'll be the only person in the car," I told him. Pansy was going to get a ride in a Lincoln.

83

THE MASTIFF sniffed the Lincoln like it was an enemy dog—circling around a couple of times, pawing at the tires, burying her giant snout in the front seat.

"It's okay," I told her, but she took her time, getting it right. Finally, she climbed into the back seat, growled a couple of times, then flopped down. She was half asleep by the time I wheeled onto Atlantic Avenue.

It was just past four o'clock when I pulled up. This time it was Bobby himself sitting on the crate in front of the garage. He raised a fist in greeting, hitting a switch to open the door so I could pull the Lincoln all the way in. My Plymouth was parked just inside, nose aimed at the street.

"I could've painted it while it was here, but I figured you'd rather keep it the way it was," Bobby said.

"That's right, Bobby. Thanks."

But I wasn't getting off that easy. He insisted on taking me through everything he'd done to the car—piece by piece. "What you got here is a *complete* tune-up, Burke. Valves adjusted, points and plugs, carb cleaned and rejetted, timing reset. And we aligned the front end, rotated and balanced the tires. Changed all the fluids—power steering, transmission. Had to bleed the brake lines—you got silicon fluid in there now. Had to adjust the bands in the tranny too. It runs perfect now."

"What do I owe you, Bobby?"

Bobby waved my offer away.

"Let's hear how it sounds," I said with an enthusiasm I didn't feel.

Bobby twisted the key—it was so smooth it sounded like a turbine. Pansy recognized the sound—her monster's head appeared in the windshield of Bobby's Lincoln. He heard something, looked.

"What the fuck is *that*?" he asked me.

"It's just my dog, Bobby." I went over and opened the Lincoln's door, slapping my hip for Pansy to come to me.

"Jesus H. Fucking Christ!" Bobby said reverently. "How much does it weigh?"

"I don't know—maybe one forty or so."

Bobby made a full circuit around Pansy, checking her lines. He didn't try and kick the tires.

"Could I pat it?" he asked.

"Pansy, jump!" I snapped at her. She hit the deck, lying prone, her murderer's eyes the color of the East River, watching Bobby the way she watches food. "Go ahead," I told him. "She won't do anything now."

Bobby had enough sense to squat down so Pansy wouldn't think he was trying to dominate her. He scratched behind her ears. "I never saw anything like this outside of a zoo," he said. Pansy made a gentle rumble in her throat—like a subway pulling into a station. "Is he mad?" Bobby asked, still stratching.

"No," I told him. "That's when she's happy."

"It's a girl?"

"Sure is," I said.

Bobby got to his feet. "The other guys are out back, Burke. Okay?"

"Okay. You want me to leave Pansy out here?"

"Fuck no," Bobby said. "She might eat one of the cars."

Bobby led the way, me following, Pansy taking the point position to my left and just slightly in front of each stride. She knew what to do now—she was working.

There was only one car in the back this time—the Mustang. And three men—two a few years older than Bobby, the other more like my age. They all had prison-faces. The older guy had a regular haircut and was wearing a dark sportcoat over a white shirt, sunglasses hiding his eyes. The other two were much bigger men, flanking the guy in the sunglasses like they were used to standing that way. One was blond, the other dark, both with longish hair, wearing white T-shirts over jeans and boots. The blond had tattoos on both arms—in case anyone could miss where he got them, he had chains tattooed on both wrists. Black leather gloves on his hands. The dark one had calm eyes; he stood with his hands in front of him, right hand holding his left wrist. On the back of his right hand were the crossed lightning bolts—the mark of the Real Brotherhood.

I stopped a few feet short of the triangle. Pansy immediately came to a sitting position just in front of me. Her eyes pinned the blond—she knew.

Bobby stepped into the space between us, speaking to the older guy in the middle.

"This is Burke. The guy I told you about."

The older guy nodded to me. I nodded back. He waved his hand back toward himself, telling me to come closer. I stepped foward. So did Pansy.

The blond rolled his shoulders, watching Pansy, talking to me.

"The dog do any tricks?" he asked.

The hair on the back of Pansy's neck stood up. I patted her head to keep her calm.

"Like what?" I asked him.

The blond had a nice voice—half snarl, half sneer. "I don't fucking know . . . like, shake hands?"

"She'll shake anything she gets in her mouth," I told him, a smile on my face to say I wasn't threatening him.

The older guy laughed. "My brother says you're okay. If we can help you, we will."

"I appreciate it," I said. "And I'm willing to pay my way."

"Good enough," he said. "What do you need?"

"I know you," the blond suddenly blurted out.

I looked at his face—I'd never seen him before.

"I don't know you," I said, my voice neutral.

"You were in Auburn, right? Nineteen seventy-five?"

I nodded agreement.

"I was there too. Saw you on the yard."

I shrugged. Auburn wasn't an exclusive club.

"You mixed with niggers," the blond said. It wasn't a question.

"I mixed with my friends," I said, voice quiet, measured. "Like you did."

"I said *niggers*!"

"I heard what you said," I told him. "You hear what I said?"

The blond rolled his shoulders again, cracking the knuckles of one gloved hand in the fist he made of the other.

"B.T., I told you what Burke did for me," Bobby put in, no anxiety in his voice, just setting the record straight.

The blond looked at me. "Maybe you just had a personal beef with *those* niggers?"

"Maybe I did. So what?"

"Maybe you *like* niggers?" It wasn't a question—an accusation.

No point keeping my voice neutral any longer—he'd take it for fear.

"What's your problem?" I asked him. That wasn't a question either.

The blond looked at me, watching my face. "I lost money on you," he said.

"What?"

"I fucking lost money on you. I remember now. You was a fighter, right? You fought that nigger . . . I forget his name . . . the one that was a pro light-heavy?"

I remembered that fight. The black guy had been a real hammer in the ring before he beat a guy to death over a traffic accident. I don't remember how it got started, but it ended up with a bet that I couldn't go three rounds with him. I remember sitting on the stool in my corner waiting for the bell to start the first round, the Prof whispering in my ear. "Send the fool to school, Burke," he was saying, reminding me how we had it worked out. I was a good fifteen pounds lighter than the black guy, and quite a bit faster. Everybody betting on whether I could last the three rounds was expecting me to keep a jab in his face, bicycle backward, use the whole ring. Make him catch me. That's what he expected too.

When the bell sounded, he came off his stool like he was jet-propelled. I threw a pillow-soft jab in his general direction and started back-pedaling to the ropes. The black guy didn't waste any time countering my little jabs—he pulled his right hand all the way down to his hip, trying for one killer punch that would end it all. That was the opening. I stepped forward and fired a left hook—caught him flush on the chin coming in, and down he went.

But then the plan came unglued. He took an eight-count, shaking his head to clear it. He got to his feet so smoothly that I knew I hadn't really hurt him. The black guy waved me in and I charged, pinning him to the ropes, firing shot after shot at his head. But he wasn't just a tough guy—he was a pro. He blocked everything with his elbows, picking off my punches until I realized I was running out of gas. I leaned against him to get a breath—he buried his head in my chest to guard against an uppercut. I collapsed all my weight on his neck, stepping on his toes, not giving him an inch of room to punch. The guard in charge of the bell rang it early—he'd bet on me too.

I let him chase me through the second round, still a step faster than he was. He wasn't going to charge again—just taking his time, punching so hard my arms ached from blocking. He caught me good at the beginning of the third round—I felt a rib go from a right hook. He doubled up, catching me on the bridge of the nose with the same hand. "Grab him!" I heard the Prof scream, and I brought my gloves up over his elbows, pulling his hands under my armpits until the referee forced us apart. He butted me on the break, aiming for my nose. I staggered back, letting my knees wobble to get closer to the ground, letting him come in. I threw a Mexican left hook—so far south of the border that I connected squarely with his cup. The black guy dropped both hands to his crotch and I threw a haymaker at his exposed head—missed by a foot and fell down from the effort. The referee wiped off my gloves, calling it a slip, killing time.

He came at me again. I couldn't breathe through my nose, so I spit out the mouthpiece, catching a sharp right-hand lead a second later. I heard the Prof yell "Thirty seconds!" just before another shot dropped me to the canvas.

I was on my feet by the count of six, with just enough left to dodge his wild lunge. He went sailing past me into the ropes—I fired a rabbit punch to the back of his head, moved against him, pinning him to the ropes with his back to me. He whipped an elbow into my stomach and spun around, hooking with both hands, knowing he had to finish it. I grabbed his upper body, feeling the punches to my ribs, driving my forehead hard into his eyes, not giving him room to punch. If I'd had to let go of him I would have fallen for good.

I was out on my feet when I heard the bell. It took four men to pull him off me. We won almost six hundred cartons of cigarettes that day. The prison even threw in a free bridge for my missing teeth.

"If you lost money that day, you bet on the other guy," I told him. "The bet was that I couldn't last the three rounds."

"I bet on you to *win*," the blond said.

I shrugged my shoulders—it wasn't my problem that some true-believer couldn't get with the program.

"You didn't even try and beat that nigger," the blond said, like he was accusing me of treason.

"I was trying to survive," I told him reasonably. Just the way I was trying to do now. "Look, pal, it's not a big deal. How much did you lose?"

"Three fucking cartons," he said. Like it was his sister's virginity.

"Tell you what I'll do. It was a few years ago, right? Figure the price has gone up a bit—how about a half-yard for each carton? A hundred and fifty bucks, and we'll call it square?"

The blond stared at me, still not sure if I was laughing at him. "You serious?"

"Dead serious," I told him, slipping my hand into my coat pocket.

The blond couldn't make up his mind, his eyes shifting from Pansy to me. The guy with the sunglasses finally closed the books. "Let it rest, B.T.," he said. The blond let out a breath. "Okay," he said.

The blond started over to me for the money—Pansy went rigid. Her teeth ground together with a sound like a cement truck shifting into gear.

"I'll give it to you when I leave," I told the blond. Even a genius like him understood. He stepped back against the fence, still flexing the muscles in his arms. Pansy was real impressed.

"Can we do business?" I asked the guy with the sunglasses.

He waved me over to the side, against the fence by the Mustang. I flatted my hand against Pansy's snout, telling her to stay where she was, and followed him over. I lit a cigarette, feeling Bobby against my back.

"One of your guys did some bodyguard work. Delivered some money to a day-care center—money was in a little satchel—like a doctor's bag."

I couldn't see the guy's eyes behind the sunglasses; he had his hands in his pockets—waiting for me to finish.

"There was a woman with the bodyguard. Maybe he was protecting her, maybe he was guarding the cash—I don't know."

"Anything else?" he asked.

"The woman, she's no youngster. Maybe my age, maybe older. And she has a house somewhere outside the city. Big house—nice grounds. Has a guy who works with her—a big, fat guy. And maybe a schoolbus-type vehicle."

"That's it?"

"That's it," I told him.

"And you want to know what?"

"All I want to know is who this woman is—where I can find her."

"You got a beef with her?"

I thought about it—didn't know if the bodyguard work was a one-shot deal or if the Real Brotherhood had a contract with her. "She has something I want," I told him, measuring out the words as carefully as a dealer putting cocaine on a scale.

He didn't say anything.

"If you've got a contract with her . . . then I'd like to ask you to get this thing I want from her. I'll pay for it."

"And if there's no contract?"

"Then I just want her name and address."

He smiled. It might have made a citizen relax; I kept my hands in my pockets. "And for us to get out of the way?" he asked.

"Yeah," I told him. "Exactly."

The blond moved away from the guy in the sunglasses, his back to the fence. Pansy's huge head tracked his movement as if she was the center of a big clock and he was the second hand.

"B.T.!" Bobby said, a warning in his voice. The blond stopped where he was—a slow learner.

"What is this thing you want?" the leader asked.

"That means you have a contract?"

"No. And I don't know where her stash is either."

"It's not dope I'm after," I told him.

The leader took off his sunglasses, looked at them in his hands as though they held the answer to something. He looked up at me. His eyes had that soft, wet glaze only born killers get—after they've fulfilled their destiny a few times. "You're a hijacker, right? That's what you do?"

I held my hands together and turned my palms out to him—cards on the table. "I'm looking for a picture—a photograph."

"Who's in the picture?"

"A kid," I told him.

He looked a question at me.

"A little kid—a sex picture, okay?"

The leader looked at the dark-haired guy standing next to him. "I thought it was powder," he said.

The dark-haired guy kept his face flat. "I never asked," he replied.

The leader nodded absently, thinking it through. "Yeah," he said, "who asks?"

I lit a cigarette, cupping my hands around the flame, watching the leader from a corner of my eye. He was scratching at his face with one finger, his eyes behind the sunglasses again.

"Bobby, you mind taking your friend inside for a couple of minutes? We've got something to talk over out here, okay?"

Bobby put his hand on my shoulder, gently tugging me toward the garage. I slapped my hand against my side, telling Pansy to come along. She didn't move, still watching the blond, memorizing his body. "Pansy!" I snapped at her. She gave the blond one last look and trotted over to my side.

Inside the garage, I opened both front doors of the Plymouth and told Pansy to climb inside.

"B.T.'s okay, Burke," Bobby said. "He's just a little nuts on the subject of niggers, you know?"

"I know," I said. "No big deal."

We waited in silence. Pansy's dark-gray fur merged into the dim interior of the garage—only her eyes glowed. She missed the blond.

The back door opened and they came inside. The leader sat on the Plymouth's hood, leaving his boys standing off to one side.

"The woman told us she had to deliver money to various places—serious cash, okay? She was worried about somebody moving on the money—taking it away from her. Victor"—he nodded his head in the direction of the dark-haired guy—"he picked up a grand for every delivery. He carried the cash. We thought it was a regular series of payoffs—she never took anything back when she turned over the money."

I didn't say anything—I had a lot of questions but it wasn't my turn to talk.

"She told Victor no weapons—if someone made a move on them with a gun, he was supposed to turn over the bag he was carrying. He was just muscle, okay?"

I nodded. The woman wasn't worried about a hijack—Victor was there to intimidate the people who supplied the kids. He could do that just by being himself.

"You're sure she has this picture?" he asked.

"No question," I told him.

"This means she has others—that she does this all the time?"

"It's what she does," I told him.

The leader was wearing his sunglasses even inside the garage, but I could feel his eyes behind the dark lenses. "I'm a thief," he said, "just like you are. We don't fuck kids."

"I know that," I said.

"Some of our guys . . . they're a little crazy . . . like B.T. He'd stab a nigger just to stay in practice, you know?"

"I know."

"But none of us would do little kids. Our brotherhood . . ."

I bowed my head slightly. "You have everyone's respect," I told him.

"We do *now*," he said, his voice soft. "If word got out that we were involved with kids like this . . ."

"It won't," I said.

He went on like he hadn't heard me. "If that word got out, we'd have to do something serious, you understand? We can't have anything hurt our name—people would get stupid with us."

I kept quiet, waiting.

"We give you the information you want—you going to try and buy this picture from her?"

"If she'll sell it."

"And if she won't?"

I shrugged.

"Victor made a lot of those cash runs for her," he said. "A couple of day-care centers, private houses . . . even a church. There has to be a fucking lot of those pictures around."

"Like I said—she's in the business."

The leader ran his fingers through his hair—I could see the tattoo on his hand. His voice was still soft. "Her name is Bonnie. The house is on Cheshire Drive in Little Neck, just this side of the Nassau County border. A big white house at the end of a dead-end street. There's a white wall all around the property—electronic gate to the driveway. Big, deep backyard, trees and shrubs all around. Two stories, full basement, maybe some room in the attic too."

"Anything else?" I asked him.

"She has that schoolbus you talked about—a little one, maybe a dozen seats in the back. She uses the big, fat guy as the driver."

"Any security in the house?"

"I don't know," he said. "The Real Brotherhood—we play it straight—we weren't even thinking about taking her off."

I handed him two grand, all in hundreds. "That square us?" I asked him.

He smiled. "I'll take B.T.'s money out of this," he said.

I held out my hand. He took it—his grip was firm, but not a bone-crusher. I wouldn't give B.T. the same opportunity.

"I'm going to move fast now," I told him.

"Do what you want," he said. "Take your time. She put down our name, you understand?"

I nodded—someday soon, B.T. was going to get the idea the woman was a front for the NAACP.

I slammed the door in Pansy's face, waved a clenched fist to Bobby to thank him, and drove the Plymouth out of the garage.

84

EVEN PANSY felt the difference in the Plymouth as it purred along, heading back to the office. Bobby had done a beautiful job. I rolled to a stop at a red light on Atlantic near the Brooklyn-Queens border. An orange G.T.O. screeched to a stop next to me—two kids in their street racer. The passenger rolled down his window, smiling at me while his partner revved the engine, waiting for the light. I raised my eyebrows in respect for their dragster, and stomped the gas just as the light changed. I heard the G.T.O.'s tires squeal, hunting for traction on the rough road, but the Plymouth leaped ahead as though their orange machine was tied to a stake. The speedometer needle flicked at seventy before I backed it off for the next red light. I heard the G.T.O. roaring behind me, letting up on the gas while still in gear to make his exhaust pipes crackle. Very impressive. This time, they pulled up on the passenger side. I hit the power window switch just in time to hear the driver shout the street racer's time-honored question, "What you got in that, man?"

Pansy popped her head up from the front seat, snarling at all the noise. I heard another squeal from the G.T.O.'s tires and it was gone. The light was still red.

It was getting dark. Time to start making the phone calls, checking my traps. I wanted to drop Pansy off at the office, but I was short of time. The leader of the Real Brotherhood seemed like a patient man, but he was raised the same places I was—places where if your name went down, your body wouldn't be far behind.

I pulled up behind Mama's, opening Pansy's door to let her out. She prowled the walls of the narrow alley, finally relieving herself against both of them. She sniffed the air, a soft growl coming from her throat. I don't know if it was the smells from Mama's kitchen or whether she missed old B.T.

I let her back in the car and went inside through the kitchen. My table in the back was empty like it always was—Mama's heavy dinner crowd didn't fill half the joint—she kept the prices high and the ambience foul to discourage yuppies.

"Trouble?" she asked, approaching my table, her voice soft.

"No trouble, Mama. But I have to make a bunch of phone calls—and I have Pansy with me. Out in the car."

"This new puppy, Burke?" She knew my old Doberman, Devil.

"She's not really a puppy anymore, Mama."

"Big dog?"

"Big dog," I assured her.

"Maybe keep puppy in basement, okay?"

"Perfect, Mama. Just for a little while, right?"

"Sure," she said, doubtfully. "I tell cooks everything okay. Come."

I followed her back to the kitchen; she fired some Cantonese at the collection of thugs.

"Go get puppy," she told me.

I snapped Pansy's leash on. She lifted her head, wondering what was going on. She only got the leash when she was going to be around citizens.

When we walked through the back door, one of the cooks made a sound like "Eigh!" and backed all the way into the stove. They all started talking at once—arguing about something. Pansy sat at my side, drooling. They couldn't be sure it was the food. Two of them were pointing at the beast's head, standing chest to chest, screaming at each other. I couldn't make out a word. I had started to the basement with Pansy when Mama held up her hand.

"Burke, what country this dog from—don't say word, okay?"

I should have known—all the screaming and yelling was about some dumb bet—and Mama was looking for the edge. Mama's alleged cooks would stab you in the stomach and then bet you how long it would take you to die.

"Pizza," I told her, under my breath.

Mama charged into the argument, adding her own voice to the din. Finally, she pointed to one of the cooks.

"Germany?" she asked me.

"No," I said.

She pointed to another.

"England?"

I said "No" again, watching their faces.

"China?" she asked, pointing to a young man in the corner.

"No," I told her again. "The dog is from Italy."

A smile broke out on Mama's face. She made me say it again, so everyone in the room would get the benefit of her wisdom. Everybody bowed to her. I didn't see money change hands, but I figured their pay envelopes would be a little short that week.

Pansy snarled her way down the steps to the basement, threatening the darkness. Mama switched on the lights—the place was filled floor-to-ceiling with boxes, some wood, some cardboard. Drums of rice stood to one side. There was still another basement below this one—I remember one time when the cops were looking for Max and they thought he was down there. They waited two days to find me to ask him to come out quietly.

"Puppy want food, Burke?"

"Sure, Mama. Whatever you think is best."

She bowed. "I come back soon," she said, and went back up the stairs. More screaming and yelling in Chinese erupted—I think the cooks wanted a rematch. She came back down with a volunteer helper; he was carrying one of those giant stainless-steel pots they use to keep the rice freshly steamed all day long. He put it on the floor, watching Pansy warily.

"This puppy good guard dog, Burke?" she asked.

"She's the best, Mama."

"She . . . this girl puppy?"

"Yep."

"Women the best warriors," Mama said, then translated it for the cook, who nodded dubiously. "Puppy guard down here?"

"If you want her to," I said. "Watch—and tell your man to keep his hands in sight, okay?"

She nodded. I slapped my side for Pansy to follow me, walking her so her back was in a corner formed by some of the stacked cartons. I took down a few cartons to make a little wall in front of her, about as high as her chest. Her face loomed above the barrier, watching. I knew just what trick Mama would love. "Pansy!" I said, my voice sharp to get her attention. "Friends!" I motioned Mama forward. "Go ahead and pat her," I said.

Mama hadn't gotten where she was by showing fear. She walked right up to Pansy, patting her head, saying "Good puppy!" a few times. Pansy stood still, her eyes on the cook.

"Okay, now step back, Mama." When she did, I got Pansy's attention again. "Guard!" I told her.

"Tell your man to approach like he's going to pat her too, Mama. But tell him not to reach over the barrier, you got it?"

She said something to the cook. His face stayed flat, but you didn't need a translator to see he was suspicious as hell. The poor bastard had gotten about five feet from the barrier when Pansy lunged at him, a blood-chilling snarl flowing between her teeth. He leaped back about twenty feet—the snap of Pansy's jaws was like a thick branch breaking.

"Pansy, out!" I yelled at her. She sat back down, her head swiveling to watch the entire room.

Mama clapped her hands. "Good trick, Burke!" she said. The cook went back upstairs. I rolled the pot of steaming food over to Pansy. "What's in this?" I asked her.

Mama looked insulted. "Beef, pork, lobster, shrimp, good vegetables, plenty rice. All best stuff."

"She'll love it," I assured Mama.

"How come she not eat, then?"

"She'll only eat when she's alone with me, Mama. Let me get her started and I'll come up and make those calls, okay?"

"Okay, Burke," she said.

I waited a minute or two before saying "Speak!" to my dog. A good survivor never shares all his secrets.

85

THE FIRST call was to SAFE. Lily was in a session—they asked if I could leave a number. I told them I couldn't and got a time to call back. They didn't seem surprised.

I got lucky with McGowan—he was in his office for a change.

"You know my voice?" I asked him.

"Sure do, pal." McGowan had a magnificent Irish baritone—he used it for sweet-talking little girls away from their pimps.

"I need a favor. You know Wolfe, the D.A. in charge of City-Wide?"

"Pal, that woman is aces with me, understand? Cases the other prosecutors won't touch—she grabs 'em up. You better not be having a problem with her."

"No problem. I just want you to put in a good word for me, okay? I need to talk with her—I figure she might do it if she knew I was all right."

"My friend, you are *not* all right if you're looking to sting that woman."

"McGowan, come *on*. You know what I do—it's part of that, okay?"

"*What* part?"

I took a breath, thinking it through. McGowan knew his phones could be tapped—he had every honest cop's fear of Internal Affairs.

"Look, all I want is for you to tell her I play the game straight. I'll tell her what I need—she can make up her own mind."

Another silence on the line. Finally his voice came back. "You got it," he said.

I started to ask him to do it tomorrow, but I was talking to a dead line.

Strega answered her phone on the first ring. "I was waiting for you," she said, her voice soft.

"How could you know it was me calling?"

"I know," she said. "I told you before—I always know."

"There's been some progress."

"Tell me," she said, her voice going throaty, playing with the words, stroking them.

"Not on the phone," I said.

"I know what you want—come to my house—come tonight—late, after midnight—come tonight—I'll have what you want."

"I just want . . ." and I was talking into another dead line.

I went back inside the restaurant, killing some time until Lily would be available. One of the waiters brought me some soup and a plate of fried rice and beef, green pea pods lancing through the mixture. Mama walked by, smiling. She tossed the *News* on the table in front of me. I scanned the headlines. Half of Queens County was getting indicted. Politicians were grabbing their lawyers in one hand and their guts in the other and dashing to the courthouse, offering everyone they knew in exchange for immunity from the deals they'd done together. That's why they call it the rat race.

The sports pages read like the front pages—one role model was using cocaine, another was going into an alcoholism rehab program. Another claimed he threw a prize fight.

But on the racing page I saw my horse again. Flower Jewel, running in the eighth race against the same collection she had faced last week. I checked my watch—not even nine-thirty yet.

Maurice didn't answer until the sixth ring—probably a lot of late action coming in.

"It's Burke," I told him.

"No kidding?" he said. Maurice didn't have the manners of a pig, but he was taking lessons and hoped to be right up there soon.

"The eighth closed yet?"

"Not until ten—where've you been, fucking Idaho?"

"Flower Jewel," I told him. "Three to win."

"Flower Jewel, eighth race. Three to win. That right?"

"Right," I said.

"Send your man around tomorrow with the money," Maurice said, slamming down the phone.

I went back to my dinner, wondering if even Pansy could eat all the food Mama had left down in the basement for her.

I lit a cigarette as the dishes were cleared away. Flood's face drifted up from nowhere, floating in the smoke—I ground it out in the ashtray, but it didn't help.

Lily herself answered when I called SAFE.

"It's Burke," I told her. "Did you speak with Wolfe?"

"Yes, I did."

"And?"

"And she gave me a number for you to call—anytime between eight and nine in the morning."

"She'll talk to me?"

"She just gave me the number to give to you."

I hadn't expected Lily to get over with Wolfe so easily—McGowan had been my backup plan. If he did get around to calling tomorrow, it wouldn't hurt. I sure as hell wasn't going to call him back and tell him to forget it—he'd be sure I was up to no good.

"Okay," I said. "The kid's been coming for treatment?"

"Right on time. But his mother doesn't want to be involved."

"The redhead?"

"Yes."

"She's not his mother."

"Oh. Will his mother . . . ?"

"I don't know. I'll see about it, okay?"

"Just so long as they keep bringing the child."

"I'll talk to his people. And thanks, Lily."

"Be careful," she said, hanging up.

I said goodbye to Mama and collected Pansy from the basement. She was still behind the barrier, but the steel container was as clean as if it had been washed. I could see her teethmarks on the rim.

Pansy was happy to be home, insisting on visiting the roof for old times' sake. I had a couple of hours before I had to meet Strega. I found a pro wrestling match on television and lay back on the couch to watch with Pansy. She growled in contentment—if she could have nailed B.T. it would have been a perfect day.

86

THE MOON's cold light never penetrated to the dark streets, but I felt it deep in my spine as I wheeled the Plymouth past the burnt-out buildings on Atlantic. The radio was talking about Marcos settling down in Hawaii. He split the Philippines a few weeks ago, traveling light—a couple of loyal subjects, and the gross national product of his entire country for the last dozen years. A major-league scumbag.

I cut the engine, letting the Plymouth coast around to the garage in back. The door was standing open. Only the BMW was there. I backed the Plymouth inside, found the button, and closed the door. Waiting in the darkness.

A door opened. I could see her back-lighted silhouette standing there, weaving slightly—a candle flame in a gentle breeze.

I climbed out of the Plymouth. When I looked up again, the doorway was empty. I went through the opening and saw her gently floating up the stairs. Her body was wrapped in some gauzy black fabric, blending into the shadows under her red hair. When I got to the top of the stairs, she was gone again.

No lights were on in the house. I found my way into her white living room and took off my coat. I took out a cigarette, scraped the wooden match into life. As I touched the tip of the cigarette to the flame, I heard her voice. "Me too," she whispered, floating into the dark room, bending her face forward to the flame. A lollipop stick of marijuana was in her mouth.

I held the light for her, watched her puff to get the joint going and then suck in a massive breath. She floated away from me to the couch—the tip of the joint was a glowing pinpoint in the dark room.

"You having a séance?" I asked her.

"You afraid of the dark?" she retorted.

"I'm afraid of a lot of things," I told her.

"I know," she said, dragging on the joint again, holding her breath, expelling it in a hiss.

"It'll be over soon," I said. "I'm getting close."

"To the picture?"

"To the person who took the picture. I can't be sure the picture is still around—like I told you. But I think I can get some answers soon."

"You want me to do something?"

"I just want an answer to something. I have a couple of more things to do—then I'm going to the people who took the picture, okay? But the picture may be with a whole bunch of other pictures. I may not have time to look through them all—you understand?"

"So?"

"So what if I just destroy *all* the pictures? Make sure there aren't any pictures left. Of anybody."

Another drag on the joint, red tip blazing, sharp intake of breath, hiss when it came out. "I want to see the picture," she said.

"I'll do my best. But I'm not hanging around if things go bad, see? Scotty wasn't the only one—I'm sure of that now. The people who took the picture, they're in the business, understand?"

"Yes."

"I don't know how much time I'll have once I get inside."

She took a last drag and the joint went out; maybe she just pinched off the tip—I couldn't tell.

"You want to get inside now?" Strega said, coming off the couch toward me.

"No," I told her.

"Yes, you do," she said, standing next to me. She dropped to her knees, the black gauze fluttering behind me. Bat's wings. Her face was in my lap, her hands at my belt. My hand dropped onto her back, feeling the fabric—and the chill.

"Don't touch me," she whispered.

I watched my hands grip the arms of the chair; the veins stood out. A picture formed on the back of my hands—below the waist I was somewhere else—the picture formed and I could see my passport into the woman's house.

I felt myself go off, but her mouth stayed locked to me for a long time. She reached back one hand, pulled off the gauzy wrapper—her body was a gleam of white.

Strega took her mouth from me, wrapping the gauze around me, cleaning me off, tossing the fabric to the floor.

"You didn't even have to ask—I know what to do," she whispered against my chest.

I stroked her back. It felt too smooth to be a person.

"I'm a good girl," she said, her voice certain and sure of itself, the way a kid gets sometimes.

I kept stroking her.

"Yes?" she whispered.

"Yeah," I said.

We stayed like that for a long time.

"I'll be right back," she said, her voice strong and hard again. "I have to get something for you." She got to her feet and padded away.

The downstairs bathroom had two matching sinks; a telephone was built into a niche near the tub. I caught my reflection in the mirror—it looked like a mug shot.

When she came back downstairs, I was standing next to the wall-size window in the living room, watching the lights in the yard. She was wearing a white terrycloth robe; her hair was wet, copper-colored in the soft light.

"This is for you," she said, opening her hand for me to see.

It was a thick gold chain the size of my wrist—each link must have weighed a couple of ounces. I held it in my hand, feeling the weight. It was solid enough to be a collar for Pansy.

"It's beautiful," I said, slipping it into my pocket.

"Put it on," Strega said, reaching into my pocket to pull it out again.

I thought of the tattoos on B.T.'s wrists. "I don't wear chains," I told her.

"You'll wear mine," she said, fire-points in her eyes.

"No, I won't," I told her, my voice quiet.

She stood on her toes, reached behind me to pull at my neck—she was so close I couldn't focus on her eyes. "I'll keep this for you—I'll sleep with it next to my body. When you come back to me—when you come back with the picture—you'll put it on."

I put my lips against her—she pulled her face away.

"Bring me that picture," she said, turning her face to the window.

I left her standing there, looking like a little girl waiting for her father to come home from work.

87

THE PLYMOUTH took itself back to the office. I had to call Wolfe in a couple of hours; no point in trying to sleep.

I kicked my feet up on my desk, a yellow pad in my hand, and jotted down notes of what I knew, telling myself I was putting it together. When I opened my eyes, it was almost eight in the morning. Somebody had written *Bruja* on the pad and crossed it out—I could read the word through the scratches.

I took a shower, waiting for Pansy to come down from the roof. Checked the phone—clear to call. The number Lily gave me for Wolfe rang a couple of times.

"City-Wide."

"Ms. Wolfe, please."

"This is she."

"It's Burke. I'd like to talk to you about something."

"Yes?"

"In your office—if that's okay."

I could feel her hesitate.

"I have something to give you—something that will be of value in your work."

"What?" she asked.

"I'd prefer to show you."

Another silence. Then:

"You know where my office is?"

"Yes."

"Make it nine o'clock. Give your name to the desk man."

"There isn't much time," I told her. "I live all the way up in West-chester County—the traffic and all . . ."

"Nine o'clock *tonight*, Mr. Burke."

She hung up. I went back to sleep.

88

THE DAY came up bleak—dirty skies, a cold wind hovering over the city, waiting its turn. I blocked it all out, walking through the case inside my head, looking for a handle to grip. I didn't walk around while I was thinking—one of the first things you learn in prison is not to pace, it just underlines that you're in a cage. If you stay inside your head, you can go over the walls.

I'd been playing this all wrong—not paying attention to all the tuition payments I'd made in jails and hospitals over the years. Something about this case was making me afraid, but that wasn't so strange. I'm scared most of the time—it keeps me from getting stupid. But I'm used to being scared of the usual things—like being shot or doing more time . . . not this *bruja* nonsense Pablo told me about. You ever watch a fighter who slugged his way into a championship bout decide he's a fucking *boxer* and blow his big chance? You have to go with what got you there. I smoked a couple of cigarettes, thinking it over. Crime had never made me rich, but it kept me free. And it was what I knew best.

I didn't get started until late afternoon, taking my time about getting ready. I picked over my clothes, looking for something that wouldn't make the people in Wolfe's building nervous. I found a black wool suit with a faint chalk stripe hanging in the closet. It was brand-new, but a bit rumpled from storage—car trunks do that. I matched it with a white shirt—genuine Hong Kong silk, which is like saying "virgin vinyl." And a plain black tie. I washed my hair and combed it the best I could. Shaved carefully. Polished the black half-boots. I checked myself out in the mirror. Clothes do make the man—instead of looking like a thug who worked the docks, I looked like a pilot fish for a loan shark.

I folded some money into one pocket, took a couple of other things I needed out of the desk, and shut the place down. Pansy raised one eyebrow, still near comatose from the cubic ton of Chinese food. I told her I'd be back late and took the back stairs to the garage.

I checked my watch. A little past six. Plenty of time to have something to eat, get my mind right for the meeting.

When I first rolled past the restaurant, the blue dragon tapestry was in the window. Cops inside. I kept going all the way down to Division Street to the warehouse. Nobody was around. I checked the desk in the back room to see if any mail had circled around the loops I set up and come in for a landing. Flood knew how to work the loop, but she'd never written. The desk was empty.

When I drove back, the white tapestry was in place. All clear. I parked around the back. A couple of the cooks looked suspiciously at me—maybe the ones who lost the bet on Pansy's nationality. I took my table in the back. Mama sat down with me, handing over a copy of the *News*.

"You had the law here, Mama?"

"Yes. Police very worried about this place. The gangs—stores have to pay for protection. They ask me if it happen to me."

You could see Mama thought the whole idea was ridiculous—the gangs only tried their shakedown racket on legitimate businesses.

"What did you tell them?"

"I tell them the truth. Nobody bother me. You want soup?"

"Sure," I told her, opening the paper as she went back to her business.

I'd almost forgotten about Flower Jewel. I flipped to the back of the paper, looking for her name. I found it, but it didn't cheer me up. She'd left early, but some other nag parked her to the first quarter in 28:4. Too fast. She was shuffled back into the pack. Then she make a big brush at the three-quarter pole, going three-wide on the paddock turn. She actually had the lead at the top of the stretch, but the little "1x" told me the story—she broke stride, looking for more speed. Finished fourth. It looked like a lousy drive to me, but Maurice would want his money, not an autopsy.

I finished my soup, ate a few of the dim sum the waiter brought, smoked a couple of cigarettes. I went up to the front desk and slipped Mama the three hundred for Maurice with another thirty for Max.

"You not such good gambler, Burke," she said, a little smile on her face.

"I don't get many chances to bet on a sure thing," I told her. "Like where dogs come from."

Mama wasn't insulted. "Only way to bet," she said.

It was time to visit Wolfe.

89

TRAFFIC WAS light on the way to the courthouse. I turned off Queens Boulevard and nosed past the D.A.'s parking lot, saw Wolfe's Audi near the door. The lot was half empty, but I didn't want to leave the Plymouth there. They have municipal parking a half-block away. It looked like a graveyard for the few cars still remaining. Dark and deserted—a mugger's paradise. I hit the switch to disable the ignition, not worrying about even the lowest-grade thief breaking in for the radio. I don't use a car alarm—they're a waste of time unless you're close by.

It was eight-forty-five when I pushed open the glass doors to the D.A.'s office. The guy at the desk looked up from his crossword puzzle. His eyes never reached my face.

"The jail's next door," he said.

"I know," I told him. "I have an appointment with A.D.A. Wolfe."

Still not looking at me, he picked up a black phone on the desk, punched in a couple of numbers.

"There's a lawyer here—says he's got an appointment with Wolfe."

He listened for a second, looked up again. "Name?" he asked.

"Burke."

He spoke my name into the phone, then put it down.

"Turn right past the divider, last door at the end of the corridor."

"Thanks," I said to the top of his head.

I found the place easy enough. Wolfe was sitting behind a big desk. The top was swept clean—a white orchid floated in a brandy snifter in one corner. Two monster piles of paper were on a shelf behind her. I guess she knew most cons can read upside down.

She was wearing a white wool jacket over a burnt-orange dress, a string of pearls around her neck. Her nails were a few shades darker than her lipstick—both red. Wolfe had a soft, pale face—one look and you could see it wasn't from fear, it was her natural color. The silver wings gleamed in her lustrous hair. When I came in the room she stood up, reached across the desk to shake hands.

"Thank you for seeing me," I said.

"I can't promise you much privacy," she replied. "There's a lot of people still working in the other offices."

I couldn't tell if it was a warning—it didn't matter.

"I've been working on something for a while," I said. "And I ran across some stuff I thought you'd be interested in."

She lit a cigarette with a cheap plastic lighter, pushing an ashtray with some hotel's name on it in my general direction. She was good at waiting.

"Anyway," I said, "I got to the point where I need some more information—another piece of the puzzle. . . ."

"And you believe I have this piece?"

"I'm sure you do," I said.

A tall black woman stalked into the office, ignoring me as if I was a lump of furniture. Her mouth was a grim line.

"It was an acquittal," she told Wolfe.

Wolfe's face didn't change. "It figured to be," she said. "Did you stand up?"

"Stand up?" the black woman asked.

I knew what she meant even if the black woman didn't. Baby-rapers have a way of smirking when the jury refuses to believe their victims—as if the jury said it was okay, what they did. A good prosecutor looks them in the eye, memorizing their faces.

"What did you do when the foreman read the verdict?" Wolfe asked the question another way.

"I went over to the defendant—I told him I'd see him again," the black woman said.

"You stood up," Wolfe told her. "Round one, remember?"

"I remember," the black woman said. "He'll be back. And I'll be ready for him."

Wolfe smiled—I could feel the heat coming off the black woman standing behind me. She knew what the smile meant.

"Want to take tomorrow off?" Wolfe asked.

"I'll take a day off when Jefferson goes down," the black woman snapped.

"We all will," Wolfe said. It was a dismissal.

I lit another cigarette. Wolfe hadn't hung around just for a meeting with me. Time to get to it.

"I'm playing it straight down the line on this. Did Lily talk to you?"

"Lily did. McGowan called me too."

"And?"

"And I still don't know what you want, Mr. Burke."

"I want . . ." I started to say. A guy about five and a half feet tall and four feet wide walked in, stepping between me and Wolfe. His hair was cropped close to his scalp—he had a round face but cop's eyes. He was wearing a black knit shirt over some gray slacks. The shirt didn't have an alligator on the front, but it did feature a shoulder holster. The

.38 was only a small dot on his broad chest. He looked like a retired wrestler or a bouncer in a waterfront bar.

"How's it going?" he asked Wolfe, never taking his eyes from me.

"Jefferson was acquitted," she said.

"Jefferson is a miserable fucking piece of slime," the big guy said, chewing on each word like it was raw meat.

Wolfe smiled at him. "This isn't Jefferson's lawyer," she said.

The big guy shrugged. It was like watching an earthquake. "You want the mutt?" he asked.

"Sure, bring him over," Wolfe told him.

The big guy walked out, light on his feet. Maybe he'd been a boxer instead of a wrestler.

Wolfe lit another smoke for herself and held up her hand, telling me to wait.

The big guy was back in a minute, holding Wolfe's Rottweiler on a short leather leash.

"Hi, Bruise!" Wolfe said. The beast walked right past me, put his paws on the desk, and tried to lick her face. She slapped him away good-naturedly. "Bruiser, go to place!" she said.

The big guy unsnapped the leash. The Rottweiler walked to a corner of the room and flopped down on the carpet. He watched me like a junkie watching a mailbox on welfare-check day.

"I'll be around," the big guy said. I got the message—as if the Rottweiler wasn't enough.

"I'm listening," Wolfe said.

"I'm looking for a picture. Of a kid. A picture of a kid having sex with a man. I talked to a lot of people, went a lot of places. I think I know where the picture is. I think you know the people who have the picture. All I want is for you to give me a name and address."

"You said you had something for me?" she asked. One look at Wolfe and you knew she wasn't talking about money—even in Queens County.

I tossed the little leather address book I took from the pimp on her desk. She didn't make a move to touch it.

"It's from a guy who sells little boys. In Times Square. First names. Initials. Phone numbers. And some kind of code."

"How did you come by this?"

"I was taking up a collection—he donated it."

Wolfe took a drag of her cigarette, put it in the overflowing ashtray, picked up the book. She turned the pages slowly, nodding to herself.

"Did he get hurt making this donation?"

"Not badly," I told her. "If you want to ask him yourself, his name's Rodney. He works out of that fast-food chicken joint on Forty-sixth off Eighth."

Wolfe nodded. "And you want to trade this book for the information?"

I took a gamble. "It's yours," I told her. "No matter what you decide."

"You have a copy?"

"No," I lied.

Wolfe tapped her nails on the desk. It wasn't a nervous gesture—something she did when she was thinking. A phone rang someplace down the hall. It rang twice, then stopped.

A tiny little woman burst into the office, her face flushed, waving a bunch of papers in her hand. "We got the printout!" she yelled, the words sticking in her throat when she saw Wolfe had a visitor. The Rottweiler snarled at the intrusion. The woman had her hair all piled on top of her head; a giant diamond sparkled on her finger. She put her hands on her hips. "Bruiser, *please!*" she said.

The big dog subsided. Wolfe laughed. "I'll look at it later, okay?"

"Okay!" the other woman shouted, running out of the office as if she was going to a fire sale.

"Are all your people so worked up?" I asked her.

"We don't have draftees in this unit," she said, her eyes watching me closely.

"Not even the dog?"

"Not even him." She fingered her string of pearls. "What do you need?"

"I know the woman I'm looking for is named Bonnie. I know she lives on Cheshire Drive in Little Neck. Maybe with a fat guy."

"That's it?"

"That's it. She's running a kiddie-porn ring—I figure you have your eye on her."

Wolfe said nothing, waiting for me.

"And if you don't," I told her, "then I just gave you some more information, right?"

Wolfe took a breath. "What is it you really want, Mr. Burke? You obviously already know how to find this person."

I lit a cigarette for myself—it was time to tell her.

"I have to go in there—I have to get that picture. If I can buy it, I will."

"And if you can't . . ."

I shrugged.

Wolfe reached behind her and pulled a bunch of papers onto her desk. Some of the sheets were long and yellow—I knew what they were.

"Mr. Burke, Lily did call me, as I said. But I did a little checking on my own before I agreed to this meeting."

"So?"

"So you are not exactly unknown to law enforcement, are you?" She ran her finger down one of the yellow sheets, reading aloud, lifting her eyes to my face every once in a while. "Armed robbery, assault one, armed robbery *and* assault. Attempted murder, two counts. Possession of illegal weapons . . . Should I go on?"

"If you want to," I told her. "I was a lot younger then."

Wolfe smiled. "You're rehabilitated?"

"I'm a coward," I told her.

"We have twenty-seven arrests, two felony convictions, three placements in juvenile facilities, one youthful-offender adjudication."

"Sounds about right to me," I told her.

"How did you beat the attempted-murder case? It says you were acquitted at trial."

"It was a gunfight," I told her. "The cops arrested the winner. The other guys testified it was somebody else who shot them."

"I see."

"Anything on that sheet tell you I don't keep my word?" I asked her.

Wolfe smiled again. "Rap sheets don't tell you much, Mr. Burke. Take this one—it doesn't even give your first name."

"Sure it does," I told her.

"Mr. Burke, this shows a different first name for every single time you were arrested. Maxwell Burke, John Burke, Samuel Burke, Leonard Burke, Juan Burke . . ." She stopped, smiling again. *"Juan?"*

"Dónde está el dinero?" I said.

This time she laughed. It was a sweet chuckle, the kind only a grown woman can do. It made my heart hurt for Flood.

"Do you have a true first name, Mr. Burke?"

"No."

Wolfe's smile was ironic. "What does it say on your birth certificate?"

"Baby Boy Burke," I told her, my voice flat.

"Oh," Wolfe said. She'd seen enough birth certificates to know I'd never have to worry about buying a present on Mother's Day. I shrugged again, showing her it didn't mean anything to me. Now.

Wolfe took another piece of paper off her desk—this one wasn't yellow.

"The FBI has a sheet on you too," she said.

"I never took a federal fall."

"I see that. But you *are* listed as a suspect in several deals involving military weapons. And a CIA cross-reference shows you were out of the country for almost a year."

"I like to travel," I told her.

"You don't have a passport," she said.

"I didn't come here to ask you for a date," I said. "I'm not applying for a job either. I admire what you do—I respect your work. I thought I could help you—that you could help me too."

"And if we can't work this out?"

"I'm going into that house," I told her, looking her full in her lovely face like the crazy bastard this case had turned me into.

Wolfe picked up the phone, punched a number. "Nothing's wrong," she said. "Come in here." She hung up. "I want to be sure you're not wearing a wire, okay? Then we'll talk."

"Whatever you say," I told her.

The bouncer came back in, the .38 almost lost in his meaty hand.

"I told you nothing was wrong," Wolfe said.

"That was a few seconds ago," he snapped. The Rottweiler growled at him. "Good boy," he said.

"Would you please take this gentleman with you and see if he has anything on him he shouldn't have," Wolfe told him.

The big guy put his hand on my shoulder—it felt like an anvil.

"There's no problem," Wolfe said to him, a warning note in her voice.

We went past a couple of offices—the tall black woman was reading something and making notes, the little lady with the piled-up hair was talking a mile a minute on the phone, a handsome black man was studying a hand-drawn chart on the wall. I heard a teletype machine clatter—bad news for somebody.

"Doesn't anybody go home around here?" I asked the big guy.

"Yeah, pal—some people go home. Some people should *stay* home."

I didn't try any more conversation-starters. He took me into a bare office and did the whole search number, working at it like a prison guard you forgot to bribe. He took me back to Wolfe.

"Nothing," he said, disappointed. He left us alone.

The Rottweiler was sitting next to Wolfe, watching the door as she patted his head. She pointed to his corner again and he went back, as reluctant as the big guy was.

"Mr. Burke, this is the situation. The woman you intend to visit is Bonnie Browne, with an 'e.' She sometimes uses the name Young as well—it's her maiden name. The man she lives with is her husband. George Browne. He has two arrests for child molesting—one dismissal, one plea to an endangering count. Served ninety days in California. She's never been arrested."

I put my hand in my pocket, reaching for a smoke.

"Don't write any of this down," Wolfe said.

"I'm not," I told her, lighting the smoke.

"We believe this woman to be the principal in a great number of corporations—holding companies, really. But she doesn't operate the way most of the kiddie-porn merchants do. You understand what I mean?"

"Yeah," I told her. "You want the pictures—videotapes, whatever— you send a money order to a drop-box in Brussels. When the money clears, you get a shipment in the mail from Denmark, or England, or any other place they're established. Then the money orders get mailed to an offshore bank—maybe the Cayman Islands—and the bank makes a loan to some phony corporation set up in the States."

Wolfe looked at me thoughtfully. "You've been at this quite a while."

"I do a lot of work—you get bits and pieces here and there—you put it together."

"Okay. But this woman doesn't work like that. Her product is special. She guarantees all her stuff is so-called collector's items. No reproduction—every picture is one of a kind."

"What's to stop some freak from copying the pictures?"

"She puts some kind of mark on every picture she takes—like this." Wolfe showed me a tiny drawing of a standing man, his hand on the shoulder of a little boy. It looked like it was hand-drawn with one of those needlepoint pens architects use. Only it was in a soft blue color. "The mark won't survive a copy—she uses something called chroma-blue ink. She puts every mark on herself—by hand."

"What's the point?"

"There's two points, Mr. Burke. The first is that she gets a minimum of five thousand dollars a picture, so she can achieve huge profits without a lot of volume."

I took a drag on my cigarette, waiting.

"The other point is more significant. She produces pictures to order."

"You mean some freak calls her and says he wants to see a certain thing go down . . . ?"

"Yes. If you want a blond boy wearing a snowsuit, you got it."

"You going to drop her?" I asked.

"We *are* going to drop her—but not soon. We're just beginning to trace pictures back to her. We don't have a prayer of getting a search warrant now."

"And if you ask for one, it might get back to her?"

Wolfe raised her eyebrows. "You are a cynical man, Mr. Burke."

"Those black robes the judges wear," I told her, "they don't change you inside."

Wolfe didn't say anything for a minute, fingering her pearls. "Do you know anything about search warrants?" she finally asked.

Now I knew why she wanted to make sure I wasn't wired. "I know if a citizen breaks in a house and finds dope or whatever, the evidence won't be suppressed unless the citizen is an agent of law enforcement."

"Um . . ." Wolfe said, encouraging me. I hadn't told her what she wanted. Yet.

"I also know that if the police are called to a location . . . say because there's a burglary in progress . . . and they find something bad, they can take it."

"And use it in court."

"And use it in court," I agreed.

Wolfe's face was flat and hard. "This woman wouldn't report a burglary," she said.

I lit a last cigarette. "You have her house under surveillance?"

"We might—starting tomorrow."

"Round the clock?"

"Yes."

I took a drag of my smoke.

"Any citizen has an obligation to rescue people when there's a fire," I said.

Wolfe held her hand across the desk. I brought it quickly to my lips before she could do anything and walked out of her office.

90

I took a couple of days to sort things out, telling myself that I didn't want to hit the filth factory in Little Neck the very first night Wolfe's people were on the job. The truth was that I wanted to get back to myself—get cautious, work the angles, find some way to get the job done with the least possible risk.

But it all jammed together in my head. I'd start to work out some scam—maybe have the Mole take out the phones in the house, walk in dressed up like a repairman, look around. Or maybe just a gentle breaking-and-entering while the two of them were out of the house in their little schoolbus. No matter what I tried on, it wouldn't fit. You can't scam humans who produce custom-tailored kiddie porn.

I thought about how out of control the whole lousy thing was. I could never have a woman like Wolfe. Flood wasn't coming back. I could live with not having the woman I wanted; I had a lot of practice at not having choices. But I couldn't live with Strega. I had to burn the *bruja*-woman out of my life before she took me down with her.

The Prof reported in. He had made a couple of runs past the target. Then he'd knocked on the door, asking if they wanted any yard work done. The woman answered the door herself—told him to get lost. No sign of security people.

I got the blueprints of the house from the city. Checked through the back files—the house was jointly owned by the woman and her husband. Purchased for $345,000 about four years ago. Conventional bank mortgage. Fifty bucks got me a look at the papers—she put down a little more than a hundred grand. Listed her occupation as "private investor." Declared an income of almost $250,000 a year.

The phone-company employees who sell information charge more—they still think of themselves as a monopoly. Two phones in the house—both numbers unlisted. Their combined bill ran about five hundred dollars a month, most of it toll calls. Just for the hell of it, I checked the numbers against the ones I'd copied from the pimp's address book I gave to Wolfe. None of them matched—they were in a different league.

It was time to be myself again.

91

I ROUNDED up most of the crew with no problems, but I couldn't find Michelle at any of her usual spots. Finally, I dropped in to The Very Idea, a transsexual bar where she hangs out when she isn't working.

"She's getting her hair cut, darling," her friend Kathy told me.

I made a face—her favorite "salon" reminded me of a parakeet's cage, feathers flying, shrill shrieking, and shit all over the floor.

"Oh, Burke, don't look like that. Nobody goes *there* anymore. Daniel has opened a fabulous new place on Fifth—here's a card."

"Thanks, Kathy," I said, throwing a twenty on the bar to cover her tab.

"See you around, handsome," she replied. I don't think it was the twenty bucks—transsexuals just have more empathy.

La Dolce Vita was a couple of flights up. It had a tiny little elevator but I took the stairs. I wasn't worried about running into anything, but if I was going to get back to myself, it was time to get started.

The joint was all pastel colors and mirrors. The waiting room was decorated with people reading the Italian edition of *Vogue* and drinking coffee from glass cups. The receptionist was inside a little island in the middle, watching the fun.

"Can I help you, sir?" she asked.

"Is Daniel here?"

"He's with a customer."

"It's the customer I want—which way?"

She pointed straight ahead. I followed her finger into a room overlooking Fifth Avenue—the windows sloped at an angle, flowers covering the broad base. Michelle was getting combed out by a slim man wearing a white sweater over blue jeans—white running shoes on his feet. She was in the middle of a heated exchange with the woman in the next chair.

"Honey, please don't go on about the Holy Coast. The only thing Los Angeles ever contributed to culture is the drive-by homicide!"

I stepped between them before it got bloody.

"Burke!" she called out. "You're just in time."

"For what?" I asked her.

"For *Daniel*," she said, like I was from another planet. "He just got a cancellation—and you need a haircut."

Daniel and I shook hands—he had a strong grip, an ironic smile on his face.

"Burke," he said. "What's your first name?"

"I'm not paying by check," I told him.

"Will you *stop* it?" Michelle snapped, turning in her chair to slap at my arm. "This isn't a poolroom."

"Can I talk to you for a minute?" I said.

"Talk."

"Not here."

Michelle sighed. "Oh, really—it's always such a big deal. Just give me a few minutes—sit down," she said, pointing to the chair next to her.

"This has to stay a few minutes anyway, Michelle," Daniel told her, patting her hairdo.

"Don't rush yourself, baby. Anyway, you have to cut my friend's hair too."

Daniel looked a question at me. I shrugged—what the hell.

"You have to get shampooed first," he said.

"Can't you just cut it?"

"It has to be wet," he said with a sideways glance at Michelle.

"He was raised in a barn," Michelle sighed.

I let some little girl lead me to another room, where she put the shampoo in my hair, rinsed it out, did it all over again. Daniel was still playing with Michelle's hair when I came back.

"How would you like this cut?" he asked.

"Just do whatever you do," I told him. I saw him glance at Michelle again. "Don't get stupid," I warned him.

He walked out of the room to get something he needed.

"Michelle, we got something on for tonight, okay?"

"A phone job for me?"

"And something with the Mole too," I told her. For once, she didn't make a crack about the Mole.

"What time?"

"We'll meet around five, five-thirty. Mama's basement, okay?"

"I'll be there, baby," she told me, giving me a quick kiss and walking out.

Daniel finished cutting my hair. With the room quiet, it was like a real barbershop—he even knew something about prize-fighting. When he was finished, I looked the same—Daniel told me it was an art.

I went out to the receptionist, asking for Michelle.

"Oh, she left a few minutes ago. She said you'd be taking care of her bill with yours."

What was I going to do? "Okay, how much for the whole thing?"

"Let's see . . ." she told me brightly, "with tax, that's a hundred and seventy dollars and fifty-six cents."

"What!"

"Michelle had a styling, a color consult, a manicure, and a pedicure," she said, as if that explained everything.

I didn't leave a tip for Daniel—if he owned that joint he had a license to steal.

92

"Hold still !" Michelle ordered. She was sitting next to me, my right hand spread out on a board she held in her lap, working carefully with a rapidograph, inking in the crossed lightning bolts of the Real Brotherhood.

The Prof peeked over my shoulder—he knew what the real thing looked like better than most.

"You should have been an artist, babe," he complimented her.

"Honey," Michelle said, "I am an artist—I give a whole new meaning to the term 'satisfied customer.'"

Max sat in the lotus position against the wall in Mama's basement. He was dressed all in black—not the ceremonial silk he usually wore for combat—some dull matte material. He fitted a hood of the same stuff over his face. It covered the back of his neck, blending into the jacket—only his eyes were visible. He was working with some black paste, rubbing it into his hands.

"Mole, you got the car?"

He nodded. We wouldn't use the Plymouth to approach the house.

Michelle was going to stash it a few blocks away—if anyone was following us, we'd switch cars, leaving the Mole's untraceable junker behind.

"The phones go down at eleven-thirty?" I asked him.

He nodded again. There was no burglar alarm, no direct connection to the local police station either. There wouldn't be.

We didn't have to go over it again. Michelle would call, act like she was a telephone solicitor, ask to speak to the man of the house. If the husband answered, she'd do her best to keep him on the phone while I was ringing the front-door bell. Max would go over the back fence, penetrate the house. He'd take out anyone he found, except the woman— I needed to talk to her. If the woman answered the door, I'd brace her right there, take her inside, and get the pictures. If the wrong person answered the door, I'd show them the pistol, play it from there while Max worked his way through the rest of the house.

And if I didn't like the look of the front of the house, I'd find my own way inside.

The Prof and I each had a little radio transmitter the Mole hooked up. When I hit the switch, the Prof would climb behind the wheel of the crash-car and start the engine. I'd come busting out the front door. And the Mole would turn the house into an incinerator. Then he and Max would go back over the fence to where Michelle would be waiting.

It should all be over by midnight.

Michelle was finished with my hand and started on my face. The heavy pancake makeup made me a few shades darker, and the black mustache changed the shape of my face even more. I'd have a hat on my head and dark glasses over my eyes.

"What did McGowan say when you brought him the kid . . . Terry?" I asked her.

She didn't answer—I saw something in her face, her mouth set and hard.

"Michelle?"

"I didn't bring him to McGowan," she said.

"What did you do with him?" I asked her, keeping my voice level.

"Burke, he couldn't go home. His father's an evil pig—he's the one who started him off."

"That's why he ran away?"

"He didn't run away—his father sold him to that pimp."

And people think it's going to be air pollution that kills us all someday.

"What did you do with him?" I asked her again.

"He's my child now," she said. "I'll take care of him."

"Michelle," I said, my voice patient but my mind screaming *trouble!*, "you can't keep that kid in your hotel. Sooner or later somebody's going to . . ."

"He's with me," the Mole said.

"In the junkyard?"

"I fixed up a place for him," the Mole said, a hurt tone in his voice.

"The Mole's teaching him, Burke," Michelle said. "He's learning all about electronics and stuff. He's real smart. You wouldn't believe how much . . ."

"Jesus Christ!"

"Burke, he's *my* boy, okay? We take him to SAFE. Lily's working with him. He's going to be fine."

"What if someone comes looking for him?"

"What if they do?" she challenged.

"Michelle, listen for a minute. You're in the life, baby. What kind of a mother could you be?"

"Better than the mother you had," she said, her voice quiet.

I lit a cigarette. Maybe the kid would never get to prep school, but the state makes the worst mother of them all.

"He's one of us," the Mole said, looking at Michelle.

I gave it up. "Just don't expect me to be his goddamned uncle," I said.

Michelle gave me a kiss on the cheek. "When I have my operation, I'm going to adopt him, Burke. He can go to college and everything . . . you can scam up some papers for him . . . I started to put money aside already. . . ."

"I know," I said. "And the Mole's going to buy him a puppy, right?"

"He has lots of dogs," the Mole said in a serious tone.

My fingers twisted into the sign for "Okay," aiming at Max. He was gone. I peered into the corner where he had been working with the black paste, wondering how he did that—and then I saw him. He hadn't moved at all—the black cloth ate the light until he was nothing but a puddle of shadow. They'd never see him coming.

The Prof came over and stood beside me. "Burke, if that old woman doesn't talk, you going to walk?"

I thought of what Mama said not so long ago. No rules. "I'm coming out with that picture, Prof," I told him. "It's the jailhouse or the graveyard. If it goes sour, do what you have to do."

"I know what I have to do," he said.

I took one last look around.

"Let's do it," I told them.

93

I LED THE two-car convoy carefully through Manhattan, me in the maroon Cadillac sedan the Mole had welded back together, Michelle following in the Plymouth. The Prof was crouched down under the dash on the passenger side of the Cadillac, keeping up a steady stream of chatter. He didn't look uncomfortable— for a guy who spent half his life pretending to have no legs, hiding under the dash was no big thing. The Mole rode next to Michelle in the front of the Plymouth. Max was in the trunk.

The City Planning map showed the cul-de-sac at the end of Cheshire Drive, but I'd gone over the ground in person a couple of times to be sure of the layout. The back of the house was separated from a little park by the same wall that went around to the front. I brought the Cadillac to a stop, checking the mirrors. Michelle pulled in behind me, getting out to pop open the Plymouth's hood as if she was having engine trouble. I took out the jumper cables, preparing to hook them up in case anyone watching got to wondering what we were all doing.

All clear. I opened the trunk of the Plymouth and Max flowed out.

He was a black blot against the white wall for a second; then he was gone.

"You remember where the phone booth is?" I asked Michelle.

Her disgusted look was all the answer I was going to get.

A black rope flew over the wall. The Mole shouldered the strap of his satchel, got a grip, and heaved himself up. The Prof and I each grabbed a leg and shoved too—the Mole isn't exactly agile. Max would probably throw him over the wall on the way out.

"You make the call—you hang up—you cruise *slowly* back here and wait for Max and the Mole to come over the wall, okay? If there's trouble, it'll be at the front of the house."

"I'll be here," Michelle said.

The Prof and I got back in the Cadillac and motored quietly away, Michelle right on our tail. I drove her past the phone booth just to be sure, waiting until I saw her brake lights flash. I checked my watch—eleven-twenty-five.

The Cadillac turned into Cheshire Drive, cruising past a black Ford with two men inside. Wolfe's people were real subtle. I thought how easy it would be for anyone to block off the street on our way back, checking the manicured front lawns of the expensive houses on each side. Plenty of room.

I used the short driveway in front of the big house to turn around, leaving the Cadillac's nose pointing back out.

"It's time," I whispered to the Prof.

I closed the door of the Cadillac quietly. The front gate was locked. I jumped up and grabbed the top, pulled myself up in a second, dropped down on the other side. I covered the path to the front door quickly, my ears hurting from listening for sirens.

The door was black—a dramatic counterpoint to the fieldstone front of the house. I couldn't see a knocker or a bell. Soft light flowed from a large bay window, but the house was quiet. I eased away from the door, peering into the front window. It was a living room that nobody ever lived in—plastic covering the furniture, every piece sharply aligned, not a cigarette butt or an old newspaper in sight. Ringing the front-door bell would be a mistake. Maybe they were all asleep, maybe even sleeping right through Michelle's phone call.

I slipped off the front step and around to the side of the house, checking through each window for humans. Nothing. The joint was as quiet as a Russian civil-rights meeting.

A double-wide driveway continued from the front around the side, sweeping in a gentle curve to someplace behind the house. I followed it along, feeling the smooth pavement under my feet, checking the string of floodlights angling from the house. They were dark now, but there had to be a switch somewhere inside. The driveway ended in a teardrop-shaped slab of concrete behind the house—a schoolbus-yellow van sat next to a dark, anonymous sedan. A sloping extension had been built off the house. It looked like a garage, but it had to be the entrance to the basement.

I did another slow circuit before I returned to the most likely prospect—the window at the back corner of the house where it was pitch-dark. There was no alarm tape around the border—I couldn't see any wires either. I put on a pair of gloves before I tried to raise the window. The wood looked pretty old—I didn't want to get splinters. It was latched. I took a roll of heavy masking tape from my coat and carefully covered the pane nearest the latch. I used three layers of tape, leaving the ends free, smoothing it down from corner to corner. Then the little rubber mallet, softly tapping, working from the corners toward the middle of the pane. My heart was beating hard, like it always does when I work, but I breathed slowly through my nose, keeping it under control. You get too impatient doing one of these jobs, you get a lot of time to think about it in a place where the windows don't have glass.

I put my hand flat against the windowpane, working the cracked glass carefully, easing it away from the frame. It made a tiny crackle, like when you crumple the cellophane wrapper from a pack of smokes. I slipped my hand inside and pushed against the tape; the broken glass clung to its other side. I found the latch. Gently withdrew my hand and started to work the window up. Every couple of inches or so I sprayed some liquid silicon into the channel to smooth the way.

When the window got to the top, I took a couple of deep breaths to steady myself. Then I put my head inside and risked a quick spray from the flashlight. It looked like a man's den, the kind you see in magazines.

Big leather easy chair, television set in one corner, some kind of plaques on the walls. The room felt musty and dead, like it was never used.

I climbed over the sill and dropped into the room, pulling the window closed behind me, adding up the crimes in my head. Breaking and entering. Burglary of an occupied dwelling. So far, not so bad. I pulled the dark nylon stocking mask over my head, adjusting it so the slits matched up with my eyes. When it felt right, I took the pistol from an inside pocket. From now on, it was going to be Felony City.

I stepped out into a long hallway running down one side of the house. To my right was an eat-in kitchen, windows on two sides. To my left was the foyer, with that plastic-covered living room off to one side. Still quiet. The whole place was covered with thick wall-to-wall carpet the same color as dirt. I think they call it "earth tones." I padded down the hall toward the front door, looking for the staircase. The stairs were carpet-covered too, but I eased my weight onto each one just the same.

Halfway up the stairs I heard the music. Some kind of orchestra stuff, but real light—all strings and flutes. I reached the top, waited, listening hard now. The music was coming from a room at the rear of the house, the only room with a light on—I couldn't see inside. I slipped around the newel post at the top of the stairs, heading in the opposite direction. The second floor wasn't anywhere near as big as the first—just two rooms that looked like bedrooms, windows looking out toward the street. Each had its own bathroom attached. I didn't risk the flash to look closely, just checked to make sure nobody was sleeping there. The rooms were all dark. Empty.

I walked toward the open door at the other end, toward the music and I didn't know what else. When I got close, I could see the door was at the far corner of the room; everything else was off to the left. I took the pistol in both hands, holding it high above my head over my right shoulder; my back was against the wall. Then I stepped inside with my left foot, pivoting and bringing the pistol down and across my chest, sweeping the room.

A short, stocky woman was sitting on a stool at a white drafting table, peering at something under an architect's lamp. The light came from behind her—I couldn't make out her face. She was wearing a pink quilted bathrobe, orthopedic shoes on her feet. She didn't even look up, concentrating on something. I was almost on top of her before she looked up.

"Don't scream," I told her, my voice calm, showing her the pistol.

She opened her mouth wide, gulped in a ton of air instead, her eyes bulging. "Oh my god!" she said, like she'd been expecting this.

"Just keep quiet and you won't get hurt," I said, still calm and quiet, gently reaching out toward her.

"What is this?" she asked, her voice shaking.

"It's about a picture, bitch," I told her, grabbing the front of her robe with one gloved hand, my voice filtered through the nylon mask. "I want a picture you have. Understand?"

She tried to pull away from me, plucking at my arm in a feeble gesture. I slapped her lightly across the face with the pistol. I put my face as close to hers as I could. "I got my orders—I bring the picture or your fucking head!"

The woman's eyes rolled up and she slumped against me—I jerked her face up again—she was breathing in gasps but she wasn't going to faint.

I grabbed her by the back of the neck, holding the pistol in front of her face with the other hand, pulling her off the stool, dragging her toward a chair near a butcher-block desk in the corner. A gooseneck lamp was shining on some papers. I shoved the woman into an oxblood leather chair and stepped back.

"Who are you?" she asked.

"I'm a man with a job, understand? I don't have a lot of time."

I tossed the picture Strega gave me on the table in front of her. Her eyes flicked over to it but she didn't make a move.

"That's the kid," I told her. "You got a picture of him somewhere in this house. I want it."

"Why would I have a picture . . . ?"

I stepped forward and backhanded her across the face, not too hard—just enough to make her focus on what she had to do.

I started pulling things out of my pocket—a small coil of piano wire, a little glass bottle of clear fluid, a strip of leather. And a straight razor. The woman's eyes were huge.

I stepped to her again—she cowered, covering her face with her hands. No rings on her fingers—no polish on her nails. I slipped the leather strip past her clawing fingers, fastening the gag in her mouth. She jumped forward—I jammed the heel of my hand into her chest—she let out a burst of air and fell forward from the waist. It only took me another minute to lash her wrists to the arms of the chair with the piano wire.

Her mouth was silent but her eyes were screaming. "You got two choices," I told her. "You see this bottle? It's ether. To knock you out. If I have to do that, I'm going to chop off the fingers on your hand. One by one. And I'm going to wait for you to wake up, bitch. You'll wake up screaming, understand?"

Her face was coming apart behind the gag.

"You understand!" I snarled at her.

She nodded her head hard enough to make it fall off her neck.

"I'm going to take the gag out now—you don't tell me what I want to know, you bleed to death right in that chair. Through the fucking stumps."

I pulled the gag from her mouth—she struggled for a breath, panting as if she'd run a mile.

I watched her face. "Don't even think about screaming," I told her.

She was more under control now. "I'm not alone in the house," she gasped.

"Yeah, you are," I said. "It's me that's not alone here."

Her eyes were on me, trying to figure out what I meant. Hard, flat doll's eyes—nobody home behind them. A thin, ugly smell came off her. Her breathing was under control. "I have no money here," she said, as if that settled everything.

I leaned close again, letting her look into my eyes. "I want the picture," I told her. "Last chance."

"Just the one picture?"

"Don't bargain with me, you fucking slime. I got my orders."

She was watching me, thinking. No good. I picked up the leather gag.

"In the safe!" she said. "Please, don't . . ."

"Where's the safe?"

"In the floor—under the work table."

I took a look—the floor under the table was all parquet squares. Four of them came away when I pulled. The combination lock was set so it was facing the ceiling.

"Give it to me," I said.

She knew what I meant. "Six left, twenty-four right, twelve left."

The safe was a deep one, maybe three feet into the floor. Video cassettes to the right, 35mm cartridges in plastic containers. And Polaroids— hundreds of them, each one in a separate plastic jacket.

"You got an index?" I asked her.

"No," she said, lifeless. She was probably lying, but I didn't have the time to find out. I knew what I was looking for. It only took a couple of minutes—a couple of minutes of looking through the worst thing on this slop basin of a planet—a little baby peacefully sleeping, a man's erect penis in his mouth as a pacifier—kids from a few days old to maybe ten or eleven, penetrated with every blunt object freakish minds could think of—smiling kids, playing with each other—a little boy, maybe six years old, his screaming face adjusted by the camera so you could see him being sodomized from behind, two strands of barbed wire drawn across his little chest to make a bloody "X." All the pictures had the tiny blue image of a man and a boy in one corner—her mark.

The picture of Scotty was just what he told Immaculata—wearing his little striped T-shirt and nude from the waist down. Sucking on a man wearing a clown suit. I put it in my pocket.

I went back to the woman. "You got what you wanted?" she asked. Her voice hard and confident now, back to something she understood.

"Yeah. I got it. And I'm going to give you something for it too." I held the razor to her throat, whispering in her ear. "You're dead, bitch. You took a picture of the wrong kid this time. I were you, I'd call the D.A. and surrender—cooperate with the Man. You know how it's done. Find yourself a nice, safe cell for a few years. But get someone to taste your food for you."

I poured the whole bottle of ether over the white cloth—the smell made me dizzy.

"You promised not to hurt me!" she screamed.

"You promised those kids a day in the country," I told her, slapping the sopping wet cloth over her mouth and nose, holding it there while she struggled, making sure she could get enough air to mix with the ether and take her down. The Mole had warned me I could kill her if I used too much. Accidents happen.

Her head lolled forward, unconscious. I unwrapped her wrists, slapping them to bring the color back. I dragged her out of the chair by the front of her robe to one of the bedrooms. Tossed her on the bed. Moved her around until she was lying face up. She looked asleep—I wasn't going to put my face close enough to her to find out.

Max and the Mole were somewhere in the house. I'd told them to give me fifteen minutes and then make tracks, but I knew they weren't going anywhere until they knew I was safe. Just like I knew the Prof would sit outside the front door with the motor running even if a SWAT team was coming up the street. I hit the stairs running. Every second in the house was a big risk now. The first floor was empty—even the kitchen looked like nobody ever ate a meal there. It was all for the neighbors, like a window display of a typical American home. The neighbors would never look in the basement.

I opened the door to the cellar stairs off the foyer and stepped through. Found myself in another small room, set up to resemble a cloakroom—coats hanging on hooks, umbrella stand in one corner. It took another minute to find the door behind the coats. Locked from the inside. I took out a credit card and slipped it between the door and the frame, working it gently, telling myself if there was a deadbolt on the other side I'd have to try another way in. But the loid worked, and the door popped open. Another couple of steps and I was at the top of a curving wrought-iron staircase. I tested my weight against the first step and then I heard a man's voice, high and shaky, like he was near the edge of something.

"Look, you guys are making a mistake, okay? I mean . . . I *know* people, understand? Whatever problem you got, I can take care of it. Just sitting here *looking* at me isn't doing you any good, right?"

I followed the staircase toward the voice. Halfway down, the darkness faded. Indirect lighting bathed the basement floor, coming from some concealed panels. A fat man was sitting in one of those huge beanbag chairs, one hand on each side for balance, staring into a dark corner like it held all life's secrets. The Mole was hunkered down against one wall at the side of the chair, his satchel open in front of him. His big head swiveled to cover the room, a stocking mask stretched over his thick glasses. He looked like a malignant frog.

The man's eyes rolled over to me as I came down the stairs. He watched me approach, relief coming into his face.

"Hey, are *you* in charge? These guys . . ."

"Don't talk," I told him.

It didn't have any effect. "What difference does it make, man? This whole place is soundproofed, okay? I mean . . . take a look around."

I did. The walls were lined with dark-brown cork, the ceiling covered with acoustic tile. Even the rug on the floor felt like it was covering a thick rubber mat.

"So nobody can hear the kids scream?" I asked him.

"Hey! What is this?" he yelled at me, trying for a hard edge to his voice.

I cocked the pistol. He winced at the sound. I stuck the gun into his fat face, depressing the skin under his right eye. "I. Don't. Have. Time," I told him, pushing at his face with every word.

"Whaaat?" he moaned. "Just tell me . . ."

"I want the *pictures*. I want the *film*. I want the *lists*. I want the *money*."

The fat man wasn't going to bargain like his wife. "It's upstairs. All upstairs. I swear . . . down here there's just some money . . . in the workbench . . . just walk-around cash. . . . It's all in the bank. . . . Tomorrow morning, when the banks open, I . . ."

"Shut up!" I told him, backing away. The workbench drawer had three short stacks of bills. I tossed the money to the Mole. It went into his satchel. The basement looked like a kid's playroom—stuffed animals, dolls, a hobbyhorse, electric trains in one corner. I checked behind the only door, but there was nothing except the oil burner and a hot-water heater. A back door opened into the extension to the house. I walked through it quickly. No windows to the outside, and the floor was concrete like the driveway. All designed so they could pull the van inside and discharge its cargo. And take pictures of kids.

It was time to disappear.

"Your wife is upstairs," I told him. "She's okay—just sleeping. I'm going to give you a shot too. When you wake up, the police will be here. You say whatever you want to say—make the best deal for yourself you can. You mention me or my people, I'll find you again, wherever you are. Understand?"

He nodded, still trying to talk. "Look . . . you don't need the shot. . . . I mean, I got a bad heart, you know? I'm on medication. Tomorrow I can get you all the money you want. . . ."

The Mole took a hypo out of his satchel, pushed the plunger, watched the thin spray, nodded to me. A shadow moved from a corner of the basement, flowed behind the fat man. He was jerked to his feet, one arm braced in front of him, veins clearly visible.

"We'll do it upstairs," I told the Mole, gesturing to Max to bring the fat man along.

I took the curving staircase first, listening. Nothing. Then came the Mole, with Max last. We stopped at the landing; the fat man stood against one wall, breathing much too fast.

"We need the fire now," I said to the Mole. "Something that started in the boiler."

He nodded, returned the hypo to his satchel, and went back downstairs.

The fat man was still having trouble with his breathing, sucking in gulps of air and trying to talk at the same time. I pulled off one glove to scratch at the mask, letting him see the tattoo.

"You guys! I know your boss . . . I mean, we have a contract, right? We got no problem. . . ."

I put the glove back on as if I hadn't noticed what set him off. "Shut up," I said, talking the way a machine talks.

The fat man never tried to make a move—combat wasn't his game. But it seemed like he had to find out mine—he couldn't keep quiet.

"What would it take?" he asked.

"I'm just doing a job," I told him, in the same mechanical voice.

"Look, you don't get it, okay? It's not like anyone got *hurt*, all right? Kids . . . they get over it. It's just a business."

I could feel the heat coming off Max, but I was empty inside. All maggots have a story to tell, and I'd heard most of them by then.

The Mole walked up the staircase, satchel in one hand. A day at the office. He held up a palm, fingers spread wide. Five minutes to ignition.

I took Scotty's picture from my pocket, held it up to the fat man's face. I was really showing Max that we'd rescued the kid, but the fat man decided I wanted an explanation.

"Hey! I remember him. Is that what this is all about? Hey, *look*, man . . . that is one sexy little kid, you better believe. . . . I mean, he *loved* lapping it up. . . . It's not like I started him off or anything. . . ."

I saw red dots in front of my eyes where his face should have been. I gripped the pistol handle so hard my hand throbbed, hearing the sound of the shot in my mind, willing myself not to pull the trigger.

"Don't!" the fat man screamed, clasping his hands in front of his chest like he was praying. I heard a sharp hiss from the darkness where Max was standing, and then a sound like a meat ax driving into bone. The fat man's neck snapped to the left—and stayed there. Max released him and the body slumped to the ground.

The Mole dropped to his knees, doing his job even though we all knew it was over. "Gone," he said.

"The jailhouse or the graveyard," I'd told the Prof. Now it really didn't matter if the old lady upstairs was dead. I gestured Max to pick up the fat man's body and we all went back downstairs. I could feel the clock ticking in my head—the boiler was going to go. "He tried to escape the flames—ran up the stairs. Slipped and fell. Broke his neck," I said to myself. We hauled the fat man halfway up the stairs, to the place where they started to curve. Leaned him across the railing and pushed him over, face first. The silent basement swallowed the sound of his fall.

"Go!" I said to the Mole, pointing to the back of the house. Max's shadow followed him back into the basement.

I pushed the button on the radio transmitter, telling the Prof I'd be hitting the front gate any minute. I still had a little piece of time left to finish what I had to do—even when the boiler went off it wouldn't reach the first floor for a while. I ran back upstairs to the big office room, grabbing handfuls of the filth, throwing it all around the hallway, dusting every room with pictures and film. I pushed a few of the cassettes back in the safe and slammed it closed, thankful for the gloves I was wearing— no time to wipe everything down.

I checked the bedroom. The woman was still lying on the bed, like she hadn't moved. Maybe she never would.

I charged down the stairs, the gun in front of me, my ears sucking in every sound, waiting for the sirens. I heard a crackling sound from someplace in the basement.

I opened the front door a narrow slit, poked my head out. The street was quiet. I made sure the door wasn't going to lock behind me, patted my pockets to check I had everything, and charged for the fence. I dropped down on the other side—the driver's door was hanging open. I dove inside and the Prof leaped out of the way—he had the car in gear, holding the brake pedal down with his hand.

I looked over my shoulder—the basement windows were full of flame. I heard an engine jump into life somewhere down the street. Wolfe's surveillance team shot straight past us, heading toward the house. I kept rolling smoothly, flipping on the headlights when I turned the corner.

The Plymouth was waiting where it was supposed to be. Nobody was following, so I flashed the lights and Michelle pulled in behind me. We took the Throgs Neck Bridge over to the Bronx, pulling off the road just past the tolls, doing the same number with the jumper cables just in case.

I left the Prof to watch the cars, pulling everyone else into the shadows.

"I got it," I told Michelle. "Anybody answer when you called?"

"Sure did," she replied. "It was a man."

"No, it wasn't," I told her, lighting a cigarette for the first time since we got out. "Any trouble?" I asked the others.

"Just the fence," said the Mole, rubbing his side. He and Michelle went back to the cars.

Max was still in the dark cloth, but the hood was off his head. He watched the Prof approach us, made the gesture of a man taking a picture, moved his hand in a "come here" sign. He wanted the Prof to see the picture. I held it out to him. The mercury-vapor lamps they use on the bridge threw a cold orange light down on all of us. Max held the picture in both hands, waiting for the Prof to look and see what he wanted. He tapped his finger against the picture of the man in the clown suit—then his head suddenly twisted to one side.

"You understand?" I asked the Prof. He had been with us—he had a right to know.

The little man nodded his head. "It means the clown went down."

94

THE MOLE took the Cadillac back to the Bronx. Max got back in the trunk—explaining his night-stalker getup to a passing cop would be too much trouble. We found a turnaround and headed home.

"I'll have the money in a couple of days," I said to the Prof. "Where should I drop you?"

"It's too late for the Men's Shelter—let me try Grand Central."

"Michelle?"

"Home, baby."

I drove the Plymouth into the warehouse. Immaculata appeared while I was opening the trunk for Max to get out.

"It's done," I told her.

Immaculata examined Max like he was a piece of jewelry she was going to buy someday—her eyes going over every inch. She touched his chest, feeling his body, making sure. Max suffered in silence, his face stony. But his eyes were soft.

I bowed to them both. As I backed out of the warehouse, I could see Immaculata patting her stomach, gesturing to Max—the life-taker was a life-maker too.

95

I<small>T WAS</small> all over the midday papers. I liked the *Post*'s version best.

FIRE REVEALS KIDDIE PORN RING!

A fire late last night that killed a Queens man and hospitalized his wife led startled firefighters to discover the couple was operating a "major kiddie-porn ring" from the comfort of their Little Neck mansion, police said.

Killed in the blaze was George Browne, 44, who lived in the house at 71 Cheshire Drive with his wife Bonnie. Mrs. Browne, 41, was taken to nearby Deepdale General Hospital suffering from smoke inhalation.

Firemen, alerted by a telephone call to the emergency 911 number, arrived shortly after the fire ignited at about 10:00 p.m., and had the blaze under control by 10:45.

It was while they were examining the damage, which a Fire Department spokesman called "moderate," that firemen made the shocking discovery of "literally hundreds of kiddie-porn photographs," the spokesman said. The firemen immediately notified the police, she added.

Captain Louis DeStefano of the 111th Precinct said that in addition to the Polaroid photographs, a "substantial amount" of undeveloped film and "several videotape cassettes" were also seized.

"I'm shocked. I'm absolutely shocked," a stunned neighbor, Elsie Lipschitz, told the Post. "They kept to themselves a lot, but they were always very polite when you saw them on the street. I can't believe it," she said.

Although the Fire Department and the couple's neighbors were caught off guard, the Post has learned that the $450,000 house at the end of the quiet cul-de-sac has been under police surveillance and that George Browne was arrested twice for child molesting in recent years.

In 1978 Browne, who listed his occupation as "entertainer," was arrested on felony molestation charges that were eventually dropped. Two years later, he was arrested again, and ultimately pleaded guilty to endangering the welfare of a minor—a five-year-old boy from upstate, according to police sources.

Browne's charred body was discovered at the bottom of the basement stairway. An apparent broken neck has led cops to theorize he was trying to escape the fire—which may have begun with an explosion in the boiler, according to firemen—when he was overcome by smoke and fell down the stairway. An autopsy is pending.

Among the first cops to arrive on the scene were detectives conducting round-the-clock surveillance for the City-Wide Special Victims Bureau. Assistant District Attorney Eva Wolfe, who heads the bureau, would only say that the surveillance was "part of an ongoing investigation." She declined to say when the investigation began.

Mrs. Browne has not yet been arrested, ADA Wolfe said, adding that charges are expected to be filed "soon."

A hospital spokesman said the woman's condition is satisfactory.

The Prof was reading over my shoulder. "When people can't learn, they're bound to burn," he said.

The blues are the truth.

96

I MADE the call the next morning. "You have my money?" I asked her when she answered the phone.

"Was that you . . ."

"You have my money?" I asked her again, cutting her short.

"I'll have it tonight. Do you have . . ."

"Tonight. Midnight, right?"

"Yes. I'll . . ."

I hung up on her. A dry run.

97

I WAS THERE on time. Fear was strong in me; I couldn't put a name to it. Nobody wants surgery, but when the disease is fatal, even the knife looks good.

The back of the house was soft, sly darkness. Shadows played their games. There was no music.

"I have you in me now," Strega said once. I called to Flood in my mind, telling her Strega had lied. Telling myself.

I had Scotty's picture in my pocket. It was enough to get me into the house—I wasn't sure it was enough to get me out.

The garage was standing open, a space ready for my Plymouth. I left it outside, nose pointing toward the drive.

I walked up the stairs to the living room. It was empty. I fired a wooden match, looking for a light switch. I couldn't find one—settled for a lamp that flowed gracefully over the couch. I bit into a cigarette, watching the match flare with the first drag, waving my hand to put it out. I put the match in my pocket, waiting.

She came into the room wearing a red slip, her feet bare. Her face was scrubbed and clean. Sat down next to me on the couch, tucking her feet underneath her. She looked like a young girl.

I took the picture from my pocket, gave it one last look, and put it in her lap. An offering—take this from me and go haunt someone else. She ran her finger lightly over the surface of the picture. "This is the one," she whispered.

I didn't want a ceremony. "You have my money?" I asked her.

"I'm going to burn this in front of Scotty," she said like she hadn't heard me. "And it will all be gone."

"It won't be gone—only the people at SAFE can do that," I told her.

"You know what I mean," she said.

She had her magic words—I had mine. "Where's the money?" I asked her again.

"It's upstairs," she said, flowing to her feet. "Come on."

A woman's hatbox was in the middle of her bed. I could see it through the canopy. A diamond floating on quicksand. She pointed to it, one hand on her hip.

I reached through the lacy fabric and pulled it out. The top came off—inside was the money, all neatly stacked. And the thick gold chain on top of the pile.

"Touch it," she whispered against me. "It's warm. Just before you came, I took a nap. I slept with it inside my body—it's warm from me."

"I don't want it," I said.

"Don't be afraid . . . take it."

"I don't want it," I said again, hearing my voice go hollow, holding on.

She pushed me to the chair in the corner. I stood hard against her, not moving. "It has to be in a chair," she whispered. "It's the only place I can do it. You have to be sitting down."

"I just want the money," I told her.

She grabbed the front of my coat with both hands, pulling at it with all her weight, her devil eyes firing both barrels at me. "You're mine," she said.

I met her eyes—something danced in there—something that would never have a partner. "I did my work," I told her, staying where I was safe. "I'm done."

"You can't walk away from me," she whispered, holding on.

"Forget it, Strega."

"You call my name—you think you know me. You don't know me."

"I know you. And don't waste your time running to Julio—there's nothing he can do."

Strega knew an exit line when she heard one. She let go of my coat, turned her back to me, one hand holding a bedpost.

"Yes, Julio," she said. "My precious uncle Julio—the great and good friend of my father."

She turned to face me. "Who do you think taught me to make nice while he sat in a chair—be a good little girl?"

"What?" I said. I've had a lifetime of keeping my thoughts off my face, but it didn't work with Strega. She answered the question I never asked.

"Julio. I was Peppina then. I loved everybody. Especially Julio—he was so good to me. When he started with me, I told my father on him," she said, her voice that of a little child.

"What did he do?"

"What did he do? He beat me with a strap for telling evil tales about Julio. Julio the Saint. He was a saint to my father . . . because of the money and the fear. And I went back to Julio."

I just looked at her, watching her eyes. Cold fire. Hate.

"They taught me—money and fear. They taught me good. One day I wasn't little stupid happy Peppina anymore."

I saw Julio in my mind, the last time we talked. I knew why he looked like that now. "That's why Julio wanted me to do this . . . get the picture for you?"

"Julio does what I want now. They all do what I want. Money and fear."

"Jina . . ."

"Strega. To you, Strega. And when you come back to me, Strega still."

"I'm not coming back," I said, putting the hatbox under one arm, holding the money against the cold.

One tear escaped her eye, ran down her cheek. "I have my Mia," she said, her voice as dead as the clown in the big white house, "and I have myself. I will always have myself."

"I've got more than that," I thought, walking out, the cold wind swirling at my back. Guarding its child.

A NOTE ON THE TYPE

This book was set in a digitized version of Granjon, a type named in compliment to Robert Granjon, a type cutter and printer active in Antwerp, Lyons, Rome, and Paris from 1523 to 1590. Granjon, the boldest and most original designer of his time, was one of the first to practice the trade of type founder apart from that of printer.

Linotype Granjon was designed by George W. Jones, who based his drawings on a face used by Claude Garamond (ca. 1480–1561) in his beautiful French books. Granjon more closely resembles Garamond's own type than does any of the various modern faces that bear his name.

Composed by PennSet, Inc., a division of
Maryland Linotype Composition Company,
Bloomsburg, Pennsylvania

Printed and bound by R. R. Donnelley & Sons,
Harrisonburg, Virginia

DESIGNED BY PETER A. ANDERSEN